**Praise for the novels of *New York Times*
bestselling author GENA SHOWALTER**

"*The Darkest Surrender* is another sure-to-please hit…
Gena Showalter knows how to keep readers
glued to the pages and smiling the whole time."
—*New York Times* bestselling author Lara Adrian

"Showalter gives her fans another treat, sure to satisfy!"
—*RT Book Reviews* on *The Darkest Passion*

"The Showalter name on a book
means guaranteed entertainment."
—*RT Book Reviews* on *Twice as Hot*

"If you like your paranormal dark and
passionately flavored, this is the series for you."
—*RT Book Reviews* on *The Darkest Whisper*

"Talk about one dark read… If there is one book
you must read this year, pick up *The Darkest Kiss*…
a Gena Showalter book is the best of the best."
—*Romance Junkies*

"A fascinating premise, a sexy hero and nonstop action,
The Darkest Night is Showalter at her finest,
and a fabulous start to an imaginative new series."
—*New York Times* bestselling author
Karen Marie Moning

"A world of myth, mayhem and love under the sea!"
—#1 *New York Times* bestselling author J. R. Ward
on *The Nymph King*

"Sexy, funny and downright magical!"
—*New York Times* bestselling author Katie MacAlister
on *The Stone Prince*

GENA SHOWALTER

The Darkest
WHISPER

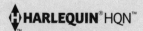

ISBN-13: 978-0-373-77799-0

THE DARKEST WHISPER

Copyright © 2009 by Gena Showalter

Recycling programs
for this product may
not exist in your area.

The character of Nix from the Immortals After Dark series
appears courtesy of Kresley Cole © 2009

Printed in U.S.A.

To Kresley Cole. A shining star,
a talent beyond compare, beauty personified and one
of the reasons I exist. I want to live inside your brain.

To Nix of the Immortals After Dark
for coming to play in my sandbox.

To Christy Foster for all your help online.

To Krystle for the wonderful title.

To Nora Roberts,
an amazingly talented woman and writer—
who just happens to be great at fixing toilets, too!

To my editors Tracy Farrell and Margo Lipschultz,
whose bountiful support blesses me
more than I can ever say.

And LAST on this list:
To Jill Monroe. I guess you're okay. Kind of. (Fine.
I love and adore you beyond what is deemed healthy.
You are a shining star, a talent beyond compare,
beauty personified and the other reason I exist.)

The Darkest
WHISPER

CHAPTER ONE

SABIN, KEEPER OF THE DEMON of Doubt, stood in the catacombs of an ancient pyramid, panting, sweating, his hands soaked in his enemy's blood, his body cut and bruised as he surveyed the carnage around him. Carnage he'd helped create.

Torches flickered orange and gold, twining with shadows along the stone walls. Walls that were now spattered with vivid red, dripping…pooling. The sandy floor was thick like paste, wet and colored black. Half an hour ago it had been honey brown, grains sparkling and scattering as they'd marched. Now bodies littered every square inch of the small corridor, the scent of fatality already rising from them.

Nine of his enemy had survived the attack. They'd already been stripped of their weapons, hustled into a corner and bound with rope. Most trembled in fear. A few had their shoulders squared, their noses in the air, hatred in their eyes, refusing to back down even in defeat. Damned admirable.

Too bad that bravery had to be quashed.

Brave men didn't spill their secrets, and Sabin wanted their secrets.

He was a warrior who did what needed to be done, when it needed to be done, no matter what was required of him. Killing, torturing, seducing. He didn't hesitate to ask his men to do the same, either. With Hunters—mortals who'd decided he and his fellow Lords of the Underworld made good whipping boys for the world's evil—victory was the only thing that mattered. For only by winning the war could his friends finally know peace. Peace they deserved. Peace he craved for them.

Shallow, erratic rasps of breath filled Sabin's ears. His, his friends', his enemies'. They'd fought with every ounce of strength they possessed, each of them. It had been a battle of good versus evil, and evil had won. Or rather, what these Hunters considered evil. He and his brothers-by-circumstance thought otherwise.

Yeah, long ago they'd opened Pandora's box, unleashing the demons from inside. But they had been punished eternally, each warrior cursed by the gods to host one of those vile fiends inside himself. Yeah, they'd once been slaves to their new, demonic halves, destructive and violent, killers without a conscience. But they had control now, human in all the ways that mattered. For the most part.

Sometimes the demons *did* fight...*did* win...*did* destroy.

Still. *We deserve to live,* he thought. Like everyone else, they suffered if their friends were hurt, read books, watched movies, gave to charity. Fell in love. Hunters, though, would never see it that way. They were convinced the world would be a better place without the Lords. A utopia, serene and perfect. They believed every sin ever committed could be laid at a demon's feet. Maybe because they were dumb as shit. Maybe because they hated their lives and were simply looking for someone to blame. Either way, killing them had become the most important mission of Sabin's life. *His* utopia was a life without *them.*

Which was why he and the others had relinquished the comforts of their Budapest home to spend the past three weeks searching every godsforsaken pyramid in Egypt for ancient artifacts that would lead to the recovery of Pandora's box—the very thing Hunters planned to use to destroy them. Finally, he and his friends had hit the jackpot.

"Amun," he said, spotting the soldier in a far, dark corner. As usual, man blended perfectly with shadow. Sabin motioned toward the captives with a grim shake of his head. "You know what to do."

Amun, keeper of Secrets, nodded forbiddingly before striding forward. Silent, always silent, as if afraid the terrible secrets he'd gleaned over the centuries would spill from him if he dared utter a single word.

Seeing the hulking warrior who'd ripped through their brethren like a knife through silk, the remaining Hunters took a collective step backward. Even the brave ones. Wise of them.

Amun was tall, leanly muscled, with a stride that was somehow both purposeful and graceful. Purpose without grace would have made him seem normal, like any other soldier. The combination allowed him to exude the kind of quiet savagery usually found in predators used to bringing their prey home between their jaws.

He reached the Hunters and stopped. Scanned the thinned crowd. Then shoved forward and grabbed the one in the center by the throat, lifting him so that they were eye to eye. The human's legs flailed, his hands clutching Amun's wrists as his skin blanched.

"Let him go, you filthy demon," one of the Hunters

shouted, jerking on his comrade's waist. "You've killed countless innocents, ruined so many lives already!"

Amun was unmoved. They all were.

"He's a good man," another cried. "He doesn't deserve to die. Especially at the hands of such evil!"

Gideon, the blue-haired, kohl-eyed keeper of Lies, was at Amun's side in the next instant, batting the protestors away. "Touch him again, and I'll kiss the hell out of you." He withdrew a pair of serrated knives, still bloody from his most recent clashes.

Kiss equaled *beat* in Gideon's upside-down world. Or was it *kill?* Sabin had lost track of Lies's code.

A moment passed in confused silence, the Hunters trying to figure out what exactly Gideon meant. Before they could decide, Amun's hostage stilled, wilting completely, and Amun dropped him to the ground in a motionless heap.

Amun remained in place for a long while. No one touched him. Not even the Hunters. They were too preoccupied with reviving their fallen cohort. They didn't know that it was too late, that his brain had been wiped, Amun the new owner of all his deepest secrets. Perhaps even his memories. The warrior had never told Sabin how it worked, and Sabin had never asked.

Slowly Amun turned, his body stiff. His black gaze met Sabin's for a bleak, tormented moment in which he couldn't mask the pain of having a new voice inside his head. Then he blinked, hiding his pain as he had a thousand times before, and strode to the far wall while Sabin watched, resolute. *I will not feel guilty. This has to be done.*

The wall looked the same as any other, jagged stones piled on top of each other and rising at a slant, yet Amun placed one hand on the seventh stone down, fingers splayed, then his other hand on the fifth up, fingers closed. Moving in sync, he twisted one wrist to the left, one to the right.

The stones pivoted with him.

Sabin observed the proceedings with awe. Never ceased to amaze him, what Amun could learn in a few heartbeats of time.

Once the stones settled into their new positions, a crack formed in the center of each, branching up, down, aligning with a streak of space Sabin hadn't noticed before. A section of the wall pulled back…back, and finally began to inch to the side. There would be a gaping doorway when it finished, wide enough for an army of hulking beasts like himself.

As it continued to widen, cool air blustered through the catacombs, causing the torches to sputter and crackle. *Hurry,* he projected to the stones. Had anything ever moved with such agonizing slowness?

"Any Hunters waiting on the other side?" he asked, sliding his Sig Sauer from his waist and checking the clip. Three bullets left. He dug a few more from his pocket and reloaded. The custom silencer remained in place.

Amun nodded and held up seven fingers before standing guard at that ever-widening chasm.

Seven Hunters against ten Lords. He didn't count Amun because the man would soon be too distracted by the new voice in his head to fight. But gods knew Amun would still (silently) demand to be included in the action. Still. Poor Hunters. They didn't have a chance. "They know we're here?"

A shake of that dark head.

No cameras watching their every move, then. Excellent.

"Seven Hunters is child's play," Lucien, keeper of Death, confirmed as he slumped against the far wall. He was pale, his mismatched eyes bright with…fever? "Go on without me. I'm fading. I'll soon have souls to escort, anyway. And then I'll have to flash our prisoners to the dungeon in Buda."

Thanks to the demon of Death, Lucien could move from one location to another with only a thought and was often forced to usher the dead into the hereafter. That didn't mean he himself was immune to destruction. Sabin frowned over at him. Studied him. The scars on his face were more pronounced, his nose out of joint. There was a bullet wound in his shoulder, one in his stomach, and from the looks of the crimson stain spreading from his lower back, his kidney.

"You okay, man?"

Lucien smiled wryly. "I'll live. Tomorrow, though, I'll probably wish I hadn't. A few organs are shredded."

Ouch. Been there, had to recover from that. "At least you don't have to regenerate a limb."

From the corner of his eye, he saw Amun flash hand signs.

"Not only are there no cameras installed, but they're in a chamber with soundproof walls," Sabin interpreted. "This was an ancient prison and the masters did not want anyone to hear their slaves screaming. The Hunters are completely oblivious to our presence, which should make it easy to ambush them."

"You don't need me for a simple ambush. I'll stay behind with Lucien," Reyes said, sliding to his ass and propping his back on a stone to hold himself up.

Reyes had been paired with the demon of Pain. Physical agony brought him pleasure and being injured actually strengthened him. While fighting. When the fight ended, however, he weakened like anyone else. Right now, he was more battered than the rest of them, with a cheek so swollen his line of vision had to be shit. "Besides, someone needs to guard the prisoners."

Seven against eight, then. Poor Hunters. Actually, Sabin suspected Reyes wanted to stay behind to guard Lucien's body from the enemy. Lucien could take it with him to the spirit world only when he was strong enough, which he probably wasn't now.

"Your women are going to give me hell," Sabin muttered. The two had recently fallen in love, and both Anya and Danika had asked only one thing of Sabin before the warriors left for Egypt: bring my man back safely.

When the boys arrived home in this damaged condition, Danika would shake her head at Sabin in disappointment as she rushed to soothe Reyes and Sabin would feel slimier than the mud on his boots. Anya would shoot him exactly as Lucien had been shot, *then* comfort Lucien, and Sabin would feel pain. Lots and lots of pain.

Sighing, Sabin eyed the rest of the warriors, trying to decide who was good to go and who needed to remain behind. Maddox—Violence—was the fiercest fighter he'd ever known. Right now the warrior was as blood-soaked as Sabin and panting for breath, but he'd already moved beside Amun, ready for action. His woman wasn't going to be any happier with Sabin than the others.

Slight shift, and the lovely Cameo came into view.

She was the keeper of Misery, as well as the only female soldier among them. What she lacked in size she made up for in ferocity. Besides, all she had to do was start talking, all the sorrows of the world in her voice, and humans were likely to kill *themselves* without her ever having to lay a finger on them. Someone had sliced at her neck, leaving three deep grooves. It didn't seem to slow her down as she finished cleaning her machete and joined Amun and Maddox.

Another shift. Paris was the keeper of Promiscuity and once upon a time, he'd been the most jovial among them. Now he seemed harder, more restless with every day that passed, though Sabin couldn't fathom what had caused the change. Whatever the reason, he currently loomed in front of the Hunters, huffing and growling and so keyed for war he vibrated with brutal energy. And though there were two gushing holes in his right leg, Sabin didn't think the warrior would be asking to rest anytime soon.

Beside him was Aeron, Wrath. Only recently had the gods freed him from a curse of bloodlust where no one around him had been safe. He'd lived to hurt, to kill. At moments like these, he still did. Today he'd fought as though that lust still consumed him, hacking at and mauling anyone within his reach. That was good, except…

How much worse would that bloodlust be when the next fight ended? Sabin feared they would have to summon Legion, the tiny, blood-hungry demon who worshipped Aeron like a god and was the only one who could calm Aeron during his darker moods. Unfortunately, she was currently doing surveillance work for them in hell. Sabin liked to keep up-to-date on Underworld happenings. Knowledge was power and one never knew what one would be able to use.

Aeron suddenly slammed a fist into a Hunter's temple, sending the human to the floor in an unconscious heap.

Sabin blinked at him. "What was that for?"

"He was about to attack."

Doubtful, but just like that, Paris cut whatever invisible tether had been holding him in place and swooped through the rest of the huddle, methodically punching the Hunters until every single one of them was down.

"That should keep them calm as Amun for the time being," he rasped darkly.

Sighing, Sabin switched his attention yet again. There was Strider, Defeat. The man couldn't lose at anything without enduring debilitating pain, so he made sure to win. Always. Which was probably why he was digging a bullet out of his side in preparation for the battle to come. Good. Sabin could always count on him.

Kane, keeper of Disaster, walked in front of him, ducking as a shower of pebbles fell from the ceiling, plumes of dust spraying in every direction. Several warriors coughed.

"Uh, Kane," Sabin said. "Why don't you stay here, too? You can help Reyes watch the prisoners." A flimsy excuse and they all knew it.

There was a pause, the only sound to be heard the scrape of stone against sand as the doorway continued that slow glide. Then Kane gave a clipped nod. He hated being left out, that much Sabin knew, but his presence sometimes caused more problems than it solved. And as always, Sabin placed victory above his friends' feelings. It wasn't something he enjoyed doing, wasn't something he'd do in any other situation. But someone had to act with cold-blooded logic or else they'd always lose.

With Kane out, that made the coming battle seven against seven. Totally even. Poor Hunters. They still didn't stand a chance. "Anyone else want to stay behind?"

A chorus of "No" circled the chamber, eagerness dripping from the different timbres. An eagerness Sabin shared.

Until Pandora's box was found, these skirmishes were a necessity. But it couldn't be found without those damn godly artifacts to show the way. And as one of the four relics was supposedly here in Egypt, this particular skirmish was more important than most. He would not allow Hunters to claim a single artifact, for that box could destroy Sabin and everyone he held dear, drawing the demons out of their bodies and leaving only lifeless shells.

Despite his confidence that he would win this day, he knew he would have to work for victory. Led as the Hunters were by Sabin's sworn enemy, Galen, a demon-possessed immortal in disguise, those "protectors of all that was good and right" were privy to information humans should not have been privy to. Such as the best way to distract the Lords…the best way to capture them…the best way to destroy them.

Finally the stone ceased sliding, and Amun peeked inside. He waved a hand to signal it was safe to enter. No one stepped forward. Sabin's men and Lucien's had only just resumed fighting together, having been separated for over a thousand years. They hadn't yet learned the best formation.

"We going to do this or just stand here and wait for them to find us?" Aeron grumbled. "I'm ready."

"Look at you, all unenthusiastic and shit," Gideon said with a smirk. "I'm not impressed."

Time to take charge, Sabin mused. He considered the best strategy. These last few centuries he'd gotten nowhere with the Hunters, rushing heedlessly into battle with only a single thought: kill. But the enemy's numbers were growing, not shrinking, and to be honest, their determination and hatred were growing, as well. It was time for a new way of battle, of cataloging his resources and weaknesses before charging ahead.

"I'll go first since I'm the least injured." He curled his finger under the trigger of his gun before reluctantly sheathing it. "I want you staggered, a less injured man paired with a more injured one. You'll work together, most injured acting as backup while the healthier takes out the target. Leave as many as you can alive," he commanded. "I know you don't want to, that it goes against every instinct you possess. But don't worry. They'll die soon enough. Once we ferret out the leader—and learn his secrets—they'll be useless to us and you can do what you want to them."

The trio blocking his path broke apart, allowing him to sail inside the narrow hallway without pause, then everyone filed behind him, their footfalls offering only the slightest whisper. Battery-powered lamps illuminated the hieroglyph-covered walls. Sabin allowed his gaze to rest on those glyphs for only a second, but that was long enough to burn the images into his mind. They showed one prisoner after another being ushered to a cruel execution, hearts removed while they still beat inside their chests.

Human scents coated the stale, dusty air: cologne, sweat, an assortment of foods. How long had the Hunters been here? What were they doing here? Had they already found the artifact?

The questions skated through his mind, and his demon latched on to them. As Doubt, it couldn't help itself. *Clearly they know something you do not. It might be enough to topple you. Your friends could very well take their last breaths this night.*

Doubt could not lie, not without causing Sabin to pass out cold. It could only use derision and supposition to topple its victims. He'd never understood why a fiend from hell couldn't utilize deceit—best he could come up with was that the demon carried a curse of its own—but he'd long since accepted it. Not that he'd allow *himself* to topple this night. *Keep it up and I'll spend the next week sequestered in my bedroom, reading so I can't think too much.*

But I need to feed, was the whined reply. The worry it caused was its greatest nourishment.

Soon.

Hurry.

Sabin held up his hand, stopped, and the warriors behind him stopped as well. There was a chamber up ahead, its doorway already open. The sound of voices and footsteps echoed, perhaps even the buzz of a drill.

The Hunters were indeed distracted and begging for an ambush. *I'm just the man to give it to them.*

Are you, really? the demon began, Sabin's threat unheeded. *Last time I checked—*

Forget about me. I've supplied you with food as promised.

There was a gleeful exclamation inside his head,

and then Doubt was opening its mind to the Hunters inside the pyramid, whispering all manner of destructive thoughts. *All for nothing...what if you're wrong... not strong enough...could soon die...*

Conversation tapered away. Someone might even have whimpered.

Sabin held up a finger, then another. When he raised the third, he and the warriors jumped into motion, a war cry echoing.

CHAPTER TWO

GWENDOLYN THE TIMID SHRANK against the far wall of her glass cell the moment the horde of too-tall, too-muscled, too-bloody warriors charged into the chamber she'd both loved and hated for over a year. Loved, for being inside of it would have meant she was out of her cell, freedom a possibility. Hated, for all the torturous deeds that had taken place there. Deeds she'd witnessed and feared.

The very men who had performed those deeds gave startled cries, dropping their Petri dishes, needles, vials and various tools. Glass shattered. Savage roars boomed, the intruders leaping forward with practiced menace, their arms slashing, their legs kicking. Down, down their targets fell. There was no question about who would win this fight.

Gwen trembled, unsure what would happen to her and the others when things settled. The warriors were clearly inhuman, like her, like all the women locked in the cells surrounding hers. They were too hard, too strong, too *everything* to be mortal. Exactly what they were, however, she didn't know. Why were they here? What did they want?

She'd known so many disappointments this last year that she didn't dare hope they'd come on a rescue mission. Would she and the others be left here to rot? Or would these men try and use them as the detestable humans had done?

"Kill them!" one of the captured shouted to the new warriors, the sound of her hard, angry voice causing Gwen to draw her arms around her middle. "Make them suffer as we have suffered."

The glass that kept the women removed from the outside world was thick, impenetrable by fist or even bullet, yet every heartbreak inside the chamber and cells was a blast inside Gwen's ears.

She knew how to block the noise, something her sisters had taught her to do as a young child, but she desperately wanted to hear her captors' defeat. Their grunts of pain were like midnight lullabies to her. Soothing and sweet.

But strong as the warriors obviously were, they never once delivered a deathblow. Oddly, they merely wounded their prey, knocking them unconscious before focusing on the next opponent. And after what seemed too-short seconds but had probably been minutes, only one human was left standing. The worst of the lot.

One of the warriors stepped forward, approaching him. Though all the newcomers had possessed lethal skill, this one had fought the dirtiest, going for the groin, the throat. He raised his arm as if to render the final blow, but then Gwen's wide-eyed gaze caught his and he paused. Slowly he lowered his arm.

Her breath caught. Brown hair soaked with blood was plastered to his head. His eyes were the color of brandy, deep and dark, and they, too, were threaded with crimson. Impossible. Surely she imagined the wild glow. His face, so roughly hewn it could only have been carved from granite, promised destruction in its every

line and hollow, though there was something almost…
boyish about him. A startling contradiction.

His shirt had been slashed to ribbons, rope after rope
of sun-kissed muscle visible every time he moved. Oh,
the sun. How she missed it, craved it. A violet butterfly tattoo wrapped around his right rib cage and dipped
into the waist of his pants. The points of its wings were
razored, making it appear at once feminine and masculine. Why a butterfly? she wondered. Seemed odd that
such a strong, vicious warrior would have chosen it.
Whatever the reason, the mark somehow comforted her.

"Help us," she said, praying the immortal could hear
through soundproof glass as she could. But if he heard
her, he gave no indication. "Free us." Still no reaction.

*What if they leave you here? Or worse, what if
they're here for the same reason as the humans?*

The thoughts filled her head suddenly, and she
frowned, perhaps even paled. The fears weren't out of
place; she'd wondered the exact same things only a short
while ago. But these were somehow different…foreign.
They were not her own, not spoken in her own inner
voice. How…what…?

Sharp white teeth sank into the man's bottom lip as
he clawed at his temples, clearly infuriated.

What if—

"Stop!" he snarled.

The thought forming inside her head halted abruptly.
She blinked in confusion. The warrior shook his head,
scowl intensifying.

Distracted as the immortal clearly was, her human
tormentor decided to act, closing the remaining distance between them.

Gwen straightened, calling, "Look out!"

Attention remaining fixed on Gwen, the granite-faced warrior reached out an arm and grabbed the human by the neck, choking and stopping him at the same time. The man—Chris was his name—flailed. He was young, perhaps twenty-five, but still leader of the guards and scientists here. He was also a man she despised more than captivity.

Everything I do, I do for the greater good, he was fond of saying, just before he raped one of the other women right in front of her. He could have artificially inseminated them, but had preferred the humiliation of forced intercourse. *I wish this was you,* he had often added. *Every one of these females is a substitute for you.*

Despite his desires, he'd never touched her. He was too afraid of her. They all were. They knew what she was; they'd seen her in action the day they came for her. Unintentionally maul a few humans to death, and a girl gained a reputation, she supposed. Rather than eliminate her, however, they'd kept her, experimenting with different drugs in the ventilation system in the hopes of knocking her out long enough to use her. They hadn't yet succeeded, but they hadn't given up, either.

"Sabin, no," a beautiful, dark-haired female said, patting the once again red-eyed warrior on the shoulder. Her voice was so laden with sorrow, Gwen cringed. "Like you told us, we might need him."

Sabin. A strong name, reminiscent of a weapon. Fitting.

Were the two lovers?

Finally that all-consuming gaze left her, and she was able to breathe. Sabin dropped Chris and the bastard fell to the ground, unconscious. She knew he still lived because she could hear the rush of blood in his veins, the crackle of air filling his lungs.

"Who are these women?" a blond warrior said. He had bright blue eyes and a lovely face that promised compassion and safety, but he was not the one Gwen suddenly imagined herself curling next to and sleeping beside peacefully. Deeply. *Safely.* Finally.

All these months, she'd been afraid to sleep, knowing Chris would have loved to take her unaware. So she'd slumbered in short, shallow spurts, never relaxing her guard. Sometimes she'd had to refrain from simply giving herself to the evil man in exchange for the prospect of closing her eyes and sinking into dark oblivion.

A black-haired, violet-eyed mountain stepped forward, eyeing the cells surrounding Gwen's. "Dear gods. That one is pregnant."

"So is that one." This speaker had multicolored hair, pale skin and eyes as brilliant a blue as his blond friend's, though this man's were rimmed with a darker shade. "What kind of bastards keep pregnant females in these conditions? This is low even for Hunters."

The females in question were banging on the glass, begging for help, for freedom.

"Anyone hear what they're saying?" the mountain asked.

"I do," Gwen answered automatically.

Sabin turned to her. That brown gaze no longer sleeked with red once more honed in on her, probing, searching...perusing.

A shiver danced the length of her spine. Could *he* hear her? Her eyes widened as he strode to her cell, sheathing a knife at his waist. Heightened as her senses were, she caught the barest hint of sweat, lemon and mint. She inhaled deeply, savoring every nuance. For so long, she'd smelled nothing but Chris and his over-powering cologne, his pungent drugs and the terror of the other females.

"You can hear us?" Sabin's timbre was as rough as his features and should have grated her nerves like sand-paper, but somehow soothed her like a caress.

Tentatively, she nodded.

"Can they?" He pointed to the other prisoners.

She shook her head. "Can you hear me?"

He, too, shook his head. "I'm reading your lips."

Oh. That meant he'd been—was—watching her in-tently, even when his head had been turned. The knowl-edge was not unpleasant.

"How do we open the glass?" he asked.

Her lips pressed in a stubborn line, and she dared a quick look at the heavily armed, blood-coated predators behind him. Should she tell him? What if they planned to rape her fellow prisoners, just as the others had done? Just as she'd feared?

His harsh expression softened. "We haven't come to harm you. You have my word. We just want to free you."

She didn't know him, knew better than to trust him, but pushed to shaky legs anyway and lumbered to the glass. Up close like this, she realized that Sabin towered over her and his eyes were not brown as she'd supposed. Rather, they were ringed with amber, coffee, auburn and bronze, a symphony of colors. Thankfully, the glow of red was still gone. Had she imagined it those times?

"Woman?" he said.

If he opened the cell as promised…if she could gather her courage and not freeze in place as was her habit…escape would finally be possible. The hope she'd denied earlier sprang to life, unstoppable and tantalizing, tempered only by the thought that she might cruelly and brutally destroy these possible saviors without meaning to.

Don't worry. Unless they try to harm you, your beast will remain caged. One wrong move from them, though…

Worth the risk, she thought, saying, "Stones."

His brow furrowed. "Bones?"

Swallowing the lump in her throat, she lifted one of her nails—a claw when compared to a human's—and carved the word *STONES* in the glass. Each etching would hold only long enough for her to finish a letter before wiping clean. Damned godly glass. She'd often wondered how the humans had acquired it.

A pause. A frown, his attention remaining fixed on her too-long, pointed nail. Was he wondering what type of creature she was?

Then, "Stones?" Sabin asked, gaze once more meeting hers.

She nodded.

He spun in a circle, eyeing the entire chamber. Though the look-over lasted only a few seconds, Gwen suspected he'd cataloged every inch of the place and could have found his way out of it in the dark.

The warriors lined up behind him, all staring at her expectantly. Mixed with the expectation, however, was curiosity, suspicion, hatred—for her?—and even lust. One step, two, she backed away. She'd take hate over lust any day. Her legs trembled so violently she feared her muscles would give out. *Stay calm. You cannot panic. Bad things happen when you panic.*

How did one combat the desire of others? There was

nothing she could do to cover herself more than she already was. Upon her imprisonment, her jeans and T-shirt had been replaced with a white tank and short skirt her captors had given her—easier access that way. Bastards. One of the tank straps had ripped months ago and the shirt now gaped. She'd had to tie it under her arm to keep her breast covered.

"Turn away," Sabin suddenly growled.

Gwen spun without thought, long red hair swaying at her sides. Breath sawed in and out of her mouth, and sweat beaded over her brow. Why had he wanted her back? To better subdue her?

There was another of those heavy pauses. "I didn't mean you, woman." This time, Sabin's voice was soft, gentle.

"Aw, come on," someone said. She recognized the rich, irreverent tone of the male with the blond hair and blue eyes. "You're not serious about—"

"You're scaring her."

Gwen peeked over her shoulder.

"But she—" the heavily tattooed one began.

Once again Sabin interjected. "You want answers or not? I said turn!"

A few groans, the shuffling of feet.

"Woman."

Slowly she pivoted back around. All of the warriors had turned as Sabin commanded, giving her their backs.

Sabin placed a palm against the glass. It was large, unscarred and steady, but streaked with blood. "Which stones?"

She pointed to a grouping in a case beside him. They were small, about the size of a fist, and each had a different way to die painted on the front. The highlights:

a beheading, limb removal, a stabbing, a pike through the gut and a wildfire climbing the body of a man nailed to a tree.

"Good, that's good. But what do I do with them?"

Now panting with the need to be free—*close, so close*—she pantomimed the placing of a stone into a hole, like a key into a lock.

"Does it matter which stone goes where?"

She nodded, then pointed to each particular stone and which cell it opened. She'd come to dread the use of those stones, as it meant she would be forced to witness another rape. Sighing, she began to scratch the word KEY into the glass when Sabin slammed a fist into the stones' case, shattering the outer shell. It would have taken the strength of ten humans to do such a thing, yet he made it look effortless.

Several cuts branched from his knuckles to his wrists. Beads of crimson appeared, but he wiped them away as if they meant nothing. By that time, the injuries were already in the process of healing, torn flesh weaving back together. Oh, yes. He was something far greater than mortal. Not fae, for his ears were perfectly rounded. Not vampire, for he didn't possess fangs. A male siren, then? His voice was rich enough, delicious enough, yes, but perhaps too harsh.

"Grab a stone," he called, never taking his focus from her.

Instantly the warriors spun on their booted heels. Gwen purposely kept her gaze on Sabin, afraid that looking at the others would cause her fear to spike. *You're in control, doing good.* She couldn't—wouldn't—falter. Already she carried too many regrets.

Why couldn't she be like her sisters? Why couldn't

she be brave and strong and embrace what she was? If necessary, they would have cut off a limb to escape—and they would have done it long before now. They would have pounded a fist through the glass, then Chris's chest, and eaten his heart in front of him, laughing all the while.

She experienced a pang of homesickness. If Tyson, her former boyfriend, had told them of her abduction—which he probably hadn't, scared as he was of her sisters—then they were looking for her and they wouldn't give up until they found her. Despite her weaknesses, they loved her, wanted the best for her. But they would be so disappointed in her when they learned of her captivity. She'd failed herself, as well as her race. Even as a child she had run from conflict, which was how she'd earned the degrading moniker "Gwendolyn the Timid."

Her palms were damp, she realized, and she rubbed them on her thighs.

Sabin directed the men, telling them which stone belonged in which hole. He got a few of the placements wrong but she wasn't worried. They'd figure it out. He was correct about hers, though, and when one man, a blue-haired, pierced punk, tried to pick up the appropriate stone, Sabin's strong, tanned fingers banded around his wrist, stopping him.

The blue-haired one locked eyes with Sabin, who shook his head. "Mine," he said.

The punk grinned. "Hating what we see, are we?"

Sabin just frowned at him.

Gwen blinked in confusion. Sabin hated looking at her?

One by one the women were freed, some crying, some attempting to hurry out of the chamber. The

males didn't let them get far, catching them and surprising Gwen by cradling them gently, even when the
women fought violently. In fact, the most beautiful man
in the group, he of the multicolored hair, approached
the women one by one, softly muttering, "Sleep for
me, sweetheart."

Shockingly, they obeyed, sagging in the warriors'
protective arms.

Sabin crouched and palmed Gwen's stone, the one
that showed the man burning alive. When he straightened, he tossed it in the air, caught it easily. "Don't run.
All right? I'm tired and I don't want to chase you, but
I will if you make me. And I'm afraid I'll accidentally
hurt you."

You and me both, she thought.

"Don't...free her," Chris suddenly sputtered. How
long had he been awake? He lifted his head and spit out
a mouthful of dirt. Bruises had already formed under
his eyes. "Dangerous. Deadly."

"Cameo," was all Sabin said.

The female warrior knew what he wanted and stalked
to the human, grabbed him by the back of his shirt and
easily lifted him to his feet. With her free hand, she
placed a dagger at his carotid. Either too weak or too
frightened, he didn't struggle.

Gwen hoped it was fear that held him still. Hoped
it with every fiber of her being. She even stared at the
tip of the knife, willing it inside the bastard's throat,
piercing skin and bone and causing unforgettable agony.

Yes, she thought, entranced. Yes, yes, yes. *Do it.
Please, do it. Cut him, make him suffer.*

"What do you want me to do with him?" Cameo
asked Sabin.

"Keep him there. Alive."

Disappointment caused Gwen's shoulders to sag. But with the disappointment came a startling realization. Her emotions were under control, yet she was very close to releasing her inner beast anyway. All those thoughts of pain and suffering were not her own. They couldn't be. *Dangerous,* Chris had said. *Deadly.* He'd been right. *You have to stay in control.*

"Feel free to hurt him a bit, though," Sabin added, his eyes narrowing on Gwen. Was he…angry? At her? But why? What had she done?

"Don't set the girl free," Chris repeated. A tremor rocked his entire body. He backed away, but Cameo, obviously stronger than she appeared, jerked him back into place. "Please don't."

"Maybe you should leave the redhead in her cell," the tiny warrior woman said. "For now, at least. Just in case."

Sabin raised the stone, stopping just short of inserting it into the hole beside Gwen's cage. "He's a Hunter. A liar. And I think he hurt her, but doesn't want her able to tell us."

Gwen blinked over at him in shock and awe. He wasn't angry at her, but at Chris—a hunter?—for what he might have done. He truly meant what he'd said. He wouldn't harm her. Wanted her free. Safe.

"Is that right?" Sabin asked her. "He hurt you?"

Cheeks heating in mortification, she nodded. Emotionally, he'd destroyed her.

Sabin ran his tongue over his teeth. "He'll pay for that. You have my word."

Slowly the embarrassment faded. Her mother, who had disinherited her almost two years ago, would rather see her dead than weakened, but this man—this stranger—thought to avenge her.

Chris swallowed nervously. "Listen to me. Please. I know I'm your enemy, and I won't lie and pretend you're not mine. You are. I hate you with every fiber of my being. But if you let her go, she'll kill us all. I swear it."

"Will you try and kill us, little red?" Sabin asked her, even more gently than before.

Used to being called "bitch" and "whore" by the men here, Gwen felt the sweet endearment drift through her mind with the potency of a rose-scented summer breeze. In their few minutes together, this man had managed to gift her with the very thing she'd dreamed about since being locked up: a white knight, determined to slay her dragons. Sure, she'd once thought that white knight would be Tyson or even the father she'd never known, but still. It wasn't every day a dream came true.

"Red?"

Gwen snapped to attention. What had he asked? Oh, yeah. If she would try and kill him and his friends. She licked her lips and shook her head. If her beast overtook her, she wouldn't just try. She would succeed. *I have control. For the most part. They'll be fine.*

"That's what I thought." With a flick of his wrist, Sabin drove the stone home. Her heart thundered in her chest, nearly cracking her ribs. Gradually the glass lifted… lifted…soon…soon… And then there was nothing between her and Sabin but air. The scent of lemon and mint strengthened. The coldness she'd grown used to gave way to a blanket of heat that seemed to wrap around her.

She smiled slowly. Free. She was truly free.

Sabin sucked in a breath. "My gods. You're incredible."

She found herself stepping toward him, reaching out, desperate for the contact she'd been denied all these months. A single touch, that's all she needed. And then she would leave, go home. Finally.

Home.

"Bitch," Chris shouted, struggling against Cameo's hold. "Stay away from me. Keep her away from me. She's a monster!"

Her feet halted of their own accord, and her gaze swung to the wretched human responsible for all the distress, all the anguish, she'd endured for the past year. Not to mention what he'd done to her cell mates. Her nails elongated to razor points. Tiny, seemingly gossamer wings sprang from her back, ripping at the cotton, fluttering frantically. Her blood thinned in her veins, rushing through every part of her, fast, so fast, and her vision tunneled to infrared, colors fading as body heat became her only focus.

In that instant, she realized she'd never had any sort of control over her beast. Her darker side. It had swirled inside her all along, mostly quiet as it waited for the opportunity to strike...

Only Chris, only Chris, please gods only Chris. The chant rang through her mind, hopefully penetrating the bloodlust of her vengeful beast. *Only Chris, leave everyone else alone, attack only Chris.*

But deep down, she knew there would be no stopping the death toll now.

CHAPTER THREE

FROM THE FIRST MOMENT Sabin had seen the lovely red-head in the glass cell, he'd been unable to remove his gaze from her. Unable to breathe, to think. Her hair was long and curled wantonly, blond streaked with thick locks of ruby. Her eyebrows were a darker auburn, but just as exquisite. Her nose was buttoned at the end, her cheeks rounded like a cherub's. But her eyes...they were a sensual feast, amber with striations of sparkling gray. Hypnotic. Black lashes spiked around them, a decadent frame.

Halogens hung from hooks in the walls and drowned her in bright light. While that would have revealed another's flaws and did in fact expose the dirt streaking her skin, it gave her a healthy glow. She was petite, with small, round breasts, narrow hips and legs long enough to wrap around his waist and hold on through the most turbulent of rides.

Don't think like that. You know better. Yeah, he did. His last lover, Darla, had killed herself and he'd vowed not to get involved again. But his attraction to the red-head had been instant. So had his demon's, though Doubt wanted her for another reason. It had sensed her trepidation and had purposely targeted her, wanting inside her mind, pouncing on her deepest fears and exploiting them.

But she was not human, they'd both soon realized, and therefore Doubt had been unable to hear her thoughts unless she voiced them. That didn't mean she was safe from its evils. Oh, no. Doubt knew how to size up a situation and spread its poison accordingly. More than that, the demon relished a challenge and would work harder to learn this girl's nuances and ruin any faith she might have.

What was she? He'd encountered many immortals over his thousands of years yet he couldn't place her. She certainly appeared human. Delicate, fragile. Breakable. Those amber-silver eyes gave her away, though. And the claws. He could imagine those digging into his back.…

Why had the Hunters taken her? He feared the answer. Three of the six newly liberated females were clearly pregnant, which brought to mind only one thing: the breeding of Hunters. Immortal Hunters, at that, for he recognized two sirens with scars along the column of their necks where their voice boxes had obviously been removed, a pale-skinned vampire whose fangs were gone, a gorgon whose reptilian hair had been shaved and a daughter of Cupid who had been blinded. To prevent her from ensnaring an enemy in her love spell, Sabin supposed.

How cruel the Hunters had been to these lovely creatures. What had they done to the redhead, the loveliest of them all? Though she wore a tiny tank and skirt, he could see no scars or bruises to indicate mistreatment. That didn't mean anything, though. Most immortals healed quickly.

I want her. Intense fatigue radiated from her, yet

when she'd smiled at him in thanks for freeing her...
he could have died from the sheer glory of her face.

I want her, too, Doubt piped up.

You can't have her. Which meant he couldn't either.
*Remember Darla? As strong and confident as she was,
you still managed to break her down.*

Gleeful laughter. *I know. Wasn't it fun?*

His hands fisted at his sides. Fucking demon. Eventually everyone caved under the intense worries his
other, darker half constantly threw at them: *You aren't
pretty enough. You aren't smart enough. How could
anyone love you?*

"Sabin," Aeron's cold voice called. "We're ready."

He reached out and motioned the girl over with a
wave of his fingers. "Come."

But his redhead had backed herself against the far
wall, her body trembling in renewed fear. He'd expected her to beat feet, despite his warning of the consequences. He hadn't expected this...terror.

"I told you," he said gently. "We mean you no harm."

Her mouth opened, but no sound emerged. And as he
watched, the golden glow of her eyes deepened, darkened, black bleeding into the whites.

"What the hell is—"

One minute she was before him, the next she wasn't,
gone as if she'd never been. He spun, gaze scanning.
Didn't see her. But the only Hunter still standing suddenly belted out an agonized scream—a scream that
halted abruptly as his body sagged, collapsing on the
sandy floor, blood pooling around him.

"The girl," Sabin said, palming a blade, determined
to protect her from whatever force had just slain the
Hunter he'd planned to interrogate. Still he did not see

her. If she could disappear with only a thought like Lucien, she would be safe. Out of his reach forevermore, but safe. But could she? Had she?

"Behind you," Cameo said, and for once she sounded more shocked than miserable.

"My gods," Paris breathed. "I never saw her move, yet…"

"She didn't…did she…how could she have…" Maddox scrubbed a hand down his face, as though he didn't believe what he was seeing.

Again, Sabin spun. And there she was, back inside her cell, sitting, knees drawn to her chest, mouth dripping with blood, a…trachea?…clutched in one of her hands. She'd ripped—or bitten?—the man's throat out.

Her eyes were a normal color again, gold with gray striations, but they were completely devoid of emotion and so faraway he suspected the shock of what she'd done had numbed her mind. Her expression was blank, too. Her skin was now so pallid he could see the blue veins underneath. And she was shaking, rocking back and forth and mumbling incoherently under her breath. What. The. Hell?

The Hunter had called her a monster. Sabin hadn't believed it. Then.

Sabin stepped inside the cell, unsure of what to do but knowing he could neither leave her like this nor lock her back up. One, she hadn't attacked his friends. Two, swift as she was, she could escape before the window closed and do serious damage to him for breaking his word.

"Sabin, man," Gideon said, grim. "You might not want to rethink going in there. For once, a Hunter was lying."

For once. Try *once more*. "Know what we're dealing with here?"

"No." Yes. "She's *not* a Harpy, the spawn of Lucifer who did *not* spend a year unfettered on earth. I *haven't* dealt with them before and I *don't* know that they can kill an army of immortals in mere seconds."

As Gideon couldn't tell a single truth without soon wishing he were dead, his entire body wrapped in agony and riddled with suffering, Sabin knew everything he said was a lie. Therefore, the warrior *had* encountered a Harpy before—and he clearly didn't mean the word in a derogatory sense—and those Harpies *were* the spawn of Lucifer and *could* destroy even a brute like himself in a blink.

"When?" he asked.

Gideon understood his meaning. "Remember when I wasn't imprisoned?"

Ah. Gideon had once endured three months of torture at Hunter hands.

"One didn't destroy half the camp before a single alarm could be sounded. She didn't take off, for whatever reason, and the remaining Hunters didn't spend the next few days cursing the entire race."

"Hold on. Harpy? I don't think so. She isn't hideous." That little nugget came from Strider, the king of stating the obvious. "How can *she* be a Harpy?"

"You know as well as we do that human myths are sometimes distorted. Just because most legends claim Harpies are hideous doesn't mean they are. Now, everyone out." Sabin began tossing his weapons on the ground behind him. "I'll deal with her."

A sea of protests arose.

"I'll be fine." He hoped.

You might not be...
Oh, shut the hell up.

"She's—"

"Coming with us," he said, cutting Maddox off. He couldn't leave her behind; she was too valuable a weapon, a weapon that could be used against him—or used by him. *Yes,* he thought, eyes widening. *Yes.* "And she's coming alive."

"Hell, no," Maddox said. "I don't want a Harpy anywhere near Ashlyn."

"You saw what she did—"

Now Maddox cut *him* off. "Yes, I did, and that's exactly why I don't want her near my pregnant human. The Harpy stays behind."

Another reason to eschew love. It softened even the most hardened of warriors. "She has to hate these men as much as we do. She can help our cause."

Maddox was undeterred. "No."

"She'll be my responsibility, and I'll make sure she keeps her claws and teeth sheathed." Again, he hoped.

"You want her, she's yours," Strider said, always on his side. Good man. "Maddox will agree because you never pressure Ashlyn to go into town and listen to conversations Hunters might have had, no matter how badly you want to."

Eyes narrowed, Maddox popped his jaw. "We'll have to subdue her."

"No. I'll handle her." Sabin didn't like the thought of anyone else touching her. In any way. He told himself it was because she'd most likely been tortured, used in the most horrendous way, and might react negatively to anyone who tried, but...

He recognized the excuse for what it was. He was

attracted to her, and a man attracted couldn't turn off the possessive thing. Even when that man had sworn off women.

Cameo approached his side, attention riveted on the girl. "Let Paris deal with her. He can finesse the cruelest of females into a good mood. You, not so much, and we clearly need this one in a perpetual good mood."

Paris, who could seduce any woman, anytime, immortal and human alike? Paris, who needed sex to survive? Sabin's teeth ground together, an image of the couple flashing through his mind. Naked bodies tangled, the warrior's fingers gripping the Harpy's wild fall of hair, bliss coloring her expression.

Would be better for the girl that way. Would probably be better for them all, as Cameo had said. The Harpy would be more inclined to help them defeat the Hunters if she was fighting by her lover's side—and Sabin was now determined to have her help. Of course, Paris couldn't bed her more than once, would eventually cheat on her because he needed sex from different vessels to survive, and that would probably piss her off. She might then decide to aid the *Hunters*.

Bad idea, all the way around, he decided, and not just because he wanted it to be.

"Just...give me five minutes. If she kills me, Paris can have a turn with her." His dry tone failed to elicit a single chortle of laughter.

"At least let Paris put her to sleep as he did the others," Cameo persisted.

Sabin shook his head. "If she were to wake early, she would be scared and she might attack. I've got to get through to her first. Now get out. Let me work."

A pause. A shuffling of feet, heavier than usual as

the warriors were carrying the other women out. And then he was alone with the redhead. Or strawberry blond, he supposed the color was called. She was still crouched, still mumbling, still holding that damn trachea.

Such a bad little girl, aren't you? the demon said, tossing the words straight into the Harpy's mind. *And you know what happens to bad little girls, don't you?*

Leave her alone. Please, he begged the demon. *She cut through our enemy, preventing them from searching for—and finding—the box.*

At the word *box,* Doubt cried out. The demon had spent a thousand years inside the darkness and chaos of Pandora's box and did not want to return. Would do anything to prevent such a fate.

Sabin could no longer exist without Doubt. It was a permanent part of him and much as he sometimes resented it, he would rather give up a lung than the demon. The first he could regenerate.

Just a few minutes of quiet, he added. *Please.*

Oh, very well.

Satisfied with that, Sabin stepped the rest of the way inside the cell. He bent down, placing himself at eye level with the girl.

"I'm sorry, I'm sorry," she chanted, as though she sensed his presence. She didn't face him, though, just continued to stare ahead, unseeing. "Did I kill you?"

"No, no. I'm fine." Poor thing didn't know what she'd done or what she was saying. "You did a good thing, destroyed a very bad man."

"Bad. Yes, I'm very very bad." Her arms tightened around her knees.

"No, he was bad." Slowly, he reached out. "Let me

help you. All right?" His fingers lightly pried at hers, opening them up. The bloody remain fell from her grasp, and he caught it with his free hand, tossing it over his shoulder, away from her. "Now, isn't that better?"

Thankfully, his action didn't send her into another rage. She merely released a deep breath.

"What's your name?" he asked.

"Wh-what?"

Still moving at an unhurried pace, he brushed a strand of hair from her face and hooked it behind her ear. She leaned into his touch, even nuzzled her cheek against his palm. He allowed the caress to linger, savoring the softness of her skin when deep down he recognized the thin ledge of danger he walked. To encourage his attraction, to crave more of her, was to condemn her to utter misery as he'd done Darla. But he didn't pull away, even when she gripped his wrist and guided his hand through the silkiness of her hair, clearly wanting to be petted. He massaged her scalp. She practically purred.

Sabin couldn't recall a time he'd been so...tender with a woman, not even with Darla. Much as he'd cared for her, he'd placed more importance on victory than on her well-being. But at that moment, something about this girl drew him. She was just so lost and alone, feelings he knew well. He wanted to hug her.

See? You're already craving more. Frowning, he forced his arm to fall to his side.

A slight cry of despair escaped her, and maintaining what little distance there was between them became even harder. How could this needy creature have so savagely slain the human? Didn't seem possible, and he wouldn't have believed it had the story simply been relayed to him. He'd had to see it. Not that there had been much to see, given how quickly she'd moved.

Perhaps, like him, like his friends, she was captive to a dark force inside her. Perhaps she was helpless to stop it from treating her body as a puppet. The moment those thoughts struck him, he knew he'd guessed correctly. The way her eyes had changed color...the horror she'd exuded when she had realized what she'd done...

When Maddox slid into one of his demon's violent rages, the same changes overtook him. She couldn't help what she was and probably hated herself for it, the little darling.

"What's your name, red?"

Her lips edged into a frown, a mimic of his. "Name?"

"Yes. Name. What you're called."

She blinked. "What I'm called." The shallow rasp in her voice was fading, leaving a dawning awareness. "What I'm—oh. Gwendolyn. Gwen. Yes, that's my name."

Gwendolyn. Gwen. "A lovely name for a lovely girl."

Traces of color were returning to her face, and she blinked again, this time dragging her attention to him. She offered him a hesitant smile, one that spoke of welcome, relief and hope. "You're Sabin."

Exactly how sensitive were her ears? "Yes."

"You didn't hurt me. Even when I..." There was wonder in her voice, wonder tinged with regret.

"No, I didn't hurt you." He wanted to add, *Nor will I,* but he wasn't sure that was true. In his single-minded quest to defeat the Hunters, he'd lost a good man, a great friend. He'd healed from countless near-fatal injuries and had buried several slain lovers. If necessary, he would sacrifice this little bird to the cause as well, whether he desired her or not.

Unless you soften, Doubt suddenly piped up.

I won't. It was a vow, because he refused to believe otherwise. And it was a reinforcement of what he'd already known: he wasn't an honorable man. He *would* use her.

Gwen's gaze skittered past him, and her smile vanished. "Where are your men? They were right here. I didn't…I…did I…"

"No, you didn't hurt them. They're just outside the chamber, I swear it."

Her shoulders sagged as a sigh of relief escaped her. "Thank you." She seemed to be speaking to herself. "I—oh, heavens."

She had just spotted the Hunter she'd slain, he realized.

She paled again. "He—he's missing—all that blood… how could I…"

Sabin purposely leaned to the side, blocking her view and consuming her entire line of vision. "Are you thirsty? Hungry?"

Those unusual eyes swung to him, now lit with wild interest. "You have food? Real food?"

Every muscle in his body tightened at the sight of that interest. There was an almost euphoric edge to it. She could be toying with him, pretending to be excited by what he offered in order to relax his guard for an easier escape. *Must you be like your demon and doubt everyone and everything?*

"I have energy bars," he said. "Not sure they can be classified as food, but they'll keep you strong." Not that she needed any more strength.

Her lashes drifted closed, and she sighed dreamily. "Energy bars sound divine. I haven't eaten in over a year, but I've imagined it. Over and over again. Chocolate and cakes, ice cream and peanut butter."

A whole year without a crumb? "They gave you nothing?"

Those dark lashes lifted. She didn't nod or reply in the affirmative, but then, she didn't have to. The truth was there in her now-grim expression.

As soon as he finished interrogating the Hunters, every single one he'd found in these catacombs was going to die. By his hand. He'd take his time with the kills, too, enjoy every slash, every drop of blood spilled. This girl was a Harpy, spawn of Lucifer as Gideon had said, but even she did not deserve the gnawing torture of starvation. "How did you survive? I know you're immortal, but even immortals need sustenance to remain strong."

"They put something in the ventilation system, a special chemical to keep us alive and docile."

"Didn't fully work on you, I take it?"

"No." Her little pink tongue slashed over her lips hungrily. "You mentioned energy bars?"

"We'll have to leave this chamber to get them. Can you do that?" Or rather, would she do it? He doubted he could force her to do anything she didn't want to without ending up cut and broken, maybe dead. He wondered how the Hunters had trapped her. How they had gotten her here and lived to tell the tale.

A slight hesitation. Then, "Yes. I can."

Once again moving slowly, Sabin clutched her arm and helped her to her feet. She swayed. No, he realized, she snuggled up next to him, seeking closer contact with his body. He stiffened, poised to pull away—*keep her at a distance, have to keep her at a distance*—when she sighed, her breath trekking through the slashes in his shirt and onto his chest.

Now *his* eyes closed in ecstasy. He even wound an arm around her waist, urging her closer. Utterly trusting, she rested her head in the hollow of his neck.

"I've dreamed about this, too," she whispered. "So warm. So strong."

He swallowed the sudden lump in his throat, felt Doubt prowling the corridors of his mind, rattling the bars, desperate to escape, to obliterate Gwen's ease with him.

Too much faith, the demon said, as if that were some sort of disease.

The perfect amount, if Sabin were being honest with himself. He liked that a woman was looking at him as if he were a prince of light rather than a king of darkness, someone she needed to run screaming from. He liked that she'd allowed him to soothe her torment.

Foolish of her, though, he had to admit. Sabin was no one's hero. He was their worst enemy.

Let me talk to her! the demon demanded, a child denied a favorite treat.

Quiet. Causing Gwen to doubt him could very well rouse the feral Harpy, placing his men in danger. That, Sabin would not allow. They were too important to him, too necessary.

Distance, as he'd realized before, was needed. He dropped his arms and stepped away. "No touching." The words were a croak, harsher than he'd intended and she blanched. "Now come. Let's get out of here."

CHAPTER FOUR

THE WOMAN WAS GOING TO KILL HIM, and not because she was stronger and more vicious than he was. Which, if he thought about it, she was. He'd never ripped a man's throat out with his teeth, and he was damned impressed that Gwen had. She'd made the Lords of the Underworld look like marshmallows.

Two full days had passed since Sabin and his crew had rescued her from the pyramid. The only time she'd seemed content was at her first glimpse of the sun. Since then, she had not relaxed. Or eaten. The energy bars she'd so wanted, she had merely gazed at with utter longing before shaking her head and turning away. She hadn't even showered in the portable stall he'd had Lucien fetch her.

She didn't trust them, didn't want to risk poisoning or the vulnerability of unconsciousness or nakedness, and that was understandable. But damn it, he was seething with the need to *force* her to do those things. For her own good. Without the shit that had been pumped into her cell, she had to be feeling every bit of her starvation. She had to be exhausted and dirty as she was—from the past two days, as well as her confinement, which was strange because the other women had been clean—she couldn't possibly be comfortable. Forcing her, however, was not an option. He liked his trachea where it was.

Only thing she'd taken from him was clothing. *His* clothing. A camouflage tee and military fatigues. They bagged on her, even though she'd rolled the arms, waist and legs, but there wasn't a female who'd ever looked better. With that wild fall of strawberry curls...those take-me-to-bed lips...she was utter perfection. And knowing the material she wore had once touched his body...

I need to end my self-imposed celibacy. Soon.

The moment he returned to Buda, that's what he'd do. Find a willing woman who wanted only a good time and, well, show her a good time. No one would get hurt because he wouldn't be sticking around. But maybe then his head would clear and he'd figure out how to deal with Gwen.

Something else that bothered him was the way Gwen had planted herself in the corner and watched him no matter who entered his tent. Him. As if *he* were the biggest threat to her now. He'd snapped at her that day in the cavern, yeah, telling her not to touch him, but he'd also ensured that she remained on her feet on the trek through the desert to set up camp. He'd stayed with her, guarded her while the other warriors went back to the pyramid to search for anything they might have missed the first go-round. Did he really deserve the death glares?

Maybe...

Shut up, Doubt! I don't need your opinions.

Don't know why you care what she thinks. You've never been good for women, now have you? Funny that I now need to remind you *about Darla.*

Crouched on the sandy floor, Sabin closed the lid

of his weapon case with a forceful snap, locked it and turned to the bag of food he'd had Paris bring him.

Darla, Darla, Darla, the demon sang.

"Like I said, you can shut the hell up, you dirty piece of shit. I've had all of you I can take."

Gwen, still in the far corner, jerked as though he'd screamed. "But I didn't say anything."

He'd lived among mortals for a long time and had trained himself to converse with Doubt inside his head. That he'd forgotten his training now, in the presence of this skittish yet deadly woman...mortifying.

"I wasn't speaking to you," he muttered.

Paler than usual, she drew her arms around her middle. "Then to whom were you speaking? We're alone."

He didn't answer. Couldn't. Not without lying. Since Doubt's inability to lie had long ago spread to Sabin, he had to stick to the truth, evade, or he'd be sleeping for the next few days.

Thankfully, Gwen didn't press the issue. "I want to go home," she said softly.

"I know."

Yesterday, Paris had questioned all the freed women about their confinement. They'd indeed been kidnapped, raped, impregnated and told their babies would be taken from them and trained to be defenders against evil. Afterward, Lucien had flashed all but Gwen—who had told Paris nothing—to their families, who would hopefully hide them from Hunters in the peace and comfort that had been denied them during their captivity.

Gwen had asked to be taken to a deserted stretch of ice in Alaska, of all places. Lucien had reached out to take her hand, despite her failure to cooperate, and Sabin had stepped between them.

"Like I said in the cavern, she stays with me," he'd said.

Gwen had gasped. "No! I want to go."

"Sorry. Not gonna happen." He'd refused to face her, afraid he'd cave and release her despite the fact that her strength, speed and savagery could win him this war, thereby saving his friends.

By gods, he'd dreamed of an end, a victorious end, for too many years to count; he couldn't put Gwen's needs and wants before that victory.

Too badly did he want Galen, the person he hated most in this world, defeated and imprisoned.

Galen, the once forgotten Lord, was the very man who had convinced the warriors to help steal and open Pandora's box. He was also the man who had secretly planned to kill them all, then capture the demons they'd freed, becoming a hero in the eyes of the gods. But things hadn't worked out as the bastard hoped, and he'd been cursed to house a demon—Hope—right alongside the other warriors.

If only that had been the end of things. But as further punishment, they'd all been kicked out of the heavens. Galen, still determined to destroy the men who'd called him friend, had quickly assembled an army of outraged mortals, the Hunters, and this endless blood feud had erupted. A feud that only intensified with every year that passed. If Gwen could aid Sabin in even the small-est way, she was too valuable to release. She, however, thought differently.

"Please," she had begged. "Please."

"I'll take you home one day, but not now," he'd told her. "You could be useful to us, to our cause."

"I don't want to help with *any* cause. I just want to go home."

"Sorry. Like I said, it's not gonna happen any time soon."

"Bastard," she'd muttered. Then she'd frozen, as if she hadn't meant to say that aloud and now thought he would launch forward and beat her. When he didn't, she'd calmed a bit. "So I've traded one captor for another, is that it? You promised you wouldn't harm me." Soft, so soft. Even sadly resigned, and that had…hurt him. "Just let me go. Please."

Obviously, the girl was afraid. Of him, his friends. Of herself and her deadly abilities. Otherwise, she would have tried to ditch him or bargained for her release. But not once had she done so. Did she fear what they would do to her if they caught her? Or what she would do to them?

Or, as Doubt liked to whisper in the dark of night, did she have more sinister plans? Was she Bait, a very convincing trap laid by the Hunters? A trap meant to ruin him?

Not possible, he retorted every time. Such timidity couldn't be faked. The trembling, the refusal even to eat. Which meant her fears, whatever they were, were real. And the more time she spent with him, the more those fears and doubts would grow. They would become all that she knew, all that she thought about. She would question every word out of her mouth, every word out of *his* mouth. She would question every action.

Sabin sighed. Others here were already questioning his actions, and not because of his demon. At her plea, Lucien's expression had hardened—a rare thing, for Lucien was always careful to contain his emotions. After ordering Paris to guard her, he'd whisked Sabin to the home they'd rented in Cairo, where they could talk away from the others. Away from Gwen.

A ten-minute argument had ensued. And because flashing always sickened him, causing his stomach to churn, he hadn't been at his best.

"She's dangerous," Lucien had begun.

"She's strong."

"She's a killer."

"Hello, so are we. Only difference is, she's better at it than we are."

Lucien frowned. "How do you know? You've only seen her kill one man."

"And yet you would ban her from our home for that very killing—despite the fact that it was our enemy she killed. Look, Hunters know our faces. They're always on the lookout for us. But the only ones who knew her are now dead or locked up. She's our Trojan horse. Our own version of Bait. They'll welcome her and she'll slaughter them."

"Or us," Lucien had muttered, but Sabin could tell he was considering the point. "She just seems so…faint-hearted."

"I know."

"Around you, that will only get worse."

"Again, I know," he growled.

"Then how can you think to use her as a soldier?"

"Believe me, I've weighed the pros and cons. Faint-hearted or not, spirit broken down by me or not, she has an innate ability to destroy. We can harness that for our own benefit."

"Sabin…"

"She's coming with us, and that's that. She's mine." He hadn't wanted to claim her, not that way. He didn't need another responsibility. Especially a beautiful, apprehensive female he could never hope to possess. But it had been the only way. Lucien, Maddox and Reyes had brought females into their home, therefore they could not deny entrance to his.

He shouldn't have done that to her, should have just let her go for both their sakes. But as he'd reminded himself already, he'd placed his war with the Hunters above everything else, even his best friend, Baden, keeper of Distrust. Now dead, gone forever. He could make no exceptions for Gwen. She was coming to Budapest, like it or not.

First, though, he was going to feed her.

Crouching a few feet in front of her, putting them at eye level, Sabin began unwrapping Twinkies and unsealing Lunchables. He poked a straw in a juice box. Gods, he missed the home-cooked meals Ashlyn prepared and the gourmet cuisine Anya "borrowed" from Buda's five-star restaurants.

"Have you ever been inside an airplane?" he asked her.

"Wh-what do you care?" She lifted her chin, yellow fire snapping in her eyes. But that hot gaze wasn't on him. It was on the food he was spreading on the paper plate beside him.

A show of spirit. He liked it. Definitely preferred it over the stoic acceptance she'd displayed earlier. "I don't. I simply want to ensure you're not going to—" Shit. How could he phrase this without reminding her of what she'd done to the Hunter?

"Attack you out of fear," she finished for him, cheeks heating with embarrassment. "Unlike you, I don't lie. You take me on a plane that isn't headed to Alaska and there's a very good chance you'll meet my…darker half." The last words were choked.

His eyes slitted dangerously, his mind caught on the beginning of her speech. He wadded up the plastic wrappers scattered around him and shoved them into the cloth trash bag. "What do you mean, unlike me? I've never lied to you." That he was still conscious proved it.

"You said you meant me no harm."

A muscle ticked in his jaw. "And I didn't. Don't."

"Keeping me here is harming me. You said you'd free me."

"I did free you. From the pyramid." He shrugged, sheepish. "And as long as you're uninjured physically, I consider you unharmed." A sigh slipped from him. "Is it really so bad, being around me?"

Her lips pressed into a thin line.

Ouch. "Doesn't matter. You're gonna have to get used to me. The two of us will be spending a lot of time together."

"But why? You said I could be useful; I haven't forgotten that. What I don't understand is what you think *I* can do."

Why not tell her everything? he thought. It could soften her toward him and his cause. Or it could frighten her even more and finally send her running. Would he be able to stop her?

Not knowing what he wanted of her had to be torture, though, and she'd suffered enough. "I'll supply you with any piece of information you want," he said. "*If* you eat."

"No. I—I can't."

Sabin lifted the plate, circled it around. She followed every movement as though entranced. Sure that he had her attention, he lifted one of the Twinkies and bit into half.

"Can't," she said again, though she sounded exactly as she looked: entranced.

He swallowed before licking away any remaining cream. "See. Still alive. No poison."

Hesitantly, as though she simply couldn't help herself any longer, Gwen reached out. Sabin placed the dessert in her hand, and she immediately snatched it to her chest. Several minutes ticked by in silence, and she did nothing but eye him warily.

"So this food is payment for listening to you?" she asked.

"No." He would not allow her to think bribery was acceptable. "I just want you healthy."

"Oh," she said, clearly disappointed.

Why disappointment?

Doubt nearly danced with the urge to crawl out of Sabin's head and into Gwen's. Much longer, and he'd lose his hold. One wrong suggestion from the demon, however, and Sabin knew she would throw the tiny morsel to the ground.

Eat it, he projected. *Please eat it.* It wasn't the most nutritious of snacks, but at this point he would have been happy if she'd eaten a pile of sand.

Finally, she lifted the golden cake and tentatively nibbled on the edge. Those long, dark lashes closed, and a tiny smile appeared. Absolute ecstasy radiated from her—the kind that usually arrived on the heels of an orgasm.

His body reacted instantly, every muscle hardening. His heartbeat picked up speed; his palms itched to touch. *My gods, she's lovely.* Quite possibly the most exquisite thing he'd ever beheld, all carnal pleasure and blissful decadence.

The rest of the cake was inside her mouth a second later, her cheeks puffing with its mass. As she chewed, she reached out, silently commanding him to give her another. He did so without hesitation.

"Shall I take half?" he asked before letting go.

Black began to swirl in her eyes, obliterating gold.

Maybe not. He raised his hands, palms out, and she stuffed the second cake into her mouth. The black faded, the gold returning. Crumbs fell from the corner of her lips.

"Thirsty?" He held up the juice box.

Again she reached out, fingers waving him to hurry. Within seconds, every drop of juice was gone.

"Slow down, or you'll make yourself sick."

Just like that, the black returned to her irises. At least it didn't bleed into the whites as it had moments before she'd slain the Hunter. Sabin pushed the plate to her, and she polished off the rest of the food.

When she finished, she settled back into the tent, that contented smile making another appearance. Rich pink painted her cheeks. And before his eyes, her body filled out. Her breasts overflowed. Her waist and hips flared perfectly, sinfully. His cock, still hard and aching, twitched in response.

Stop. Now. His erection would probably terrify her, so he remained in the crouch, his knees together, his chest hunched.

What if she liked it? What if she asked you to close the distance and kiss her? Touch her?

Zip it.

But then Gwen began to pale. Her smile fell, becoming a frown.

"What's wrong?" he asked.

Without a word, she jerked up the bottom tent flap, leaned outside and retched, heaving, every drop and crumb leaving her. Sighing, he pushed to his feet and gathered a rag. After soaking it with the contents of a water bottle, he shoved it into her fingers. She eased the rest of the way into the tent and wiped her mouth with a trembling hand.

"Knew better," she mumbled, returning to her former position. Arms locked around her legs, holding them to her chest.

Knew better than to eat too quickly? Well, yeah. 'Cause he'd warned her.

Sabin cleared his throat and decided to feed her again once her stomach had settled. For now, they could finish their conversation. After all, she'd lived up to her side of the bargain. She *had* eaten.

"You asked what I needed you to do. Well, I need your help finding and killing the men responsible for your... treatment." *Tread carefully. Don't rouse her dark side with painful memories.* But there was no way around it. "The others, they told us what had been done. The fertility drugs, the rapes. How there were other women once locked in those cages. Women who were raped as well, their babies taken away from them. A few seemed to think this has been going on for years already."

Gwen's back was pressed against the sand-colored tent flaps, yet she tried to scoot backward, as though she needed to escape from his words and the images they evoked.

Sabin himself had cringed, hearing the stories. He

might be half demon, but he had never done anything as terrible as what had been done to the women in that cavern.

"Those men are vile," he said. "They need to be destroyed."

"Yes." One of her arms fell from her legs, and she drew little circles in the dirt beside her hip. "But I... wasn't." The words were so softly spoken, he had to strain to hear them.

"You weren't, what? Raped?"

Nibbling on her bottom lip—a nervous habit of hers?—she shook her head. "He was too afraid to open my cage, so he left me alone. Physically, at least. He... took the others in front of me." There was guilt in her tone.

Ah. She felt responsible.

Sabin felt only relief. The thought of this fae-like creature being held down, her legs pried apart while she cried and begged for mercy, mercy that would never have been given... He anchored his hands on his thighs, his nails elongating into claws and cutting past fatigues.

When he returned to Budapest, the Hunters in his dungeon would suffer untold agonies, he thought for the thousandth time. He'd tortured men before, considered it a necessary part of war, but this time he would truly enjoy it.

"Why did he keep you, then, if he was afraid of you?"

"Because he hadn't given up hope that the right drugs would make me biddable."

Blood beaded where claw met skin. She'd lived in terror, he was sure, of that very thing happening. "You can avenge yourself, Gwen. You can avenge the other women. I can help you."

Her lashes lifted, the sand she played with clearly forgotten, and then those amber orbs were probing all the way to his soul. "So can you. Avenge us, I mean. Obviously those men did something to you. You came here to fight them, didn't you?"

"Yes, they did something to me and mine, and yes, I came here to fight them. That doesn't mean I can destroy them on my own." Otherwise, he would have done so by now.

"What did they do to you?"

"They murdered my best friend. And they hope to murder everyone else I hold dear, all because they believe the lies of their leader. I've been trying to obliterate them for centuries," he admitted. The fact that the Hunters continued to thrive was like a dagger in his side. "But I kill one, and five more take his place."

When she didn't blink at the word *centuries,* he realized she knew he, too, was immortal. But did she know what he was?

No way she's guessed. Like most every other woman in your life, she would despise what you are. How could she not? And look at her now. So sweet, so gentle. No evidence of hatred. Yet. The last emerged in a singsong.

Doubt. His constant companion. His cross to bear.

"How do I know you aren't one of them?" she demanded. "How do I know this isn't simply another way to try and gain my cooperation? I'll help you fight your enemy and you'll rape me. I'll get pregnant, and you'll steal the child from me."

Doubts. Courtesy of his demon?

Before he could think up a reply, she added tightly, "I watched you fight those men. You hurt them, claim to hate them, but you didn't kill them. You let them live.

That isn't the action of a warrior who wants to annihilate his enemy."

As she spoke, an idea sprouted. A way to prove himself. "And if we'd killed them, you would have been convinced of our hate for them?"

More nibbling on that lush bottom lip. Her teeth were white and straight and a little sharper than a human's. Kissing her would probably draw blood, but part of him suspected every drop would be worth it. "I—maybe."

Maybe was better than nothing. "Lucien," he called without removing his attention from her.

Her eyes widened, and again she tried to scoot back. "What are you doing? Don't—"

Lucien stalked through the front flaps, glancing between them expectantly. "Yes?"

"Bring me a prisoner from Buda. I don't care which."

Lucien's brow furrowed in curiosity, but he didn't reply. He simply disappeared.

"I can't help you, Sabin," Gwen said, sounding agonized. Imploring him to understand. "I really can't. There's no reason to do whatever it is you're about to do. I shouldn't have yelled at you the way I did. All right? I admit it. I shouldn't have insulted you with my doubts. But I seriously can't fight anyone. I freeze up when I'm scared. And then I black out. When I wake up, everyone around me is dead." She gulped, squeezed her eyes shut for several seconds. "Once I start killing, I can't stop. That's not the kind of soldier you can rely on."

"You didn't kill me," he reminded her. "You didn't kill my friends."

"I honestly don't know how I pulled myself back. That's never happened before. I wouldn't know how to do it again." She paled.

Lucien had reappeared, a struggling Hunter at his side.

Reaching behind his back, Sabin withdrew a dagger and stood.

When Gwen saw the glinting silver, she gasped. "Wh-what are you doing?"

"Was this man one of your tormentors?" Sabin asked the now trembling female.

Silent, her gaze moved from one man to another in dread. She clearly knew what was coming, but this wasn't the heat of battle. It would be straight-up murder.

The Hunter kicked and punched at Lucien. That failed to gain him his freedom, so he began sobbing. "Let me go, let me go, let me go. Please. I only did what I was told. I didn't mean to hurt the women. It was all for the greater good."

"Shut it," Sabin said. This time he'd be the one to show no mercy. "You didn't save them either, now did you?"

"I'll stop trying to kill you. I swear!"

"Gwendolyn." Sabin's voice was hard, uncompromising, a roar compared to the Hunter's pleading. "An answer. Please. Was this man one of your tormentors?"

She gave a single nod.

Without word or warning, he cut the Hunter's throat.

CHAPTER FIVE

SABIN HAD MURDERED a man in front of her.

Several hours had since passed and they'd even switched locations, but the bloody image of that human falling to his knees, then to his face, gurgling then silent, so silent, refused to leave her mind.

Gwen had known that kind of fierceness churned inside of Sabin—the same kind of fierceness that had driven *her* to murder. She'd known he was hard and harsh and untouched by softer emotion. His eyes gave him away. Dark and cold, utterly calculating. The moment he'd led her out of her cell those two days ago, she'd begun to notice the way he surveyed the scene around him and decided who and what he could use to his advantage. Everything else was debris.

She must have been debris. Then. Now he wanted her help.

But she couldn't forget that he'd pushed her away at their first meeting. Oh, that had embarrassed her. One simple brush of his callused fingertips and she'd glued herself to the side of a man who wanted nothing to do with her. But he'd been so warm, his skin buzzing with energy, and she'd been without contact for so long that she hadn't been able to help herself.

No touching, he'd said, and he'd looked capable of slaying her if she dared reach out again.

His cruel treatment had reminded her that her rescuers were strangers to her, that their intentions could be every bit as nefarious as her captors'. So she'd kept her distance, using the past two days to study them and eavesdrop on their most private conversations. Her mental ear blocks were back in place, noise levels at a bearable pitch, allowing her to listen to men who didn't want to be listened to without grimacing and giving herself away.

One of those conversations, which had taken place this very morning, constantly replayed through her mind.

"We've been here nearly a month with no sign of an artifact. How many pyramids do we have to search before we find it? I thought we'd hit the jackpot with that last pyramid, since Hunters were there, but..."

Again, the men had referenced a hunter. It's what they'd called Chris. Why?

"I know, I know. All that work, and we're no closer to finding the box."

Artifact? Box?

"Should we pack up?"

"Might as well. Until our Eye gives us another clue, we're directionless."

Strange phrasing. Their eye could offer clues? To what? And whose eye were they referring to? Maybe the one called Lucien; she'd noticed he had one blue eye and one brown.

"Hopefully Galen hasn't found anything, either. Well, other than a pike through the heart. That, I'd like to help him find."

Who was Galen? Did it matter? These warriors were...odd. Half of them spoke as though they'd stepped straight from the pages of *Medieval Times* magazine. The other half could have been members of a street gang. They loved each other, though, that much was clear. They were solicitous of each other's needs, either joking and laughing together or fiercely guarding each other's backs.

Three men and the female warrior, Cameo, had sneaked inside Sabin's tent while Sabin was off speaking with Lucien. Each of them had delivered the same message to her: Hurt the warrior and suffer. They hadn't waited for her reply, but had stomped out. The woman's voice... Gwen shuddered. She *had* suffered just listening to it.

As much time as she'd spent alone in the tent, she could have escaped. Probably should have tried. But mile after mile of desert, glaring sun and who knew what else surrounded her, and fear had held her in place.

Even though she'd grown up in the ice-mountains of Alaska, she could have dealt with the sand and the sun. She hoped. It was the unknown that intimidated her. What if she stumbled upon a vicious tribe? Or a pack of hungry animals? Or another group of treacherous men?

Besides, striking out on her own to follow her then-boyfriend Tyson to another state had been the catalyst to her ending up the unwilling guest of that glass cage. Still. Had the warriors hurt her, she would have risked it. Again, she hoped. But they hadn't touched her, not in any way. And she was happy about that. Really. The fact that Sabin had kept his word—no touching—was like a gift from the heavens. Really.

"You okay?" The warrior named Strider plopped down in the plush leather seat beside hers. They were inside a private jet, high in the sky, and there was quite a bit of turbulence.

Surprisingly, that didn't faze her.

Gwen suppressed a bitter laugh. A shadow could send her into hiding, but rattle-your-bones, fall from the sky instability made her yawn. Maybe because she herself could fly—kind of—though she hadn't attempted the skill in forever. Maybe because as much as she'd been through this past year, crashing seemed like child's play.

"You're pale," he added when she remained silent. He whipped a pack of Red Hots from his pocket, downed a mouthful, then offered some to her. She smelled cinnamon, and her mouth watered. "You need to eat."

At least she didn't cower from him. Still. What was with these men and their need to shove junk food in her face? "No thanks. I'm fine." She hadn't yet recovered from the Twinkies.

Oh, she didn't regret eating them. The sugary taste… the fullness of her stomach…it had been heaven. For those few precious seconds, anyway. But she'd known better than to eat food freely given to her. Cursed by the gods, like all Harpies, she could only eat food that she had stolen or earned. It was penance for crimes her ancestors had committed and completely unfair, but there was nothing she could do about it.

Well, she could starve.

She was too afraid of the consequences to steal from these men, as well as too afraid of what they'd make her do to earn a few precious morsels.

"You sure?" he asked, then tossed a few more of the candies in his mouth. "These are small, but they pack a hell of a punch." Of all the men, he'd been the most gentle with her. The most concerned with her care. Those bright blue eyes never regarded her with disdain. Or fury, as was sometimes the case with Sabin.

Sabin. Always her mind returned to him.

Her gaze sought him. He reclined in the lounge across from her, his eyes closed, spiked lashes casting shadows over the hollows of his sharp cheeks. He wore fatigues, a silver chain necklace and a leather man-bracelet. (She was pretty confident he'd want the "man" distinction.) His features were relaxed in slumber. How could someone look at once harsh and boyish?

It was a mystery she wanted to solve. Maybe when she did, she'd stop seeking him out. Five minutes couldn't pass without her wondering where he was, what he was doing. This morning, he'd been packing his things, preparing for this trip, and she'd imagined her nails digging into his back, her teeth sinking into his neck. Not to hurt him, but to pleasure *her!*

She'd had a few lovers over the years, but those kinds of thoughts had never plagued her before. She was a gentle creature, damn it, even in bed. It was him, his I-don't-care-about-anything-but-winning-my-war attitude that was causing this…darkness inside her. Had to be.

She should have been disgusted by what he'd done, slicing the human's neck as he had. At the very least, she should have screamed for him to stop, protested, but part of her, that darker side, the monster she couldn't escape, had known what was about to happen and had been glad. She'd *wanted* the human to die. Even now, there was a spark of gratitude inside her chest. For Sabin. For the wonderfully cruel way he'd dispensed justice.

That was the only reason she'd willingly stepped

onto this plane. A plane headed not for Alaska but Budapest. That, and the respectful distance the warriors had maintained from her. Oh, and the Twinkies. Not that she could give in to their sweet temptation again.

Maybe she should, though. Maybe she should strap on her big girl panties and steal one, risking punishment. Her skills were rusty, but now that she was out of the cell, her hunger pangs were strong, her body growing weaker. Too, if the warriors hurt her that would finally spur her into action. Going home.

She'd have to decide quickly, though. Pretty soon, she wouldn't have the strength or clarity to appropriate a fallen crumb, much less an entire meal, and she definitely wouldn't have the strength to leave. What made it worse was that she wasn't simply battling hunger, she was also battling lethargy.

She wasn't cursed to stay awake forever or anything like that, but sleeping in front of others was against the Harpies' code of conduct. And with good reason! Sleeping left you vulnerable, open to attack. Or, say, abduction. Her sisters didn't live by many rules, but they never deviated from that one. She wouldn't either. Not again. Already she'd embarrassed them enough.

But without food and without sleep, her health would continue to decline. Soon the Harpy would take over, determined to force her into wellness.

The Harpy. While they were one and the same, she considered them separate entities. The Harpy liked to kill; she didn't. The Harpy preferred the dark; she preferred the light. The Harpy enjoyed chaos; she enjoyed tranquility. *Can't let her out.*

Gwen gazed around the plane, searching for those Twinkies. Her eyes, however, stopped on Amun. He was the darkest of the warriors, and someone she'd never heard speak a word. He hunched in the seat farthest from her, his hands over his temples, moaning as though in great pain. Paris, the one with the brown and black hair—the seductive one, as she'd come to think of him, with his azure eyes and pale skin—was beside him, staring pensively out the window.

Across from them was Aeron, the one covered from head to foot in tattoos. He, too, was silent, stoic. The three of them could have been spokesmen for misery. *And I thought I had it bad.* What was wrong with them? she wondered. And did they know where the Twinkies were?

"Gwendolyn?"

Strider's voice pulled her from her thoughts with a jolt. "Yes?"

"Lost you again."

"Oh, sorry." Had he asked her something?

The plane hit another bump. A lock of sandy hair fell over Strider's forehead, and he brushed it aside. Another cinnamon-scented breeze followed the motion. Her stomach grumbled. "I know you won't eat," he said, "but are you thirsty? Would you like something to drink?"

Yes. Please, yes. Her mouth watered even more, but she said, "No, thanks."

"At least accept a bottle of water. It's capped, so you don't have to worry that we've done something to it." He produced a glistening, ice-cold bottle from the cup holder beside him and waved it in front of her face. Had it been there the entire time?

Inside, she wept. *Looked so good...* "Maybe later." The words were croaked.

He shrugged as if he didn't care, but there was disappointment in his eyes. "Your loss."

Surely there was something nearby that she could steal. Once again, she searched the plane. Her gaze snagged on the half-drunk cherry-flavored water beside Sabin. She licked her lips. *No, it will be Sabin's loss.* Soon as Strider left her, she'd go for it, damn the consequences.

Maybe. No, she would. But he was here now, and she might as well get some answers out of him. She could also use the time to build her courage. "Why are we flying?" she asked. "I saw the one called Lucien disappear with the other women. We could have reached Budapest in seconds."

"Some of us don't handle flashing all that well." His eyes darted pointedly to Sabin.

"So some of you are babies?" The words were out before she could stop them. It was something she would have said to her sisters, the only people in the world she could be herself around without fear of recrimination. Bianka, Taliyah and Kaia understood her, loved her and would do anything to protect her.

Rather than offend Strider, however, her words amused him. He barked out a laugh. "Something like that, though Sabin, Reyes and Paris prefer to think they catch a virus whenever they're flashed somewhere."

Twins Bianka and Kaia were the same way. They'd rather believe they were stricken by infirmity than cop to a limitation. Taliyah, cold as ice and twice as hard, simply didn't react to anything.

Slowly Strider's merriment faded and he studied Gwen intently from head to toe. "You know, you're different than I expected."

Hold your ground. Don't squirm. "What do you mean?"

"Well…wait, will what I say offend you?"

And cause her to erupt, was what he was really asking. Seemed he was as afraid of her dark side as she was. "No." Maybe.

His intense stare probed all the deeper as he weighed the legitimacy of her claim. He must have seen the determination in her features because he nodded. "I think I've said this before, but from what little I know, Harpies are hideous creatures with misshapen faces, sharp beaks and the lower half of a bird. They're spiteful and pitiless. You…you're none of those things."

Had he so easily forgotten what she'd done to Chris?

She glanced over at Sabin, who hadn't budged. His breathing was deep, even, his lemon and mint scent wafting to her. Hadn't he reminded Strider that not all legends were completely true? "We have a bad rap, that's all."

"No, it's more than that."

For her, yeah. Not that she could tell him. Her sisters—lucky as they were—had shape-shifter fathers. Taliyah's was a snake, the twins' a phoenix. Hers, on the other hand, was an angel—a fact she was forbidden to talk about. Ever. Angels were too pure, too good for her kind to respect, and Gwen had enough weaknesses. As always, the thought of her father had her flattening a palm over her heart.

While Harpies were mainly a matriarchal society, fathers *were* allowed to see their children if they so wished. Both of her sisters' fathers had chosen to be part of their daughters' lives. Gwen's hadn't gotten the chance. Her mother had forbidden it. She'd merely given Gwen a portrait of him to warn Gwen of what she would become—too morally superior even to steal her own food, unable to lie, concerned about others rather than herself—if she wasn't careful. And after Tabitha had washed her hands of Gwen, labeling her a lost cause, Gwen's father still hadn't tried to make contact. Did he even know she existed? A tide of longing swept through her.

All her life she'd had dreams of her father fighting any and everything to reach her, to whisk her into his arms and fly her away. Dreams of his love and devotion. Dreams of living in the heavens with him, protected forevermore from the world's evil and her own dark side.

She sighed. Only one name was to be mentioned when speaking of her lineage and that was Lucifer. He was strong, wily, vengeful, violent—in short, a poor enemy to have. People were less likely to mess with her, with any of them, if they thought the prince of darkness would be gunning for them.

And, to be honest, claiming him as family wasn't technically a lie. Lucifer was her great-grandfather. Her mother's grandfather. Gwen had never met him, for his year on earth had ended long before her birth, and she hoped they never crossed paths. Even the thought made her shudder.

Carefully considering her next words, she breathed deeply, taking in Strider's aroma of wood smoke and all that delicious cinnamon. Sadly, even that lacked the decadence of Sabin's scent. "Humans place a negative connotation on everything they cannot understand," she said. "In their minds, good always conquers evil, so anything stronger than they are is evil. And evil is, of course, ugly."

"Very true."

There was a wealth of understanding in his tone. Now was as good a time as any to determine just what he understood, she supposed. "I know you are immortal, like me," she began, "but I haven't figured out exactly *what* you are."

He shifted uncomfortably, glancing at his friends for support. Everyone listening quickly looked away. Strider sighed, an echo of the one she'd released earlier. "We were once soldiers for the gods."

Once, but no longer. "But what—"

"How old are you?" he asked, cutting her off.

Gwen wanted to protest the abrupt change of topic. Instead, coward that she was, she weighed the pros and cons of admitting the truth, asking herself the three questions every Harpy mother taught her daughters: Was it information that could be used against her? Would keeping it secret award her some type of advantage? Would a lie serve just as well, if not better?

No harm, she decided. No advantage, either, but she didn't mind. "Twenty-seven."

His brow puckered, and he blinked over at her. "Twenty-seven *hundred* years, right?"

If he were speaking to Taliyah, yes. "No. Just twenty-seven plain, ordinary years."

"You don't mean human years, do you?"

"No. I mean dog years," she said dryly, then pressed her lips together. Where was the filter that was usually poised over her mouth? Strider didn't seem to mind, though. Rather, he seemed stupefied. Would Sabin have had the same reaction were he awake? "What's so hard to believe about my age?" As the question echoed between them, a thought occurred to her and she blanched. "Do I *look* ancient?"

"No, no. Of course not. But you're immortal. Powerful."

And powerful immortals couldn't be young? Wait. He thought she was powerful? Pleasure bloomed inside her chest. In the past, that word had only been used to describe her sisters. "Yeah, but I'm still only twenty-seven."

He reached out—to do what, Gwen didn't know, didn't care—and she shrank back in her seat. While she'd craved Sabin's touch from the beginning—why, why, why?—and had even pictured herself doing those very wicked things to him this morning, the thought of anyone else putting their hands on her held no appeal.

Strider's arm dropped back to his side.

She relaxed, her eyes once again seeking Sabin. He was now red-faced, his jaw clenched. Bad dreams? Did all the men he'd killed clamor inside his head, tormenting him? Perhaps it was a blessing Gwen wasn't allowing herself to sleep. She had experienced those types of nightmares herself and hated every second of them.

"Are all Harpies as young as you?" Strider asked, reclaiming her attention.

Was this information that could be used against her? Would keeping it secret award her some type of advantage? Would a lie serve just as well, if not better? "No," she answered truthfully. "My three sisters are quite a bit older. Prettier and stronger, too." She loved them too much to be jealous. Much. "They wouldn't have been captured. No one can make them do anything they don't want. Nothing scares them."

Okay, she needed to shut up now. The more she

spoke, the more her own failures and limitations were brought to light. It'd be better if these men assumed she had *some* cojones. *But why can I not be like my sisters? Why do I run from danger when they race* to *it?* If one of them had been attracted to Sabin, they would have viewed his distance as a challenge and seduced him.

Wait. Stop. That was craziness. She wasn't attracted to Sabin. He was handsome, yes, and she'd even imagined herself making love to him. But that stemmed from a sense of gratitude. He'd set her free and slain one of her enemy. And yeah, she was also baffled by him. He was all that was violent and hard, yet he hadn't once hurt her. But admit to an attraction to the immortal warrior? Never.

When Gwen started dating again, she would pick a kind, considerate human who didn't rouse her darker side in any way. A kind, considerate human who preferred board meetings over swordplay. A kind, considerate human who made her feel cherished and accepted, despite her faults. Someone who made her feel normal.

That's all she'd ever wanted.

SABIN'S ATTENTION WAS zeroed on Gwen. Had been since they'd boarded the plane. Okay, fine. Since the moment he'd met her. He'd thought she refused to relax because he intimidated her, so he'd pretended to sleep. He must have been right because she'd let down her guard and opened up. To Strider.

A fact that irritated the hell out of him.

He didn't dare "wake up," though. Not even when he'd heard Strider try to touch her, and Sabin had wanted to drive his fist into his friend's nose, smashing cartilage into brain tissue. Their conversation fascinated him.

The girl—and that's what she was, a girl, only twenty-seven fucking years old, which made him feel like Father fucking Time—considered herself a failure in every possible way, and her sisters paragons. Prettier? Not likely. Stronger? He shuddered. They wouldn't have been captured? Anyone could be taken unaware. Himself included. Nothing scared them? Everyone had a deep, dark fear. Again, even Sabin. He feared failure as much as Gideon feared spiders.

Timid as Gwen was and as shocked as she'd been that day in the cavern, he'd known she had doubts about her own strength and her feral abilities, but he'd had no idea how deep they actually ran. The way she compared herself to her sisters proved she had doubts on top of doubts. Girl was riddled with them. And being around him would only make them worse.

All of his past lovers had been confident, self-reliant women. (Aged thirty-five and up, damn it.) He'd chosen them for that very reason, their confidence. But they'd quickly changed, his demon sinking sharp claws of uncertainty through them and cutting deep. A few, like Darla, had even committed suicide, unable to bear the constant scrutiny of their appearance, their wit, the people around them. After Darla, he'd given up on females and relationships once and for all.

Then he'd seen Gwen. He desired—oh, did he desire. He could maybe allow himself one night with her and be able to justify it in some way, he thought. But he doubted one night would be enough. Not with her. There were too many ways to take her, too many things he wanted to do to that curvy little body.

Her lush beauty fired his blood every time he glanced at her, made his mouth water and his body ache. Her insecurity roused his protective instincts as much as his demon's destructive urges. Her sunshine scent, buried underneath the grime she'd yet to wash off, continually wafted to him, summoning him closer…closer still…

To give in was to destroy her. *Don't forget.*

Perhaps I'll be good. Perhaps I'll leave her alone.

At the sweet cajoling, Sabin bit his tongue, drawing blood. The demon wanted him to doubt its malicious intent. *I fell for that once. I won't again.*

"You do that a lot," Strider said now to Gwendolyn, pulling Sabin from his musings.

"What?" Her voice was breathless, raspy. At first, Sabin had thought her fatigue responsible for such a timbre. But no, that hoarseness was all her. And pure sex.

"Watch Sabin. Are you interested in him?"

She gasped, obviously outraged. "Of course not!"

Sabin tried not to scowl. A little hesitation would have been nice.

Strider chuckled. "I think you are. And guess what? I've known him for thousands of years, so I've got dirt."

"So," she sputtered.

"So. I don't mind spilling. I mean, I'd be acting as a friend to both of you if I changed your mind about him."

Your friend undermines you, Doubt said, *perhaps wants her for himself. Trusting him after this might not be wise.*

Sabin experienced a moment of unease before he shook the feeling off. *He warns her away for her own good. For* my *own good. Just as he claimed. Now shut it.*

"I want nothing to do with him, I assure you."

"Then you won't care if I leave you without telling you what I know." Through his narrowed eyes, Sabin watched Strider push to his feet.

Gwen grabbed his wrist and jerked him back down. "Wait."

Sabin had to grip the arms of his seat to stop himself from leaping up and separating them.

"Tell me," she said, and released the warrior of her own accord.

Slowly Strider eased back into his chair. He was grinning. Even as limited as Sabin's line of sight was, he could see the bright gleam of Strider's teeth. He suddenly wanted to grin himself. Gwen was curious about him.

Probably wants to learn the best way to kill you.

Shut up, damn it!

"Anything particular you'd like to know?" Strider asked her.

"Why is he so…distant?" She was still looking over at him, her gaze burning him, probing deep. "I mean, is he like that with everyone or am I just a lucky girl?"

"Don't worry. It's not you. He's like that with all females. He has to be. See, his demon is—"

"Demon?" Gwen gasped out. Her back jerked ramrod-straight, and her face leeched of color. "Did you just say demon?"

"Oh, uh…did I say that?" Strider once again glanced around the plane helplessly. "No, no. I think I said seaman."

"No, you said demons. Demons. Demons and Hunters and that butterfly tattoo. I should have guessed the moment I saw that tattoo, but you seemed so nice. I mean, you didn't hurt me, and thousands of people have butterfly tattoos." She, too, gazed around the plane, studying the warriors through new, wild eyes. On her feet a second later, she jumped away from Strider and backpedaled toward the bathroom. She extended her arms, as though the puny action could keep everyone at bay. "I—I get it now. You're the Lords, aren't you? Immortal warriors the gods banished to earth. M-my sisters told me bedtime stories about your evils and conquests."

"Gwen," Strider said. "Calm down. Please."

"You killed Pandora. An innocent woman. You burned ancient Greece to the ground, filling the streets with blood and screams. You tortured men, removed their limbs while they still lived."

Strider's expression hardened. "Those men deserved it. They killed our friend. Tried to kill us."

"If she screams, wonderful things are going to happen," Gideon said, grim, easing to Strider's side. "Don't try and knock her out, and I won't help, okay?"

"Wait. Before we do any manhandling and maybe lose our throats, let's try something else. Paris!" Strider barked, his gaze never leaving Gwen. "You're needed."

A determined Paris approached just as Sabin gave up the pretense of sleeping and popped to his feet. "Gwen," he said, hoping to cajole her to calm before Paris could work his wiles. But she was having trouble catching her breath, hysteria curtaining her features. "Let's talk about—"

"Demons…all around me." She opened her mouth and screamed. And screamed and screamed and screamed.

CHAPTER SIX

DEMONS. LORDS OF THE UNDERWORLD. Once beloved soldiers of the gods, now reviled plagues of earth. Each man carried a demon inside his body, a demon so vile that even hell had been unable to contain it. Demons like Disease, Death, Misery, Pain and Violence. *And I'm trapped inside a small aircraft with them,* Gwen thought, her hysteria reaching new heights.

The plane, on the other hand, was shuddering and tilting, losing altitude at an alarming rate. That didn't stop the Lords. They were closing in around her, encircling her, pinning her. Her heart drummed heavily in her chest, causing blood to surge through her veins and roar in her ears. If only that roar dulled the wild screech of the Harpy... No such luck. There was a tumultuous symphony inside her head, clanging, tolling, wiping away her sanity, tossing her down...down...into a black void where only death and destruction reigned.

Brutal and powerful as these warriors were, she should have suspected they were possessed by demons. The red eyes the first time she'd seen Sabin...the jagged butterfly tattoo on his ribs...

I'm so stupid.

Though Gwen had been watching these men the past few days, she must have been too tired, too hungry, too relieved by her liberation to notice the tattoos on the others, wherever they were. That, or she'd been too caught up in Sabin's appeal. Actually, now that she thought about it, the warriors had always been fully dressed in her presence, as if they'd sympathized with what she'd been through and hadn't wanted to frighten her by showing too much skin. But now she knew the truth. They'd simply been hiding their marks.

What demon possessed Sabin? she wondered. What demon had she observed, fascinated by every word and action? What demon had she imagined herself kissing and touching, clawing and writhing against?

How could her sisters adore these princes of evil? Well, the idea of them, anyway. To her knowledge, they'd never met. Who would have survived if they had? They were men without mercy or remorse, capable of any dark deed, and they were engaged in a never-ending war that stretched from past to present, sea to sea, death to death.

Each time she'd been told about them, her fear of predators skulking in the night and fiends hiding in the sunlight had multiplied. That was when she'd begun to fear the predator inside herself, for that was why she'd been told those stories. So that she might emulate the warriors. Even as Gwen had recoiled at the thought, the Harpy had soaked up every word, ready to prove itself.

I have to escape. Can't stay here any longer. Nothing good can come of it. Either they'll kill me next or my Harpy will fight all the harder to be like them. She might have been better off in the hands of their dastardly enemy.

"You have to stop screaming, Gwen."

The harsh, familiar voice penetrated the chaotic mire flooding her mind, but still the shrieks persisted.

"Shut her up, Sabin. My fucking ears are bleeding."

"Not helping, asshole. Gwendolyn, you have to calm down or you'll hurt us. Do you want to hurt us, darling? Do you want to kill us after we saved you, sheltered you? We might harbor demons, but we aren't evil. I think we've proven that to you. Did we not treat you and the others better than your captors? Have I touched you in anger? Forced myself on you? No."

What he said was true. But could she trust a demon? They loved to lie. *So do Harpies,* a voice of reason piped up. Part of her did want to trust them; the other part of her wanted to jump from the plane. The still shuddering, still plummeting plane.

Okay, time to think logically. She'd been with them for two days. She was alive and well, with not even a scratch. If she continued to panic, the Harpy would break free from her hold, controlling her, hungry to wreak havoc. She'd most likely take out the pilot—perhaps even herself—in the inevitable crash. How foolish would she be, having survived captivity *and* the Lords only to end up offing herself?

Logic achieved.

As calm nudged its way into her mind, her high-pitched screams faded. Everyone stood frozen. In, out she breathed—or tried to, her throat felt swollen, blocked—now hearing the frantic alarm coming from the cockpit. Before she could work up another panic, the plane evened out and then everything quieted.

"That's a good girl. Now back off, guys. I've got her." Sabin didn't sound confident, just determined.

Light winked into her awareness, and colors quickly followed suit, real life painting itself around her. Holy hell. Her vision had gone infrared, and she hadn't even known it. The Harpy had been close, so damn close, to breaking free. It was a miracle that she hadn't.

Gwen was still standing in the back of the plane, a grouping of red leather chairs around her. Only Sabin remained in front of her. The others had moved away, but they hadn't turned their backs. Afraid to? Or were they protecting their leader?

Sabin's chocolate gaze was leveled on her, fiercer than it had been even inside the catacombs, his daggers thrusting at men she now knew were Hunters. He had his hands raised, empty, palms out. "I need you to calm some more."

Did he? she thought dryly. Maybe she would if she could draw enough air through her nose or mouth, but she still couldn't manage it. Dizziness was creeping up on her, black once again sneaking into her line of vision.

"What can I do to help you, Gwen?" There was a shuffle of footsteps as he closed the rest of the distance between them. His heat seeped into her.

"Air," she was finally able to force past the knot in her throat.

Sabin's hands settled atop her shoulders, gently pushing. Her legs were too weak to offer any type of resistance, so she tumbled down—straight into one of those chairs. "I need air."

With no hesitation, Sabin dropped to his knees. He inserted his big body between her legs and cupped her face, forcing her to focus on him. Intense brown eyes became the new center of her world, an anchor in a turbulent storm.

"Take mine." His callused thumb caressed her cheek, abrading lightly. "Yes?"

Take his…what? she wondered, and then she didn't

care. Her chest! Constricting, pinching bone and muscle together. A sharp pain tore through her ribs and slammed into her heart, causing the organ to skitter to a momentary halt. Gwen jerked.

"You're turning blue, darling. I'm going to place my mouth over yours, give you my breath. All right?"

What if this is a trick? What if—

Shut up! Even in her haze, she knew the eerie, ghostly whisper was not her own. Thankfully, it heeded her command and quieted. Now, if only her lungs would open up. "I—I—"

"Need me. Let me do this." If he feared her response, he gave no indication. One of his hands trailed to the base of her neck and drew her forward, even as he leaned into her. Their lips pressed together, a heated tangle. His hot tongue pried her teeth apart, and then warm, minty air was sliding down her throat, soothing.

Her arms wound around him of their own accord, holding him captive, meshing them together chest to chest, hardness to softness. His necklace was cold, even through her shirt, and made her gasp. She greedily took his breath. "More."

He didn't hesitate. He blew inside her mouth, and another warm, calming breeze moved through her. Little by little the dizziness faded; her head cleared, darkness once more giving way to light. The frantic dance of her heart slowed to a gentle waltz.

A need to kiss him, truly kiss him and learn his taste, filled her. His origins, forgotten. His past, of no consequence. Their audience, vanished as if they'd never been present. Only the two of them existed. Only the here and now mattered. He'd calmed her, saved her, gentled her, and now, here in his arms, real life slipping away, the fantasy she'd had of him, of them, played through her mind. Bodies wrapped around each other, straining. Skin slick with sweat. Hands roaming. Mouths seeking.

She threaded her fingers through the silkiness of his hair and tentatively brushed her tongue against his. Lemon. He tasted of sweet lemons and a hint of cherry. A moan escaped her, reality so much more decadent than she could have dreamed. So heady...so...heavenly. Pure and good and everything a girl could want from a lover. So she tilted her head and did it again, sinking deeper, silently demanding more.

"Sabin," she breathed, wanting to praise him. Maybe thank him. No one had ever made her feel so protected, cherished, safe, needy, so needy. Not with something as simple as a kiss. A kiss that left no room for fear. Perhaps she could let go, even be herself, and not worry about her dark side...about hurting him. "Give me more."

Instead of obeying, he jerked his head away and tugged her arms from him until there was no longer any physical link between them. "Touch me again!" she wanted to shout. Her body *needed* him, needed contact.

"Sabin," she repeated, studying him. He was panting, trembling, his face pale—but not from passion. Fire didn't dance in his eyes, determination did.

He hadn't kissed her back, she realized. Her own desire-haze faded, just as the dizziness had done a bit ago, leaving the harsh realities she'd foolishly forgotten. Voices clamored around her.

"—didn't see that one coming."

"Should have."

"Not the kiss, idiot. The calming. Her eyes had turned, and her claws had emerged. She was poised to strike. I mean, hello. Am I the only one who remembers what happened to the Hunter who tangled with her?"

"Maybe Sabin's a portal to heaven like Danika," someone said dryly. "Maybe the Harpy saw a few angels while receiving mouth-to-mouth."

Male chuckles abounded.

Gwen's cheeks heated. Half of what they'd said escaped her understanding. The other half mortified her. She'd kissed a man, a demon, who clearly wanted nothing to do with her—and she'd done it in front of witnesses.

"Ignore them," Sabin said, his voice so guttural it scraped against her eardrums. "Focus on me."

Their gazes clashed together, brown against gold. She scooted as far back in her chair as she could, putting as much distance between them as possible.

"Are you still afraid of me?" he asked, head tilting to the side.

She raised her chin. "No." *Yes.* She was afraid of what he made her feel, afraid that what he was would again cease to matter. Afraid he'd never crave her the way she suddenly craved him. Afraid that the wonderfully protective man in front of her was nothing more than a mirage, that evil waited just below the surface, ready to devour her whole.

Such a coward you are. How the hell could she have kissed him like that?

One of his brows arched. "You wouldn't be lying, would you?"

"I never lie, remember?" Ironically, that was a lie.

"Good. Now listen closely, because I don't want to have this discussion again. I have a demon inside my body, yes." He gripped her armrests so tightly his knuckles slowly blanched. "It's there because centuries ago I stupidly helped open Pandora's box, unleashing the spirits inside. As punishment, the gods cursed me and all the warriors you see on this plane to carry one inside ourselves. In the beginning, I couldn't control that demon and did some…bad things, as you said. But that was thousands of years ago, and I now have control. We all do. Like I told you in that cell, you have nothing to fear from us. Got me, red?"

Red. Earlier, during her panic attack, he'd called her something else. Something like…sweetheart? No. Tyson used to call her sweetheart. Dearest? No. But close. Darling? Yes! Yes, that was it. She blinked in surprise. In delight. This hard warrior who could cut a man's throat without hesitation had referred to her as precious treasure.

So why hadn't he kissed her back?

"We've reached our destination, guys," an unfamiliar voice dripping with relief said over the intercom. The pilot, she figured, and experienced a wave of guilt for the trouble she had caused. "Prepare for descent."

Sabin remained in place, an indomitable rock between her legs. "Do you believe me, Gwen? Will you still willingly travel to our home?"

"I was never willing."

"But you never tried to escape."

"Should I have braved a strange land by myself, with no provisions?"

He frowned. "I've seen for myself how skilled you are. And we've offered you provisions time and time again. For whatever reason, part of you wants to be with us or you wouldn't be here. You know it, and I know it."

Logic she couldn't deny. But…why? Why would part of her want to stay? Then or now?

You know the answer to that, though you've tried to deny it. Him. Sabin. Not attracted to him? Ha! She studied him, noting the thin lines of strain branching from his eyes, the spiky shadows cast by his lashes, the muscle twitching in his jaw. The erratic pound of his pulse, now so loud in her ears. Maybe he was just as attracted to her, but was fighting it, as she was. The thought pleased her.

Did he have a woman waiting for him in Budapest? A wife?

Gwen's hands fisted, the nails digging deep, cutting. She was no longer pleased. *This doesn't matter. You* shouldn't *want him.*

"Gwen. Will you?"

The way he said her name was a slap and a caress at the same time, jarring her, making her shiver. She liked that he sought her cooperation, though she suspected he would try and force her to his will if she declined. "Maybe I *should* have run."

"To what? A life of regrets? A life of wishing you had acted against the ones who hurt you? I'm offering you a chance to help me kill Hunters. And just so you know, killing them won't be the only benefit," he said.

"What do you mean?"

"I can help you control your beast the way I control mine. I can help you channel it for a good cause. Don't you want to be in control?"

All her life, she'd wanted only three things: to meet her father, earn her family's respect and learn to control her Harpy. If Sabin could deliver on that promise, she would finally, after all these years, have achieved one of the three. He was probably overreaching and destined to fail, but it was a temptation she couldn't resist.

"I'll go with you," she said. "I'll help you as best I can."

Relief pulsed from him as he closed his eyes and smiled. "Thank you."

That smile relaxed the stark edges of his face, making him appear boyish once again. As she drank him in, the plane jolted abruptly. Sabin was pushed back; she was propelled forward. To her delight—dismay— the distance between them never widened.

"On one condition," she added when they settled.

His relief hardened into something cruel. "What?"

"You have to invite my sisters." Maybe not right away. She was embarrassed by her circumstances and didn't want her sisters to see her like this, to know what had happened to her. But she missed them like crazy, and knew her homesickness would soon outweigh her embarrassment.

"Invite your sisters? You mean you want me to have to deal with *more* of you?"

"That had better be happiness in your tone, not disgust," she said, offended. "My sisters have castrated men for less."

Sabin pinched the bridge of his nose. "Sure. Invite them. Gods save us all."

CHAPTER SEVEN

PARIS SLOUCHED IN the backseat of an Escalade, Strider at the wheel and completely unaware of speed limits. Though the sun was shining on downtown Budapest, you couldn't tell it from where Paris was sitting. The windows were tinted so thickly the interior was cast in gloomy shadows. Anya, Lucien's lover and the minor goddess of Anarchy, had stolen the vehicle from gods knew where—along with a matching second and a Bentley for herself—just before they'd left for Egypt.

You don't have to thank me, she'd said, smiling beatifically. *Your horrified expressions are gift enough. The cars are very upscale gangster, if I do say so myself. And let's face it. You guys were in serious need of a makeover and these wheels do the job.*

Unfortunately, Paris had gotten stuck in the same car as Amun, who was gripping his head as if it was about to explode; Aeron, who couldn't stop glowering—dude needed his little demon friend, Legion, like, stat—as well as Sabin and his Harpy.

Sabin couldn't keep his eyes off the dangerous, throat-eating woman, and hadn't lost his hard-on since kissing her on the plane. Understandable, sure. She was incomparably lovely, with golden eyes almost diamond-like in their purity, lips as red as Eve's apple had probably been and a body that defined the word *temptation*.

And that strawberry hair was a miracle all its own. But she was a Harpy who'd been found in the enemy's camp and therefore not to be trusted for any reason.

Maybe she'd been abused like the other prisoners. Maybe she despised the Hunters as much as he did. Maybe…

But maybe wasn't good enough to earn his trust. Not anymore. She could be Bait, a pretty trap the Hunters had set and the Lords had welcomed with open arms.

Paris didn't want Sabin ending up like him: craving an enemy with every fiber of his being but unable to have her.

A minute, an hour, a month, a year ago—he didn't know, time no longer mattered to him—he'd been ambushed by Hunters and imprisoned. Because he played host to the demon of Promiscuity, he needed sex to survive. Sex every day, at least once, but never with the same woman. In that cell, strapped to a gurney, he'd grown so weak opening his eyes had become a chore. Not wanting to kill him before they found Pandora's box—without it, the death of his body would have freed his demon, allowing it to wander the earth, crazed, unfettered—they'd sent *her* in. Sienna. Plain, freckled Sienna with her elegant hands and untapped sensuality.

She'd seduced him, strengthening him exponentially. And for the first time since his possession, Paris had gotten hard for the same woman twice. In that moment, he'd known she belonged to him. Known that she was his—his reason for breathing. The reason he'd been spared death all these thousands of years. But her own people had shot her down as Paris absconded with her.

She'd died in his arms.

Now Paris was still forced to bed a new woman every

day, and if he couldn't find a woman, he had to find a man, even though he'd never been attracted to his own sex. A fuck was a fuck to the demon of Promiscuity. A fact that had long since plunged him down a spiral of shame.

Yet nowadays, no matter who his bed partner was, he had to picture Sienna's face to get hard. He had to picture her face to finish the job, because every cell in his body knew the person underneath him was wrong. Wrong scent, wrong curves, wrong voice, wrong texture. Wrong *everything*.

Today would be the same. Tomorrow, as well. And the next day and the next. For an eternity. There was no end in sight for him. Except death, but he didn't deserve death yet. Not until Sienna was avenged. Would she ever be?

You didn't love her. This is madness.

Wise words. From his demon? Himself? He didn't know anymore. Could no longer distinguish one voice from the other. They were one and the same, two halves of a whole. And both of them were at the breaking point, ready to snap at any moment.

Until then…

Paris patted the bag of dried ambrosia in his pocket and let out a sigh of relief. Still there. He now carried the potent stuff with him wherever he went. Just in case he needed it. Which, more often than not, he did.

Only when the ambrosia was mixed with human wine did the alcohol do what it was supposed to do and numb him. If only for a little while. Every day, though, it seemed like he had to add more to achieve the same buzz.

He'd just have to ask his friend to steal more. Gods

knew he deserved a few hours of peace, a chance to lose himself. Afterward, he would be refreshed, stronger, ready to fight his enemy.

Don't think about that now. Soon as he reached the fortress, he had a job to do. That came first; it had to. He forced his eyes to focus on his surroundings, his mind to blank. Gone were the multihued palaces, humans traipsing from one side of the streets to another. In their place were thickly treed hills, abandoned, forgotten.

The SUV popped a rocky ledge and ascended one of those hills, dodging trees and the little presents he and the others had left for any Hunter stupid enough to come gunning for them. Again, that is.

About a month ago, they'd stormed inside and blasted the hell out of his home, a home he'd lived in for centuries, forcing the warriors to patch up quickly before heading out on another trip, another battle. New furniture had been needed. New appliances. He didn't like it. There'd been so much change in his life lately—women in residence, the return of an old frenemy, the eruption of the war—he couldn't handle much more.

The fortress came into view, a towering monstrosity of shadow and stone. Ivy climbed the jagged walls, blending home into land and making it nearly impossible to differentiate between the two. The only thing that set them apart was the iron gate that now surrounded the structure. Another addition.

Eagerness suddenly saturated the cool air. Bodies tensed, mouthfuls of oxygen were held. So close…

Torin, who watched them from inside the fortress on monitors and sensors, opened that gate. As they meandered toward the tall, arching front doors, Aeron squeezed his armrest so tightly it snapped.

"A wee bit excited, are you?" Strider asked, glancing at him from the rearview mirror.

Aeron didn't reply. There was a good chance he hadn't even heard the question. His tattooed face registered determination and anger. Not the usual indulgent expression he wore when about to see Legion.

When the vehicle stopped, the entire group jumped out. Glaring sunlight beat down on his body, making him sweat under his T-shirt and jeans. Gods, was it even this hot in hell?

Soon as she emerged from the car, the little Harpy stepped to the side, delicate arms around her middle, eyes wide, face pale. Sabin tracked her every movement, not even looking away when he jerked out a bag and another toppled to his feet.

How could something as vicious as a Harpy be so timid? It just wasn't possible; it didn't fit. She was like two pieces of two different puzzles, and now Paris was thinking the girl should have been blindfolded on the way to the fortress.

Hindsight. They could always cut out her tongue to keep her from talking, he supposed. Maybe cut off her hands to keep her from signing or writing.

Who are *you?*

Before Sienna, he would have been the one fighting to *protect* the female. That he wasn't now, that he actually wanted her injured, should have filled him with guilt. Instead, he was angry that he hadn't done a better job of guarding his friends against her. All possible threats had to be eliminated. Throughout the years, the other warriors had tried to convince him of that but he'd always resisted. Now, he understood.

It was too late to do anything to her, though. Sabin

wouldn't allow it. Guy was wasted. Even before the rift that tore Lucien's group from Sabin's, Paris didn't recall ever seeing Sabin this intent on a woman. Which wasn't necessarily a good thing. If the girl's timidity wasn't an act, then Sabin would destroy her, one bit of her self-esteem at a time.

Maddox emerged from the second Escalade, a dark slash in Paris's periphery. The keeper of Violence didn't bother grabbing his bag but pounded swiftly up the porch steps. The doors swung open and his pregnant female flew outside, laughing and crying. Ashlyn leapt into his arms, a blur of gold, and he swung her around. They were locked in a heated kiss seconds later.

It was tough to imagine the savage Maddox as a father—even if the baby ended up half demon like the Lords.

Next came Danika, who halted in the doorway and scanned the crowd for Reyes. The lovely blonde spotted him and squealed. As if that squeal was a mating call of some kind, Reyes palmed a dagger and stalked to her.

Possessed as he was by the demon of Pain, Reyes could not feel pleasure without physical suffering. Before Danika, the warrior had had to cut himself twenty-four/seven to function. During their stay in Cairo, he hadn't had to injure himself once. Being away from Danika was pain enough, he said. Now that they were reunited, he'd have to cut himself again, but Paris didn't think either of them minded.

With a growl, Reyes swept her into his arms and the two disappeared inside the fortress, Danika's giggling the only remaining evidence they'd been nearby.

Paris rubbed at a sudden ache in his chest, praying it would go away. He knew it wouldn't, though. Not until he'd had his ambrosia. Every time he was around these couples so obviously in love, the ache sprouted and stayed, a parasite that sucked the life right out of him, until he drank himself into a stupor.

There was no sign of Lucien, who had flashed home rather than endure the long plane ride. He and Anya were probably locked inside their room. One small favor, at least.

He noted that the Harpy had watched the couples as intently as he had. Because she was fascinated or because she hoped to use the information against them?

No other females were in residence, thank the gods. No one Paris could seduce and eventually hurt when he screwed her over for someone else. Gilly, Danika's young friend, now lived in an apartment in town. The kid had wanted her own space. And they'd pretended to give it to her, not telling her that her home was wired to Torin's surveillance systems. Danika's grandmother, mother and sister had left, as well, and were now back in the States.

"Come," Sabin said to the Harpy. When she failed to comply, he motioned her to his side.

"Those women…" she whispered.

"Are happy." Confidence layered every syllable. "Had they not been so eager to be reunited with their men, they would have greeted you personally."

"Do they know…?" Once again, she had trouble finishing her sentence.

"Oh, yes. They know their men are possessed by demons. Now come." He waved his fingers.

Still she hesitated. "Where will you take me?"

Sabin pinched the bridge of his nose with his free hand. He was doing that a lot lately, it seemed. "Come inside or don't, but I'm not waiting out here for you to make up your mind." Angry footsteps, the slam of the door.

Anyone else he simply would have picked up and thrown over his shoulder, Paris suspected. Her, he allowed to choose. Smart of him.

The Harpy glanced left and right, and Paris braced himself to give chase. Not that he thought he could catch her if she decided to kick it into hyperdrive as she'd done inside that cavern. But he was prepared to fight her if necessary.

Another red flag started waving in his mind. She could get away, here and now. Even earlier, before they'd boarded the plane. Hell, she could have escaped while they camped in the desert. Why hadn't she? Unless she was Bait, as he'd suspected, here to learn everything she could about them.

Though she had denied it, Sienna had been Bait. She'd kissed him even as she'd poisoned him—and she'd merely been human. What kind of damage could this Harpy do?

Let Sabin worry about this one for now. You have enough on your plate o' fuck.

Finally, she decided to follow Sabin and headed inside, her steps tentative.

"The prisoners are in need of interrogating," Paris said to no one in particular.

Cameo flipped her dark hair over one shoulder and bent to grab her bag. No one tried to help her. They treated her like one of the guys because she preferred it that way. At least, that's what he'd always told himself. He'd never tried to treat her as anything else because he'd never wanted to sleep with her. Perhaps she would have liked to be pampered upon occasion.

"Maybe tomorrow," she said, her tragic voice nearly making his eardrums bleed. "I need to rest." Without another word—thank the gods—she marched inside.

As well as Paris knew women, he knew beyond any doubt that she was lying. There'd been a sparkle in her eyes, a rosy flush to her cheeks. She'd looked aroused, not tired. Who did she plan to meet?

She'd been hanging with Torin a lot lately and... Paris blinked. No, surely not. Torin couldn't touch another being skin to skin without infecting it with disease—as well as everyone that person encountered, causing a plague to sweep the land. Not even an immortal was safe from harm. That immortal wouldn't die, but would become like Torin, unable to know the caress of another without severe consequences.

Didn't matter what they were up to, really. He had work to do. "Anyone?" Paris said to those remaining. He wanted this shit over with, like, now. The sooner he finished beating information out of the Hunters, the sooner he could barricade himself inside his room and forget he was alive.

Strider whistled under his breath, pretending not to hear him as he edged toward the front door.

What the hell? No one appreciated violence better than Strider. "Strider, man. I know you heard me. Help me with the interrogation, yeah?"

"Oh, come on! At least wait until tomorrow. Not like they're going anywhere. I just need a little me time to recover. Like Cameo, I'll be ready to go bright and early. Swear to the gods."

Paris sighed. "Fine. Go." Were Cameo and Strider a couple, then? "What about you, Amun?"

Amun nodded his assent, but the action tossed his equilibrium into the shitter and he collapsed on the bottom step of the porch with a moan.

Barely a second later, Strider was at his side and wrapping an arm around his waist. "Uncle Stridey is here, don't you worry." He hefted the usually stoic warrior to his feet. Would have carried him if it had been necessary, but with Strider as a crutch Amun was able to throw one foot in front of the other, only stumbling occasionally.

"I'll help with the Hunters," Aeron said, stepping up to Paris. The offer surprised the hell out of him, truth be told.

"What about Legion? Girl probably misses you."

Aeron shook his head. His hair was cropped to his scalp and that scalp glistened in the sunlight. "She'd be on my shoulders right now if she were here."

"Sorry." No one knew better than Paris how it felt to miss a female. Though he had to admit he'd been surprised to discover the wiry little demon *was* a female.

"It's for the best." A veined hand scrubbed Aeron's tired face. "Something's been…watching me. A presence. Powerful. Started about a week before we left for Cairo."

Paris's stomach tightened in dread. "First, you have a nasty habit of keeping that kind of information to yourself. You should have told us the first time you noticed it, just as you should have told us what happened with the Titans the moment you returned from your heavenly summons all those months ago. Whoever's watching you could have alerted the Hunters about our trip. We could have—"

"You're right, and I'm sorry. But I don't think it, whatever it is, works for the Hunters."

"Why?" Paris demanded, unwilling to let it go.

"I know the feel of those hateful, judging eyes on me and this isn't like that. This one is…curious."

He relaxed somewhat. "Maybe it's a god."

"I don't think so. Legion isn't afraid of the gods but she's damn afraid of whoever this is. That's one of the reasons she's so amenable to going to hell for Sabin's recon work. She told me she'd return when the presence was gone."

There was worry in the guy's tone. Worry Paris didn't understand. Legion might have been a tiny demon with a penchant for tiaras—which they'd discovered not long ago, when she'd stolen one of Anya's and paraded around the fortress in it, proud as could be—but she could take care of herself.

Paris turned in a circle, intent. "Is your shadow here? Now?" Like they needed another enemy. "Maybe I can seduce whoever, whatever, it is away from you." And kill it. No telling what it had learned already.

A single shake of Aeron's head. "I honestly don't think it means us harm."

He paused, slowly released a pent-up breath. "All right, then. We'll deal with that later. Just let me know when it returns. Right now, we'll take care of the dungeon full of shitheads."

"You sound more human every day, you know that?" Aeron had said that before, but for once, he didn't sound disapproving. There was a whistle as he unsheathed a machete from the loop at his back. "Maybe the Hunters will resist."

"Only if we're lucky."

TORIN, KEEPER OF DISEASE, sat at his desk, but he faced the door of his bedroom rather than the monitors that linked him to the outside world. He'd watched the SUVs pull into the driveway and had instantly grown hard. He'd watched the warriors emerge and had had to palm himself to assuage the sudden ache. Watched as one by one they'd entered the fortress. Any moment and—

Cameo slipped quietly inside his chamber and shut the entrance with a soft snick. She flipped the lock, and for several ticks of the clock, kept her back to him. Long dark hair tumbled to her waist, curling at the ends.

Once, she'd allowed him to twirl a few of those ends around his gloveless finger, careful, so careful not to touch her skin. It had been his first true contact with a woman in hundreds of years. He'd almost come, just from the feel of those silky strands. But that small touch was all she'd permitted, all she could ever permit and all he could ever risk.

Actually, he was surprised they'd risked even that much. With his gloves on, sure. The chance of infecting her was nil. But tendrils against skin, silk against warmth, female against male? That required bravery and trust on her part and desperation and foolishness on his. Hair wasn't skin, but what if he'd slipped? What if she'd fallen against him? For some reason, neither of them had been able to make the consequences matter.

Last time he'd touched a woman, an entire village had been wiped out. Black Plague, they'd called it. That's what was inside him, swirling in his veins, laughing in his mind. For years afterward, Torin had scrubbed his skin until the black blood poured from him. Cleansing himself of the virus proved impossible, however.

Over the ensuing centuries, he'd learned to suppress the constant feeling of being dirty, tainted, hiding it with smiles and wry humor, but never had he suppressed the longing for what he couldn't have: companionship. Cameo, at least, understood him, knew what he was dealing with, what he could and could not do, and didn't ask for more.

He wished she would ask for more, and he hated himself for it.

Slowly she turned to him. Her lips were red and wet, as if she'd been chewing them, and her cheeks were flushed to a dusty rose. Up and down her chest lifted and fell in quick, shallow pants. His own breath blistered his throat.

"We're back," she said on a wispy catch of breath.

He remained seated, arching a brow as if he hadn't a care. "You're unharmed?"

"Yes."

"Good. Take off your clothes."

Since the caressing of her hair those few months ago, they'd become best friends. With benefits. Pleasuring-themselves-at-a-distance-while-watching-the-other-do-the-same benefits, but benefits all the same. It complicated the hell out of everything. The here and now…the future. One day she'd want a lover who could truly touch her, make love to her, pound in and out of her, kiss her and taste her and wrap himself around her, and Torin would have to step aside and not kill the bastard.

Until then…

She hadn't obeyed.

"Maybe I wasn't clear," he said. "I want you to take off your clothes."

Later, she'd punish him for ordering her around. He knew her well, knew how diligently she fought to prove she was just as powerful as her male counterparts. Now, need was upon her. He could smell the sweetness of her arousal. She wouldn't be able to resist much longer.

Sure enough, shaky fingers curled around the hem of her shirt and tugged it over her head. A lacy black bra. His favorite.

"That's a good girl," he praised.

Her eyes narrowed, zeroing in on the erection straining past the waist of his pants. "I told you to be naked when I got here. *You* were not a good boy."

Used to her sorrowful voice, he didn't flinch as the others always did. Inwardly or outwardly. That voice was a part of who she was—warrior to her core, beautiful disaster…unintentional nightmare. To him, it was a soulful melody, one that echoed within his own soul.

Torin pushed to his full height, his muscles coiled, his bones taut. "When am I ever good?"

Her pupils dilated fully, her nipples hardened. She liked it when he challenged her. Maybe because she knew the value of a prize increased the more you had to work for it.

He only wished he had the fortitude to win a battle with her—once, just once. In the end, she always won. He had little experience with women, was too desperate for what transpired here. But he always made a good showing.

"I'll strip when you're bare," he said, voice hoarse.

"Not a moment before." Strong words he couldn't possibly see through.

"We'll see…" Black hair swished as she sauntered to his dresser. She kicked one booted foot on the chair in front of her, gaze devouring him. Never had the unlacing of shoes been so sexy an act. The first boot she threw at him, he dodged with only a slight head tilt. The second he allowed to smack him in the chest. Tearing his gaze from her to avoid impact, even for a second, was not an option.

Ziiip. Down went the pants. She stepped out of them.

Black lace panties to match her bra. Perfection. Weapons, everywhere. Delightful.

Her breasts were small and pert and he knew her nipples were like rosebuds. She had an oval-shaped mole on her right hipbone. What he would have given to lick it… But what drew the hottest fires of his fascination was the glittery butterfly tattoo wrapped around her hips.

If studying only one side of her, or even the front of her, it was almost impossible to tell what the shimmery, incandescent design was. Only when she had her back to him did the shape take form. Oh, how he longed to trace his tongue over every sharp peak and hollow.

He had a matching tattoo on his stomach, though his was onyx framed in crimson. Actually, all the warriors here had a butterfly tattoo, but no one's demon mark resided in the same location. And not once had he ever yearned to have his hands, lips and body on the other men's brands.

When Cameo finished removing her weapons, a small pile rested beside her. She arched a brow at him. "Your turn." There was a tremor to her words, as if she were more affected by what was about to happen than she wanted him to know.

He took selfish comfort in that. "You aren't bare."

"I could be."

He should put a stop to this, send her on her way, *something,* because they both knew this was as far as it could ever go and that it would never be enough for either of them, but...he stripped.

Cameo gasped as she always did at this point, gaze locked on his swollen erection. "Tell me everything you want to do to me," she commanded, already cupping her breasts. "Don't leave anything out."

He obeyed, and her fingers acted as his, moving over her own body. Only when she'd come twice did he touch himself, his fingers acting as hers. But not once did he forget that this was all he could ever have, that more would never be his.

CHAPTER EIGHT

"I WANT A ROOM of my own."

"No."

"Just like that? No hesitation?"

"That's right. You're staying here." The words *with me* weren't said, but then, he didn't have to say them. His meaning was clear. "I haven't lived in Buda long, haven't stayed in this room much, but it's mine." *As are you.* Again, unsaid but there.

Gwen sat on the edge of an unfamiliar yet opulent bed in an unfamiliar yet terrifyingly masculine bedroom in an unfamiliar yet massive fortress with a very familiar yet fascinating man she had kinda sorta kissed and wanted to kiss again but couldn't because he wanted nothing to do with her. And really, it wasn't her that craved the kiss but the Harpy. At least, that's what she told herself. The Harpy liked dangerous and dark, and demonic Sabin certainly fit the bill.

Gwen liked staid bordering on boring.

She watched as the completely *un*staid Sabin unpacked his bag, his movements as stiff as his tone had been. *His distance is for the best,* she told herself. For the Harpy's benefit, of course. Kissing the intoxicating and infuriating Sabin again would not have been wise. He was too intense, too much a mystery for her peace of mind. But damn, he was sexy—the act of unpacking, even as torqued as he clearly was, practically foreplay. The way his muscles moved…

Stop watching him. Not like you can start a relationship with him. Who'd said anything about starting a relationship? As afraid as she was of her dark side, Gwen had always been the get-in-get-what-you-want-and-get-out type of girl. Her six-month commitment to Tyson had been an anomaly.

What was Tyson doing now? Was he with someone else? Married, even? And how would she feel if he was? Did he ever think of her? Ever wonder where she was or why she'd been abducted? She should probably call him.

Mind on the task at hand. "Why do I have to share your room?" she asked Sabin.

"Safer this way."

For who? Her? Or his friends? The thought depressed her. Oh, it was good that the men feared her. They'd leave her alone. But demons finding her too lethal to hang with? It should have been laughable. "I already promised to stay in Budapest. I'm not going to run."

"Doesn't matter."

Her eyes narrowed on him, her lashes fusing together. His clipped replies were annoying. "Do you have a girlfriend like the others? A wife?" *Bitch,* she couldn't help but think. "I'm sure she'll have something to say about this situation."

"I don't. And if I did, it wouldn't matter."

She gaped at him, positive she had misheard. "Wouldn't matter? Why? Your girlfriends aren't worthy of your kindness or consideration?"

His knuckles were tight around a velvet bag of… throwing stars? They clanged together ominously as he walked them to a chest and locked them inside. A second velvet bag he left anchored at his waist. "I've never cheated on a lover. I'm faithful, always. But the war comes before anyone's feelings. Every time."

Wow. Battle before love. Without a doubt, he was the most unromantic male she'd ever met. Even more so than her great-grandfather, who had laughingly burned her great-grandmother to death after she'd given birth to Gwen's grandmother. Gwen's head tilted to the side as she studied Sabin more intently. "Would you cheat on your girlfriend if it helped you win the war?"

Back at his suitcase, he lifted a pair of combat boots. "What does that matter?"

"I'm just curious."

"Then yes."

She blinked in surprise. One, he hadn't sounded apologetic. Two, he hadn't hesitated. "Yes, as in you would?"

"Yes. I would. If cheating meant gaining a victory, I would cheat."

Double wow. His honesty…depressed her. He was a demon, but she'd somehow expected—wanted?—more from him. No way would she be able to date a man who might cheat. Not that she planned to date Sabin.

Gwen wanted to be the one and only. Always. Sharing had never been easy for her; it went against every instinct she and the others of her race possessed. That's why she'd finally pushed past her fears and accepted a relationship with Tyson.

To her knowledge, he had been faithful to her. The sex had been good, if tame, because, while she might have convinced herself she could handle a relationship, she'd known losing herself to pleasure would be disastrous. He'd loved her, at least, and she thought she'd loved him. Now, thanks to all these months apart, she realized she'd only loved what he'd represented: normalcy. Plus, they were very similar. He worked for the IRS and was hated by his peers. She was a Harpy who despised confrontation and was pitied by her race. Similarity, though, was not a good enough reason to stay together. Not forever.

Gwen had a feeling she would be able to let go—somewhat at least—with Sabin. He hadn't backed down from her Harpy either in the cavern or on the plane. And strong as he was, he could take more than a human. But even though he was both brave and immortal, she doubted he could take everything she dished. No one could.

Still, she found herself wondering what he'd be like in bed. Not tame, that much she could guess. He'd get down and dirty and insist on the same from his lover. How much *could* he take from her?

"So you don't have a wife, but are you currently single?" she asked, the words a croak. She couldn't imagine anyone being crazy enough to date him. Yeah, he was handsome. Yeah, his kisses alone would take a woman to the gates of heaven. But momentary pleasure with him would only result in heartbreak. Surely she wasn't the only one to realize that.

"What's with all the questions?"

"Just filling the silence." A lie. It seemed she was full of them lately. She'd been—was still, despite everything—beyond curious about him, this warrior who had saved her.

"Nothing wrong with silence," he grumbled, head nearly inside his bag.

"Are you single or not?"

"I liked you better when you were afraid of, well, everything," he muttered.

She *had* been less timid around him than usual, she realized. Seeing the love his friends possessed for their women must have empowered her somehow. For the moment, at least. "Well? Single?"

He sighed, clearly giving up. "Yes, I'm single."

"I can believe it," she muttered. His last girlfriend had probably dumped him on his ass. "Well, that doesn't mean we can bunk together. You'll have to find somewhere else to sleep because I'm taking the bed." Brave words. She just hoped he didn't call her bluff.

"Don't worry. I'll be on the floor." He threw several wrinkled shirts into the laundry basket beside the closet. A demonic warrior sorting laundry; now there was something you didn't see every day.

"What if I don't trust you to remain there?"

He laughed, and it was a cruel sound. "Too bad. I'm not leaving you alone all night."

Not comforting. He hadn't vowed to stay away from her, and he hadn't claimed to want nothing to do with her sexually.

Did he?

And did she want him to?

She studied his profile, gaze traveling the length of his nose. It was a little longer than what was considered average, but regal because of it. His cheekbones were sharp, his jaw square. Overall, a very rough-looking face, with no hint of the boyishness she'd sometimes imagined.

His eyes, though, were heavily, almost femininely, lashed. She hadn't noticed that before, she realized, but those lashes were so thick his eyes appeared lined in soot.

Drawing her arms around her middle, she tore her gaze from that intriguing face and focused on his body. All those muscles… Again she found herself fascinated by them. Veins throbbed in his biceps as he lifted a shaving kit. The black leather and metal links of his man-bracelet hugged the thickness of his wrist. His long legs ate up the distance to the bathroom. Hopefully he'd take off his shirt and she'd get another peek at those ropes of muscle. Maybe see more of that butterfly tattoo that stretched along his ribs and disappeared into the waist of his pants.

"Now it's my turn to question you," he said from the bathroom doorway. He propped a shoulder against the frame. "*Why* haven't you run? Or tried to, at least. I know you said you didn't want to face the unknown out in that desert. That, on some level, I get. But then you discovered our dirty little demon secret and still you stayed. Even said you'd help me."

Good question. She *had* considered bolting for the woods the moment the plane landed, then again when the SUV had stopped. Then those human females had raced from the fortress, throwing themselves at their men, clearly madly, deeply in love, and she'd paused. The demon warriors had been gentle with them, caring. Utterly reverent, as though they were prized.

That, more than anything, had made her reevaluate her perception of demons.

These men were the complete opposite of what she'd expected, honorable in their own right (so far) and almost kind. They seemed to want to protect her. Better, they didn't gaze at her with disappointment, blatantly wishing she were stronger, braver, more violent.

It's the angel in her, her mother would *tsk* every time Gwen refused to hurt an innocent. *I knew better than to sleep with him.* Her sisters would come to her defense, loving her as fiercely as they did, but she knew they, too, considered her feeble. The truth always shone brightly in their eyes.

Had he known her, her father would have been proud of her, she thought defensively. Surely he would have applauded such benevolence.

"Well?" Sabin prompted.

"I could answer you the way you've been answering me," she said now, raising her chin. *I'm strong. I can stand up for myself.* "Why haven't I run from you? Because. That's why." *There. Take a little of your own medicine.*

Sabin ran his tongue over his teeth. "I'm not amused."

"Well, neither am I!" *That's it. That's the way.*

"Darling, talk to me."

The way he said the endearment...like a caress, a fantasy and a curse all rolled into a chocolate éclair. Stolen, of course. "I feel safe with you," she finally admitted. Why she had opted for the truth, she didn't know. "Okay?"

He scoffed, surprising her. "That's ridiculous. You don't even know me. But if you really are that foolish, why did you want your own room? Why question me like this?"

Heat burned in her cheeks. She *was* foolish. "Why does it seem like you're trying to talk me out of staying when I'm here at your request? Do you want me to run or something?"

A single, clipped shake of his head.

"Then can you at least pretend to be nice? Consistently?"

"No."

Again, he didn't hesitate. That was really starting to annoy her. "Fine. But tell me why you're nice one minute and cruel the next."

A muscle ticked in his jaw, as if he was grinding his teeth together. "I'm no good for you. Trusting me will only bring you pain."

And he didn't want to bring her pain? "Why do you say that?"

No reply.

"Because of your demon?" she persisted. "What demon do you carry?"

"Doesn't matter," he growled.

So again, no answer. There was no answer that would make sense, anyway. Except, perhaps, that he was lying and he really did want to bring her pain because he was a demon and that's what demons did. Yet he couldn't be truly evil. He genuinely loved his friends. That much was obvious every time he looked at them.

"Tell me again what you think I can do for you," she said, just to remind him that he did indeed want something from her and she didn't have to help him if she didn't want to. "Tell me why you want to keep me around."

For once he seemed happy to respond. "To kill my enemy, the Hunters."

A laugh bubbled from her. "And you honestly believe I can do something like that? Purposely," she added quickly, not needing another reminder of what she'd unintentionally done inside that cavern.

His dark gaze leveled on her, piercing with the sharpness of a blade. "Under the right conditions, I think you can do just about anything."

Right conditions. Aka fearing for her life, aka pissed as hell. He'd do it, too. Place her in danger or anger her to the point of total loss of self. Anything to win his war. "What happened to teaching me control?"

"I said I'd try. Not that I'd succeed."

Never had there been a better reason to try and escape him. He was far more dangerous than she'd thought. But she couldn't leave now, when she'd only just realized that part of her did want to help him. Not to kill, she wanted no part of the actual fighting, but she didn't like that there were men like Chris out there, perhaps preying on other immortal females. If she could play some small role in stopping them, wasn't it her obligation to do so?

"You don't fear for your life?" she asked. "If I give in to the Harpy, you might not live to gloat about the Hunters I've slain. Even immortals can be killed *under the right conditions*."

"It's a chance I'm willing to take. Like I told you, they killed my best friend, Baden, the keeper of Distrust. He was a great man, undeserving of the death they delivered."

"What kind of death was that?" After what they'd done to her fellow captives, she could only imagine.

"They sent a female to seduce him, and in the middle of the act they ambushed him and cut off his head. But if you want a more recent reason, the Hunters blame me and my brethren for every disease contracted, every loved one's death, every lie uttered, every violent act committed. They have tortured humans I was stupid enough to care for and they will do anything to bury me. Anything. Destroy anyone or thing, all while calling *me* evil."

"Oh," was all she could think to say.

"Yeah. Oh. Still think you won't be able to help me?"

SABIN WAS UTTERLY RIVETED by the lovely girl in front of him. All that strawberry hair tumbling down her arms, spilling into her lap. Those golden eyes flecked with shimmery silver and shining brightly. That rosy color burning in those round cheeks.

More than her appearance, he liked this newfound spirit. Despite his earlier grumblings to the contrary. Strength was damn sexy. Especially strength that didn't come naturally. Though she was timid by nature, afraid of him, this house, even her own shadow, she was sitting calmly on his bed, questioning him, head high, refusing to back down. She was truly a remarkable creature.

If she's not the world's greatest actress, that is. Doubt.

Sabin growled. Gwen wasn't an actress. She'd been imprisoned and tortured by Hunters; she wasn't helping them. *You're irritating me with your suspicions.*

Maybe I'm keeping you and your friends alive. Better to be on guard than dead. After all, Danika came here under the guise of rescue while she was, in fact, feeding the Hunters information.

Sabin swallowed.

Let me at the Harpy! I'll break her and get the truth.

He pictured Reyes and Danika as they were now. Happy, in love. Proof that bad intentions could morph into good. *You'll zip it. That's what you'll do.* As for him…

He glanced at Gwen, knowing—beyond a doubt—that he wasn't destined to have a fairy-tale ending like Reyes. Watching a man cut himself, a woman could get over. Losing all sense of self-respect, she could not. Gwen was already too close to that point.

What else had shaped her into the girl she was? Or rather, woman. She was older than both Ashlyn and Danika, after all.

He was curious about her, every little detail of her life. Family, friends, lovers. And she was curious about him, too, a discovery he liked more than he should have. Way more than he should have, actually. He'd wanted to answer all her questions, tell her everything, but knew the dangers of that. His self-directed irritation had made him snappier than usual. Snappier, but not any less aroused.

Just standing here, he felt desire heat him up from inside out. He wanted that hair tangled in his fingers, that lush body shivering beneath him, on top of him, her cries of bliss in his ears.

To stop himself from reaching out, he folded his arms over his chest, his shirt straining. Her gaze fell, locking on his left bicep. Damn. If she wanted him the way he wanted her, they were going to be in trouble. Lots and lots of pleasurable, oh, so wrong trouble.

Again his demon began pulling at its reins, desperate to get to her, to invade her mind and fill it with doubts. In fact, the whispers had already started: *You're not good enough, not pretty enough, not strong enough.* It took every ounce of his strength to keep them inside his own head. If they reached hers…

He knew how to battle the demon and quash the

doubts; she didn't. She would crumble, just as the demon wanted.

Why couldn't she calm his torments as Ashlyn had for Maddox? Why couldn't she charm his dark side as Anya had for Lucien? Why couldn't she curb the cravings for evil as Danika had for Reyes? Instead, Gwen roused the beast inside him to a fever pitch.

"I honestly don't know if I can help you the way you want, but I do know I'm sorry for your loss," she said, and there was genuine sorrow in her voice.

"Thank you." How…sweet. He frowned. She needed to better protect her heart and her emotions. Hurting for him could do her no good. He paused. Now he was thinking like a boyfriend. Speaking of… "Do you have a boyfriend?"

"Used to. Before."

Before her captivity, he guessed. How had the relationship worked? Had the poor man had to watch his every word and action so he wouldn't rouse her beast? "Do you miss him?" There'd been a trace of sadness in her tone.

"I did, yes."

Okay, that…aggravated him. "Did he cheat on you? That why you asked all those silly questions?"

"Silly?" The pink tip of her tongue swiped angrily at her lips, and his cock jerked in response, imagining it elsewhere. On him. Say, midway down his body. "No, he didn't cheat on me. *He* was honest."

For some reason, the comparison caused his aggravation to spike. "I'm honest. I told you before, I didn't lie about what I will and will not do. I can't."

One of her brows arched. "What do you mean, you can't?"

"Not going there," he gritted out. Gwen might need to further protect her heart, but he needed to better guard his words.

"Telling the truth about your willingness to cheat doesn't make you a better person than my human. Under no circumstances would Tyson have strayed. He loved me."

Her human? Her human! "His name is Tyson? I hate to break it to you, but you dated a brand of chicken. And I wouldn't be so sure about his sense of honor. I bet he was nailing tail the moment your back was turned. And if he loved you so much, why didn't he try and find you?" Sabin inwardly cursed and pressed his lips together. The terrible words had not been his, but his demon's. Since he had the bastard on a tight leash, not allowing it to seep into her head, it had decided to escape another way.

Gwen blanched. "H-he probably tried."

Guilt and shame overshadowed any lingering hints of his annoyance. For all her bravado, she was still fragile. But really, this just proved his suspicions. A few measly doubts and she'd looked ready to crumble. He had to stay away from her.

Could he, though? He was drawn to her. He'd already arranged for her to sleep in his room. With him. Alone. Stupid! But it was the only way to guard her—from the others, from herself. And foolishly, he liked the thought of being near her. He enjoyed her. More than her beauty, she was witty—when she wasn't scared and silent, anyway—and endearingly sweet.

He had to wonder if all Harpies were as tempting and distracting as Gwen. Guess he'd find out, since he'd promised to bring her sisters here. A promise he hadn't wanted to make. At first. More Harpies meant more danger. More hassle. But then he'd realized that more Harpies also meant more weapons against the Hunters. Somehow, some way, he'd convince her sisters to help him destroy the men who had hurt their beloved sibling.

If *they love her,* Doubt said. *Did they even search for her when she was taken?*

Damn. He hadn't thought of that. Gwen had been inside that cell for a year. They hadn't found her, hadn't saved her. Neither had that bastard Tyson.

His hands fisted at his sides. If the sisters didn't want to help him, fine. He had Gwen. He knew firsthand what she was capable of.

"Look, I'm sorry for what I said," he forced out— apologizing sucked—and moved toward the door. "You want the room to yourself, fine. I can give you a few hours. Don't you dare leave this chamber, though. I'll have food sent up."

She moaned in obvious pleasure, in want, but said, "Don't bother sending anything up. I won't eat it."

He stopped, keeping his back to her. The more he looked at her, the quicker he softened toward her. "You're going to start eating, Gwen. Do you understand? I don't want you to think I'm like your captors, deliberately starving you."

"I don't think that," she said stubbornly. "But I won't eat. And you're just leaving me here, where the demons can get to me? Where are you going?"

"*I'm* a demon," he said, ignoring her other question. He was getting good at that.

"I know." Her voice was hesitant, barely audible.

His stomach clenched. She knew, but it didn't matter? More potent words had never been spoken. "I'll be close by if you need me. Just call. Actually, I have a better idea. I'll send Anya to sit with you. She and Lucien have had hours to…reunite. She'll keep you safe." And trick Gwen into eating if necessary. If anyone could convince someone to do something they didn't want to do, it was the mischievous Anya. "Stay put."

Only as he shut the door behind him, barricading Gwen inside lest she decide to risk bumping into one of his friends to explore, spy or even search for a phone to call the Hunters—*she's not working for them, damn it!*—did he realize he was about to knowingly pair a Harpy with the goddess of Anarchy. Great. He'd be lucky if his head was still attached in the morning.

CHAPTER NINE

SABIN STALKED THROUGH THE FORTRESS, pained moans rising from the dungeons below and echoing off the walls. Someone was interrogating the prisoners. He should be down there, helping, but had to speak with Anya first.

Yes, he realized he was placing a woman before his duty, but this was a tiny thing, ensuring Gwen's comfort, and it shouldn't take too long. Never again, though, he assured himself. Next time there was some torturing to be done, he'd be the first one in line, Gwen be damned.

Still. Strangely, leaving Gwen felt…wrong. Part of him, a big part—fuck it, a very big part—thought he should be with her, easing her fears, assuring her that everything would be all right.

I can't assure a female of anything but misery, he thought darkly. Especially a female he was desperate to kiss again.

That kiss on the plane had nearly slayed him. Nothing had ever been sweeter—or held the potential to be so amazingly explosive. But allowing himself to participate would have meant loosening his iron hold on Doubt, and had he done so, the demon would have drawn mental blood; it was the one outcome he didn't have to doubt. Already she'd been in a fragile state, frightened of who and what he was. Another kiss would be the epitome of stupid.

And why the hell had he made things worse, tainting her memories of her ex? How low was he, telling her there was no way the man she'd trusted had been faithful to her, no matter that his demon had driven him to say it? Worse, with every moment that passed, Doubt's determination to destroy what little confidence Gwen had strengthened. Maybe because Sabin had made her the forbidden fruit, constantly commanding the demon to stay away from her.

There was no help for that, though. If he stopped reining the demon in, Gwen's already shaky self-esteem would vanish. Her confidence would be obliterated. And he couldn't let that happen. He had to protect his weapon. Surely that was the only reason he cared about her state of mind.

He just had to figure out the best way to use her. Maybe he'd convince her to pretend to join the Hunters and cut them down from the inside. That certainly had possibilities.

Hunters had been trying such a strategy for thousands of years, Baden their greatest success. It was past time he used their own wiles against them.

Would he be able to convince Gwen to do it, though?

The question plagued him as he maneuvered through the fortress. Stained glass windows cast colorful prisms over the hallway and illuminated the dust dancing through the air.

Sabin hadn't lived here long, but even he could tell the new female residents had breathed life into the place. Their decorating had somehow chased away the gloom he'd noticed when he'd first arrived here. Ashlyn had selected the furniture. Sabin didn't know a lot about that sort of thing, but suspected they were expensive pieces, as they reminded him of the years he'd spent in Victorian England.

No longer was every piece a shade of red to hide the blood that Reyes spilled when forced to cut himself. Now there was an off-white lounge, a chair draped in pink velvet, a carousel horse, and a walnut-and-marble desk. There was even a nursery next door to Maddox and Ashlyn's room.

Anya had supplied the…extras. The bubblegum machine in the far corner, the stripper's pole he had to sidestep and the Ms. Pacman arcade at the side of the staircase.

Danika had painted the portraits lining the walls. Some were of angels, soaring through the heavens, some were of demons, skulking through hell, but each depicted a vision that she, as the All-Seeing Eye, had once had. Through those paintings, they were learning more about the spirits inside themselves, as well as the gods who now controlled them.

Of course, interspersed with the visions of heaven and hell were more "extras" from Anya. These happened to be portraits of naked men. To everyone's consternation, she'd managed to save them from the Hunters' bomb blast. Only once had Sabin attempted to take one down. The next day, he'd found a naked portrait of *himself* in its place. How the goddess had had it painted so quickly—and so accurately—he would never know. He would also never take down another of her pictures.

Sabin rounded a corner and stalked past the open doorway of the entertainment room, intending to take the second flight of stairs up to Lucien and Anya's bed-room. From the corner of his eye, he spotted someone tall and slender, and backtracked. He stopped in the entrance, Anya coming into focus. Dressed in an ul-trashort leather dress and tall, spiked boots, she was as perfect as a female could be. Not a single flaw to her. Except her warped sense of humor.

At the moment she was playing Guitar Hero with her friend William. Her head was bobbing to the erratic beat of music, tendrils of hair dancing all around her. William was immortal and had long ago been kicked out of the heavens just as the Lords had. While they had nearly destroyed the world with their misdeeds, his crime had simply been seducing the wrong woman. Or two. Or three thousand. Not unlike Paris, he'd bedded any woman who would have him, married or not. Even the god queen. King Zeus had found them together and, as William liked to say, "flipped out."

Now his fate was bound to a book, a book Anya had stolen from him and liked to give back a handful of pages at a time. A book that supposedly predicted that a curse—one involving a woman—would befall him.

True to form, as he pounded on the drums, the war-rior was eyeing Anya's ass like it was candy and he had a sweet tooth that had been long denied. "I could do this all day," he said, eyebrows waggling.

"Pay attention to your notes," Anya admonished. "You're missing them and dragging down the band."

There was a pause, and then they both laughed.

"Don't praise him, Gilly! He didn't do *his best*. Only a girl with a cru—uh, never mind. Just—tell him how awful he is!" Anya twirled, fingers never slowing over the guitar.

Gilly was here? Sabin glanced around, but saw no sign of her. Then he noticed the earpieces both Anya and William sported and realized they were playing long-distance with Gilly.

Sabin leaned a shoulder against the door frame, crossed his arms over his chest, and waited impatiently until the end of the song. "Where's Lucien?"

Neither Anya nor William spun or gasped or acted as though they were surprised by his presence in any way.

"He's escorting souls," Anya said, tossing her guitar on the couch. "Yes! I hit ninety-five percent. Gilly, you hit ninety-eight and poor William only hit fifty-six." Pause. "What'd I tell you? No praising the man who harshed our mellow. Yeah, you too. Until next time, chica." She removed her earpiece and threw it beside the guitar. Then she lifted a carton of cheese tots from the coffee table and started eating slowly, eyes closing in ecstasy.

Sabin's mouth watered. Cheese tots—his favorite. Somehow, she'd known he'd come here, seek her out; she meant to torture him, the tease. "Give me a bite," he said.

"Get your own," she replied.

William tossed his sticks in the air, caught them, then placed them atop the drum set. "Doesn't matter how many notes I miss, I still manage to make some beautiful music."

"Ha! I totally carried you." Anya downed the rest of the tots, her amused gaze on Sabin. She threw herself onto the couch, legs swinging over the side. "So, Sabie, I've been looking for you. Lucien tells me we have a Harpy in the house!" She clapped excitedly. "I adore Harpies. They're so wonderfully naughty."

He didn't point out that she'd been playing games, not looking for him. "Wonderfully naughty? You didn't see her rip out the throat of a Hunter."

"No, I didn't." Her lips fell into a familiar pout. "I miss all the fun babysitting Willy."

William rolled his eyes. "Thanks a lot, *Annie*. I stayed here, kept you company, helped you guard the females, and you wish you'd been off fighting. Gods, the blow you've just dealt me. I might even be tearing up."

Anya reached over and patted his head. "Take a moment, collect yourself. Meanwhile, mommy is gonna chat with Doubtie poo. 'Kay?"

William's mouth quirked at one corner. "Does that make me the daddy?"

"Only if you want to die," Sabin said.

A laugh booming from him, William trekked to the seventy-three inch HDTV and plopped into the plush recliner in front of it. Three seconds later, a flesh fest was in full swing, moans abounding. Once, Paris had loved those movies. But in the weeks before their jaunt to Egypt, only William had gone near them.

"Tell me everything about the Harpy," Anya said, leaning toward Sabin, her face alight with interest. "I'm dying to know."

"The Harpy has a name." Was that…irritation in his voice? Surely not. What did he care if everyone referred to her as the Harpy? That's how *he* referred to her. "It's Gwendolyn. Or Gwen."

"Gwendolyn, Gwendolyn. Gwen." Anya tapped her chin with a long, sharp fingernail. "Sorry, not familiar."

"Gold eyes, red hair. Well, strawberry-blond hair."

Her bright blue gaze suddenly glittered. "Hmm. That's interesting."

"What? The hair color?" Didn't he know it! He wanted to plow his fingers through it, fist it, spread it over his pillow, his thighs.

"No, that you called it strawberry-blond." A tinkling laugh bubbled from her. "Does little Sabin have a crush?"

His teeth ground together in irritation as heat flooded his cheeks. A blush? A fucking blush?

"Aww. How precious. Look who fell in love while searching all those pyramids. What else do you know about her?"

"She has three sisters, but I don't know their names." The words were raw, filled with violent warning. He was *not* in love.

"Well, find out," she said, clearly exasperated that he hadn't done so already.

"Actually, I was hoping you'd find out. I need you to keep her company." *Guard her,* a part of him wanted to beg. *Keep her safe.* Wait. Part of him wanted to beg? Seriously? "But William stays here. William does not go near her."

Leather rubbed against denim as William turned in the chair. He practically glowed with intrigue. "Why can't I go near her? Is she pretty? I bet she's pretty."

Sabin ignored him. It was either that or kill him, and killing him would upset Anya. Upsetting Anya was the equivalent of placing your head in a guillotine.

At times like this, Sabin found himself longing for the dull routine of battling and training that had comprised his life pre-Lords reunion. Then he had only five roomies and no annoying women—beyond Cameo, but she didn't count—or their horny friends to deal with. "Also, see if you can get her to eat," he added. "She's been with me for several days and has only eaten a few Twinkies, but she threw them up immediately afterward."

"First, I never said I'd babysit your woman. And second, of course she won't eat. She's a Harpy." Anya's tone suggested he was a moron.

Maybe he was. "What are you talking about?"

"They only eat what they steal or earn. Duh. If you're offering her food, she *has* to turn it down. Otherwise she'll…drumroll please…throw up."

He waved a hand in dismissal. "That's ridiculous."

"No, that's their way of life."

But that…surely it wasn't…hell. Who was he to say something was impossible? For years Reyes had had to stab Maddox in the stomach at midnight and Lucien had had to escort the dead warrior's soul to hell—only to return it the next morning to a healed body and do it all over again the next night.

"Help her steal something, then. Please. Isn't petty theft your forte?" Later, he'd make sure food was lying around his room and easy to "pilfer."

Suddenly a high-pitched cry of agony ripped through the walls, a sound that soothed Sabin's very soul. The Hunter interrogation had just reached a new level. *I should be there, helping.* Instead, he remained rooted in place, curious, desperate for answers. "What else should I know about her?"

Pensive, Anya stood, walked to the pool table and dug one of the balls out of a pocket. She tossed it into the air, caught it, tossed it again. "Let's see, let's see. Harpies can move so quickly the human eye—or immortal eye, as the case may be—can't register a single motion. They love to torture and punish."

Both of those he'd already witnessed firsthand. The speed with which she'd killed the Hunter…the brutal way she'd attacked him…that had been all about torture and punishment. Yet every time Sabin mentioned attacking the other Hunters responsible for her treatment, she paled, a trembling mass of fear.

"Like any other race, Harpies can have special gifts. Some can predict when a specific person will die. Some can pull a soul from a body and carry it into the afterlife. Too bad more of 'em can't do that—it'd make my honey's job so much easier. Some can time travel."

Did Gwen possess a special ability?

Every time he learned something about her or her origins, a thousand other questions presented themselves.

"But don't worry about your woman," Anya added as if reading his thoughts. "Those types of powers don't develop until late in life. Unless she's a few hundred years old—or is it a few thousand? I can't remember—she probably hasn't tapped into her ability yet."

Good to know. "Are they evil? Can they be trusted?"

"Evil? Depends on your definition. Trusted?" Slowly she grinned, as if she relished her next words. "Not even a little."

Not good for his main objective. But damn, he couldn't picture sweet, innocent Gwen playing him. "From what Lucien told you, do you think Gwen could be working with the Hunters?" He hadn't meant to ask that; he truly didn't believe her capable of it. The only reason the thought was in his mind was Doubt. Doubt, for whom confidence and assurance were vile curses.

"Nah," Anya said. "I mean, you found her locked up. No Harpy alive would willingly allow herself to be caged. To be captured is to be ridiculed, found unworthy."

How would her sisters treat her when they arrived, then? He wouldn't allow them to castigate her. And shit. He'd left her locked in his bedroom. A spacious bedroom, but a prison all the same. Did she now view him as she viewed the Hunters? His stomach churned.

"Will you stay with her? Please."

"Hate to break it to you, sweet chops, but if she doesn't want to be here, even I can't keep her here. No one can."

Another human cry ripped through the room, followed quickly by immortal laughter. "Please," he repeated. "She's frightened and needs a friend."

"Frightened." Anya laughed. But his intent expression never wavered, so that laughter began to fade. "You're kidding me, right? Harpies are never scared."

"When have I ever demonstrated a sense of humor?"

As disdainful of mysteries as she was, Anya shook her head. "You've got me there. Fine. I'll babysit her, but only because I'm curious. I'm telling you, a frightened Harpy is an oxymoron."

She would soon learn the error of that. "Thank you. I owe you one."

"Yes, you do." Anya smiled sweetly. Too sweetly. "Oh, and if she asks about you, I'm going to tell her everything I know. Every detail. And I do mean *every.*"

Dread instantly speared him. Already Gwen was wary of him. If she knew half the things he'd done in the past, she would never help him, never trust him, never again look at him with that intoxicating blend of desire and uncertainty.

"Deal," Sabin said darkly. "But you are in desperate need of a spanking."

"Another one? Lucien gave me a good one this morning."

In that moment Sabin admitted to himself that he'd never gain the verbal edge with Anya. He'd never intimidate her, either. No reason to even try. "Just…be gentle with her. And if you have any shred of mercy inside that gorgeous body, don't tell her I house Doubt. She's already afraid of me."

Sighing, he turned and stomped to the dungeon below.

"WHERE ARE THEY?" Paris demanded.

A moan of pain was his only answer.

They'd been at it for what seemed like days, with no real results. Aeron's demon, Wrath, was flashing all kinds of sick images in his head, wanting to punish this man for his sins. Soon Aeron wouldn't be able to stop himself. If that happened, he wouldn't get answers. He was ready to stop, regroup and try again tomorrow, allowing the remaining Hunters—they'd already accidentally killed two—to imagine what would soon be done to them. Sometimes, the unknown proved more intimidating than reality. Sometimes.

Paris, though, didn't look ready to quit. The man was possessed. By more than his demon. He'd done things to these humans that even Aeron, cold warrior that he was, couldn't have stomached. But then, Aeron was not the man he used to be.

Months ago the gods had commanded him to slay Danika Ford and her family and he'd fought diligently against the bloodlust that had subsequently consumed him. Fought against the images of those sweet deaths that invaded his head, his hand slicing their throats, his eyes watching their blood pour from them, his ears registering their last, gurgling breath. Gods, he'd craved those things, more than anything else in the world.

When the lust had finally left him—though he still didn't know why it had—he'd been afraid of taking another life, any life, lest he morph back into the beast he'd been. Then he and the other warriors had traveled to Egypt and a battle had raged. He'd been unable to stay his hand, the lust he'd feared overtaking him yet again, driving him.

Thankfully, he'd calmed down without harming one of his friends. But what if he hadn't? He would not be able to live with himself. Only Legion was capable of soothing him completely, and he was currently without her company.

His hands fisted. Whoever, whatever, was watching him had to be stopped before Legion could return. Somehow. Sadly, those invisible, penetrating eyes were not on him now. He was covered in blood and had a wadded-up rag in his pocket—a rag that cradled one of the dead Hunters' fingers. The sight of him might have driven the voyeur away for good.

At first he'd thought it was Anya, playing a prank. She'd done something similar to Lucien. Legion was not afraid of Anya, though. Which made her probably the only fortress resident aside from Lucien who could make that claim.

"One last chance to answer my question," Paris said calmly, tapping his dagger against the Hunter's pale cheek. "Where are the children?"

Greg, their current victim, whimpered, a stream of saliva gushing from his lips.

They'd isolated the Hunters, one to a cell. That way, the screams they elicited from one would drive the others mad, making them wonder what exactly had been done to their brethren. The scents of urine, sweat and blood already saturated the air, another added bonus.

"I don't know," Greg blubbered. "They didn't tell me. I swear to God they didn't tell me."

Hinges creaked. Footsteps echoed. Then Sabin was strolling into the cell, features tight with determination. Now things would get really bloody. No one was more determined than Sabin. With a demon like Doubt, that determination was probably the only thing that kept him sane.

"What have you learned?" the warrior asked. He pulled a velvet pouch from the back of his waist and gently placed it on the table, slowly unraveling the material to reveal the sharp gleam of different metals.

Greg sobbed.

"The only new information is that our old friend Galen—" Aeron said the name with a sneer "—is aided by someone he calls…you aren't going to believe this. Distrust."

Sabin froze in place, the words obviously playing through his mind. "Impossible. We found Baden's head, minus his body."

"Yes." No immortal could have survived that. A head was not something that could be regenerated. Other body parts, yes, but not that. "We also know his demon is now wandering the earth, crazed from the loss of its host. There's no way it could have been found without Pandora's box."

"It offends me that such words were even spoken. You punished the Hunter for lying, of course."

"Of course," Paris said with a satisfied grin. "He's the one who had to eat his own tongue."

"We should put this one in the cage," Aeron suggested. The Cage of Compulsion. An ancient, powerful artifact—and one that would supposedly aid them in their quest to find the box. Anyone they placed inside it had to do whatever the warriors commanded, no exception. Well, almost no exception. When Aeron had been consumed by bloodlust, he'd begged someone in the heavens to place him inside and command him to stay away from the Ford women.

But Cronus had appeared before him and said, "Think you I would create something as powerful as this cage and allow it to be used against me? Anything I set into motion cannot be stopped. Even with the cage. That's the only reason I agreed to leave it here. Now. Enough of this. Now is the time to act."

Aeron had blinked and found himself inside Reyes's bedroom, a knife in his hand, Danika's neck so beautifully close…

"Nope," Sabin said. "We agreed."

They would not show the cage to Hunters—even doomed ones—for any reason, so that Hunters would never see what it could do. Just in case.

"Learn anything else?" Sabin asked, changing the subject.

But Aeron saw the gleam in the warrior's eye. Because the cage had been mentioned in mixed company, this Hunter would die after their session. "Just a confirmation of what the captive women told us. They were raped, impregnated, their babies meant to be used to one day fight us. Already there are half-immortal children out there being raised as Hunters, but Greg there doesn't want to save his fingers and toes and tell us where."

The sobs became silent, the Hunter so scared his throat was closing. Any moment, he'd pass out.

Paris gripped him by the neck and shoved his head between his legs, the rope that bound him pulling tight on his wrists. "Breathe, damn you. Or *I* swear to the gods I'll keep you lucid another way."

"At least he still has his voice box," Sabin said dryly. He held a curved blade up to the light and flicked the tip. Blood instantly beaded on his finger. "Unlike his friend in the cell to the left."

"My bad," Paris said, but he didn't sound repentant. There was an almost maniacal gleam in those blue eyes.

"How's he supposed to answer our questions if he can't speak?"

"Interpretive dance," was the wry response.

Sabin snorted. "You could have used your powers." His faculty for seduction worked even on men.

"I could have, but didn't." Paris scowled. "And I won't do so now, so don't ask. I hate these bastards too much to lay on the charm, even for information. I still owe them for the time I spent as their prisoner."

Sabin glanced at Aeron, an unspoken *why didn't you stop him* drifting between them. Aeron shrugged. He had no idea how to deal with the fierce, violent soldier Paris had become. Was this how the others had felt about him?

"So right now we're determined to learn the location of the kids?" Sabin asked. "That it?"

"Yes," Aeron replied. "One of the Hunters admitted that they range in ages, anywhere from infancy to teenager. And yeah, they've been raping immortals that long. They were able to do so without getting caught because of their location. That cavern in Egypt was once a temple to the gods. It's protected, though no one knows by who—or how we bypassed that protection.

"Supposedly the kids are faster and stronger than any Hunter that has come before. Oh, and get this. Most of the incubators, as this bastard called them…they were immortals Ashlyn found."

Ashlyn had the unique ability to stand in one location and hear every conversation that had ever taken place there. Before coming to Budapest, she'd worked for—hell, dedicated her life to—the World Institute of Parapsychology, an agency that had used her skills to hunt immortals. For "research," they'd told her.

"We can't tell her," Aeron added. "She would be devastated." Learning she'd inadvertently been working for Hunters must have been bad enough; the discovery that her abilities had been used to help breed new Hunters might be too much for the gentle pregnant woman.

"We'll tell Maddox and let him decide what to leak to her."

"Please, let me go," Greg begged, tone desperate. "I'll take the others a message. Any message you want. A warning, even. I'll tell them to stay away from you. To leave you alone."

Sabin lifted a vial of dirty-looking liquid from that velvet pouch. "Now why would I let you give them a warning that I can deliver myself?" He popped the cap with his thumb and poured the stuff over his blade. There was a hiss and sizzle.

Greg tried to scoot his chair back but it was nailed in place. "Wh-what is that?"

"A special kind of acid I like to mix myself. It'll eat through your flesh, burn you from inside out. Vessels, muscle, bone, it doesn't matter. Only thing it can't eat through is this metal, because it's straight from the heavens. So, are you going to tell us what we want to know? Or am I going to shove this blade into the bottom of your foot and work my way up?"

Tears streamed down the trembling man's face, landing on his shirt and blending with the blood already caked there. "They're in a training facility. Everyone calls it Hunter High. It's a subsidiary of the World Institute of Parapsychology. A boarding school where the kids are kept as far from their mothers as possible. There they are taught how to fight, how to track. Taught to hate your kind for the millions you've murdered with your diseases and lies. The millions who have killed themselves because of the misery you spread."

Excellent. Now he was sounding like the Hunters Aeron so loathed.

"And where is this facility located?" Sabin asked flatly.

"I don't know. I honestly don't know. You have to believe me."

"Sorry, but I don't." Slowly Sabin approached him. "So let's see if I can jog your memory, shall we?"

CHAPTER TEN

IF ONE MORE PAIN-FILLED, gut-wrenching scream echoed off Sabin's bedroom walls, Gwen was going to hurt someone! It had been going on forever, it seemed. Didn't help that fatigue beat heavy fists all over her, weighing down her eyelids, fuzzing up her brain, making this seem like an endless nightmare. But she was determined to keep both her eyes and ears open, just in case one of the Lords decided to sneak in and hurt her.

Like they were hurting the man currently begging for mercy. Beyond any doubt, she knew the Hunters were being tortured. *That's* where Sabin had gone. That's why he'd abandoned her so quickly. His "work" was the most important thing in his life.

Know him so well, do you? No. But she knew he despised the Hunters, knew he craved their destruction as much as she craved normalcy and would do anything, *anything* to ensure it.

She understood his desire. They'd taken something from him, a loved one. More than one loved one, actually. They'd taken something from her, too. Many somethings. Her pride, the normal life she'd just started to carve out for herself. She hated them as much as Sabin did. Maybe more.

They'd watched Chris rape those women with lust in their eyes, wanting a turn of their own. They hadn't stopped him, hadn't even protested his despicable actions. So even though the screams were driving her insane, stopping Sabin wasn't on her to-do list. Those Hunters deserved what they got. However, each and every one of those screams reminded her that Sabin wanted her to help him purposely end life.

Could she?

Just the thought caused bile to rise in her throat and fear to infuse her blood, turning the cells to acid and blistering her veins. Over the years, she had killed. Oh, had she killed.

At nine, she'd killed her tutor for giving her an F. At sixteen, a man had followed her into a building, had jerked her into an empty room and locked the door. He'd lasted thirty seconds against the Harpy. At twenty-five, she'd moved from Alaska to Georgia, following Tyson—which was what prompted her mother to cut all ties—and finally started college, something she'd wanted to do years earlier. She couldn't handle that rowdy a public, her sisters had said. And they were right. A married professor made a pass at her, that was all, yet she'd ripped into him as if he'd tried to slice her throat. Her third week of college had been her last.

Her sisters claimed the Harpy would not be so volatile if Gwen stopped combating what she was, but she didn't believe them. They were a bloodthirsty lot, constantly fighting, with a body count that staggered her. She loved them, but though she envied their confidence and strength, she didn't want to be like them. Most days.

Another agonized scream.

To distract herself, she explored the bedroom, picked the lock on the weapons chest and pocketed a few of the throwing stars Sabin had hidden there, only yawn-

ing three times—an improvement. Some skills a girl
never forgot, and B and E was something her family
took very seriously. *Should have done this sooner.* She
picked the door lock, as well, and sneaked into the hallway—only to backtrack into the bedroom the moment
she heard footsteps.

Why am I such a coward?

Another scream, this one fading into a gurgle.

Trembling, yawning again, she eased onto the mattress, forcing her fuzzy mind to consider what was
around her rather than what she was hearing. The bedroom was a surprise. Hard and masculine as Sabin was,
she'd expected sparse furnishing, blacks and browns,
nothing personal. And on the surface, that's what she
saw.

But under the dark brown comforter were vibrant
blue sheets and a feather-top mattress. In the closet, he
had an array of funny T-shirts. *Pirates of the Carib-
bean.* Hello Kitty. One that said *Welcome to the Gun
Show,* with arrows pointing to his biceps. Behind a veil
of lush plants was a sitting area he'd rigged with a pil-
lowed floor that looked up to a ceiling mural of castles
in the clouds.

She liked the conflicting sides of him. Like the harsh
yet boyish aspects of his face.

"Hello, hello, hello," a female called. The door she'd
just shut flew open and a tall, gorgeous woman strolled
inside, a tray of food balanced in her hands. Judging by
the scent wafting from the plate, there was a ham sandwich, a handful of Baked Lays, a bowl of grapes and a
glass of—Gwen sniffed—cranberry juice.

Her mouth watered. Maybe it was her intense hunger or perhaps her lack of sleep, but the intruder wasn't even a blip on her radar. "Wh-what do you have there?"

"Pay no attention to the food," the stranger said, placing the tray on the dresser. "This is for Sabin. The jerk conned me into making him a meal. I was told you weren't to touch anything, I'm sorry."

"Uh, no problem." It was hard to speak, her tongue felt so swollen. "Who are you?" She couldn't pull her gaze from that tray.

"I'm Anya, goddess of Anarchy."

No reason to doubt the statement. Otherworldly power radiated from the woman, practically sparking in the air. But what was a goddess doing with demons? "I—"

"Oh, fiddlesticks. Will you excuse me? I hear Lucien—Lucien's my man, so hands off him—calling for me. Don't go anywhere, 'kay? I'll be right back."

Gwen hadn't heard anything, but she didn't protest. The moment the door closed behind the goddess, she was at the dresser, stuffing Sabin's sandwich into her mouth, washing it down with the juice, then scooping the chips in one hand and the grapes in the other. She scarfed them as though she'd never tasted anything so fine.

Maybe she hadn't.

It was like having a rainbow in her mouth. A mélange of flavors, textures and temperatures. Her stomach greedily accepted every morsel and begged for more of the stolen goods.

Anya was only gone a minute, maybe two, but when she reentered the chamber, the food was gone and Gwen was seated on the bed, wiping her face with the back of her wrist and swallowing the final bite.

"Now then. Where were we?" Without sparing the tray a glance, Anya strolled to the bed and perched beside Gwen. "Oh, yeah. I was making you comfortable."

"Sabin told me he was sending you, but I thought he'd changed his mind. I, uh, don't need a guard. Honest." *Please don't notice the tray.* "I'm not going to try and escape."

"Please." The beautiful goddess waved a dismissive hand. "As I said, I'm the goddess of Anarchy. Like I'd lower myself to such a station. Besides, nobody sends me anywhere I don't want to go. I'm merely bored and curious. Now one question has been answered in my mind, at least. You're unbelievably pretty. Look at this hair." She sifted a few of the strands between her fingers. "No wonder Sabin chose you as his female."

Gwen's eyelids drifted closed, her head leaning into the goddess's touch. The Harpy was quiet, lulled first by the meal, and now by the companionship. All she needed now was to leave the fortress, just for a few hours, and catch a few Zs. "He didn't choose me as his female." But something inside her liked the thought of it, she realized. Her nipples had hardened, and heat had bloomed between her legs, spreading like wildfire.

"Of course you're his." Anya's arm fell away. "You're staying in his room."

Her eyelids popped open, and she barely held back her whimper. Why did no one want to continue touching her? "I'm here by force."

Anya laughed as if she'd just cracked a joke. "Good one!"

"Seriously. I asked for my own room but he wouldn't give it to me."

"Like anyone could force a Harpy to stay somewhere she didn't want to stay."

That was true of her sisters. Her? Not so much. At least there'd been no hint of disdain in Anya's tone when she'd said the word Harpy. So many creatures of "myth" and "legend" considered Harpies beneath them, mere killers and thieves.

"Believe me, I'm nothing like the rest of my family."

"Ouch. There was enough disgust in your voice to flay the skin from someone's body. Don't like our origins or ourself?"

Gwen's gaze fell to her hands, which were twisting in her lap. Was this information that could be used against her? Would keeping it secret award her some type of advantage? Would a lie serve just as well, if not better?

"Either," she finally replied, deciding it was safe to tell the truth. She missed her sisters beyond belief, and here was a female, listening to her, seeming to care. At this point, whether Anya truly cared or not didn't matter. Sharing her feelings was nice. Hell, *talking* was nice. Twelve months had passed since anyone had listened to her.

Sighing, Anya flopped back against the mattress. "But you guys are, like, the coolest things ever. No one disses you and lives to tell about it. Even the gods pee their pants when you approach."

"Yeah, but making friends is impossible because nobody wants to come near us. Worse, showing your true self in a romantic relationship is a no-no because you might actually eat your boyfriend." Gwen fell beside the goddess, their shoulders brushing. She couldn't help herself; she cuddled closer.

"And that's a bad thing? When I was a girl, I was

utterly reviled by my peers. They called me a whore, some even refusing to stand in the same room as me, as if I'd somehow taint their precious lives. I wanted to be a Harpy so badly I could taste it. Then no one would have messed with me. Guaranteed."

"*You* were reviled?" This beautiful, gentle, utterly kind female?

"Yeah. Imprisoned, too, then banished here to earth." Anya rolled to her side, tucking her hands under her cheek and peering over at Gwen. "So what clan are you part of?"

Was this information that could be used against her? Would keeping it secret award—*Oh, shut up.* "The Skyhawks."

Anya blinked, long black lashes momentarily casting shadows over her cheeks. "Wait. You're a Skyhawk? With Taliyah, Bianka and Kaia?"

Now Gwen rolled to her side, staring over at the goddess with simultaneous twinges of hope and dread. "You know my sisters?"

"Hell, yeah. We had some good times together back in the, oh, sixteen hundreds, I believe. In all my centuries, I have only called a handful of people friend, and those girls reached the top of the list. We fell out of touch, though, a few hundred years ago. One of my human pets died, and well, I didn't handle it well. Shut myself off from almost everybody." Anya's azure gaze became intent, gauging. "You must be a new addition."

Was she comparing Gwen to her beautiful, smart, amazingly strong siblings? "Yes. I'm just twenty-seven mortal years."

Anya sat up, clicking her tongue against the roof of her mouth. "You're just a baby, then. But with that kind of age gap between your sisters and you, wouldn't your mom have long passed the age to hatch another rugrat?"

"Apparently not." Gwen followed her upright, a spark of irritation kindling in her chest. She wasn't a baby, damn it. A coward, yeah, but a grown, adult coward. These immortals would never see her any other way, that much was clear. Even Sabin had to consider her a child. A child too young even to kiss.

"Do the girls know you're here?" Anya asked.

"Not yet."

"You should call them. We can party."

"I will," she said. And she would. Just not yet. The more she thought about it, the more she realized that her fear of admitting what had happened to her was justified. It really was going to be humiliating. They were going to lecture her, punish her as was their right as her elders and maybe even command her home, forever, where they could watch and protect her. They'd never admit that the latter was just another kind of cage.

That's exactly what she'd gone to Georgia to escape. She'd told herself she'd left to be with Tyson, who had been vacationing in Anchorage when they met. But these last few months, alone in her cell, she'd had nothing to do but think and she'd realized she'd simply wanted out. Freedom.

For once, she'd put on her big girl panties and acted on her own with no safety net. Yeah, she'd failed. But at least she'd tried.

The thought of putting off the call caused guilt to swim through her. Her sisters were probably worried about her lack of communication, whether they knew what had happened or not. No matter how humiliating it was going to be, she would have to contact them soon.

"You said you've fallen out of touch with them," she couldn't help but say. "But did you keep tabs on them? Do you know how they're doing? What they're doing?"

"I didn't and I don't. I'm sorry. But knowing them, they're panties-deep in trouble."

They shared a laugh. Gwen could easily recall the time Bianka and Kaia had painted a hopscotch square in their backyard. Rather than toss stones, they'd tossed cars. Taliyah had used semis.

"Good news is, they'll approve of your choice of beefcake. Sabin's just the sort of wicked they'd like, no doubt about it. Pun intended, of course."

Pun? What pun? And Sabin was not her boyfriend. A good thing he wasn't; because she'd left her sisters for Tyson, they'd probably slay her next boyfriend on principle alone. "My guess is they'd be dining on his liver five minutes after meeting him." Another reason to put off her phone call, despite her guilt. Sabin wasn't in her Fave Five at the moment, but she didn't want him dead.

"That's okay. He'd just grow a new one. Besides, you're not giving my boy enough credit. When it comes to battle, he fights dirtier than anyone I know. Including myself, and I stabbed my BFF in the stomach just for the giggles!"

Okay. Maybe Anya wasn't as kind and gentle as she'd supposed. "I've seen him fight. I know he's fierce."

"But you worry for him?" Anya studied her intently.

Yes. No. Maybe.

"Well, don't. He's half demon, after all."

"Which demon possesses him?" she asked, unable to hide her impatience to know.

But Anya continued as if she hadn't spoken. "Let me give you a little background info. See, Sabin's been clashing with Hunters—the men who held you captive—for thousands of years. They blame the Lords for the world's evil, sickness, death, you name it, and will stop at nothing to obliterate every single one of them. Murder humans—" her gaze turned shrewd "—rape immortals."

Gwen had to look away.

"Right now there's a race to find four artifacts that once belonged to king Cronie, the shithead, because they'll lead the way to Pandora's box, the one thing guaranteed to kill the Lords. It'll suck their demons right out of them." There at the end, worry had seeped from her tone.

"That sounds like a good thing." What she wouldn't give to have the Harpy sucked out of her. But it wasn't another entity, much as she liked to pretend otherwise. It was *her.* The deepest part of her.

"Oh, no. Not good. It'll kill their bodies. Those demons are like another heart. Without it, they can't function."

"Oh."

"Don't sweat it, though. Threesomes are fun. I should know." Anya's smile was dreamy. "My man was ordered to kill me by Cronus himself, but Lucien just couldn't do it. He fell in love with me instead. And oh, I love the way he loves me."

No one, not even Tyson, had ever made Gwen smile like that. Which meant she had never loved or been loved like that. And though she'd already come to that conclusion in prison, the fresh reminder stung.

"Now, enough lying around like lazy bums," Anya said. "C'mon, I'll give you a tour of the fortress. I'll even tell you everything I know about Sabin."

Sabin. Her heart skipped a beat, just the mention of his name able to affect her. How was that possible? He was everything Tyson was not: fierce, dominating, vengeful, passionate. He was everything she'd never wanted. "But…Sabin told me to stay put."

"Oh, please. Gwen—can I call you Gwen?—you're a Harpy, and Harpies do not take orders from anyone, especially bossy demons."

She bit her lip and eyed the door. *You considered sneaking out once already. What's a second time?* "A tour does sound kind of wonderful. *If* you can guarantee the Lords will leave me alone."

"I can, so come on." Anya hopped to her feet, dragging Gwen up behind her. "I'll give you ten minutes to shower and then we'll—"

"Oh, I don't need a shower." Or rather, she wouldn't take one. Not in this house.

"You sure? You're all…icky."

Yes, and she wanted to keep it that way. During her captivity, she'd made sure to dust herself with the sand off the ground every few days. Otherwise, everyone would have seen the true color and texture of her skin. Much as she was curious to see Sabin's reaction, she didn't want to deal with the aftereffects. And there were always aftereffects. "I'm sure."

If she were home, either in Georgia or Alaska, she could shower and use her makeup to blend in. Since she wasn't, she couldn't. Dirt was her only buffer.

"Fine, then. Lucky for you I'm not a clean freak." Anya linked their arms and kicked into a leisurely stroll.

For half an hour, they wandered the fortress, upstairs, downstairs, the wide, open kitchen—Gwen tried and failed to picture any of the Lords in there cooking—

the library, an office, a covered garden of bright multi-colored blooms, and into private bedrooms that didn't belong to either of them. Nothing was sacred to the goddess. In two of them, couples had been sleeping, arms and legs tangled. Gwen's cheeks had burned bright until the doors were shut, the nakedness blocked.

But not one secret of Sabin's did Anya reveal.

By the time they reached the media room—"entertainment" room, as the goddess called it—she was ready to break down and ask. Instead, she forced herself to focus and look around, trying to learn more about Sabin and his friends through their possessions. There was a huge flat-screen TV, assorted video game systems, a pool table, a refrigerator, a karaoke machine, even a basketball hoop. Popcorn kernels littered the floor, scenting the air with their buttery goodness.

"This is amazing," she said, spreading her arms and twirling. The men must not be the all day/all night war hounds she'd thought they were.

"Well, hello, ladies. I do believe this room isn't the only thing that's amazing."

The deep voice filled the spacious chamber as the recliner in front of the TV swiveled. Then a gorgeous man with dark hair and blue eyes was peering over at her, assessing her every curve. Gwen panicked, automatically reaching for one of the stars she'd hidden in her pocket.

"Gwen, meet William. He's an immortal, but not demon-possessed. Unless you count his sex addiction as his own personal demon. William, meet the woman who is going to bring Sabin to his knees."

William's sensuous lips dipped into a pout. "I

wouldn't mind being brought to my knees. So if you change your mind about being with the warrior..."

"I won't," she rushed out, even though she'd denied Anya's claim earlier. Encouraging an admirer could lead to problems. Bloody, life and death problems.

"I'd take excellent care of you, I swear it."

"For a day. Maybe a day and a half," Anya retorted dryly. "He's a love-'em-and-leave-'em kind of guy. And though he's not a Lord, he does have a curse hanging over his head. I have the book to prove it."

William growled low in his throat. "Anya! Must you share my secrets with everyone?" He flattened his palms on the arms of his chair. "Fine. If you can spill, I can, too. Anya's the reason the *Titanic* sank. She was playing chicken with the icebergs."

Scowling, Anya anchored her hands on her hips. "William had a bronze made of his penis and placed it on his mantel."

Rather than embarrass the man, her words spurred him on. "Anya visited the Virgin Islands a few years ago and after that, all the natives started calling them the Islands."

"William has a tattoo of his own face on his back. He says it's 'cause he doesn't want to deprive the people behind him of his beauty."

"Anya—"

"Wait!" Gwen said with a laugh. Their easy banter had chased away her nervousness. "I get the point. You're both depraved. Now enough about you two. Someone tell me something about Sabin. You said you would, Anya."

"Did she now?" William immediately gave her his full attention, blue eyes sparkling. "Allow me to help her out. Sabin once stabbed Aeron, the tattooed warrior with the buzz cut, in the back. Not in a playful gesture, either, but to kill him."

"Did he?" she asked. William seemed outraged by that fact. Gwen thought perhaps she should be, as well, but Sabin was the kind of man who fought dirty—as both she and Anya had remarked—and that, well, impressed her. Her sisters were like that; sometimes, despite her instinctive fear of violence, she secretly wished *she* were like that, where nothing mattered but victory.

"Bor-ing," Anya said. She rubbed her hands together, as if she was happy to have her turn.

"Wait. Tell me why Sabin stabbed him," Gwen said.

"You're digging William's story, then? Fine." Anya sighed. "I'll finish it for him. The Lord/Hunter war had just erupted. In ancient Greece, in case you're wanting a timeline, before those delicious gladiators. Anyway, Hunters, being human, were losing and so they began using women as Bait to draw, trap and slaughter the Lords. They managed to kill Sabin's BFF, Baden."

Gwen's fingers fluttered over her throat. "He told me." He must have been more devastated by the loss than she'd realized.

"He did?" One of Anya's eyebrows winged up. "Wow. He's usually so tight-lipped. But why do you look close to tears? You didn't even know the man."

"Something's in my eye," she rasped.

Lips twitching, Anya said, "Sure. Whatever you say. But back to my story. Sabin and the other warriors pounced on the Hunters responsible and destroyed them. Afterward, Sabin wanted to continue the killing spree. The others didn't. Wait, that's not true. Half agreed with Sabin, half craved peace. Aeron was going on and on about dropping things, starting a new life away from the Hunter war, blah, blah, blah, so Sabin, in his grief and fury, plunged his dagger into the man's back."

"Did Aeron retaliate?" Gwen pictured the warrior in her mind. Tall, muscled and heavily tattooed, as William had said. Hair cropped to his scalp, violet eyes stark and gloomy. He seemed cold but quiet. Almost unassuming. Yet she'd seen the way he'd viciously attacked those Hunters.

Who would win a fight between the two?

"Nope," Anya said. "And it pissed Sabin off even more. He then went for Aeron's throat."

Was it bad that she was relieved? She didn't like the thought of Sabin being hurt. Or assaulted.

"Still want to be his female?" William interjected, sounding almost hopeful. "My offer is still good. I can make all your naughty dreams come true."

If she *were* Sabin's, which she wasn't, yeah, she'd still want to be with him. William was beautiful, didn't intimidate her like the others, but he also didn't tempt her in any way. Her eyes craved the sight of rugged, sometimes boyish Sabin. Her ears craved the sound of his hard voice. Her hands itched to touch that sun-kissed skin. *Silly girl.* He couldn't have been any clearer about wanting to keep her at a distance.

What would she do if he changed his mind, though? He was everything she feared and there'd be no controlling him.

"Oh, and just so you know," William added, grinning wickedly, "he's possessed by the demon of Doubt. So anytime you find yourself battling insecurities, he's the reason. I, however, will make you feel special and loved. Cherished."

"No, you won't," the very voice she'd been dying to hear suddenly proclaimed from behind her. "You won't be seeing another morning."

CHAPTER ELEVEN

SABIN KNEW HE looked like a monster. Blood coated him like a second skin, his eyes gleamed wildly, feral—they always did after something like this went down—and he smelled like old pennies. He'd meant to shower before approaching Gwen, not wanting to frighten her further. First, though, he'd gone to check on Amun. The man had stopped writhing but had not stopped moaning, still bound to his bed and clutching his head. He must have stolen more secrets than usual. Darker secrets. Usually he'd recovered by now.

Sabin felt guilty for having asked his friend to fill his head with more chaos, more voices. He soothed himself only with the knowledge that Amun knew what he was doing and wanted to defeat the Hunters as much as Sabin did.

When he left, he'd decided to sneak a peek at Gwen and see how she was doing. Had Anya fed her? Frightened her? Learned more about her? The questions had taken residence inside his head and refused to leave, somehow overshadowing his desire to force more information out of the prisoners.

Except Gwen hadn't been in his room.

Furious, he'd begun to hunt. Thinking Paris, who had left the dungeon soon after Sabin appeared, had used Sabin's distraction to his advantage and seduced her, Sabin had stomped to the warrior's bedroom, violence brewing inside him. Sabin had claimed Gwen as his. *His*. No one else would touch her. Not because he was jealous or possessive of her, of course, but because, as he'd already assured himself, he planned to use her as a weapon. Wouldn't do to have one of the warriors pissing her off. Yes, that's the only reason his vision had burned bright red and his fists had clenched, his nails elongating into his claws, his muscles gearing for confrontation.

Paris hadn't been in bed with her, however, which had saved his life. He'd been alone, drinking himself into oblivion, practically mainlining ambrosia—drug of choice for the gods.

Sabin was still shocked by the sight. Paris was the upbeat one, the optimistic, caring one. What the hell had happened to him?

The misuse of the heavenly substance would have to be dealt with, for an intoxicated warrior was a sloppy warrior. Again, Sabin had meant to act, to knock some sense into the warrior, then speak with Lucien about it. *Then* he'd heard laughing female voices and had followed the sound, helpless to do anything else, his curiosity simply too great. Yes, curiosity—not desperation to finally see Gwen's lovely face lit with amusement rather than shadowed by fear and trepidation.

Now here he stood in the entrance to the entertainment room, gaze darting between her and William, seething with fury, his demon snarling in his head. Doubt might crave Gwen's destruction, but it wanted to be the one, the only, to deliver it. Wanted to be the only male around her. Everyone else was an interloper and worthy of punishment.

Let me have the warrior, the demon snarled. *He'll regret his actions. He'll beg for mercy.*

Soon. Sabin had just killed a man, violently and cruelly, and should have abhorred the thought of adding another slaying to his ever-increasing list. Besides, Gwen wasn't ready to witness another violent dispute.

Gone was her amusement—what had made her laugh?—and in its place was more of that hated trepidation. Was it directed at Sabin? Or William, who had just blatantly propositioned what belonged to Sabin? And to think Sabin had started to like the womanizing bastard, had admired his cheeky wit. Now, not so much.

"Sabin, my man," the bastard in question said, popping to his feet with an irreverent smile. "We were just talking about you. Can't say I'm happy to see you, though."

"No, and very soon you won't be saying much at all. Gwen, return to my room."

Anya jumped in front of the man, acting as his shield. "Now, Sabin. He didn't mean any harm. He's borderline stupid. You know that."

Rather than shove her behind him as was honorable, William offered Sabin a cocky, come-get-me-now wave from behind the goddess. "I kind of did mean harm. She's pretty and it's been a while for me. Like several hours."

"Gwen, go. Now." Narrowed gaze never leaving the warrior, Sabin withdrew the blade sheathed at the back of his waist and wiped any remaining blood on his pants. "Doesn't matter who you hide behind. You've seen your last sunrise."

Gwen gasped, snapping out of whatever frozen state the confrontation had inflicted. When Sabin stalked forward, she even held out an arm to stop him. He allowed the action, the feel of her arm against his stomach somehow more erotic than another woman's mouth on his cock.

"Please," she whispered. "Don't."

Indecision suddenly reigned. Gwen wasn't going to leave. Too much determination wafted from her. How strongly must this timid little creature feel to stand her ground like this? But did she hope to protect William? Sabin's desire to punish the warrior intensified exponentially.

"If you think about it," William said in that same amused tone, hands on Anya's shoulders as if to taunt him, "I didn't do anything wrong. She's not yours. Not really."

Sabin's nostrils flared, his muscles jerking in their frenzy to finally attack. Somehow he managed to remain in place. Perhaps because Gwen trembled against him, her fingers spreading over his chest, hot and insistent. "And why do you say that?" he found himself demanding.

"I've been around enough women to know when one has been claimed. Not that that ever stopped me from pursuing them, admittedly. But Gwen is fair game, my man. For me, for everyone."

Gwen waved her hands in front of his face. "Nothing happened," she told Sabin imploringly. "I don't know why you're upset. You and I aren't even…we're not…"

"You are mine," he said, his gaze still on William. "Mine to protect." He would mark her, he decided, put a brand on her so that William and the others understood beyond any doubt that she was now and forever off-limits. "Mine to claim."

It would mean nothing. He wouldn't let it. But it had to be done.

"Come." He twined their fingers and turned, pulling her behind him. William laughed. Thankfully, Gwen didn't protest. Had she, he would have thrown her over his shoulder and carried her fireman style—after stalking back to William and knocking a few teeth loose.

"Idiot," he heard Anya growl. A smack sounded, as though she'd slammed her open palm into the back of William's fat head. "Do you want to be kicked out? Who do you think Lucien will side with if it comes down to you or Sabin, huh?"

"Well, you," the warrior said. "And you'll side with me."

"Okay, bad example. Don't forget I've got your precious book. Every time you act like this, I'm going to rip out another page!"

A low growl. "One day I'm going to…"

Their voices faded, leaving the echo of Gwen's shallow breathing and heavy footfalls.

"Where are we going?" she asked nervously.

"My room. Where you should have stayed to begin with."

"I am not a prisoner, I'm a guest!" she said.

Up the stairs he climbed, slowing his gait so that she could keep up. Along the way they ran into Reyes and Danika, Maddox and Ashlyn, who were headed toward the kitchen. Both couples tried to stop and talk to him, the smiling females wanting an introduction to Gwen, but he kept moving without a word.

"Why are you so upset?" Gwen's fingers tightened around his. "Why couldn't I talk to them? I don't understand what's happening."

He was proud of her. She recognized the danger he posed right now, but didn't try to escape and didn't seem in jeopardy of losing control of her Harpy. "I'm not upset." *I'm enraged!*

"Do you normally threaten to kill men who don't upset you?"

He ignored the question, one of his own springing to mind and refusing to leave. "Did he touch you?" The words were ruthless, his tone biting. Walking away from the impending fight had been acceptable because he'd thought William had merely used words to try and gain Gwen's affections. Anything more, and he would turn around as he'd wanted before, grind the bastard into hamburger and feed him to the wild animals roaming the hills.

"No. He didn't. Your nails, they're hurting me."

Instantly Sabin relaxed his grip, willing his nails to sink back into their beds. They snaked a corner, and his pace increased. Urgency rushed through him, as potent and strong as a flooded river.

"Did he scare you?" This time, the question was merely gruff.

"Again, no. And if he had, I—I could have handled him."

His lips twitched in his first stirring of humor that evening. As if. When she was Gwen, the Harpy dormant, she was the most docile creature he'd ever encountered. It was, at times, endearing. His life was death and dishonor, cruelty and might, yet she was all that was serene and good.

"And how would you have done that?" He didn't ask to taunt her but to force her to admit she needed a guardian. Him. Here, in this house, even out in the world, she needed him. The day she learned to control her Harpy, of course, that would change. And he was glad. Yep. Glad.

A little gasp of irritation escaped her and she tried to rip her hand from his. He held tight, strangely unwilling to end the physical connection. "I'm not a total washout, you know?"

"I wouldn't care if you were as strong as Pandora once was. You are desirable, and some of the men here like to believe they are irresistible. I don't want you dealing with them. Ever."

"You find me…desirable?"

Had she not heard the warning in his voice? To stay away from the warriors, or else?

"Never mind," she muttered, his hesitation clearly embarrassing her. "Let's talk about something else. Like your home. Yes. Perfect. Your home is lovely." She was panting now, the long walk likely more exercise than she'd gotten in her year of confinement.

He gave his surroundings a cursory glance. The stone floor was polished and veined with gold—like her eyes. The end tables were cherrywood—as glossy a red as her hair. The walls were smooth, inlaid with multihued marble and utter perfection—like her skin, even dirty as it was.

When had he begun to compare everything to her?

When they hit the landing of the second staircase, his bedroom door entered his line of vision and he breathed a sigh of relief. Almost there… How would she react to what he was about to do? Go Harpy?

He'd have to tread carefully. At the same time, he couldn't—wouldn't—back down.

What if he hurts you? the demon was suddenly whispering into her mind. *What if he—*

"Shut the fuck up!" he snarled, and Doubt laughed gleefully at the damage it had already caused.

Gwen tensed. "Must you curse like that?"

"Yes." He tugged her now reluctant form through the door, shutting and locking it behind her. They faced off. She was pale, trembling again. "Besides, I wasn't talking to you."

"I know. We've had this conversation before. You were talking to your demon. To Doubt."

A statement, not a question. He massaged the back of his neck, wishing his fingers were curled around the goddess of Anarchy's neck instead. "Anya told you." He didn't like that Gwen knew, would have liked for her to have time to get used to *him* first.

A shake of her beautiful head. "William did. So the demon wants me to...doubt you?" She twirled the ends of her hair. Another nervous gesture?

"It wants you to doubt everything. Every choice you make, every breath you take. Everyone around you. It can't help itself. The indecision and confusion of others is where it derives its strength. A moment ago, I could hear it shooting its poisoned barb into your mind, trying to make you believe I'll hurt you. That's why I felt the need to curse."

Her eyes widened, those silver striations expanding and overshadowing the amber. "*That's* what I'm hearing, then. I wondered where the thoughts were coming from."

His brow furrowed as he processed her words. "You're able to distinguish its voice from your own?"

"Yes."

Those who knew him often recognized the demon simply by its word choices. But for a virtual stranger to separate him from his demon… How could she tell the difference between them? "Not many can do so," he said.

Her eyes widened. "Wow. I actually have a skill most don't. And an impressive one, at that. Your demon is sneaky."

"Insidious," he agreed, surprised that she hadn't fainted, screamed or demanded to be released from his despicable clutches. She even seemed proud of herself. "It senses weakness and pounces."

Her expression became pensive. Then depressed. Then angry. She'd discovered the hidden meaning to his words: she was weak and the demon knew it. He preferred her pride.

His gaze snagged on the tray resting on his dresser. An empty tray. He nearly grinned. Anya had gotten her to eat, thank the gods. No wonder her color was higher, her cheeks sweetly fuller. What else was different about her? he mused, studying her. At her waist, there were several slight bulges—but those, he was sure, weren't the result of her recent meal.

A quick scan of the room revealed his weapons case was three inches to the right of its normal mark. She must have disabled the lock and pilfered the contents. The little thief, he thought, eyeing her again.

She squirmed under the scrutiny, cheeks pinkening. "What?"

"Just thinking." Let her keep them, he decided. Hopefully, they made her feel safer. And the safer she felt, the less likely it was that he'd have a confrontation with the Harpy.

"You're making me nervous," she admitted. She rubbed her palms on the front of her thighs.

"Then let's speed things along and assuage your fears." Gods, she was lovely. "Take off your clothes."

Her mouth fell open on a strangled gasp. "Excuse me?"

"You heard me. Strip."

One step, two, she backed away from him, holding her hands up and out. "Not just no but hell, no." Her knees hit the back of the bed and she fell onto the mattress, gaping up at him in horror. "I fell! That was an accident, not an invitation," she rushed out, popping to her feet.

"I know. The *hell, no* gave you away. But it doesn't matter. We're going to shower." She needed to clean up and he needed to mark her. They could knock out both objectives at the same time.

"Feel free." Her voice trembled. "Alone."

"Together. And that's not an invitation, either. It's a fact." He reached behind him and dragged his shirt over his head. His favorite necklace, a gift from Baden, bounced against his chest as the material pooled at his feet.

"Put that back on!" she said, her gaze locking on his butterfly tattoo. "I don't want to see you." Her pupils dilated, belying her words.

Good. She was intrigued, if panicked. He toed off one boot, then the other. They landed with echoing thumps. He unsnapped his pants and shoved them to his ankles. "This is going to happen whether you agree or not, Gwendolyn."

She gave a violent shake of her head, those strawberry curls flying. Still her gaze remained on him. Between his legs now. Her breath emerged faster, raspier. "You said you meant me no harm."

"And I don't. There's nothing menacing about a shower. It's…cleansing."

"Ha!"

He stepped out of the fatigues, now totally and completely naked. And yeah, he had an erection. He willed it away, if only to relax her, but the stupid thing refused to obey, remaining long and hard and thick.

She swiped her tongue over her lips, a telling reaction, like a neon sign that read *I Want Some of That.* Her borrowed T-shirt was baggy but he could see that her nipples were hard. Another tell.

After the way she'd kissed him on the plane, he'd suspected she desired him. Now, he knew for certain. She did. And he was glad. It was foolish, wrong, and could only hurt them both in the end, but he couldn't make himself care just then.

"I'm not going to fuck you," he said, purposely being crude. Anything to snap her out of the staring contest she had going with Little Sab.

It worked. Amber met brown in a heated clash. "Wh-why not sex? And what are you going to do to me?"

Kiss you. Touch you. Give you a hickey—and an orgasm that will make you scream the roof down. No way William could question his claim on the girl after that. The lack of sex, well…Sabin's control would snap and his demon would have free rein if he allowed himself to experience too much pleasure. So he'd do what he could: a little petting for him, a lot of petting for her.

Sure you have what it takes to please one such as her? Pretty as she is, she's probably had scores of men. They've probably done things to her you've only dreamed about.

His jaw clenched. Old as he was, he didn't have a tremendous amount of experience with women. While living in the heavens, he'd been too busy defending the gods to pursue his own pleasures. When first cast to earth, he'd been too evil, too crazed to want anything besides destruction. And once he'd gained a measure of control over the wickedness inside him, he'd quickly learned how bad he was for the opposite sex.

A few times, though, he'd considered himself in love and had chased the women shamelessly. Single, married, it hadn't mattered. He supposed he and William had that in common. If he'd wanted them, he'd gone after them because the want had been such a rare thing.

Darla was the most recent—and devastating—example of his destructive impact. She had been married to a Hunter, Galen's right-hand man. She'd come to Sabin with information, knowledge of where her husband and men kept their weapons, what they were planning. She'd seen the hypocrisy of the Hunter code, she'd said, and had wanted the war to end. At first, Sabin had thought she meant to act as Bait. To lure him and his men into a trap. But she hadn't. Everything she'd told him had been accurate.

They'd soon become lovers. He'd wanted her to leave her husband, but she had refused because she would have been unable to help Sabin. He hated to admit this, but part of him had been glad about her decision. He hadn't lost his mole. But every time she'd visited him, every time he'd taken her to bed, she'd left with a little less sparkle. All too soon, she'd become clingy, needy, desperate for a kind word. He'd tried, gods had he tried, to boost her confidence back up, telling her how beautiful and brave and intelligent she was. She had, of course, doubted him, so in the end it hadn't mattered.

She'd called him after slashing her wrists.

He hadn't gotten to her in time. No, Stefano beat him there and kept Sabin from seeing her one last time. He hadn't even been able to attend her funeral, not wanting Hunters to catch sight of him.

Eleven years had passed since her death, but his guilt was as fresh and clear as if it had happened yesterday. He should have left her alone. If he had, Stefano might have grown tired of the chase and the battles and bowed out. Instead, fueled now by vengeance as much as fanaticism, the Hunter was as savagely determined to win as Sabin.

Sabin hadn't been with anyone since, avoiding female companionship entirely. Until Gwen. Could she handle him, though? Even a little?

"W-well?" she stammered. "What are you going to do?"

He forced the demon's worries from his mind. "I'm going to clean you."

Again she shook her head. "I don't want to be clean. I swear I don't."

"I don't care," he said, and advanced.

Panting, she fell back onto the bed once more and scrambled backward, not stopping until her shoulders hit the headboard. "I don't want to do this, Sabin."

"Yes, you do. You're just afraid."

"You're right. What if I kill you?"

"I've handled Hunters for thousands of years. What's a lone Harpy?" Brave words, but he couldn't admit the whole truth. That he didn't know what she'd do, how he'd react or what would happen if they were forced to fight each other. But he was willing to risk her wrath to see this done.

White-hot desire pushed itself into her eyes, lighting them up. "You truly think you can defeat a Harpy in attack mode?"

Up he climbed on the bed, closing more and more of the hated distance between them. "Hopefully, it won't come to that. If it does, well, we'll find out together."

"No! That's not good enough." Her foot slammed into his chest, but rather than shove him away, the action sealed her fate. His fingers twined around her ankle and jerked her closer.

"We'll never know unless we try."

Then a tear escaped the corner of her eye and slid the length of her cheek, and his chest constricted. "Please," she rasped brokenly. "I wouldn't be able to live with myself if I hurt you."

Don't back down. "Like I said, there's only one way to prove to you that I can handle anything you throw at me." He hardened his heart against her tears; he had to. For her, for him, for peace inside this fortress, this had to be done. She had to be marked. *Wanted* to be marked, whether or not she admitted it. And like the warrior he was, he would see it through to the end. No matter what.

CHAPTER TWELVE

GWEN COULDN'T BELIEVE IT. Sabin, the man she'd kissed, fantasized about, craved, relied on, viewed as a protector, a villain, the man she didn't want to desire but desired anyway, had stripped her despite her shouted protests and wild kicking and hauled her ass into the shower stall before climbing in behind her. Pissed as she'd been—was, damn it—she hadn't turned Harpy.

At first, she'd been shocked. Then nervous. Then excited. Each emotion had lasted only a few minutes, but each had been world-shaking. Why hadn't she hurt him? Because Sabin had yet to make a threatening move? Because the Harpy loved physical contact as much as Gwen did and would take it wherever and however she could get it?

Right now steam enveloped her and Sabin, thick as clouds. Hot water cascaded down the planes and curves of her body. Nothing had ever felt so amazing—except for the naked man behind her, pinning her in, keeping her inside. She would *not* hook up with a demon, no matter how sexy he was. Would she? Her life didn't need more weird. Did it?

Why couldn't she make a decision? His demon wasn't even pestering her, so she had no excuse.

Gwen wrapped her arms around her middle, not bothering to cover her breasts or the tiny triangle of hair between her legs. Why bother? Sabin was stronger and could pry her hands away in an instant if he so desired—and part of her wanted him to see her, to crave her. Still…

"Do you not realize you could have morning-after regrets in the form of shredded skin and organs?" she asked.

Soapy hands settled on her shoulders, hot and wet, massaging. "You feel like silk. I doubt I'll be regretting anything." His voice was husky, rich…drugging.

Mmm, more. Her muscles loosened, her head lolling back and propping against the hollow of his neck. *Stop. Tense up! Fight his allure.* She tried, she really did, but her body refused to obey her mind. His ministrations simply felt too damn good.

I wonder if he finds you attractive. Or ugly.

Okay. Finally, she tensed. There was that beguiling, destructive voice. The demon, Doubt. So different in tenor from her own inner voice. Her jaw clenched painfully, and the Harpy squawked at the unwelcome intrusion. "Any way you can cap your friend? He's annoying."

"Such spirit. I like it. And the demon is hardly my friend." Sabin's thumbs traced her collarbone. He leaned down, his mouth at her ear, his breath a beautiful caress. "I don't mean to change the subject, but have I told you yet that I find you utterly lovely?"

Gwen gulped, unsure of how to reply. Part of her still wanted to encourage him and part of her still wanted to shove him away before she forgot exactly why she had to resist him. He represented everything she hated about her life. Darkness, violence, chaos. More than that, he planned to use her to hurt his enemy. Nothing came before his hatred of the Hunters, not even the love of a woman.

"Let's get to it, shall we?" Sabin released her, and she had to press her lips together to cut off a whimper. Then those sensual fingers tangled in her hair, working in shampoo, the scent of lemon dancing from them. Her eyes closed in ecstasy. No wonder he always smelled so edible.

"You go Harpy when you're scared. What about when you're aroused? Or climaxing?"

Such a blunt and personal question. But he'd picked the perfect time to ask. As they were currently naked, she didn't mind answering. "S-sometimes she tries to make herself known. I try to be careful, though, and stop her."

"Don't try to stop her with me." Before she could respond, he changed the subject again. "William told you about my demon." He shifted his hips, his erection brushing the curve of her spine. An accident? "Did Anya tell you about my past?"

A shiver stole through Gwen. "Do you mean, did she tell me that you stabbed your friend in the back? No. She left that part out."

His nails dug deeply in her scalp, and she gasped. Immediately he released her with a muttered, "Sorry."

Damn it. Her sarcastic tongue kept creeping out at the worst times. Soon someone (cough Sabin cough) was going to take exception and try and cut it out. And really, suppressing that side of her nature shouldn't be hard. She'd been doing it her entire life. For the first time, however, there was a spark of resentment in her chest. If she weren't such a coward crybaby, she wouldn't fear people's reactions, wouldn't fear her own response and could just be herself.

Herself. Did she even know who that was anymore?

"Duck your head under the water," Sabin said suddenly, gruffly.

He didn't give her time to obey, but cupped the back of her neck and shoved her under the hot stream. Sudsy droplets sprayed into her mouth, and she sputtered.

"Close your eyes or they'll—"

"Ow, ow, ow!" She squeezed her eyelids tightly closed.

"Burn," he finished with a laugh.

Gwen rubbed her eyes, perturbed despite herself by his casual attitude about all this. He'd been so jealous about William—at least, that was the only emotion that had made any sense. And his gaze had scorched her as he'd stripped her, promising incomparable pleasure.

So why wasn't he copping a feel?

Motions clipped, businesslike, he soaped her from neck to toes. His palms glided over her breasts and hardened nipples without pause, then delved between her legs. Though his touch was somehow detached, he still managed to leave her trembling and achy, breathless and needy.

"I can clean myself," she muttered.

"You had the chance yesterday and the day before that. Hell, you had the chance this morning. You didn't take it." He shifted, his erection brushing her once again. "Why is that?"

Her blood heated as she pressed her lips together. No reason to tell him what he wanted to know. He would deduce the answer on his own any moment now. And, to be honest, she was almost excited to witness his reaction. Already he'd admitted he found her lovely. What would he think of her without the mask of grime? Would he finally make a freaking move?

When he finished cleaning and rinsing her, he stilled. His breath seemed to catch in his throat, and she felt a swirling heat seep into her, spreading, intensifying. Here it was, his reaction. He'd noticed. "Your skin…"

"I tried to warn you."

"Well, you should have tried harder." He spun her around, gaze perusing her swiftly, then more leisurely.

Seeing him, she realized just how wrong she'd been. There was nothing casual about him. His eyes were bright, hot as fire, his lips pulled back over his teeth, thin lines of strain bracketing his mouth.

"Your skin…" he repeated.

She didn't need a mirror to know that without the grime, she glowed. There was a translucent sheen to her that made her look like a freshly polished opal.

Tentatively, as though in a trance, Sabin reached out. His fingertip traced her jawline, dipped to her neck, between her breasts. She didn't back away. No, she stepped forward. Closer. Craving more. Unable to stop. Goose bumps broke out, and all thoughts of resisting him vanished.

"Smooth and warm and luminous," he whispered reverently. "Why do you hide—" His teeth pressed together and the reverence mutated into anger before her eyes. "Men can't keep their hands off you, can they?"

A lump formed in her throat, preventing her from replying. She shook her head. What would Sabin do and say next? He changed moods faster than anyone she'd ever met. *Touch me.*

But he wasn't done with his line of questioning. "Do your sisters have skin like this?"

"Yes."

"All Harpies?"

"Yes." Hopefully he was finished now.

"Have you called them?"

Nope. Not done. "Not yet."

"You'll do it the moment we leave this shower. I want them here, in this fortress, within the week."

She gaped at him, shocked to her core. She was naked, her skin at its most alluring, and he wanted to speak of her sisters? To *meet* them? Why did he—the answer slid into place and her shock faded. Of course he wanted them here. He probably thought they'd help him with his war. Or maybe he wanted a harem of Harpies.

Something dark and powerful bloomed in Gwen's chest. Something poisonous. It caused her nails to elongate, the Harpy to screech and her teeth to sharpen. Red spotted her vision.

"You're angry." He blinked in confusion. "Why?"

"I'm not angry." *I will kill you if you try and bed them.*

"You're gripping me so tightly, my palm is bleeding."

Part of her registered that he didn't sound upset or frightened. The rest of her was still too furious to admire his courage under fire.

"You want to sleep with my sisters," she snarled. Snarled? Her, Gwendolyn the Timid?

He rolled his eyes. "No, I want my friends to sleep with them."

She blinked just as he had done, not under…standing. Oh. *Oh.* All of her fury drained as swiftly as her shock had, leaving the sweetest sense of pleasure. If his friends were occupied with her sisters, they would leave *Gwen* alone. Was Sabin *that* possessive of her?

"Were you jealous?" he asked, as though the prospect intrigued him.

"No. Of course not." That was not information he needed, could be used against her, and in this instance a lie would absolutely serve her better than the truth. "I was…thinking of Tyson, wishing I was with him."

Sabin's eyes narrowed, but through the thick shield of his lashes she could see the brown irises edging with crimson. "You will not think of him. Do you understand? I forbid it."

"I—okay." She didn't know what else to say. Never had Sabin looked more capable of murder. But why wasn't she scared?

However feeble her response, it seemed to pacify him. "I'd already decided to mark you." There was determination in his tone. Determination so cold and hard she doubted a blade could cut through it. "But this…" His gaze swept over her body. "By gods, I'll mark you every day if I have to. You will only ever think of me."

"Wh-what do you mean, mark me?" Mark, as in slash? Punish? Now she had no problem backing away. And what did he mean, every day? How much did he expect her to endure?

His hand whipped out, fingers curling around her wrist and dragging her back. "I'm going to sink my teeth into that pretty skin, gently, but enough to leave an imprint."

Once again her fear drained, leaving only white-hot thrums of wicked bliss. It had been so long. So long since a man had held her, made her feel cherished and special and hot enough to writhe against him.

"Do you want that?" he asked softly.

Did she? Hell, yes. She might not know who she was anymore, but she did know her body hungered for this male. Could she allow it, though?

Time to find the logic. Sabin was strong, immortal and claimed he could handle anything she dished. She was strong enough to enjoy him and stay distanced. She hoped. The "marking" would keep the other warriors away from her. And it was nice to feed the Harpy what it wanted once in a while so that it, in turn, would behave.

Logic achieved.

Before she could form an answer, however, Sabin's nostrils flared as if he could already smell her desire. "If anyone else touches you, they'll die."

He was willing to hurt his friends for her? Lord, just the thought melted her.

Slowly, he tugged her forward, not stopping until her nipples brushed the strength of his chest. He moaned.

"Your demon—"

"Will be kept on a tight leash, so no worries. Now. Choose."

She didn't have to think about it anymore. "Yes," she said breathlessly. Gulping, she reached up, twined her arms around his neck, pressing her wet body against his. "You don't have to worry, either. I'll be careful with you."

"Please don't." He swooped in, his mouth taking possession of hers. It was not the soft, one-sided kiss from the plane. This was consuming, raw, his tongue plunging inside, *participating,* deep and hard and demanding a response. She gave it to him, helpless to do otherwise. One hand tangled in the dark silk of his hair, the other kneaded his back, probably leaving marks of her own.

Don't lose yourself completely. The warning blasted through her mind. *Enjoy, but stay focused.* The Harpy was purring, happy with what was happening, wanting more, more, more. But when Gwen commanded her breathing to slow, her body to still, to accept Sabin's touch, to enjoy but nothing more, those purrs turned to growls. More, more, more.

Sabin gripped her chin and angled her head, prying her mouth open even wider, refusing to allow her to withdraw, even slightly. Their teeth banged together with the force of his next thrust. Though she groaned, he didn't pull back. Didn't soften. On and on the kiss continued, until she was breathless, shaking, arching into him, moaning, groaning again, ready to beg for more just like the Harpy.

For the second—third?—time she tried to distance herself, to calm her body so that she didn't fall too deeply under his spell.

"Oh, no you don't. Stay with me."

"No, I—"

"Will only feel. No thinking. That's for later." Slowly he backed her into the tiled wall, and the coldness made her gasp. He swallowed the sound, his mouth already on her again, taking everything she had to give and demanding more. Behind them, the shower continued to rain, battering against the porcelain.

With one hand he corralled both her wrists and pinned them above her head. With the other he cupped her breast, rolling the nipple between his knuckles. Her stomach quivered, her knees weakened. She would have fallen, but he jammed his thigh between her legs, holding her up. Except, the core of her rubbed against the rough skin of his knee and that weakened her further.

"You like?"

"Yes." No reason to lie now. She couldn't hide her body's reaction.

Down, down his fingers traced, swirling around her navel. Back and forth she rocked against his leg, little breathless moans escaping her lips. *More. More. More!* The Harpy's cries blended with her own, until they were a single voice inside her head.

"I'm going to bite you now."

He didn't give her time to accept or deny, sinking his teeth into the tender cord at the base of her neck. At the same time, he removed his thigh from between her legs and replaced it with his hand. Two fingers plunged inside her, deep, so wonderfully deep.

"Sabin!"

"Gods, darling. You're hot. Tight."

"I'm going to…I can't…I shouldn't…" So close already. From just two fingers, pumping and grinding inside her.

"Let yourself go. I won't let anything bad happen. Swear."

What if she—what if the Harpy—damn it! Her thoughts were fragmenting, her mind focusing only on the pleasure of having those thick fingers working her.

"Come for me." His thumb brushed her clitoris, and there was no more fighting it. She climaxed, screaming, pumping against him, then biting him back until she tasted blood.

As she spasmed, he released her hands and grabbed onto her hips, forcing them forward, ramming her into his erection. No penetration, just friction, but damn, it was good. She sank her nails into his back, digging deep, cutting.

He hissed through his teeth, repeated the action of jamming her against him, and hissed again. She loved the sound. Needed to hear it again. And again. Soon she was moving on her own, meeting him halfway, pounding against him with all of her strength, sharp teeth back in his flesh, beads of blood coating her tongue.

"That's the way," he praised. "Just like that. You feel so good, so damned good." He was babbling. To remind her of where she was, who she was with? "I wasn't going to let things go this far. Not for me. But I'm going to explode. I know it. Shouldn't be this good. Shouldn't—"

Then he was kissing her again, his tongue plunging, hot seed spurting onto her stomach, his body quaking and hers erupting again just from the thought of his pleasure. They clung to each other, panting, moaning.

Finally she collapsed against him, amazed that she'd lost control. Amazed that they hadn't had sex, yet this little shower had been world-shaking. Amazed that the Harpy hadn't turned vicious. Amazed that the Harpy only wanted more. Most of all, she was amazed that, even though she'd just experienced two intense orgasms, she, too, still wanted more.

CHAPTER THIRTEEN

SABIN CARRIED GWEN to the large bed in his room and snuggled her against him. Neither of them said a word as they watched the night sky give way to dawn through the room's only window. They lay there, naked, intertwined, each stiff and strained and lost in their own thoughts.

"What happened to sleeping on the floor?" Gwen finally asked him, breaking the silence.

"I never actually fell asleep. Technically I didn't break my word."

"True."

After that, silence enveloped them again. But again, neither slumbered.

He'd expected her to drift easily; there were bruises under her eyes, more prominent than ever, and he'd seen her yawn earlier. But once again, she surprised him. She pretended to sink into oblivion once or twice, but she never actually fell.

He knew why *he* couldn't relax: his demon was crazed inside his mind, more desperate than ever to reach her, to hurt her. To make her question everything that had happened between them. Just as it had done to all the others before her. Women who had either left him or killed themselves.

I should leave before something like that happens.

The moment he thought it, denial roared through him, sharp and cutting, as if it had teeth, and all the reasons he should stay popped into his head. One, Paris could come looking for him and stumble upon her, then seduce her. Promiscuity just couldn't help himself. Two, a Hunter could escape from the dungeon, grab her and bolt. Three, she could begin to regret what they'd done in the shower and bolt on her own.

All excellent reasons. But they weren't the reason he ended up settling more deeply into the feathered mattress. Gwen felt too soft and warm against him, smelled too delicious, like lemons, his favorite, and kept uttering wanton little sighs he yearned to swallow.

Already he wanted her again. Wanted *all* of her this time. Wanted to sink in and out of her, pounding softly, then hard and harsh, a never-ending rhythm that would bind them together. No woman had ever aroused him so thoroughly, tasted so sublime, fit his body so perfectly. And none had ever clutched him with such abandon, bit him, drawn blood and had him panting for more.

Even though he hadn't sealed the deal, they'd both found release. He'd suspected once would never be enough, and he'd been right.

Hearing her cries in his ears had been sweeter than pumping inside another woman. And that skin…it was like a drug for the eyes. One glance, and you had to have another, and another. Looking away was painful, the desire to look again a constant urge.

She probably hates you now, probably wants nothing to do with you. I wouldn't be surprised if she thought about her human boyfriend while you kissed her and that's why she was so passionate. Didn't she tell you he

*was in her thoughts? Clearly the human is everything
she wants for her life. You are not.*

Sabin's arm tightened around Gwen, squeezing, and
she expelled a pained puff of air. Instantly he forced
his grip to loosen, and placed a block on his mind to
silence his demon. There'd been no thoughts of the ex-
boyfriend, emphasis on *ex;* he was sure of it, and neither
Doubt nor Gwen's own earlier words would convince
him otherwise. It had been Sabin's name Gwen had
called. Doubt was surly, that was all, and lashing out
at him, desperate for a target. At least, like him, Gwen
could distinguish the demon from her own insecurities.

"Can we stop pretending to relax like happy lovers now?" Gwen asked suddenly, once again cutting
through the quiet.

He sighed, dislodging several strands of her hair and
causing them to dance over his chest, tickling the skin.
If only they *were* happy lovers. No demon, no Harpy,
no war, just two people enjoying their time together.

Sabin blinked, the thought completely foreign to him.
Never, in all his thousands of years, had he wished to
be anything other than what he was. An immortal warrior. Powerful, extraordinary, eternal. Yes, he'd made
a mistake, helping the other Lords steal and open Pandora's box. And yes, he'd been kicked from the heavens
and suffered constantly because of the demon inside
him. But it was a suffering he accepted and deserved.
A suffering he willingly endured because it made him
stronger than he'd ever been while serving Zeus. So
why wish otherwise now?

"Yes, we can stop pretending. We can even talk.
And by talk, of course I mean I'll ask the questions

and you'll answer them. Let's begin now, shall we? You never sleep. Why?"

"Bossy baggage," she muttered. "For your information, I don't need to sleep." In a fluid move she must have been waiting hours to perform, she rolled to her back so that only their shoulders touched. He'd noticed that usually she wanted all the contact she could get. What had changed?

Didn't matter, he supposed. After Darla, he'd promised himself he'd always keep his distance from the females he found himself attracted to. For eleven years, he had. Now Gwen was helping him with that. There was a definite spark of irritation in his chest at the thought that *she* had been the one to get them back on track.

"You refused to eat though you were hungry. You refused to shower though you were dirty. Not for one moment do I believe your body—" *your luscious body* "—needs no rest."

Is he saying that because you resemble the walking dead? Because you appear tired, worn out, haggard?

Sabin heard the degrading thought leave him and drift to Gwen, unable to stop it.

A moment later, she stiffened. "Your demon is a bastard."

"Yes." *And you had better shut up, you rotten piece of shit. You've already been warned. Remember the box?*

There was a heavy pause, then an aggravated growl of acceptance.

"Well?" she gasped out. "Do I?"

Resemble the walking dead? Hardly. "You are the loveliest woman I've ever beheld." Truth. And it didn't even bother him that he sounded like Lucien when the warrior spouted pretty nonsense to Anya. Nonsense Sabin had always rolled his eyes at.

"I don't believe you." Gwen shifted to her side, peering over at him and tucking her hand under her cheek. "You have to say I'm pretty."

"Yeah, because I'm a gentleman," he said dryly. He, too, shifted to his side so that he could meet her gaze. Those exotic curls framed her face and delicate shoulders, her dazzling skin catching the red hue and making her look deliciously flushed. "You think it can be said that I'm always polite, never want to hurt anyone's feelings and spout sweet lies because I like the people around me to be docile? Oh, and if I do accidentally insult someone, because I'd never do it on purpose, I absolutely refuse to take what I want from them by force?"

Lush lips twitched into a half smile—lips he'd kissed, sucked and nibbled—and her eyes swirled hypnotically. Eyes he'd nearly drowned in. Seeing that smile Sabin experienced an instant, unwanted hard-on, immensely grateful for the sheet that covered his lower half. And he was supposed to be the dangerous one in this relationship, he mused darkly.

Not a relationship, self-preservation piped up. He wouldn't let it be anything more than a business transaction. He would convince her to fight for him, protect her from his friends while she did so, and when the war was at last over he would stop thinking about her, stop lusting for her.

"Maybe you don't care about other people's feelings, but you do want my help. You're trying to butter me up like toast."

"You'll agree to fight the Hunters whether I butter you up or not," he said, striving for a confident tone. It was a confidence he didn't feel, but had to believe in. He could accept no less. "Need I remind you that you've already promised to help?"

Tired of lying dormant, Doubt pounced. *She nearly faints at the sight of blood. Help you fight? I think not!*

"You will," he reiterated for the demon, for himself.

"I don't mind helping you with the clerical aspects of your campaign. Like researching on the Internet and filing paperwork. If you keep records of your, uh, kills, I could be in charge of that. I could even research those artifacts you're looking for. That's what I did before I was abducted. I worked in an office, taking notes, fact-checking, that sort of thing. And I was damn good at it."

Never had he heard more pride in someone's tone. But was she proud of her work or her ability to fit into the normal world?

"And you liked this work?" he asked.

"Of course."

"You weren't bored?" The real question was, how had her Harpy handled the monotony? Sabin considered Gwen's dark side very much like his own, a driving force, a curse, a sickness, but a part of her that craved excitement and danger. A part of her that grew twitchy if ignored for too long.

"Well, maybe a little," she admitted, twirling a strand of hair around her finger.

He almost laughed. He'd place money on the fact that she'd been bored out of her freaking mind. "I'll pay you for your aid," he said, recalling Anya's words about the Harpies' need to steal or earn their food. He wanted her in the field, fighting, but wouldn't mind using her for research, as well. At least at first. "Name what you want and it's yours."

Several minutes passed in silence before she said, "I'm drawing a blank. I'll have to think about it."

"There's nothing you want?"

"No."

Knowing how badly he craved victory, she could have asked him for anything, the moon and the stars even. Yet she couldn't think of a single thing. Odd. Most people would toss out an astronomical sum and bargain from there. He wondered what sort of thing was prized among her people. Money? Jewels? "What do your sisters do for a living?"

Her lips pressed together in a thin line.

What was this? She didn't want to tell him or she didn't like what they did? "Hookers?" he guessed, not just to get a rise out of her but also to test how far he could push her before the Harpy began demanding his head on a platter.

She gasped, slapped him, then jerked her hand back quickly, as if she couldn't believe she'd done such a thing. Afraid he'd retaliate for such a puny action? Silly girl.

"You deserved to be hit, so I won't apologize. They aren't hookers."

"Killers?"

No gasp. No slap. A simple narrowing of her eyes, lashes fusing together. Bingo.

"They're mercenaries." Not a question. What amazing luck.

"Yes," she said through gritted teeth. "They are."

Sabin wanted to laugh. If one Harpy could destroy an entire army, what could four do? He could pay for their services. He had the money, no matter their price.

"I see the wheels turning in your head." Her free

hand drummed the pillow cushioning her own head. "But you should know that they love me and won't take a job if I ask them to turn it down."

Now *his* eyes narrowed, probing. She wore an innocent expression, if edged with tendrils of anger. "Is that a threat, darling?"

"Take it however you wish. I don't want them fighting those despicable Hunters for any reason."

"Why? Like you said, they're despicable. Evil. They would have found a way to drug you into a stupor, rape you and steal your baby if I hadn't saved you. You should be begging your sisters to fight them."

"You've already tortured them for what they did to me and the others." The words rasped from her.

"And that's enough for you? When someone hurts me, I want to be the one to hurt them back. I want to make sure it's done right. Didn't you feel *some* satisfaction when you tore the throat out of—"

"Yes, okay. Yes. But allowing someone else to do it *has* to be enough. Otherwise I'll spend my life hunting them, killing them, never really living." Her nostrils were flared, her chest heaving. With every inhalation, the sheet slipped and revealed the top of a pink nipple. He had to force himself to look away before he ended their conversation.

Was she saying his life was empty? Well, it wasn't. It was full, damn it. "Better to live a life of hunting and killing than to bury yourself in fear."

She raised her palm as if she meant to strike him once more. She was shaking, the muted anger she'd radiated before now a red-hot fury. He'd finally pushed her hard enough. The Harpy was there, in her eyes.

"Do it," he told her. It would be good for her. Show

her that she could lash out and he wouldn't break. He hoped.

Slowly her hand lowered; the shaking ceased. With a deep breath, her eyes returned to normal. "You'd like that, wouldn't you? Like me to be like you? Well, it's not going to happen. No one would survive if it did. No one. Not even my sisters."

He caught the hidden meaning and arched a brow. "Fought them and hurt them, have you?"

A reluctant nod. "I was just a child and they were merely playing with me, taunting me as sisters do. I erupted and tore them up pretty badly."

"I thought you said they were stronger than you."

"They are. They can control who they kill, even while fully Harpy. *That* is true strength."

He thought about it a moment, tangling a hand back and forth through his hair. "I bet *I* could take your Harpy. I mean, like your sisters, I'm immortal and heal quickly." Yeah, he remembered what she'd done to the Hunter and yeah, he remembered how swiftly she'd moved. But why had he counted himself out before, even for a moment? He had brute force, thousands of years of experience and a determination matched by few. As long as she didn't take his head, he'd recover.

"You're an idiot." She must not have realized what she'd said until a few seconds later because she froze as the words echoed off the walls.

"Nothing you say will provoke me enough to hurt you," he told her, torn between tenderness and exasperation.

Gradually she relaxed, but the tension between them remained.

"Do you regret what happened in the shower?" he

asked, in part to turn the conversation in another direction and in part, well, because his curiosity demanded to be assuaged. She'd just made it very clear that she didn't like what he was or what he did.

"Yes," she replied, cheeks heating.

No hesitation from her, and that seriously irritated him. "Why? You liked every moment of it."

Hadn't she?

His hands curled into fists, the bones suddenly brittle. That damn Doubt. But he feared that for once the insecurity was his own, not the demon spreading its poison.

Her gaze skittered away from him. "It was okay, I guess."

He popped his jaw. It was okay. She guessed. She fucking guessed. By gods, he'd give her another demonstration. He'd kiss her, every inch of her this time, just the way he wanted. He'd dance his tongue between her legs, bite her, finger her, make her beg for his cock and then, only then, would he give it to her. He'd flip her to her stomach, grip her hips and—

Make love to her if he continued down this path. Mistake, mistake, mistake. Worth it, though, he thought next. There'd be no stopping him, and she'd love every minute of it. He'd pump inside her, spill his seed, deep and hot, and—

Again hear her tell you it was okay. She guessed. Doubt laughed, and in that moment the demon actually respected her.

"It was more than okay, but we'll table that discussion until later." Sabin hopped from the bed, unabashed as the sheet fell away, leaving him bared to her gaze. Suddenly shy, she slapped a hand over her eyes. But if he wasn't mistaken, she was peeking through her fingers. He could feel the heat of those eyes, the smoldering desire.

He stalked to the closet. After weaponing up as was his custom—if fifteen blades strapped to his ankles, wrists, waist and back was being too careful, then give him the Too Careful award—he tugged on a pair of jeans and an *I'll See You in the Afterlife* T-shirt.

He grabbed a pair of sweatpants and a plain white tee and tossed them at Gwen. "Get up, get dressed."

"Why?" She sat up, hair tumbling around her, and gathered the clothing.

"You're going to call your sisters." Time to get that little chore over with. "Anya told me a bit about your culture, and if you're afraid they'll try and harm you for allowing yourself to be captured, don't be. I won't let them." He didn't give her time to respond. "When you're done with the call, we're going downstairs to eat. And you will eat, Gwen. That's an order." There'd be none of that only eating what she stole nonsense. He might have considered leaving things lying around so she'd feel like she'd stolen them, but he wasn't in the mood to placate her now.

"After that," he continued, "I need to call all the men together for a meeting, tell them what I've learned about the Hunters. You'll sit in on that, too. Because you're part of this now."

Her chin rose stubbornly. "I'm not one of your men to order around."

"If you were one of my men, I'd be ashamed of my thoughts right now." His gaze lowered, lingering on her breasts, her stomach…between her legs. He spun on his heel before he could do what he really wanted and stalk to her, cover her and penetrate her. "Now hurry up."

There was a long pause, then a swoosh of material, a bounce of the bed, a sigh. "Okay. I'm ready." She sounded resigned.

Once more Sabin faced her—and stopped breathing. Just like before, the clothing bagged on her. Now that she was clean, however, the white cotton caused her skin to gleam like a pearl. His mouth watered for a taste; a single lick would suffice. Would have to suffice, he thought, entranced, already walking to her, reaching out.

What the hell are you doing? Snap out of it, asshole! He stopped abruptly, teeth grinding. It took a moment for him to gather his wits and recall what he'd wanted her to do. When he did, he crossed the room to his dresser and swiped up his cell. There was a missed call and a text message. He scrolled the menu. The call had come from Kane. The text…Kane, as well. The warrior was spending the day in town but said to call if he was needed and he would rush home. It was a miracle that Kane had been able to use his phone twice in a row without frying it to hell.

After Sabin cleared the screen, he threw the phone at Gwen. She missed.

"Start dialing," he told her.

GWEN LIFTED THE PHONE with a trembling hand, tears burning her eyes. The entire year of her imprisonment, she'd wanted to do this, had *needed* to hear her sisters' voices. But she was still ashamed about what had happened to her and still didn't want them to know.

"It's morning here, so it's nighttime in Alaska," she said. "Perhaps I should wait."

Sabin showed no mercy. "Dial."

"But—"

"I don't understand your reluctance. You love them. You want them here, even made it a condition of your staying with me."

"I know." She traced her finger over the glowing numbers on the little black device. Her guilt was returning. Guilt for making her beloved sisters wait for news of her—or, if they didn't know she'd been taken, simple contact from her.

"Will they blame you for what happened? Want to punish you? I told you I wouldn't let them."

"No." Maybe. What she did know was that they'd demand Sabin allow them to join his war, just as he wanted. *They'd* want Hunter ass on a platter, served raw and fresh. But if they were injured because of Gwen… she'd hate herself forever and still another eternity.

"Call," Sabin said.

Get over yourself, she thought. With a sigh, she dialed Bianka's number. Of the three, Bianka was the most kindhearted. And by kindhearted, Gwen meant that Bianka would toss a glass of water at the person she'd just lit on fire.

Three rings later, her sister answered. "I have no idea who is calling me from this number but you had better haul ass or—"

"Hey, Bianka." Her stomach clenched painfully, the voice so hauntingly familiar and so well loved the tears that had been burning her eyes finally spilled over, rushing down her cheeks. "It's me."

There was a pause, an inhalation of breath. "Gwennie? Gwennie, is that you?"

She swiped at her cheeks with the back of her wrist, very aware of Sabin's hot gaze on her, practically eating her up. What was he thinking? Warrior that he was, her show of weakness—more weakness, that is—probably disgusted him. And that was a good thing. Really. They'd kissed and touched in the shower and she'd been ready to go further, take more, take all, *give* all, despite the kind of man he was and the things he'd said to her, the things he would ultimately do to her.

"Hey, you still there? Gwennie? Are you okay? What's going on?"

"Yep, it's me. The one and only," she finally replied.

"My gods, girl. Do you know how long it's been?"

Twelve months, eight days, seventeen minutes and thirty-nine seconds. "I have an inkling. So how are you?"

"Better, now that I've heard from you, but pissed as hell. You are gonna pay big-time when Taliyah finds you. A while back we called your phone, you know, to say hi and threaten to bitch slap you if you didn't come home. No answer. So we called Tyson. He said you had moved out and he didn't know how to reach you. We searched and searched, all over the damn world, but no luck. Finally we paid Tyson a personal visit and he told us you'd been taken against your will."

"Did you torture him?" She wasn't mad at him, didn't want him hurt. He'd merely been protecting himself, something she understood.

"Well…maybe a little. Not our fault, though. He wasted precious time."

She moaned; then she pictured Bianka, black hair

twisted around her head, amber eyes glowing, red lips lifted in a wicked smile, and she couldn't help but grin. "He's alive, though. Yes?"

"Please, girl. As if we'd lower ourselves to kill that puny little shit. I never knew what you saw in him."

"Good. He didn't know where I was. Not really."

"Who took you, anyway? What'd you do to them to punish them, huh, huh? They are dead, right? Tell me they're dead, baby girl."

"I'll, uh, get to that." Truth. "Some other time." Again, truth. "Listen," she added before Bianka could probe too deeply, "I'm currently in Budapest, but I want to see you guys. I miss you." There at the end, her voice cracked.

"Then come home." Bianka had never pleaded for anything—that Gwen knew of—but she sounded ready to beg just then. "We want you home. Not knowing where you were nearly destroyed us. Mom moved out months ago 'cause we wouldn't stop pestering her about you, so you don't have to worry about the cold-shoulder treatment."

That she'd kept them waiting longer than necessary... guilt rose again, hotter than before, and Gwen tumbled straight into a shame spiral. *I did this. I did this to my strong, proud sister.* "I don't care about Mom." And she didn't. Not really. They'd never been close. "But you're going to have to come to me. I'm with the, uh, Lords of the Underworld, and they'd like to meet you. You know, they're the guys that are—"

"Demon-possessed?" Bianka whooped with excitement, then grew suddenly somber. "What are you doing with them? Are they the ones who took you?" There was murder in her tone.

"No. No. They're the good guys."

"Good guys?" She laughed. "Well, whatever they are, they aren't your usual bag o' fun. Unless your personality has undergone a huge overhaul this past year and a half?"

Not really. "Just…will you come?"

No hesitation. "We're on our way, baby girl."

CHAPTER FOURTEEN

THE KITCHEN LOOKED as if it had been bombed. Hungry warriors were savages, Sabin thought. Before coming down, he'd texted each of them—gods, he loved technology; he'd even brought technophobe Maddox into the twenty-first century—calling a meeting at noon to discuss what the Hunters had told him about both Distrust and the boarding school for the half-human, half-immortal children, as well as the impending arrival of Gwen's sisters.

The sisters. Tears had filled Gwen's eyes the moment one of the Harpies had answered the phone, turning the bright gold to melted bullion. Relief, hope and sadness had played across her face, and Sabin had had to fight the urge to go to her, to wrap her in his arms, offering whatever comfort he could. Every warrior instinct he possessed had been needed to hold himself in place.

He hoped the rest of the day was easier. With a flick of his wrist, he closed the refrigerator door. Warm air instantly blanketed him. He faced Gwen, who was staring down at the marble countertops. Or maybe the stainless steel sink, perhaps wondering why so ancient a home had been modernized in some places and left to age in others.

He'd had the same thought himself upon arriving in Budapest a few months ago. He'd made some improvements since moving in, and planned to have the entire monstrosity pimped out by the end of the year. It was funny. He'd traveled all over the world, had a base of operations in many places, but this fortress had quickly become his home.

"Empty," he announced.

Her gaze snapped to his and a moment passed before she focused. When she did, she ran a hand through her still-damp hair as though embarrassed. "I'll be fine without food."

"No." No way he'd allow her to go without. For a year, she'd endured the horrors of starvation. Not one more day would she do so while in his care. Her every need was his to meet. Because he desired her help and cooperation.

He was in a better mood than before, so he supposed he could placate her with "stolen" goods, after all. "We'll go into town," he added. Paris, whose job it was to shop, was probably still jacked out of his mind. "After we cover you from head to toe." No way he wanted people seeing that precious-gem skin.

"Makeup will take care of my face," she said, guessing his intentions. "And anyway, Anya brought you a tray…uh, what I mean to say is that I had food earlier."

So that's how Anya had gotten her to eat. Claiming the food was for him, ensuring that eating it was stealing it. For once Sabin applauded the goddess's trickery. "One meal won't satisfy you forever. Besides, we can grab you some clothes that fit while we're out."

Pleasure consumed her expression and that amazing skin seemed to glint with all the colors of the rainbow. His cock hardened painfully, his blood heated dangerously and images of her naked body, wet and glistening, flashed in his mind. Suddenly he could taste her decadence in his mouth, hear her cries in his ears.

"Clothes?" she said. "Of my very own?"

Her happiness was too much for Doubt, who decided to pounce, using Sabin's distraction to its advantage and ripping free of its leash. *New clothes won't make your situation better. They might even make it worse. How are you supposed to pay for them? With your body? Or maybe your sisters will be the ones to pay. What if Sabin desires them? He didn't penetrate you, even though he was primed. What if he takes your sisters to bed instead?*

Usually the demon was more circumspect, a gentle whisper, a quiet supposition, each designed to destroy the listener's confidence. Now it was using what had happened between them in the shower to ignite jealousy and feminine pique. Gwen didn't have to like him or even desire more of him for it to work, either. No one enjoyed the thought of their would-be lover in bed with someone else. Sabin was already prepared to cut out the eyes of anyone who even admired Gwen.

You knew this would happen. Knew Doubt would continue to go after her. "Gwen," he said, jaw clenched. "Those thoughts…I'm sorry." *I'm going to hurt you for this, you sick fuck.* "You won't owe me anything for the clothes. No one will."

Her pupils were thickening, black consuming gold… white… Soon she would be Harpy. Not knowing what else to do, he cupped the back of her neck and jerked her into his body. It had worked on the plane. Maybe…

His other hand snaked around her waist, fitting her against his still-hard cock. "Feel that? It's for you. No one else. I can't stop my reaction to you, crave only you." He nuzzled the side of her neck. "It's stupid, we can't be together, but I can't make that matter. I only want you." He'd say it a thousand times if necessary. He only wished the words were a lie.

Nothing. No response.

He pressed a soft kiss to her lips, lingering, savoring. Even chaste as the kiss was, it rocked him. The feel of her…knowing the skin that lurked underneath her baggy clothes, the pink little nipples that liked to be licked.

She sucked in a breath—his breath. Ever so slightly, she arched into his touch, and her arms wound around him, holding tight, tugging him closer. Just like that, her pupils began to thin. Her breathing became less choppy, her muscles less stiff.

His words hadn't reached her; his touch had. The Harpy must calm when given physical contact. He'd have to remember that.

But with the realization came a fury so hot his organs were blistered. A year, a full year, without contact must have been hell for this girl who so hated her darker side. The Harpy must have been a screaming voice inside her head, a constant hated companion.

It was one more link between them. Although Sabin didn't hate his demon. Not all the time. He certainly enjoyed the torment it could bring to Hunters. Right now, if he were honest (and he had to be), hate could not be denied. The bastard refused to leave Gwen alone, provoking her when she deserved only peace.

"Good?" he asked.

A shuddering breath escaped her. Abruptly she released him, cheeks heating. "That depends. Have you put a muzzle on your friend?"

"Working on it. And as I've told you, the demon isn't my friend."

"Then I'm fine now, yes."

There'd been resentment in her tone. "Sure?" He traced his thumb along her hairline.

"Sure. You can let go of me now."

He didn't want to; he wanted to hold on forever. And that's exactly why he released her, stepping away. He'd already marked her. Anything else was overkill. Unnecessary and dangerous to his ultimate goal.

Doubt whimpered in disappointment, receding to the back of his mind to decide on its next point of attack.

AFTER SHE APPLIED a layer of makeup to cover her skin, makeup Sabin borrowed from one of the female residents, Gwen and Sabin left the fortress. He touched her constantly. A brush of his arm here. A caress of his fingers there. She never wanted him to stop. She knew the magic he could work, after all.

She shivered. The stimulation and memories were almost—almost—enough to distract her from the beauty of Budapest. There were castlelike homes, modern buildings, green trees, bricked streets and birds eating crumbs from them. There was a murky river, an iron-enclosed bridge and a chapel that dusted the sky with its points. There were columns and statues and multi-hued lights.

Sabin almost managed to distract her from the townspeople, as well. They regarded him with awe, stepping out of his way but still trying to connect with him, any part of him. Some even gasped, "Angel" when he passed.

They shopped for several hours, and not once did he

seem irritated with her need to try everything on, to draw every piece of material across her cheek and twirl in front of the full-length mirrors. Often she caught him smiling.

After deciding on several pairs of jeans, a handful of colorful T-shirts and glittery pink flip-flops, as well as her own set of makeup, they moved on to the food. But who cared about ever eating again? She was wearing her new clothes! A snug pair of denims and a lovely pink T-shirt.

She'd never been so happy with how she looked. After a year in that skimpy white tank and skirt, she felt beautiful and comfortable and, well, normal. Human. As they left the grocery store with their bounty, Sabin eyed her as though she was his favorite ice cream cone.

Of course, then the whispers began.

Are you sure you look okay? I wonder if your breath smells bad. How many women has Sabin been with? How many were prettier and smarter and braver than you?

Gwen's happy mood faded, edginess taking its place. The whispers continued, and soon even the Harpy's feathers became ruffled. If a total meltdown happened, havoc would invade this lovely town and Sabin would be hurt. Much as Sabin irritated her, Gwen still didn't want a single drop of his blood spilled.

Right now he was loading their groceries into the back of the car, his muscles bunching with every movement. Breads, meats, fruits and vegetables abounded. The scents were divine. Several times in the store the temptation had proven to be too great, her mouth watering, and she'd pilfered. But her skills were seriously rusty, for Sabin had caught her every time. He hadn't protested, though. No, he'd encouraged her with a smile or a wink, as if he were proud of her. That had shocked her—shocked her still.

Gwen leaned a hip against the taillight. "Your demon is very close to ruining my entire day."

"I know. I'm sorry. For the record, you look amazing, your breath is fresh, I haven't been with that many and there are none prettier or smarter than you."

He didn't mention braver, she noticed. "Distract me. Tell me more about the artifacts you're looking for."

He paused, a bag suspended midair. Sunlight cascaded all around him, dark hair shimmering, lifting in the breeze. His eyes narrowed on her—something they did a lot, she mused. "That isn't something I can discuss out in the open like this."

Was that just an excuse to keep her in the dark?

Or was his demon rubbing off on her, and she doubted him just because?

Argh! "You can tell me. I'm working for you now." Wasn't she? Hadn't they decided she would do the clerical stuff? She hadn't named her price, but that was because the first thing that had come to mind was room and board in his fortress. For, like, ever. How dumb was that? "I'm helping you find them."

"And I'll tell you about them. Later."

Okay, so maybe the demon *was* rubbing off on her.

Sabin returned to the bags, finesse gone as he tossed them inside with a flick of his wrist. She winced when she heard the eggs crack.

"By the way, we never reached an agreement about your duties," he said.

Gwen propped her elbow above her head, resting her head in her hand, nails digging into her scalp. "Do you not think I'm capable of clerical work or do you just not respect me enough to let me prove myself in that way?"

"Wait. Did you just throw out the *R* word in a discussion about clerical work?" His jaw worked left and right, popping. "What is it with women? Make out a little, and suddenly everything you do means you lack respect for them."

"That's not true." He'd had to go there, hadn't he? Just talking about it, she felt the hot drops of water on her skin, felt his hands caressing her, his teeth biting at her. *He's not the kind of man you want for yourself.* It was sad that she needed the reminder. And would probably need it again. And again. "One, I've been offering to help and you claim you want me to, but you've never actually told me how I can get started. Two, the shower has nothing to do with anything. In fact, let's make a pact never to discuss what happened in there again."

He turned to her, bags completely forgotten now. "Why?"

"Because I don't want to physically fight your enemy."

"No, not why do you think I don't respect you or why do I want you to do clerical work, but why don't you want to discuss the shower?"

Cheeks heating, she straightened, looked away. "Because."

"Why?" he insisted.

Because I'll want more. "Mixing business with pleasure is more dangerous than we are," she said dryly.

A muscle ticked below his eye and he stared over at her, taking her measure, she was sure, and waiting for her to back down. She didn't, and that surprised her. She wasn't afraid of him, she realized. Not even a little.

"Get in the car," he commanded.

"Sabin."

"Car."

A curse on domineering men!

When they were buckled inside, he started the engine but didn't pull out onto the road. He shielded his eyes with sunglasses, placed a hand on her thigh and faced her. "Now that we're alone, I don't mind telling you about the artifacts. But the moment you know, it means you're stuck with me. You're not leaving with your sisters, you're not venturing away from the fortress by yourself. Understood?"

Wait. What? "Just how long are we talking about here?"

"Until they're found."

Which could be a few days. Or eternity. Which she'd secretly wanted, but not because she had no choice. "I'm not agreeing to any such thing. I was imprisoned for a year already and have no desire to live that way again. I do have a life to return to, you know." Well, kind of. Not that she'd even tried. Or wanted to. "There are things to do, people to see."

He shrugged. "Then you'll get nothing out of me." With that, he maneuvered the vehicle onto the road. He drove slowly, easing into traffic. His caution seemed… odd. Against his live-on-the-edge personality. Was this for her benefit? To keep her safe? The thought was kind of sweet.

Don't you dare soften toward him!

"You like staying at the fortress. Admit it," he said.

Was this information that could be used against her? Yes. Would keeping it secret award her some type of advantage? Yes. Would a lie serve just as well, if not better? Yes. But when she opened her mouth, the truth spilled out. "Fine. I admit it. I've been alone and afraid for a year. You and your friends came and suddenly I wasn't alone. I was still afraid, but no one hurt me or threatened me, and that feeling of safety is just so wonderful I can't bring myself to leave."

"You could have gotten the same feelings from your sisters." His tone had softened; his fingers massaged her leg. "Right?"

"Right." Kind of. "I could have lied about what happened, I suppose, so there'd be no tension, but they've always been able to see right through me. I can lie to anyone but them." And Sabin, it seemed. "You guys are like a vacation away from life. Only, you want me to work on my vacation. And that's okay," she rushed out, "as long as it's desk work."

He sighed, loud and long, the sound of it echoing through the vehicle. "Listen up, because I'll only offer this information once. There are four artifacts. The Cage of Compulsion, the Paring Rod, the Cloak of Invisibility and the All-Seeing Eye. Somehow, when all four are together, they'll point the way to Pandora's box. We own two. The cage and the eye."

"What are they, exactly? I've never heard of them."

"Whoever's locked inside the cage is forced to do whatever is commanded of them. Anything and everything, nothing is too sacred, as long as it doesn't hurt Cronus. Since he had the thing constructed, he somehow made sure it couldn't be used against him."

Wow. Gwen had to admire anyone with that level of power. She couldn't even control her own dark side.

"We're not sure what the rod does. The cloak is pretty self-explanatory and the eye shows us what's happening in heaven. And hell." He rested his head on the back of the seat, eyes still on the road. "Danika is the eye."

Okay, double wow. The petite blonde who looked so normal could see the wonders of heaven and the horrors of hell? Poor thing. Gwen knew what it was like to be different, to be…more. Maybe they could be friends, throw back a few cold ones and whine about their troubles. How cool would that be? She'd never had that before. "So how'd you find the cage and the eye?"

"We followed clues Zeus left behind so that he himself could one day reclaim them."

Like a treasure hunt. *Très* badass. "Can I see the cage?" She couldn't disguise the excitement that laced her voice. Her sisters, paid mercenaries that they were, had often left her home, alone, while they traipsed the world on hunts of their own. She'd always wanted to go. Or, at the very least, enjoy the spoils of their victories with them. But they'd always passed the item to its new owner before returning home, so she'd never gotten her wish.

Sabin's attention flicked briefly to her, and she could feel the heat of his gaze. "There's no need," he said sternly.

"But—"

"No."

"What could it hurt?"

"A lot, actually."

"Fine." Once again, she was to be left out. She tried to hide her disappointment. "What are you going to do with Pandora's box when you find it?"

His fingers whitened around the wheel. "Smash it to pieces."

The answer of a warrior. She was glad. "Anya men-

tioned it could draw the demon out of you, killing you
and locking away the demon."

"Yes."

"What happens if you're killed without the box?
Does the demon die, too?"

"So many questions," he *tsk*ed.

"Sorry." She traced a circle over her knee. "I've always been too curious for my own good." That curiosity had nearly gotten her killed a few times. Once, as a
young child, she'd been exploring her family's mountain and she'd stumbled upon a calm, serene river. If
she were submerged, would she be able to see the fish
swimming through it? she'd wondered. And if so, how
many would there be, what color would they be and
would she be able to catch one?

The moment she dove in, the icy water had completely depleted her strength. It hadn't mattered that
there was no current. She hadn't had the energy to keep
herself afloat. The Harpy had taken over, but the water
had frozen her wings to her back, preventing her from
flying out.

Kaia had heard her panicked cries and saved her, and
she'd received the thrashing of a lifetime. But that hadn't
stopped her from wondering about those silly fish.

"—listening to me?" Sabin said, his voice cutting
into her thoughts.

"No, sorry."

His lips twitched. She loved when they did that.
Made the larger-than-life male seem, well, human.
"What I'm telling you is privileged information, Gwen.
You do understand that, don't you?"

Oh, yes. She understood. It could be used against
him, given to Hunters to hurt him. "You saved me. I'm

not going to betray you, Sabin. But if you think I'm capable of that, why do you even want me on your team?" The fact that he didn't believe in her bruised her more than she would have thought possible. *Maybe he can't help himself. Maybe his demon keeps him from trusting in* anyone. She blinked at that. Made sense, and didn't sting quite so much.

"I do trust you. But you could be captured and tortured for the information. You're strong and fast and I don't think it will come to that, but they were able to get to you before, so..."

Every drop of moisture in her mouth dried. "I—uh..." Tortured?

"That's not to say I would allow that to happen."

Slowly she calmed. Of course he wouldn't let it happen. She wouldn't, either. She was a coward, but she was also vicious when she needed to be, and she'd learned her lesson on evasion well. "I still want the info."

"Good, because I was testing you and you passed. This can't be used against me since Hunters already know. If I'm killed and the box is not around, the demon will be free. Crazed, insane and more dangerous and destructive than ever, but free."

Her eyes widened. "That's why they want to capture you rather than kill you."

"How do you know that?"

"Different troops were always coming and going in the catacombs, but every time one regiment would leave to fight—I didn't know who at the time—they would remind each other not to kill, only to injure and—"

"Shit," he suddenly spat, cutting her off. "We're being followed. Damn it!" He banged a fist into the steering wheel. "I allowed myself to be distracted or I would have caught them before now."

Ignoring the accusation in his voice and the new stream of hurt that came with it, Gwen spun in her seat, peering out the darkened glass. Sure enough, there were three cars following them around a corner. Each had tinted windows, so she couldn't see inside to count the number of men bearing down on them. "Hunters?"

"Absolutely. Shit!" Sabin growled again, and it was the only warning she had before a fourth car pulled out in front of them. *Boom. Crunch.* Metal crashed against metal.

She was thrown forward, saved from injuries by her seat belt and the airbag.

"You good?" Sabin demanded.

"Yes," she managed. Her heart was drumming uncontrollably, her blood like ice in her veins.

Sabin was already reaching for the blades strapped to his body, the silver tips gleaming in the sunlight. "Lock yourself inside," he said. He dropped two blades on the dash between them. "Unless you want to fight?" He didn't give her time to reply, just jumped from the car, slamming his door shut behind him.

Bile rose in Gwen's throat as she locked the door. Bile mixed with shame and fear. How could she sit here, allowing him to fight—she scanned the groups emerging from the now stopped vehicles, running for him, guns raised—fourteen men on his own? Dear Lord. Fourteen!

She couldn't.

Pop. Whiz.

I'm a Harpy. I can fight. I can win. I can help him.

Her sisters wouldn't have hesitated. They would have

been on top of the cars, ripping the roofs to shreds before the wheels had even stopped turning. *I can do this. I can.* With a shaky hand, she lifted the weapons. They were heavier than they appeared, their handles like lava against her too-cold skin.

This one time. She'd fight this one time. But that was it. After that, she was going on full-time clerical duty. Another *pop.* Another *whiz.* Then a loud *thunck!* She yelped. *Yes, I can do this. Maybe.*

Where the hell was the Harpy? Her vision was normal, not infrared, and there wasn't a need for blood inside her mouth.

The lazy bitch was probably sated by food and touch, sleeping even. If Gwen hadn't spent so much time suppressing the dark side of her nature, she might have known how to summon it. Now, it seemed, she was on her own.

Pop. Scream.

Can't stay in here forever. Gulping, trembling, she emerged from the car. A horrific sight instantly greeted her. Sabin, locked in a lethal dance, arms slashing, knives cutting, blood spraying. Hunters, shooting him full of holes. To his credit, he never slowed.

"Stupid, going out alone, demon," one of the strangers said. "Give us back our women, and we'll be on our way."

Gwen should have known Hunters would retaliate for what had happened in those catacombs.

Sabin snorted. "Your women are gone."

"Not the redhead. We saw her with you. That whore certainly cozied up quick."

"Call her that again. I dare you." There was so much

fury in his voice, Gwen was surprised the Hunters didn't bail then and there.

"She's a whore and you're a bastard. I'm gonna jam you up with copper, revive you and spend the rest of my life making you pay for what you did in Egypt."

"You murdered our friends, you son of a bitch," someone else piped in.

Sabin didn't say another word. Just continued to pound forward, eyes glowing bright red, a flash of sharp, gnarled bones suddenly visible beneath his skin. Bodies toppled around him, but how much longer could he last? There were—eight more. Eight still shooting at him. Not to kill, but to incapacitate, going for his calves, his upper arms.

Gwen could almost hear his demon tossing danger-ous little insecurities in their ears: *You can't really beat him, you know that, right? There's a very good chance your wife is going to have to identify your body tonight.*

Blocking the sound, drawing on every ounce of cour-age she possessed, she inched forward. She'd distract the Hunters, allowing Sabin to pounce. Yes, yes. Good plan. Okay. How best to distract them so Sabin could swoop in and work his magic, though? Without getting killed or maimed in the process, she qualified.

The answer came to her, and she almost vomited. No, no, no. *There's no other way,* one part of her said.

This is stupid and suicidal, the other part replied. Didn't matter. She was doing something, acting brave for the first time in her life, and it felt…good. Really good, actually. She was still scared, still trembling, but that wasn't going to stop her. Not this time. Sabin had saved her from the Hunters, so she owed him one. More than that, as she peered over at the men partly responsible for her year-long confinement, she felt a sense of entitlement mixed with an urge to hurt.

Sabin had been right. It would feel good to destroy her enemy, up close and personal. The only problem: she wasn't a trained soldier like her sisters. She knew what to do, but could she actually succeed?

Gotta try. What was the worst that could happen, anyway? Well, she could die. Gwen sucked in a breath, straightened and waved her arms in the air, blades glistening in the sunlight. "You want me? Come and get me."

The dance of death ceased. Every gaze swung in her direction, and she tossed a knife. It soared through the air as if it meant to do major damage, then landed on the ground uselessly. Damn it!

She ducked, but one of the Hunters fired off a shot before she was fully covered, his friend yelling, "Don't kill her," and shoving at his arms to change the direction of his aim. But it was too late. The bullet lodged in her shoulder, and a sharp pain tore through her, throwing her backward.

She lay there for a moment, utterly dazed, panting, arm stinging. Being shot wasn't as bad as she'd imagined, she realized. Yeah, it hurt like a bitch, but the pain was manageable. Especially when her vision began to wink in and out, the blue sky and white clouds there for a few seconds, gone the next few. She heard footsteps pounding from a distance, cars swerving. Hopefully, she'd distracted the Hunters enough to give Sabin his victory.

"Hold him back," someone shouted. "I'll get the girl."

Sabin roared, an unholy sound that nearly made her ears explode. Then a bullet ricocheted off the tire rim and ate its way into her chest. Another sharp ache blasted through her. Okay, that pain wasn't so manageable. Her entire body was trembling, the muscles seizing into hard knots. But what bothered her most was the fact that warm blood was soaking her pretty new T-shirt. A T-shirt she herself had picked. A T-shirt she'd been so proud and happy to wear. A T-shirt that Sabin had peered at with lust in his eyes.

It's ruined. My beautiful new shirt is ruined. At that, even the Harpy stirred in anger, finally rousing.

It was too late, though. Gwen's strength was draining from her, along with her lifeblood. Her vision went completely black, no more peeks of color. Sleep pulled at her, beckoning, lulling, but she fought it. *Can't sleep. Not here, not now.* There were too many people around her. She'd be more vulnerable than ever. A disgrace to her family. A target once again.

"Gwen!" Sabin called. In the distance, there was a sickening rip, as if limbs were being torn from a body, followed by an ominous thud. "Gwen, talk to me."

"I'm…fine." The darkness finally swallowed her whole, and this time there was no fighting it.

CHAPTER FIFTEEN

THE MEETING WITH SABIN was due to kick into gear any moment, yet Aeron hadn't seen any sign of Paris. No one had, and the different sets of lovebirds had been stumbling from their rooms at different times, coming from all different directions.

He'd worried about the warrior all night. Never had he seen the usually optimistic man so bleak. Wasn't right. Wouldn't be tolerated. Which was why Aeron now stood in front of Paris's bedroom door, knocking insistently.

There was no answer. Not even the sound of footsteps echoing.

He raised his fist to knock again, this time louder, harder.

"My Aeron, my sssweet Aeron."

Hearing that familiar, childlike voice, hope flooded him and Aeron spun. And there she was. His baby. Legion. He'd only known her a short time, but she'd already become his favorite part of himself, weaseling her way into his heart with her unquestioned loyalty to him. She was the daughter he'd always secretly wanted.

When his gaze collided with the waist-high, green-scaled, bald, red-eyed, clawed, fork-tongued little she-demon all his worries melted away, Paris momentarily forgotten.

"Get over here, you," he said gruffly.

That was all the encouragement she needed. Grinning widely—and baring those sharp little teeth—she leapt at him, landing on his shoulders and winding herself around his neck. She squeezed him tightly, cutting off his air, but he didn't mind. The boa-like embrace was her version of a hug.

"Missssed you," she cooed. "Ssso much."

He reached up and scratched behind her ears the way she liked. Soon she was purring. "Where have you been?" He liked having her nearby, liked knowing she was safe.

"Hell. You know that. Me told you."

Yes, he'd known that, but he'd been hoping she had changed her mind and gone somewhere else. Hell was a place she despised, but a place Sabin kept convincing her to return to—to "help" Aeron through recon work, the warrior always said. Bastard. Her brethren there sensed the good in her and thrilled in hurting her, taunting her as if she were a damned soul rather than one of their own.

"Anyone hurt you?" he demanded.

"Try. Me run."

"Good." He would have found a way inside that fiery cavern if they'd harmed a single scale on her body.

She slithered up, propping her elbows on his shoulder and her cheek against his. The touch was hot, like a brand, but he didn't push her away. Nor did he flinch when she ran the tip of a poisoned fang against his jaw stubble. For whatever reason, Legion adored him. She would rather die than hurt him, and he would rather die than injure her feelings.

The only time Legion had gotten upset with him was

when he'd traveled to the edge of town to watch the citizens. A habit of his. Their weaknesses and frailty both disgusted and entranced him. They seemed oblivious to the fact that they were destined to die, some that very day, and he wanted so badly to understand their thought processes.

Legion had assumed he'd been on the lookout for a potential bedmate and had flipped out. *You belong to me. Me!* she'd cried. Only after he'd assured her that he'd never offer himself to creatures so feeble had she calmed.

"You eyesss gone." Relief dripped from her tone.

His eyes—his stalker. And yes, his "eyes" were gone. But for how long? That gaze bore into him randomly, never at the same time of day or night. Last time he'd felt them, he'd been stripping for a shower. Before he'd removed his briefs, he'd found himself alone.

"Don't worry. I'm going to find out who or what it is." Somehow, some way. "And I'm going to stop them." By whatever means necessary.

"Oh, oh. I learn for you!" Legion clapped happily, but then began to pout. "Ssshe a girl. An angel." Gag, shudder.

He blinked, sure he'd misheard. "What do you mean, an angel?"

"From…" Another gag. "Heaven." Another shudder.

Why would an angel from the heavens be watching him? A female, at that? In appearance, he had to be everything such a being would deplore. Tattooed, pierced…rough. "How do you know this?"

"Everyone talking in hell. That'sss why I come back, sssso'ssss I can warn you. They sssaying angel in trouble for following Lord of Underworld. Sssaying ssshe about to fall."

"But…why?" And what happened to angels when they fell?

"Don't know. But ssshe be in big trouble. Big big trouble."

"They have to be mistaken." He could understand a god or a goddess watching his every move. They wanted the artifacts; they wanted the box. Cronus, king of the Titans, liked nothing more than to use the warriors for his own gain, demanding they kill his enemies or suffer.

As Aeron well knew.

"Hate her," Legion spat.

If his shadow were indeed an angel, that certainly explained why Legion couldn't remain in his presence. Angels, he'd learned from Danika, were demon assassins. They weren't controlled by the gods, but by a single being no one had ever seen. Only…felt.

"Perhaps she's here to kill me," he mused. Ah, now that made sense, considering what he was. But why him, rather than another demon-possessed Lord? Why now? He and the other warriors had been walking the earth for thousands of years. The angels had always left them alone.

"No! No, no, no. Me kill *her!*" was the fervent reply.

"I don't want you to challenge her, sweet." Aeron patted the top of Legion's head. "I'll think of something. You have my word. And I'm grateful to you for the information." He wouldn't accept a death sentence easily; he had Legion to protect. He wouldn't allow the artifacts to be snatched from his friends, either, if that's what the angel wanted. Too many lives were at stake.

What he *would* do was talk to Danika, learn all he could about his new shadow. And how to destroy it.

Gradually Legion relaxed against him. He was gratified to learn that he calmed her as thoroughly as she calmed him. "What you doing here, anyway? Me want to play catch and claw."

"I can't. Not yet. I have to help Paris."

"Oh, oh." She clapped excitedly again, long nails clacking together. "Let'sss play with him!"

"No." He hated to deny her, but he liked his friends alive. And when it came to Legion and games, death was usually involved. "I need him."

A moment passed in silence. Then she sighed. "Fine. Me be bored just for you."

Aeron was chuckling as he turned back to the door. When Paris failed to answer his next summons, he twisted the knob. The lock held steady. "Stand over there, sweet. I'm going to bust it in."

"No, no. Me fix." Legion slithered down his chest, the lower half of her body still anchored around his neck while she reached out and used her claws to disable the cylinder. *Click.* Hinges squeaked, the wood gliding open. A giggle.

"That's my girl."

As she preened, he strolled inside the bedroom. Once, it had been a sensual haven. Blow-up dolls, sex toys and silk sheets had abounded. Now, the dolls had holes in them—and not the good kind. They'd been slashed. The toys were piled in the trash bin and the bed had been stripped of every amenity.

A quick search, and he found Paris in the bathroom, hunched over the toilet and moaning. His hair, a beautiful mix of black and golden brown, was tied in a knot at the base of his neck. Normally pale, his skin was now pallid, the veins bright and thick. There were dark half moons under his eyes, his irises a dull blue.

Aeron crouched beside him and spotted the bottles and Baggies littering the onyx floor. Ambrosia and human alcohol, and lots of each. "Paris?"

"Quiet." Moans growing in velocity, Paris rose on his haunches and emptied the remaining contents of his stomach into the toilet.

When he finished, Aeron said, "Can I do anything for you?"

"Yeah." Barely audible. "Leave."

"Watch you tone, you—"

Aeron motioned for Legion to hush, and surprisingly enough, she did. She even slid off him and perched in the corner of the bathroom, arms crossed over her chest and lower lip trembling. The intensity of his sudden guilt almost had him reaching for her. *Take care of Paris first.*

"How long since you had sex?" Aeron asked his friend.

Another moan. "Two—three days." Paris wiped his mouth with the back of his wrist.

Which meant Paris hadn't had a female since before their return. But Aeron knew Lucien had flashed the warrior into town every night they'd spent in the desert for just that reason. Had the warrior had trouble finding a willing partner?

"Let me take you into town. You can—"

"No. Only want Sienna. My female. Mine."

Uh, what now? Far as Aeron knew, Paris was as single as ever, plowing his way through the female population one at a time—sometimes two or three at a time.

Probably just the ambrosia talking, Aeron decided. Still, it wouldn't hurt to humor the man. "Tell me where she is, and I'll go get her."

Bitter laugh. "Can't. She's dead. Hunters killed her."

Okay, that was a little too specific to be fueled by ambrosia. But Aeron had never met this Sienna, never even heard of her.

"Cronus was going to give her back to me, but I picked you instead. Knew you hated the bloodlust. Knew Reyes would die without the blonde. So I gave her up. Never going to see her again."

All of the pieces suddenly fell into place. The reason for Paris's recent behavior, the reason Aeron's bloodlust had left him so suddenly. Paris must have met the girl in Greece, while searching the Temple of the All Gods for the box. Dear gods. He'd given up his lover for Aeron.

Aeron didn't have a female of his own, had never wanted one, but he'd seen the way Maddox was with Ashlyn, Lucien with Anya, Reyes with Danika. They would die for each other. In Ashlyn's case, she had. Each constantly thought of the other, craved the other and went crazy when alone.

Staggered, Aeron's knees gave out and he plopped onto the cold tile. The enormity of Paris's actions settled like a heavy weight across his shoulders. "Why would you do such a thing?"

"Love you."

That simple.

"Paris—"

"Don't." The warrior pushed to shaky legs and swayed.

Aeron was on his own feet in an instant, wrapping an arm about his friend's waist and holding him upright. When he tried to step forward, leading Paris to the bed, the warrior groaned and clutched his stomach. So Aeron swung him up, holding him steady against his chest.

Rather than carry him to bed, Aeron set him in the tub. Soon hot, steaming water was beating down, washing away the evidence of sickness. After Paris struggled out of his clothes, Aeron handed him a rag and soap and waited until the warrior cleaned himself from head to toe. Through it all, Paris stared past the stall, past the bathroom, as if, mentally, he were in a different place altogether.

"It pains me that you've done this to yourself," Aeron said softly. "And for me. I don't deserve it."

"I'll recover," Paris said, but Aeron didn't think either one of them believed it.

After he switched off the water, he handed his friend a towel. He would have dried Paris himself, but didn't think the big guy's pride would appreciate it.

"Just go," Paris said, crawling out of the stall.

"Either walk to the bed or I'll carry you," Aeron said.

Paris growled low in his throat, but stood without comment. He stumbled to the bed and flopped onto the mattress, bouncing once. Aeron followed close at his heels, then stared down at him, unsure what to do next. Never had Paris looked more fragile or lost, and the sight brought tears to his eyes. After all, he owed this man his life. Not just for what Paris had given up for him, but for his friendship, for fighting beside him, taking bullets and knife wounds for him, listening to him bitch about life—this and their other, when they'd been warriors for the gods and he'd wanted, well, more.

He couldn't leave him like this. Which meant he had to go into town on his own and find Paris a woman.

Leaning down, he smoothed a strand of hair from the warrior's brow. "I'll make this better. I will."

"Score me another bag of ambrosia," was the weak reply. "That's all I need."

"Oh, oh," Legion said happily, suddenly done with her sulking. She raced into the room and hopped onto the bed. "Me know where to get sssome!"

Paris groaned yet again as the mattress shook. "Hurry."

Aeron frowned at Legion and her smile faded. Head hanging, she climbed back on his shoulders. "What wrong now?"

"Don't encourage him. We don't want him sicker, we want him better."

"Sssorry."

He scratched her behind the ears. "I'll return," he told Paris, and left the room, shutting the door behind him. Thankfully everyone was in the entertainment room, waiting for the meeting to start. If it hadn't already. He made it to his chamber without bumping into anyone and hugged Legion tight before settling her on the ruffled lounge he'd had Maddox build for her.

"Stay here," he said, stalking to his closet. In seconds, he was weighed down with knives. He wanted to take a gun, just in case, but didn't want the human, whoever he chose, having access to it while he was preoccupied with flying.

"But—but— Me just got here. Me misssed you."

"I know, and I missed you, too. But the townspeople are already afraid of me. I think they'd riot at the sight of both of us." It was true. They'd never regarded Aeron's heavily tattooed face with the same reverence they bestowed upon the other warriors. "I need to find a female for Paris and fly her back here."

"But you can carry two. Me and her."

"No. I'm sorry."

"No!" She stomped her foot, red eyes bright. "No femalesss alone with you."

He knew she wasn't jealous romantically, but jealous like a child was when its parent remarried. "We've talked about this, Legion. I don't like human females." When he gave himself to a woman, it would be a strong immortal, one who was hard, resilient and not easily destroyed.

How Paris and the others could bed the humans, knowing they were doomed by disease, stupidity, carelessness or cruelty at the hands of another of their kind, he didn't know. They would die. They always did. Even Ashlyn and Danika, to whom the gods had promised immortality, had weaknesses.

"I won't be long," he said. "I plan to grab the first female I find. Someone completely unattractive to me."

She traced a claw over the emerald velvet. "Promissse?"

"Promise," he assured her.

That mollified her somewhat, and she sighed. "Okay. Me ssstay. Me..." Her thin lips curved into a frown.

An instant later, Aeron felt a pair of invisible eyes boring into him. Hot, curious, insistent.

Legion trembled, scales paling, fear curtaining her features. "No. *Nooooo!*"

"Go," he commanded, and she did without hesitation, disappearing with only a thought.

Slowly he spun, searching for any hint of the...angel? There was nothing, no shimmery outline, no heavenly scent. Everything was as it had always been. His jaw clenched. So badly he wanted to curse at the creature, demand it emerge and state its business with him. But he didn't. There wasn't time. Later, though…

He pulled off his shirt and tossed it to the floor, looking down at his tattooed chest. Battle scenes, faces. He never wanted to forget the things he'd done. The people he'd seen led to slaughter. Otherwise he feared he would become the very evil he'd always fought against. He would become his demon, Wrath.

No time for these grim thoughts. With only a mental command, his wings exploded from the hidden slits in his back, black, gossamer, deceptively fragile in appearance but incredibly strong. In that moment, he thought he heard a feminine gasp. Then warm hands were stroking those wings, learning every curve and hollow. Just like that, his cock hardened, a traitor to his resolve.

Hell. No. Desire a demon assassin? Not in this lifetime. "Don't touch," he snarled.

The phantom hands jerked away.

If only the creature would obey him in all things. "If you hurt my friends or think to steal from me, I will carve you up, piece by piece. It would be better for you to leave and never return."

There was no response. That white-hot gaze remained.

Teeth grinding together, he strode to the double doors overlooking his balcony.

Outside, warm air enveloped him, fragrant with the scents of nature. Trees towered around the fortress, stretching to the sky. In the distance, he could see the red rooftops of the town shops and cathedrals. Those soft, hot hands never returned to him, and he was grateful. He was not disappointed, he assured himself.

Determined, he leapt from the balcony. Down, down he fell. He flapped his wings once, and rose. Again, and soared higher. He angled toward the left, turning to the north. That's when the front of the fortress came into view and he saw Sabin, jumping out of the SUV with a bleeding, unconscious Gwendolyn in his arms.

Aeron wanted to stop, to help, but instead flapped his wings faster, harder. Paris came first. Now and always, Paris would come first.

CHAPTER SIXTEEN

SABIN HAD MEANT to keep at least one Hunter alive for questioning, perhaps a little torturing. Then they'd shot at Gwen, and that desire had vanished. The second bullet had been an accident, but rage had consumed him, more rage than he'd ever experienced before. He'd slaughtered them like cattle, one by one, their throats opening under the slick pressure of his blade. Hadn't seemed like enough, then or now.

On the way to the fortress he'd phoned Lucien, who had flashed Maddox and Strider to the scene for cleanup, then had gone back to the fortress to gather Gideon and Cameo to search for any other Hunters that might be lurking about. Sadly, there'd been no sign of more. That didn't mean they weren't there, only that they were well-hidden.

He wanted to slaughter another dozen or so.

Only a handful of times in the past two days had Gwen regained consciousness. Fuzzy as she'd been, he'd vacillated over and over again: take her to the hospital in town or keep her here? In the end, he always chose to keep her in his bedroom. She wasn't human. Doctors could do her more harm than good.

But *why* wasn't she recovering faster? She was immortal, a Harpy. Anya knew the race and swore they healed as swiftly as the Lords. But even though he'd removed the bullets, the holes in Gwen were still gaping, still raw.

After fussing over her this morning, Danika and Ashlyn had suggested he place Gwen in the Cage of Compulsion and command her to heal. Finally hopeful, he'd done it. But she'd only gotten worse. That was not how the cage was supposed to work, and he'd realized that though they thought they'd known the artifact's abilities, they actually had much to learn.

Sabin had tried summoning Cronus, but evidently the god king was ignoring him. Damn gods. Only showing up when *they* wanted something. He now found himself praying for the arrival of her sisters. They would know what to do—if they didn't butcher everyone inside the fortress first. The number Gwen had dialed the other day was stored in his phone, so he'd called it, too, intending to solicit advice, tell the girls to hurry. But the woman who answered had nearly gone up in flames when she discovered it was not Gwen on the line. And when he was unable to produce Gwen, the threats to his manhood had started.

Not a good omen of things to come.

"Can I get you anything?"

The question came from the door and Sabin jerked in surprise. Normally, a spider couldn't sneak up on him. Lately, anyone and anything could. Damn Hunters. They'd been lurking in town, watching him, waiting for him to mess up so they could snatch Gwen. And he hadn't fucking known.

"Sabin?"

"Yes." He lay on the bed, Gwen tucked into his side. She'd stopped moaning in pain, at least. *My charge, and I failed her.* Worse, he'd promised her that the Hunters would never hurt her again. Hadn't he? If he hadn't, he should have. Guilt ate at him.

Did you expect anything less?

Doubt had long since turned its evil on Sabin, not giving him a moment's rest.

"Sabin."

Hands fisting, he regarded Kane, who stood in the entryway. Dark hair, hazel eyes. There was a smear of white on his left cheek. Probably from plaster. Ceilings loved to cave in on the keeper of Disaster.

"You good?"

"No." He should be planning his next move against his enemy. He should be with his men, gearing up for battle. He should be on the streets, hunting. Instead, he could barely force himself to leave his bedroom. If his eyes weren't on Gwen, if he wasn't watching her chest rise and fall, his mind simply fried, unable to fend off Doubt with logic.

What the hell was wrong with him? She was just a girl. A girl he wanted to use. A girl who would probably die fighting his enemy—a girl he'd *asked* to fight his enemy. A girl he couldn't have. A girl he'd only known a short while.

Being with her now, guarding her, wasn't putting her above his mission, he assured himself. After he trained her, she'd be a killing machine. There'd be no stopping her. *That's* why he was here, unable to leave, desperate for her recovery.

"How's she doing?" a female voice suddenly asked.

Again, he was blinking as he refocused. Damn, but his mind wandered a lot lately. Ashlyn and Danika had returned—he'd lost count of the number of times they'd visited—and now stood beside Kane.

"Holding steady." Why wasn't she healing, damn it? "How'd the meeting go?" Because of the attack, it had been put off until this morning.

Kane shrugged, and the action seemed to piss off the lamp in the far corner because the lightbulb sparked. Then exploded. The women yelped and jumped out of the way. Used to such things, Kane continued as if nothing had happened. "Everyone's in agreement. There's no way Baden can be alive. Each of us held his head in our hands before we burned it. Either someone's impersonating him or they're starting the rumor to distract us from our purpose."

The latter made sense. How like the Hunters. Because they weren't as strong as the warriors, their best weapon was trickery.

Danika strolled to Gwen and smoothed the hair from the sleeping beauty's face. Ashlyn joined her and clutched Gwen's hand, probably willing her strength into that frail little body. Their concern touched him. They didn't know her, not really, yet they still cared. Because he cared.

"Galen knows that we know he's leading the Hunters," he told Kane. "Why hasn't he attacked again?"

"He's planning, probably. Gathering his forces. Spreading lies about Baden to confuse us, definitely."

"Well, I'm going to kill him."

"Maybe sooner than you think. I saw him last night in my dreams," Danika said without looking up. "He was with a woman. The scene was so vivid I painted it when I woke up this morning. Do you want to see?"

Poor Danika. She was faced with grisly visions nearly every night. Demons torturing souls, gods battling other gods, loved ones dying. Delicate human that she was, the horrors she witnessed had to scare her, yet she endured them with a smile because they helped her man's cause.

What would Gwen do if she had such visions? he found himself wondering. Would she tremble as she had that day in the pyramid? Or would she attack, teeth bared, like the Harpy she'd been born to be?

"Sabin?" Kane asked. "Your distraction is screwing with our egos."

"Sorry. Yes, please. I want to see it."

Danika made to stand, but Kane stopped her. "Stay there. I'll get it." He disappeared down the hall, only to return a few minutes later, holding a canvas that stretched the length of his arm. He held it up, light gleaming off the dark colors.

Looked to be some sort of cave, the jagged rocks splattered with scarlet and soot. A few bones were scattered across the twig-and dirt-laden ground. Human, most likely. And there, in the far corner, was Galen, feathered wings outstretched. His pale head faced the viewer, and he was holding a… Sabin had to squint to see. A piece of paper?

There was indeed a female beside him, though only a sliver of her profile could be seen. She was tall, thin, with black hair. Blood dripped from the corner of her mouth. She, too, was studying the sheet.

"I've never seen her before."

"None of us have," Kane said. "There's something oddly familiar about her, though, don't you think?"

He studied her more closely. None of her features were familiar, no. But the way she frowned…the crease at the corner of her eye…maybe.

"I wish I had gotten a better view of her," Danika said.

"That you saw anything at all is a miracle," Ashlyn assured her.

Kane nodded. "Torin's gonna scan her face into his computer, work some of his magic to form a complete composite and try to figure out who she is. If she's immortal, she probably won't be in any human databases, but it's worth a try."

"Why are they in the portrait?" Sabin asked, pushing the female from his mind and concentrating on their surroundings.

"Not sure, but we're looking into that, too." Kane rested the painting on the tops of his boots. "Finding Galen has become Priority One. If we can kill him, we think we can put an end to the Hunters once and for all. Without his guidance about all things immortal, they should crumble."

Gwen shifted against him, knee rubbing his thigh.

He froze, not even daring to breathe. He wanted her to awaken, but he didn't want her in pain. But several minutes passed and she remained just as she was.

My guess is she'll die.

Fuck you.

You're the one to blame, not me.

That, he couldn't refute. "What about our search for the box?" he asked Kane. "What about the training facility or boarding school or whatever it is for the half-ling children? And I wanted to go back to the Temple of the Unspoken Ones, search it again." The temple was in Rome and had only recently risen from the sea—a process that had begun when the Titans overthrew the Greeks to seize control of the heavens. Because of Anya, he knew those temples were intended to be used as a place of worship, a means of returning the world to what it once was: a playground for the gods.

"Those are priorities two, three and four," Kane said, "though knowing Torin, he's running several different searches on several different computers. A few more days, and we'll probably be back in action."

Would Gwen be recovered by then? "Any news on the third artifact?" Sometimes there weren't enough hours in the day to do everything that needed doing. Fight Hunters, find ancient relics of the gods, stay alive. Heal one tiny female.

"Not yet. Maddox and Gideon are taking Ashlyn out and she's going to listen."

Hopefully the Hunters that had come for Gwen had been vocal about their plans. Like where they'd planned to take her. He'd blow the place up on principle alone.

"Keep me updated on any progress."

Kane nodded again. "Consider it done."

"Sabin."

It was a rough, scratchy entreaty—and it had come from Gwen. His head swung in her direction. Her eyelids were flickering open as she tried to focus.

His heart sped up, his skin tightening, his blood heating.

"She's waking up," Danika said excitedly.

"Maybe we should—" Kane pressed his lips together as the bottom half of the painting careened to the floor. Scowling, he gathered the second piece. "I'm so sorry, Danika."

"No worries." She jumped up, closed the distance between them and gently took the pieces from him. "It can be taped."

Ashlyn moved beside them, rubbing her growing

belly along the way. "Come on. Let's give these two some time alone."

And then they were gone, the door closing behind him.

"Sabin?" A little stronger this time.

"I'm here." He slid his fingers up and down Gwen's arm, offering what comfort he could. His relief was palpable. "How are you?"

"Sore. Weak." She rubbed the sleep from her eyes and gave herself a once-over. A black T-shirt covered her, and she sighed in relief. "How long have I been out?"

"A few days."

She scrubbed a hand over her tired face, still too pale for his liking. "What? Really?"

Her surprise was genuine. "How long does it normally take for you to heal?"

"I don't know." Weak as she was, she was unable to hold up her arm for any length of time. It flopped to her side. "I've never been injured. Damn it, I can't believe I fell asleep."

Her claim baffled him. "That's not possible. The never-being-injured thing." Everyone, even immortals, scraped their knees, banged their heads, broke their bones at some point in their lives.

"With sisters like mine, protecting me at every turn, it is."

So her sisters had done a better job of ensuring her safety than he had. That rankled.

Did you expect something different?

I hate you today, you know that, right? They had let her be captured, he reminded himself. *He* had saved her.

"I thought I told you to stay in the car," he found himself growling.

Amber eyes landed on him, a little glazed with pain but mostly edged with anger. "You told me to stay in the car or help you. I chose to help you." With every word, her voice became weaker. Her lashes were fluttering again, ready to close for another too-long slumber.

His anger drained. "Stay awake for me. Please."

Her eyes opened at half-mast and her lips curled into a tired smile. "I like when you beg."

Didn't bode well that he was suddenly eager to beg for a few kisses. "Anything you need to help you stay awake?" Thanks to Anya, Danika and Ashlyn, he had everything a patient could desire on the bedside table. "Water? Pain meds? Food?"

She licked her lips and her stomach rumbled. "Yes, I—no." There was longing in every word. "Nothing. I need nothing."

Her fucking rules, he realized. Though he wasn't hungry, he grabbed the turkey sandwich and bit into the edge. He lifted the glass of water to his lips and sipped. "This is mine, but the rest is for you," he told her, motioning to the bowl of grapes that remained.

"Told you. Not hungry."

Not once had her attention wavered from the food in his hand. "Fine then. We'll eat later." He set the sandwich and the glass back on the tray and grabbed his cell, as if he couldn't wait to send an important text. "I'll be just a moment."

He rolled from the warmth of her body and sat up, typing, T, call when have new intel.

The reply was nearly instantaneous. Duh.

HE LAY BACK down. The sandwich was gone and the water drained. He'd never even seen her move. He pretended not to notice the missing food as he stuffed the phone in his pocket. "Sure you don't need anything?"

She swallowed audibly, and he almost laughed. "I need a bathroom. And a shower."

"No shower. Not without me. You're so weak you'll fall." Sabin gathered her up. He expected her to protest but she burrowed her head in the hollow of his neck. So trusting. Damn, but he liked that.

"I won't shower, then. Things happen when we shower together."

As if he needed a reminder. "I'll control myself," he told her.

"But will your demon? I don't have the strength to fight him. Just…give me ten minutes," she said when he set her down. Her curls were knotted around her head. "Come to my rescue only if you hear bone slam into porcelain," she added as she gripped the sink for balance.

He felt his lips twitch, beyond relieved that she was strong enough to tease him. "I will."

Nine minutes later, she emerged, face damp, the scent of lemons wafting from her. His mouth watered for a taste, a deeper, fuller taste than he'd gotten last time. She'd brushed her hair, and it cascaded down her back. "Feel better?"

Her gaze remained fixed on the floor, her cheeks bright with color. "Much. Thank you." She tried to walk, but both of her knees collapsed.

Sabin had her snuggled against his chest before she hit the ground. Once more, she welcomed his attention. So did he.

"I got my ass handed to me, huh," she said, wincing when her wounded shoulder brushed the sheets.

"Yes." He stood at the side of the bed, arms crossed over his chest. "But we can fix that. I'll train you." Whether or not she ever fought again, she needed the necessary skills to protect herself.

Whether or not she ever fights again—like it's a question now? I thought you wanted her to fight, no matter what. He couldn't blame the hesitation on Doubt. It was all his.

"Okay," she said, surprising him. Her eyelashes were drifting shut once more. "I'll let you train me, because you were right. I like the thought of hurting Hunters."

Not what he'd expected her to say. "You may change your mind before I get through with you. I'll hurt you, even though it won't be intentional, make you bleed and break you down." But she would be stronger because of it, so he wouldn't go easy on her.

Are you trying to talk her out of it?

No, he just wanted her prepared. He wasn't hard-wired like the other warriors to view female soldiers as weak, fragile and in need of protection. He didn't coddle them, either, and never had. Maybe that's why Cameo had chosen to go with him when he and Lucien had split the group. He even treated female Hunters the same way he treated male ones. Had he tortured a few? Yeah. And he wasn't sorry. He'd do it again, do more if necessary.

With Gwen, however, he *was* a bit uneasy. She wasn't just any other female soldier and she wasn't his enemy.

No reply.

"Gwen?"

A breathy sigh. She'd fallen asleep again. He covered

her more securely and settled in beside her, resigned to the now familiar task of waiting for her to wake up.

"MOVE EVEN AN INCH, and I'll take your goddamn head off."

Sabin came awake instantly. Cold steel pressed into his jugular, a bead of blood trekking down his neck. His bedroom was dark, the curtains over the window drawn. He drew in a breath and caught a scent—female. The intruder smelled of ice and wintry skies. Her long hair tickled his bare chest.

"Why's my sister in your bed? And why is she sleeping—and injured? Don't tell me she's fine or I'll make you eat your own tongue. I can smell the wounds on her."

The other Harpies had arrived.

Apparently they'd blown through Torin's state-of-the-art security without a single problem, because none of the alarms were screeching. Still more proof that he needed these women on his team—assuming he still had a team. "Are my men still breathing?"

"For now." The blade pressed deeper. "Well? I'm waiting, and I'm not the most patient of creatures."

Sabin remained utterly still, not even trying to go for the weapon under his pillow. *Some help here,* he said to Doubt.

I thought you hated me.

Will you just do your job?

He swore to the gods the demon sighed inside his head. *Are you sure you want to hurt this man?* Doubt asked the Harpy. *What if he's Gwen's lover? Gwen might hate you forever.*

Her hand trembled against him, loosening slightly.

Good boy. It was moments like this that made him appreciate the beauty of his curse. "She's here because she wants to be here. And she's injured because my enemy came after us."

"And you didn't protect her?"

"You're one to talk." His teeth ground together. "No. I didn't. But I learn from my mistakes and it will never happen again."

"You're right about that. Did you give her blood?"

"No."

There was an irritated growl. "No wonder she's sleeping with you in the room! How long ago was she injured?"

"Three days."

A gasp of outrage. "She needs blood, you ass. Otherwise she'll never recover."

"How do you know? She told me she's never been injured."

"Oh, she's been injured, she just doesn't remember. We made sure of it. And just so you know, you're going to pay for every mark on her. Oh, and if I find out you're lying, that you're the one who hurt her…"

"I haven't personally injured her." Yet. The thought sobered him as nothing else could have.

She eyed him from top to bottom. "Look, I might be impressed by the stories I've heard about you, but that doesn't mean I'm stupid enough to trust you."

"Talk to Gwen, then."

"I will. In a minute. So tell me. Which demon are you?"

He debated the wisdom of replying. If she knew the truth, she would know to guard herself against Doubt.

"I'm waiting." The tip of the blade pressed into his carotid.

What the hell, he decided. If he had to unleash the demon, she wouldn't stand a chance even if she knew what it was. No one did, not even him. "I'm possessed by Doubt."

"Oh." Was that disappointment in her tone? "I was hoping for Sex, or whatever you call him. The stories of his conquests are my favorite."

Yep, disappointment. "I'll introduce you." Maybe a good bedding from Paris would lighten the woman's attitude. For that matter, maybe a good bedding from the woman would lighten *Paris's* attitude.

"Don't bother. I won't be here long enough to make any memories. Gwen." In the next instant, Gwen's body was quaking against him.

The sister was fucking shaking her, he realized with a snarl. Sabin latched on to the Harpy's wrist. "Stop. You'll hurt her worse."

Abruptly the knife left him, her arm ripping free of his grip, and the light was switched on. His eyes watered and he blinked. The Harpy was once again at his neck, but he hadn't had time to move.

When his vision cleared, he studied her. She was lovely, her skin as luminous as Gwen's was. But for some reason, Sabin wasn't transfixed, wasn't overcome with the urge to bed her. She had bright red hair, not streaked with blond like Gwen's. They possessed the same amber-gray eyes, though, and the same sensual red lips. Yet where innocence always drifted from Gwen, this woman pulsed with centuries of knowledge and power.

"Listen," he began, only to be silenced as the knife cut past his skin.

"No. You listen. I'm Kaia. Be glad it's me who's wielding the blade rather than Bianka or Taliyah. You phoned Bianka, refused to let her speak with Gwennie, and now she wants to beat you—with your own limbs. Taliyah wants to feed you to our snakes, piece by piece. Me, I'm willing to give you a chance to explain. What were your plans for her?"

He could talk, tell her what she wanted to know, but he wouldn't. Not like this. If Gwen's sisters were going to hang around—for despite Kaia's anger, he thought that they would—and if they were going to fight for him, he had to assert himself as commander.

Without even a twitch of muscle to alert her to his plans, Sabin jerked Kaia on top of him. The blade sank deep, hit a tendon, but he didn't slow. He rolled her over, away from Gwen, and pinned her with his muscled weight.

Rather than fight him, she laughed, the tinkling sound like candy for his ears. "Smooth move. No wonder she's in your bed. Must say I'm a little disappointed you didn't go for my head, though. I expected better of a Lord of the Underworld."

The bouncing mattress must have finally woken Gwen, because she gasped weakly. Croaked out, "Kaia?"

Kaia shifted her attention, a beauteous smile playing at her lips. "Hiya, baby. Long time no see. And I know you're thinking I'm mad at you right now for falling asleep, but you're wrong. I know where to place the blame. In fact, your man and I were just working out a few details about your stay here. How are you?"

"You're underneath him. You're underneath Sabin." Gwen's pupils were bleeding into gold…white… Her nails were elongating, sharpening. Her teeth gleamed menacingly in the light.

Kaia gaped. "She's…is she really…"

"Yep. Going Harpy." Shit. Sabin shoved Kaia from the bed with all of his might. She landed on the floor with a thwack, but he didn't care. The moment his arms were free, he pulled Gwen into the heat of his body, one hand winding loosely around her neck and caressing her face, the other stroking the soft contours of her belly, where her shirt had ridden up.

Those claws latched on to his shoulders and sank all the way to bone, but he gave no reaction to the pain. She could have done far, far worse.

"We were only talking. I wasn't going to hurt her. I pinned her to get her blade out of my neck, nothing more. She's here to help you, wants the best for you."

"Do you want her?" Gwen rasped.

Bastard that he was, he was pleased by her jealousy. "No. I don't. And she doesn't want me, either. I swear it. You know I only want you."

From the corner of his eye, he saw that Kaia had stood and was now watching him raptly.

Gradually, Gwen's nails receded, leaving wide, bleeding gashes. Her gaze cleared. And through it all, Doubt was strangely silent. Like, dead silent, as if it had hidden in the deepest part of Sabin's mind.

"Wow," Kaia finally said, and there was an edge to her tone. "Impressive. You talked a Harpy from her rage. You know what that means, don't you?"

He didn't spare her a glance. He kept his attention on Gwen and slid his hand down her leg, then he angled her so that her knee was propped on his hip, cradling their lower bodies together. "No. I don't."

"You're my sister's consort. Congratulations."

CHAPTER SEVENTEEN

GWEN HAD NEVER BEEN more nervous in her life. Not in her prison cell. Not even when she'd faced the Hunters with Sabin.

After watching Sabin calm the Harpy, Kaia had summoned Bianka and Taliyah with a sharp whistle. Apparently, they'd been in the hallway, making sure no one approached while Kaia rescued Gwen. Then the three sisters had barricaded themselves inside Sabin's bedroom for a little "chat."

"No one else knows we're here," Bianka had said. "So it's just gonna be the five of us."

Gwen would have protested the coming chat, the isolation—this kind of scenario always ended in bloodshed for the Skyhawks—but several things stopped her. One, Sabin had a death grip on her, keeping her pinned against his side. Why? Did he think she would race to her sisters and demand they slaughter him? Two, she was as weak as a newborn kitten, barely able to hold up her eyelids. Plus, her shoulder and chest burned painfully. If Sabin *had* let her go, she would have collapsed against the headboard. And three, she planned to be brave one more time and act as Sabin's shield. If her sisters, who were angry at her treatment and seemed to have conveniently forgotten they'd once admired the Lords, came after him...

Why she cared, she didn't know. Only minutes ago, he'd been embracing Kaia. Hadn't he? The memory was fuzzy, as if she'd watched the couple on a screen rather than in real life. Real or not, though, it had pissed the hell out of her. Sabin belonged to Gwen. For now, at least. And not because they'd showered together and he'd given her the best orgasm of her life. But because, well, she didn't know. He just did.

"Before we start talking, let's take care of baby girl." Kaia strode to her now, cutting her wrist along the way, and held it to Gwen's mouth. "Drink."

She'd drunk from her sisters throughout her childhood, "to be safe from any injury you might obtain," they'd always told her. They themselves drank from any boyfriend they had at the time before heading to a battle or any kind of job. So it wasn't an odd command. After all, vampires weren't the only race that required blood, though Harpies only needed it for healing or to prevent injuries. But just as she fit her lips over the dripping wound, Sabin grasped her by the neck and spun her around so that she was facing him.

"Hey," Kaia growled.

His neck had a long, thick gash, a gash he'd now reopened with a slash of his razored nail. "If she needs to drink, she'll drink from me."

He didn't give anyone time to protest, but jerked Gwen forward, holding her head completely immobile to prevent her from turning away. Like she would. Already she could smell the sweetness of his scent. Lemons and blood. It filled her nostrils, drifted into her lungs and spread through the rest of her, leaving a trail of tingling warmth.

Unable to stop herself, mouth watering, she traced

her tongue over the wound. Ecstasy. A fruity dessert. Her eyes closed and she fit herself against his body, arms wrapping around him to hold him captive, knees caging his legs. The angel side of her knew this was wrong, that she shouldn't do it and certainly shouldn't like it, but the Harpy side of her sang happily, desperate for more, for nothing had ever tasted like *this*. Like heaven and hell, perfect and wicked and sure to be her downfall.

On and on she sucked, drawing the liquid decadence into her mouth, down her throat. With every swallow a little more of her strength returned. The ache in her wounds began to ebb, the tissue weaving back together. How had she ever lived without this? Thankfully, blood didn't have to be stolen to be enjoyed. It was a source of medicine, not food. She should have thought to drink from Sabin before.

Through it all, Sabin remained still. Between her legs, however, she could feel the hard length of his erection. His fingers had fallen to her hips and were digging deep, holding her immobile.

She could hear his breath raging in her ears, could even hear a few of his thoughts: *yes, yes, more, don't stop, so good, must...bed...mine.* Or maybe they were her own.

"Don't drain him, baby girl," Bianka said, breaking through the mire of Gwen's new addiction. "We have a few questions for him first."

Nails dug into her scalp, and her head was torn away from Sabin's neck. She yelped, blood trickling from her parted lips.

He snarled low in his throat, glaring over at Bianka

while tightening his grip on Gwen. "Touch her like that again and you'll be saying goodbye to your hands."

Grinning, Bianka twirled a strand of black hair around her finger. "Now there's the Lord of the Underworld I've heard so much about. I almost believe you'll do it, demon. Well, try to do it."

"I never make a threat I don't intend to see through," he said, turning Gwen and smashing her against his side once more.

She almost moaned. Her sisters never—never—backed down from a challenge. "I'm so glad you're here," she said, hoping to distract them.

"The big guy not taking care of you?" Kaia strolled around the room, lifting knickknacks, opening dresser drawers. "Oh, sweet. Black briefs are my favorite." She even crouched in front of Sabin's weapons case, broke the lock with a twist of her wrist and flipped open the lid. "Hmm, lookie what I found."

"He's taking care of me," Gwen said, oddly defensive of him. He'd released her from captivity, guarded her, planned to teach her how to defend herself. The Hunter thing was her own fault. She should have stayed in the car. She couldn't regret that she'd emerged to help, though. He was alive. Safe.

Are you being truthful with your sisters, because I can think of several instances that Sabin—

"Sorry," Sabin muttered.

Good thing he'd shut that stupid demon up, because the Harpy had started squawking the moment its voice had filled her head.

Bianka joined Kaia at the chest, and they oohed and ahhed over the guns and knives. Weapons were their kryptonite. Taliyah stepped to the edge of the bed, staring down at her, expression blank, emotionless. No one was more beautiful than Taliyah. She possessed white hair, white skin, eyes of the palest blue. She was like a snow queen—and many a person had actually accused her of having ice in her veins. Not that they'd lived long afterward.

"I know your situation with the Hunters," she said to Sabin. "I've heard tales of your viciousness and have admired you for it. I've even hoped to meet you. But now I want to kill you for bringing my sister into this mess. She isn't a fighter."

"She could be." Several seconds passed, but Sabin didn't add anything else. Didn't try to defend himself.

He was going to leave it at that? Let them think she'd shacked up with him and he'd placed her in danger for no reason, rather than tell them the truth, that she'd been stupid, caught and caged? That he'd saved her? If he told them the truth, he would guarantee their participation in his war. A war he placed above everything else in his life, even love. Why would he do that? For her?

Tears suddenly burned her eyes, threatening to spill over. Well, she could do something for him. "Actually, the *Hunters* brought me in," Gwen admitted, twisting the sheets.

"Gwen," Sabin said. A warning.

"They need to know everything." For his sake, and her own. Gathering her strength, she told her sisters about her confinement, leaving no detail out. As she spoke, the tears fell freely. Only a few minutes passed, but they were the most mortifying minutes of her life. Sabin, like her sisters, admired strength. Ferocity. Yet here she was, broadcasting her weakness to the only people who mattered to her.

He surprised her by tenderly wiping away the salty beads that cascaded down her cheeks with the pad of his thumb. That made her cry even harder.

When she finished, silence encompassed the room. Tension thickened the air, creating a crackling suspension of time.

Taliyah was the first to speak. "How did they get you?"

The cold tone of her voice sent a shiver through Gwen. "Tyson forgot his cell phone one morning when he left for work, and I knew he'd want it. But he was too far down the road for me to catch at human speed so I…" She gulped. Such a stupid mistake, one she'd regretted every day since. "I used my wings and beat him to his office. Hunters saw me when I stopped, thought I had magically appeared, though I didn't know it at the time. I guess they followed me home, waited until later that night when Tyson and I—" she gulped "—fell asleep."

"You slept in bed with Tyson?" three female voices said at once.

"What's with you Harpies and sleep?" Sabin stiffened against her. "Not that I think you're wrong to be disgusted by anyone in bed with chicken man. It's that bastard Tyson who needs to die. He didn't protect her."

"Neither did you," Taliyah said flatly.

"I'm alive because of Sabin." Gwen offered him a shaky smile. "And Tyson's not a bad guy. He tried to save me before they knocked him out." Even though he'd been upset with her.

When he'd come home from work that evening, he hadn't wanted to talk about what had happened. She'd utterly freaked him out by beating him to his office—

because he'd already begun to notice other, weirder things about her.

She'd hidden her dark side as best she could but sometimes it had emerged despite her, and he would come home to holes in the wall, ripped sheets, smashed dishes. Once, during a silly argument about whose turn it was to pick what DVD they'd watch, she'd even shoved him into a wall and the plaster had collapsed on him. They'd kissed and made up, but that had been the beginning of the end.

"Anyway," she continued, "I found myself wrapped up, unable to move, barely able to breathe as the Hunters flew me to Egypt. They locked me up and twelve months later Sabin and the other Lords set me free and brought me here."

"You killed the men responsible for her torment, of course?" Taliyah asked Sabin.

He nodded. "Gwen killed one. I killed some of the others."

Her powder blue eyes flared in anger. "Why not all? And good job, Gwen," she added with a nod of approval.

Before she could admit it had been an accident, Sabin said, "The survivors are being held in my dungeon and tortured for information."

Taliyah's shoulders relaxed somewhat. "That's all right, then." She turned back to Gwen. "Have you eaten?"

Gwen cast a sideways glance at Sabin. Very clearly she recalled stealing his sandwich and stuffing it into her mouth. "Yes."

Thankfully, he gave no reaction. With Tyson, she'd stolen their food from nearby restaurants and passed it off as her own cooking. He'd never known. He would have rebuked her. Would Sabin? She didn't think so. He'd smiled at her when she'd taken things from the store.

"You ready to go home, then?" Kaia jumped onto the side of the bed, causing the mattress to bounce. "'Cause I'm more than ready to blow this joint. I know you like your demon, so you can bring him if you want. Whether he wants to come or not. We'll get you tucked safely away and come back for the Hunters. They will pay for what they did to you. Don't worry."

"I—well…" Did she want to go home? Hidden, safe, everyone else taking care of things? Hadn't she gone to Georgia in part to escape just that? And while she liked being with Sabin, she knew he would be miserable trapped in Alaska with no one to fight. He would grow to resent her.

So if she went home, she'd have to go alone. The thought left a hollow ache in her chest. What she and Sabin had done in the shower…she wanted it again. *I thought there could be no more of that. I thought it was too dangerous.* But faced with the possibility of going without it, without him, of never knowing what it would be like to be possessed by him, totally and completely, none of the reasons for staying away from him seemed to matter.

"She's not going anywhere," Sabin said.

Lord love domineering men. Sometimes. "Right. I'm staying." Gwen peered over at her sisters, silently beseeching them to understand, to accept. They watched her for a long while, as quiet as she was.

Bianka was the first to speak. "Fine. But where should we store our gear?" she asked on a sigh.

Gwen had known they'd want to stay, as well, and

that both delighted and worried her. Sabin, at least, didn't bat an eye. "There's an empty room beside this one. Mind sharing?"

He was giving them a room of their own after denying Gwen the same privilege?

"No, we don't mind," Taliyah said. "But tell me, what are your plans for the Hunters?"

"To kill them. All of them. We'll never know peace as long as they're alive."

She nodded. "Well, lucky you, you've got yourself three new soldiers."

"Four," Gwen rushed out before she could stop herself. She'd meant what she said, she realized. She really did want to stop the Hunters. She wanted to protect her sisters and Sabin from them. And for once, she wanted to prove herself worthy.

Once more, everyone focused on her. Sabin, with anger—though she didn't know why. He wanted her to do this, didn't he? Bianka and Kaia, with indulgence. And Taliyah, with determination.

"Well, don't just lie there," Kaia said, arms lifting and dropping at her sides in exasperation. "Get up. We've got a war to win."

Sabin ran a hand down his suddenly drawn face. "Welcome to my army, girls."

HE WAS GWEN'S CONSORT, her sisters had said. Sabin took that to mean they thought she belonged to him. He wasn't sure he believed it himself, but damn if he didn't like the thought. He still couldn't keep her, though, not without destroying her. At least, not as things stood.

She spent the rest of the day and night in bed, though she never fell asleep again. Determined to find out why, he left her alone the next morning and went in search of Anya. He found her in the entertainment room, finishing another video game with Gilly. He told her about the arrival of their guests and she clapped happily.

"Lucien told me you texted him about guests, but I had no idea they were more Harpies!"

"Now you know. They're in the gym. So what's the deal with Harpies sleeping?"

She laughed in his face. "Figure it out on your own," she said, sauntering to the door. "I've got a Skyhawk reunion to see to."

He followed her into the gym, curious as to how such a reunion would go down.

The trio—who had already made themselves at home, with everything—spotted the goddess, stopped tossing and catching barbells as if they were tiny stones, and ran to her, throwing their arms around her.

"Anya! You took off without a word, you bitch!"

"Where have you been?"

"What are you doing here?"

They threw the questions at her simultaneously, but Anya seemed unfazed. "Sorry about that, girlies. I've been all over the world. You know, seeing the sights, causing trouble and falling in love with Death himself. I'm here because this is home. Like what I've done with the place?"

They continued to hug and talk and laugh. Sabin tried to butt in a few times, but was steadfastly ignored. Finally he gave up and left them to it, meaning to find Anya later and once again ask her about Harpy sleeping arrangements. Asking the sisters was out of the question. Harpies, he'd already learned, lived by their own set of rules, and he didn't want to inadvertently demean Gwen with his ignorance.

Gwen.

Every minute with her was dangerous. Last night had been the worst. He'd remained by her side, smelling her femininity, hearing the cotton glide over her skin, but they'd kept their distance from each other, remaining on separate sides of the mattress. He would have taken her—he was weak where she, that luscious body and that lickable skin were concerned; there, he'd finally admitted to a weakness—but every time he'd reached for her, Doubt had begun spreading its poison.

Will she die if you keep her? Will she want more than you can give, then leave you when you can't give it?

Once again, he hated the demon.

Only around her sisters did the little shit quiet, and Sabin didn't know why. He would figure it out, though. He was determined. Because, if he could somehow work it so that Doubt shut the hell up around Gwen, he could have her. Maybe forever.

After he checked on the prisoners—who were still too weak to endure any more torture and survive—he went to the kitchen to fix Gwen something to eat. All the food was gone. Talk about déjà vu. Nothing was left, not even a bag of chips. The Harpies had been here, he supposed.

With a sigh, he strode to his bedroom. Gwen was no longer in bed. Frowning, he began hunting her. He found her on the roof with Anya and her sisters—the latter of whom were playing Who Can Fall From The Roof And Break The Least Amount Of Bones.

"I leave you for less than an hour," he said to Gwen. "Don't you dare jump."

"I'm just watching," she assured him with a grin. A grin that made his chest ache.

A smattering of warriors stood on the ground below, watching as well. They wore resigned expressions, but mixed with the resignation was awe. They were drinking in that Harpy skin like it was wine.

"Enough of this," Sabin said before one of the Harpies could jump again. "We have training to do."

They didn't agree graciously, but they did agree and soon nearly every occupant of the fortress was on the ground, grunts and groans saturating the air, the scent of blood and sweat chasing nearby animals away.

Sabin stood on the sidelines, once again simply watching the happenings. Torin had just texted him and was on his way down.

Finally the warrior arrived. Keeping a good distance between them, Torin stopped at his side. "Everyone's been so busy, I knew calling another meeting would do no good, so I've been trying to catch everyone individually."

"Find something?"

"Oh, yeah." He waggled his black eyebrows, which were a startling contrast to his white hair. "Found an obscure tabloid article about a school for gifted children in Chicago. Children who can lift cars, get people to do whatever they want simply by speaking and move faster than the eye can see. And get this. The entire thing was denied by the World Institute of Parapsychology."

Sabin's eyes widened. "Hunter High. Just like our prisoner told us."

"Yep. Can't be a coincidence, you know?"

"We need to search that facility."

"I agree. That's why I'm making arrangements for

departure in two days. Some of you need to go, but some should stay and search for the people listed on the scrolls. I just need to know who's doing what."

He'd been geared up to say he'd go—kill Hunters, rescue those kids and maybe finally draw Galen out of hiding—when the rest of Torin's speech penetrated his mind. "Wait. Scrolls?"

A soft breeze moved between them, ruffling Torin's hair. He smoothed the strands from his face with a glove-covered hand. "Cronus just paid me a visit."

Sabin's stomach clenched. "I tried to summon him, but he ignored me."

"Lucky you."

"What'd he say?"

"You know the drill. 'Do as I command or I'll torture everyone you love,'" Torin said in a superior, arrogant tone.

The impersonation was dead-on. "Yeah, but what'd he order you to do? Find people, you said?"

"I'll get to that. You know he wants Galen dead as much as we do, right, since Danika predicted Galen will be the one to kill him? Well, the scrolls he gave me provide a list of names. Names of the other demon-possessed immortals. You won't believe how many there are. There are blank lines, though, as if several names were erased. Weird, huh? Think that means they somehow died?"

"Maybe." Only recently—through Danika—had he and the others learned that they weren't the only demon-possessed immortals running around. Seemed there had been more demons in Pandora's box than warriors in need of punishment, and so the remaining spirits had been placed inside the prisoners of Tartarus. Prisoners who were now missing.

"Anyway, Cronus thinks we can find our brethren and use them to contain Galen once and for all. They can help us lock him up, stop him from causing trouble."

Sabin shook his head. "They were prisoners, which means even the gods couldn't control them. We can't trust them enough to use them. Besides, much as we want Galen dead, we all know how dangerous it would be to unleash his demon on the world. But what's to stop these strangers from doing just that?"

"Point taken. And yeah, we're merciful enough to allow him to keep his head for now, but Galen might not reciprocate in kind. These men are exactly the kind of creatures he would want for his army, which means we still need to find them before he does."

Sabin knew they also needed to make Cronus happy. Bad things happened when the god king didn't get his way. "We also have to find the remaining artifacts, and they seem a little more important at the moment."

"We can't find them if we're overrun by immortal kids determined to destroy us," Torin said. "So, first and foremost, we have to find that school and neutralize the threat. You staying or going?"

"I'm—" Sabin's gaze locked on Gwen, who fell to her ass to dodge her sister's poorly—and purposely, he was sure—aimed sword thrust. His hands curled into fists. *Hurt her and die,* he projected at the Harpy, though he knew the woman was caging the brunt of her strength. More than that, he knew he was a hypocrite for even thinking such a thing when he'd vowed not to go easy on Gwen himself.

If he went to Chicago, he would have to leave Gwen

behind. She just wasn't ready for battle yet. He could take her sisters with him, using them to safely gather the kids. Kids who would most assuredly fight him and the other Lords, since they had probably been raised to hate them. Or he could leave the Harpies behind to guard her. Neither option satisfied him. He didn't like the thought of Gwen alone. Well, not alone, but without him. And he didn't like the thought of unnecessarily scaring those kids.

Clang. Click.

The clash of metal against metal pulled him from his musings. Gideon and Taliyah were sparring, their expressions dark, serious. So far, it was a draw. Strider and Bianka were throwing punches at each other, and Bianka was laughing. At first, Strider resisted a full-out clash with her; he held back, pulled his punches even though losing to her would mean a few days in bed, writhing in pain and crying for a mommy he'd never had. Then Bianka broke his nose and kicked his balls into his throat. The fight was suddenly on.

Amun was finally up; he sat off to the side, polishing an ax and watching…someone. Sabin wasn't sure who. Yet. He suspected it was one of the Harpies.

"Who do you have lined up so far?" Sabin asked Torin.

"You're the first person I've asked."

Before he could talk himself out of it, he said, "I'll go." War came first. "Get me five other warriors. I'll try to get us a Harpy." That would leave two sisters here to protect Gwen, while giving him a small advantage.

Torin nodded and was off.

Decision made, Sabin strode forward. "You're babying her," he snapped at Kaia. Not exactly the correct way to get on the woman's good side, but he didn't care. Gwen's future well-being was too important for niceties. Sabin was only glad he wasn't *thanking* the Harpy for her gentleness.

The redheaded Harpy swung around, tossing a dagger at his heart. "The hell I am! I've thrown her six times."

Yes, and all six of those times he'd wanted to throw Kaia. Scowling, he caught the hilt of the blade just before contact. "You relax your elbow just before striking. You're not teaching her the proper technique or even allowing her to learn your strengths and counteract. Hell, you're showing her that fighting unfairly and winning at any cost is wrong. Just…go find someone else to play with," he told her. "I'm taking over Gwen's lesson. You've done enough damage. And if you dare interfere, you'll regret it. I don't care what you see, what you disagree with or don't like, you stay back. This is for her own good."

Kaia's mouth hung open, as if she couldn't believe someone had spoken to her like that. Then she was stalking to him, murder in her gaze, nails bared, sharp teeth gleaming in the sunlight. "I'm going to snap your neck like a twig, demon."

"Bring it," he said, waving his fingers at her in a mocking salute.

An earsplitting squawk suddenly erupted from sweet little Gwen.

Both he and Kaia froze. Even Taliyah and Bianka stopped their sparring to face Gwen as she crouched, sights locked on her redheaded sister. The whites of her eyes had already turned black.

"Are you freaking kidding me?" Kaia gasped out. "I think she's going to attack me. What'd I do?"

"Threatened her man," Taliyah said coldly. "You knew better. I hope she claws her way to your spine."

Her man. Just the words had him rock hard, and it was freaking embarrassing. He couldn't allow her to hurt her sister. She'd never forgive herself. Sabin walked to Gwen, each step slow, measured. "Gwen, you will calm down. Understand?"

She snapped her teeth at him and almost nailed his chin. Only his quick reflexes saved him a severe biting. "Gwendolyn. That wasn't very nice. Shall I bite you?"

"Yes."

Okay, now he was *harder* than a rock. "Well, I won't have anything left to bite if you don't calm down."

Somehow, that reached her. She licked her lips, eyes fading to normal, body straightening. A tremor moved through her, and she swayed on her feet. He didn't touch her, not yet. He wouldn't want to stop and they had witnesses.

A deep breath shuddered through her nose. "I'm sorry," she said brokenly, reminding him of the incident in the pyramid. "I'm sorry, I didn't mean…I shouldn't have…did I hurt anyone?" Watery eyes lifted to him, the gold like the sun yet the gray like storm clouds.

"No."

"I'll—I'll go back to our room. I'll—"

"You're going to stay here and fight me."

"What?" Expression shocked, she stumbled backward. "What are you talking about? I thought you wanted me calm."

"I do. For now." He gripped his shirt and tugged it over his head, then dropped the material at his feet.

Automatically her gaze lowered to his ribs, where the points of his tattoo stretched. "We're going to fight. You're not allowed to hurt anyone but me."

"I'd rather study your tattoo," she said huskily. "I didn't get a chance to trace it in the shower, and I've been dreaming of tracing it."

Dear Lord. Talk about the ultimate come-on. Rather than pounce on her as he wanted, he forced himself to kick out a leg, slamming her ankles together and sending her hurtling to the ground. "First lesson. Distraction will get you killed."

Air shot from her parted lips, and she gazed up at him with disbelief. Even…betrayal?

Gods. Had he really done that? *Harden your heart, asshole. Treat her like Cameo. Like her sisters. Like any other female.*

She'll hate you. She'll—

Not another word.

But—

Silence!

"You tripped me," she said.

"Yes." And he'd do much, much more before they were finished. Had to be this way. He couldn't show her any mercy. Otherwise, she'd never learn. Would never be safe.

Thankfully her sisters maintained their distance and didn't try to stop him.

"Up." He held out a hand, and she grasped it. But he didn't help her to her feet. He jerked her into his body, rattling her brain and pinning her arms at her sides. "Second lesson. An opponent will never aid you. He might act like he wants to, but never, ever believe him."

"Fine. Now let go." She struggled, and he released

her, letting her fall back to the ground. Immediately she popped to her feet, eyes shooting fire at him. "You're going to kill me!"

"So dramatic. Toughen up. You aren't human. Everything I dish, you can take. You know that deep down."

"I guess we'll see," she grumbled.

For the next hour, he worked her over. Hand to hand combat, daggers. To her credit, she didn't complain, didn't beg to stop. She did wince several times, yelp once and twice he thought she verged on tears. His chest had constricted painfully at that, and he'd found himself pulling back, not using all of his strength.

Just as Kaia had done.

Pussy. That's what he was. A disgrace to himself and his men. He was ready to quit, something he'd never done before. Something he'd be teased about for the rest of his endless life.

All of the Lords, all of the Harpies, William, Ashlyn, Anya and Danika were now watching avidly. Some were throwing popcorn at them. Some were placing bets on who would win. William was hitting on Gwen's sisters—not literally. Gwen was shaking, her every strike tentative. She wouldn't last five minutes in a real battle.

"You aren't even close to hurting me," he barked. "Come on. Make me work for it. I'm all over you and you're taking it. Letting me. Almost welcoming me."

"Shut up!" Sweat dripped from her face, and her shirt was plastered to her chest. "I'm not welcoming you. I hate you."

Everyone he'd ever trained had said that at one point or another, but this was the first time he'd ever felt the words in his soul, burning, aching. "Then why haven't you given up? Why are you doing this? Why are you trying to learn to fight?" he demanded, easily tripping her again. He wanted her to voice her reasons for pushing herself so hard. Maybe it would motivate her. "You could be hurt. By me. By Hunters."

She went down, but quickly jumped back up, spitting dirt. Cuts and bruises marred her from head to toe. Her jeans had been ripped to shreds from her many tumbles.

"Hunters deserve to die." She remained in place, panting. "Besides, I've already been hurt. I survived. I healed."

Because of his blood. It was the hottest thing he'd ever done, giving his essence to a woman. He wanted to give her more, every drop. The craving had grown with every hour that passed.

Sabin scoured a hand down his face, wiping away grime. "This isn't working." She couldn't take much more, and he wasn't sure how much more he could dish. "We need to try something new."

"The only thing we haven't tried is unleashing my Harpy. Then you'd be sorry. She's desperate to get her hands on you." There was relish in her tone.

His eyes widened. Of course. "You're right. If you plan to fight Hunters," which he wasn't sure he would allow anymore—wait, where had that thought come from?—"you'll have to learn to summon your Harpy quickly. Which means you need to summon her now and train with her."

Every speck of color in Gwen's lovely face drained. She shook her head. "I was taunting you, trying to scare you. I wasn't serious."

"You might want to rethink this, demon," Bianka called from the sidelines, tossing her black hair over her shoulder. "She hasn't learned to control her Harpy yet. Piss her off, and she might eat even you."

He turned, giving Gwen his profile. Part of him hoped she would attack him, prove she'd been listening and go for blood the moment her opponent's attention veered. But she didn't. Too softhearted, he supposed. "And you have? Learned to control it?"

Her lips curled into a smile. "Yes. Only took me twenty years, but then, I like that part of myself and Gwen never has."

Great. He realized in that moment that he couldn't leave Gwen when he traveled to Chicago, not even with two of her sisters guarding her. If she accidentally lost control of her Harpy, she could hurt the warriors who'd remained behind. He was the only one who seemed capable of calming her. Could he take her with him, though, and leave her somewhere while he traipsed off to war? Alone? Unprotected?

Shit. He was going to have to stay here with her.

Surprisingly, the decision brought relief rather than irritation.

"How did you finally learn?" he asked Bianka.

"Practice. Regrets." The last was said with a hint of sadness. She'd probably killed people she cared about, even as Gwen feared doing.

He focused fully on Gwen. "Well, we're gonna have to put you on an accelerated program. So let the Harpy out. She and I are going to play."

"No." Violently she shook her head again, even backed away from him, palms outstretched to keep him at bay. "No way in hell."

Very well. He popped his jaw. *This is for her own*

good. Do it. You have to. A deep breath, then, *Doubt. Have at her.*

Happy to finally get to work without restriction, the demon swooped on her in a single heartbeat. *He had your sister pinned to a bed yesterday. She's so pretty, so strong. I wonder if he wishes you'd never woken up. If he wishes he'd never fed you his blood to make you strong. I wonder if he's imagining Kaia in bed with him even now, all that hair spread over his thighs as she sucks him dry. Maybe that's why he's pushing you so hard—so you'll walk away from him, leaving the field wide open for your sister. Or maybe he hopes you'll be so sore, you won't protest if he decides to make another go at her. Tonight. All night.*

One second Gwen was in front of him, the next she was gripping him, flying him through the air, forest buzzing past, a blur. After an eternity, his back slammed into a tree trunk, and breathing became an impossible dream.

Her teeth were bared, her claws ripping away his pants. He grabbed Gwen by the shoulders, not knowing whether to push her away or draw her closer. She was Harpy, totally and completely, her eyes a perfect night sky, hair feathered back from her wild expression.

"Gwen. We need to go back to the field."

"Don't move," she said, her voice high-pitched, and then her teeth were deep in his neck and he couldn't have moved to save his life. "You're mine. Mine!"

CHAPTER EIGHTEEN

GWEN'S MIND WAS a whirl of activity. Most of it turbulent, dark. Last night, she'd tried to ignore Sabin's appeal because he hadn't seemed to want her. He'd slept next to her—his lemon and mint scent in her nose, his heat wafting to her, his raspy breaths ringing in her ears, her body attuned to his every movement, skin itching for a touch, a single touch, heart racing—but he hadn't made a move. Ignoring him was no longer an option.

She was becoming obsessed with him. She wanted to learn more about him. She wanted to spend every minute of every day with him. She wanted to possess him. *Will possess him,* a voice screeched in her mind. The Harpy. The one now pulling her strings, urging her to do all the naughty things she'd been fantasizing about. So what that Sabin wasn't what she'd always wanted for herself. So what that he would betray her in an instant if it meant winning his war. There was nothing wrong with enjoying the here and now. With him. If he thought to take her sisters...

She'd known the demon of Doubt had whispered those terrible things to her. She'd recognized its poisonous murmur, but had been unable to stop the flood of violence that raged through her. Sabin and Kaia—hell, no. No one touched him, including her loved ones. Might be irrational of her, but she didn't care.

Several times he'd claimed to desire only Gwen. Well, he was damn well going to prove it.

She had him pinned to a tree, and there was nothing he could do to escape. He was hers. Hers, hers, *hers* to do with as she pleased. And right now, she wanted him naked. He'd already removed his shirt on the field, so all that remained were his pants. She worked at buttons, then the zipper. In seconds, the denim was nothing more than ribbons in the warm breeze.

He wasn't wearing underwear.

"I think my briefs were stolen," he said sheepishly, following her gaze.

His erection sprang free, long, thick, proud, and she gasped in pleasure. His testicles were heavy and drawn up tight. Sunlight poured over him, turning the bronze of his skin to a delicious gold. Today he'd pushed her around, and she'd taken it without (much) complaint. Deep down, she'd known she needed his brand of training. Never again did she want to be shot up like a turkey at Christmas. Plus, part of her really did want to defeat the men who'd abused her. *Plus,* she'd wanted to impress Sabin. He valued strength.

"Mine," she said, wrapping her fingers around his cock. She didn't recognize her voice. It was higher, raspier. A bead of moisture coated her hand.

He arched his hips forward, forcing her hand to slide to the base of his shaft. "Yes," he gritted out.

Her grip tightened. Her vision was a bit distorted, fuzzed to infrared, so she could see the heat pulsing from him. "Tell your demon to keep his mouth shut or I'll gut him."

"He's been quiet since you rammed me."

Good. She must have scared the forest animals and

insects, as well, because there wasn't a chirp or foot-fall to be heard. She and Sabin were completely alone, about a mile from where they'd been training. "Rip off my clothes. Now."

Unused to taking commands, he reacted slowly to hers. She released him to do it herself, and he growled. "Put your hand back."

The moment she did, he was tugging at her clothes, doing whatever was necessary to remove them without disrupting the connection between them. Finally, she was naked, their heated skin was touching and he was moaning.

"Beautiful." He ran his hands down her back, paused. "Wings?"

"Problem?" Warm air caressed her, hardening her nipples, stoking the wet ache between her legs. A constant ache. One that hadn't left since that time in the shower.

"Let me see." He spun her around. For a moment, there was nothing, no reaction, no comment; he didn't even breathe. Then he placed a soft kiss on one of the tiny, fluttering protrusions. "They're amazing."

No man had ever seen her wings. She'd even kept them hidden from Tyson, never letting them peek from the slits in her back. They set her apart, proved how different she was. But under Sabin's gaze, she felt... proud. Shivering, she pivoted on her heel, returning to her former position. "Let's get started."

"Sure you want to do this, Gwendolyn?" His voice was husky and thick, almost drugged.

"Can't stop me." Nothing would stop her, actually, not even a protest from him. She was going to have him, know his taste, feel him inside her, today, now, this moment. Part of her knew she was not herself just then, but the other part of her didn't care. Once Sabin had thought to mark her to keep his friends away from her. Now *she* was going to mark *him*.

"Sure you want it and not just your Harpy?"

He wouldn't make her feel guilty about this. "Stop talking. I'm going to have you. I don't care what you say."

"Very well." Her world spun, and then jagged bark was cutting into her back. Sabin kicked her ankles, shooting her legs apart. He quickly inserted a thigh, placing her clitoris right above his knee. "There'll be consequences. I hope you know that."

"Why are you talking?" Because his erection was so thick, she hadn't been able to close her fingers around it and easily lost her grip. That pissed her off, and she snarled. "Give back."

"No."

"Now!"

"Soon," he vowed, biting her earlobe. To distract her, the diabolical man? Didn't matter, it worked.

As she cried out at the exquisite sensation, he descended, claiming her mouth with his own. His tongue plunged deep, taking, giving, demanding, seeking, begging, rolling, branding every inch of her. The taste of mint hit her first, then lemons, then the flavors became a part of her, his breath hers.

Her fingers tangled in his hair and drew him closer. Their teeth scraped, and he angled, sinking deeper. Her breasts rubbed against his chest, the friction so decadent her legs were trembling. And then her legs weren't holding her up anymore—his were. She had propped herself completely on his knee, was gliding up and down, back and forth, zings of sensation rocketing through her.

"That's a tight grip," he rasped out.

Took every ounce of humanity inside her, but she loosened it. Disappointment filled her, and the Harpy squawked, demanding she *make* him like it.

Sabin frowned down at her. "What are you doing? It's a tight grip, but I want tighter. You're not going to break me, Gwen." As he palmed and squeezed her ass, urging her on, he ducked his head and sucked hard on one of her nipples.

She cried out, her belly quivering, her hands back in his hair and tugging forcefully. His words…damn, they were as beautiful as a caress, freeing in a way she'd never imagined. "I love how strong you are."

"Same here. I want everything you have to give." He kicked at her ankles and she tumbled to the ground. Sabin followed her down, never slowing his quest to her core. When he reached it, he spread her legs as far as they would go and just looked at her.

"Touch," she commanded.

"So pretty. So pink and wet." His eyelids had dropped to half-mast, and he licked his lips as though he could already imagine her taste. Those dark eyes were luminous. "You've had a man?"

No reason to lie. "You know I have."

A muscle ticked in his jaw. "That fucker Tyson treated you properly?"

"Yes." How could he have done anything but, as tame as they'd been with each other? But right here, right now, she didn't want tame. As Sabin had said, she couldn't break him. Anything she gave, he could take…he wanted. Though he hadn't even entered her, her pleasure soared to a new level.

"I think I'm going to kill him," he muttered, rolling her nipples between his fingers. "Do you still think of him?"

"No." And she didn't want to talk about him, either. "Have you had a woman?"

"Not many, considering how old I am. But perhaps more than a human will ever have."

At least he was honest about it. "I think I'm going to kill them." Sadly, that was not an empty boast. Gwen had always abhorred violence, had always fled from a fight, but right now she happily could have sunk a dagger into the heart of every woman who had tasted this man. He belonged to her.

"No need," Sabin said, ghosts in his eyes. Then he dove for her, licked the core of her and groaned, his expression flooding with pleasure.

Her back arched, her gaze shooting straight to the heavens. Sweet fire, that felt good. She reached behind her and latched on to the base of a tree, instinctively knowing she needed to hold on for the ride of her life.

"More?" he asked huskily.

"More!"

Over and over he tongued her, and then his fingers joined the play, spreading her, sinking deep. She didn't have to ask him if he liked it; he was lapping her up as if she was candy and she was arching in to every sensual glide.

"That's right," he praised. "That's the way. I've got my cock in my hand, can't help myself, imagining it's your hand, while I've got heaven in my mouth."

Her cries echoed through the forest, each more hoarse

than the other. Almost there…so close… "Sabin. Please."
His teeth grazed her clitoris, and that was all it took.
She climaxed, skin tightening, muscles jumping in joy,
bones locking together.

He lapped until he'd sucked down every drop.

As she panted, Sabin flipped her over and propped
her on her hands and knees. He teased her with the tip of
his shaft, running it along her folds but not yet entering.

"I want to see you."

"I don't want to hurt your wings."

Sweet man. "Let *me* taste *you*," she said, and he
groaned. She wanted to lick his tattoo, as well. It drew
her, was an aphrodisiac all on its own, yet she'd never
gotten a chance to study it the way she craved.

"You taste me, and I won't be able to make love to
you. I really want to make love to you. But the choice
is yours." He pressed his chest into her back, his face
only an inch away from hers.

His shaft in her mouth or between her legs. Hard
choice, literally. In the end, though, she opted for what
she'd spent last night fantasizing about. She had to know
what it was like to be his woman. Completely. Otherwise, she'd regret the lack for the rest of her life. However long or short that was. Being shot and realizing
she did indeed want to help bring those Hunters down
had taught her one thing: time wasn't a guarantee, even
for immortals.

"Next time, then." She reached around, clamping
down on a handful of his hair and jerking his mouth to
hers. His tongue plunged deep again, and this time he
was flavored with her.

He positioned himself at her entrance, but just before sliding home, he stiffened. Cursed. "I don't have a condom."

"Harpies are only fertile once a year, and this isn't it." Another reason Chris had been willing to hold her for so long. "Inside. Now."

In the next instant, Sabin's shaft was buried all the way to the hilt. The kiss halted as she gave another cry of pleasure. He stretched her, filled her up, touched every part of her, and it was even better than she'd dreamed.

He bit her earlobe. Still reaching around, she dug her nails into his shoulder, felt warm blood trickle as he hissed in a breath. Hmm, the sweet smell of it drifted to her and her mouth watered. "I want—I need—"

"Anything you want is yours." On and on he pounded inside her, forward and back, fast, hard, his testicles slapping at her.

"Want...all. Everything." With the feel of him, she became mindless, lost, no longer Gwen or the Harpy but an extension of Sabin. "Want your blood," she added. Only his. The thought of anyone else's left her hollow, unsatisfied.

Sabin withdrew from her completely.

A whimper escaped her. "Sabin—"

He was lying on the ground, fitting her over him, deep inside her, pumping, sliding, gliding a second later. One of her knees dug into a twig and got cut, but even that seemed to lull her into a state of utter sensation. Pleasure, pain, didn't matter. Each fed off the other and dragged her further and further into a black sea of bliss.

"Drink," he commanded, gripping her head and forcing her mouth to his neck.

Her teeth had already sharpened. Without hesitation,

she bit him. He roared, loud and long, and she sucked the warm liquid deep into her throat, her tongue dancing over his skin. Like a drug, it spread through her, the warmth becoming a sizzle, blistering, scorching her veins. Soon she was trembling, writhing against him.

"More," she said. She wanted everything he had, every drop. Had to have it. Would—kill him, she realized, forcing herself to jerk upright. His cock slid even deeper, and she shivered. "I almost drank too much."

"No such thing."

"You could have—"

"I won't. Now give me more. Everything, like you said."

Up and down she rode him, his fingertips clutching her so tightly they nearly broke skin. The fear of hurting him faded, leaving only a consuming sense of neediness.

"That's the way. So good…so very good…" He was panting, grinding against her, his thumb stroking her clit. "Don't want it…to end."

Neither did she. Nothing had ever consumed her like this. Nothing had ever taken over her mind and body so fervently, to the point that nothing else mattered. Her sisters could find them, could be searching even now. Swift as they moved, they could be here already. *Can't stop. Need more.*

Her head fell back, the ends of her hair brushing his chest. Reaching up, he cupped and kneaded her breasts, applying a little pressure to arch her backward. She complied, anchoring her hands on his thighs.

"Turn around," he commanded roughly. "I want *your* blood."

Perhaps she hesitated too long—what exactly did he

want? Had she heard correctly? He palmed her knees, lifting, and spun her. His cock remained inside her. When she was facing the other direction, away from him, his fingers curled around her neck and drew her down. Her back to his chest. His teeth were in her neck a second later, and she was spasming, screaming at the bliss.

He didn't suck her long, just enough to experience his own orgasm, hips hammering up and into her, one hand flat on her stomach to grind her against him. Nothing compared. Nothing was as wild, as necessary, as liberating. She and the Harpy soared through the heavens, lost in the pleasure of another climax.

An eternity passed before she collapsed, fully and completely spent, unable to breathe. Her chest was too constricted. Sabin's inhalations were choppy, as well, his grip on her now weak.

The Harpy was quiet, had quite possibly passed out. Gwen didn't roll off him, even though she wanted to pass out, as well. She'd been fighting sleep for so long, restful sleep untainted by pain and injury, but now it was creeping up on her, determined to consume her.

She lay exactly as she was, head cushioned by Sabin's neck, his arms wrapped around her, his shaft still inside her. Stars winked in front of her eyes—or maybe it was the sun dancing between the clouds.

What they'd just done…the things they'd done…

"I didn't rape you, did I?" she asked softly. Her cheeks burned. Without the cloud of lust, she admitted that she'd been jealous, attacked him, and had decided to have sex with him whether he wanted it or not.

He laughed. "Are you kidding me?"

"Well, I was kind of forceful." Her eyelids were so

heavy she blinked—closed, open, closed—and then they refused to open again, as though they were glued together. If her sisters found her asleep, they'd freak out. They'd be disappointed in her, and they'd have every right. Had she learned nothing from her capture?

"Actually, you were kind of perfect."

Words to make her melt. Instead, she stiffened, still fighting with all her might to remain awake for just a little longer. Anytime she and Sabin relaxed together, no anger between them, Doubt usually pounced.

"What's wrong?" he asked, suddenly concerned.

"I was waiting for Doubt to try and tear me down." Were her words truly as slurred as they sounded to her? "You say something nice, and he's knocking on my door to point out why you're wrong."

Sabin pressed a soft kiss into the side of her neck. "He's afraid of your Harpy, I think. She comes out, and he goes into hiding." Joy and awe had entered in his tone there at the end, as if he'd reached some sort of decision with those words. But what?

"Someone afraid of me." She grinned slowly. "I like the sound of that."

"Me, too." He stroked between her breasts, his index finger grazing a nipple. "Do Harpies have any weaknesses I should know about?"

Yes, but to admit it was to court punishment. Her sisters would cut her off as her mother had; they would have to. It was a rule that couldn't be broken. Lethargy fragmented her thoughts before she could reason things out. She yawned and settled more snugly against him, fading…still struggling…

"Gwen?"

A soft entreaty, but it pounded through her mind, and she grabbed on to it like a life preserver. "Yes?"

"I lost you there for a moment. You were telling me about a Harpy's greatest weakness."

Was she? "Why do you want to know?"

"I want to make sure you're protected so no one can use it against you."

Good idea. *I can't believe you're actually considering this.* But this was Sabin, the man who'd just kissed and touched her everywhere. The man who wanted her strong, invincible. And she didn't like that she had such a weakness, either. It was how the Hunters had subdued her, though they had never realized exactly what they'd done. It was what flooded her with worry every time her sisters decided to hire out their services.

"You can tell me," he said. "I won't use it to hurt you. I swear it."

Once he'd admitted to forsaking his honor if it meant winning a battle. Would he forsake this vow? She sighed, sinking further under the blackness. *Stay awake. You have to stay awake.* This came down to one decision: to trust him or not. He desperately wanted her to help destroy his enemy. No way would he jeopardize that by betraying her.

"Our wings. Break them, cut them off, bind them, and we're powerless. That's how the Hunters got me. They didn't know it, but when they wrapped me in that blanket to abduct me, they paralyzed my wings, thereby weakening me."

He squeezed her tight. In comfort? "Maybe we can design something to protect them, something that still allows them to move freely. But you're also going to need to train with them bound. It's the only way to…"

His voice faded completely, the darkness thicker than ever. Lord, she'd done so many bad, bad things this last hour. She'd given him her body and snuggled in as though he were a comfortable couch. Harpy rule: always leave afterward.

If she fell asleep, Sabin would have to carry her out of the forest, past her sisters, who would see her zonked out and vulnerable, just as she'd feared.

I'm a failure in every way.

"Don't...let...them see," she managed before sinking into oblivion.

CHAPTER NINETEEN

DON'T LET THEM SEE…what? Sabin wondered as he gathered the sleeping Gwen in his arms. A mewling sound parted her lips, soft and oddly erotic. He tightened his grip, feeling oddly protective.

Don't let the Lords see her naked body? Done. He would rather die than allow another man a peek at her beauty.

Don't let her sisters see her like this? Again, done. They would ask questions he wasn't ready to answer. More than that, they tended to react negatively to the thought of Gwen snoozing. Why? It still made no sense to him.

Another mewl, this one quieter, breathy. His stomach clenched in desire, because it was a sound she'd made while grinding on his erection. The sun stroked her, highlighting the glimmer of her skin, her rosy nipples. Her hands were folded over her belly, her body loose, her head resting trustingly at the base of his neck. Strawberry curls tumbled over his arm, his stomach, and it felt as if he were draped in silk.

Should he dress her? No, he thought a moment later. He didn't want to jostle her and accidentally wake her. Finally, she was resting. Truly resting. And all he'd had to do was pleasure her senseless, he thought dryly. Then he grinned. If he had to, he would pleasure her senseless every night. Girl needed her rest, after all. And (cough, cough) he was used to making sacrifices.

He didn't even consider dressing himself. He would have had to put her down and coverage wasn't a good enough reason to risk a twig poking her or a bug crawling on her.

Sabin kissed her temple, unable to help himself, and stalked forward. Remaining in shadows, he edged toward the back of the fortress, always careful of the cameras, pits and trip wires he and the other warriors had designed to keep Hunters out.

What had just happened between him and Gwen... He'd never experienced anything like it before. Not even with Darla, whom he had loved.

And unlike Darla, Gwen just might be strong enough to cope with his demon over the long term. It had been a startling, and welcome, revelation.

Do you really think you can keep her? How long will she love you, if she's ever stupid enough to love you? You might betray her. And you're always rushing off to fight. Worse, you plan to fight beside her sisters. What if they're killed? Gwen will blame you, and rightly so.

The doubts didn't float through him. They screamed, pounding into his temples, beating at his skull. He cringed from the sharp ache of it. Now that Gwen was asleep, her Harpy tethered, Sabin's demon had come out of hiding, pissed and desperate to feed.

What better to feed on than the secret fears Sabin only then realized he'd harbored? And now that they'd been forced to the forefront of his mind, there was no blocking them; they nearly swallowed him whole.

Did he want Gwen to love him?

To have those amber eyes regard him softly, today,

tomorrow, forever…to have that luscious body in his bed every night…to hear that sparkling laughter…to protect her…to awaken her to the strength of her true nature…

Yes, he wanted her to love him. She could handle his demon in mental combat, as he'd just discovered. Hell, she'd frightened the beast into submission.

Part of him had loved her since the moment he'd seen her, he realized. When she'd been captive, helpless, his every instinct had clamored to save her. Then, as she'd struggled to keep her Harpy under tight control, to follow the rules of her people, he'd found himself fascinated by her. But he'd never really understood her, had mistakenly thought her weak. Now, he saw her for what she really was: stronger than her sisters, stronger than him.

For most of her life, she'd suppressed a seemingly insuppressible brute. Sabin had trouble caging his demon for more than a day. She'd left her family to pursue her own dream. She hadn't run from him, even when she'd discovered his origins and even though she'd been afraid.

Oh, yes. There was more courage in this tiny female than anyone had realized. Even Gwen. Now, because of him, she wanted to attack the Hunters. She wanted to place herself in danger, each and every day.

If she were injured, she would heal. That, he knew. Rationally, at least. The thought of her injured, bloodied, broken, however, nearly had him roaring as he snuck in one of the back entrances to the fortress. *I'm a fucking idiot!*

No argument here.

Frowning, he made his way to a secret passage, a passage Torin monitored.

Sabin stared up at one of the hidden cameras and shook his head, a command for his friend's silence. Never once did he slow his gait, though. When he reached his bedroom, he barricaded the door. Did Gwen love him? She was attracted to him, otherwise she wouldn't have given herself to him. And so passionately, at that, gifting him with the best orgasm of his long, long life. She trusted him, otherwise she wouldn't have admitted her greatest weakness. But love?

If she did love him, could that love withstand the trials they were sure to face? Yes or no, he realized he wouldn't let her go. She belonged to him now, and he belonged to her. He'd warned her there would be consequences to giving herself to him.

He wanted to know everything about her. He wanted to see to her every need. Pamper her. Kill anyone who hurt her—even her sisters.

He'd once told her that he could—and would—sleep with a woman other than the one he loved if it meant aiding his cause. How silly he'd been. How naive. The thought of bedding another woman left him cold. Even sick. No one would feel, sound and taste like his Gwen. More than that, it would hurt her, and he couldn't hurt her. And the thought of Gwen bedding another man— touching him, kissing him, enjoying him—just to win a battle sent Sabin into a killing rage.

What if she wants another man? Desires him? Craves—

Another word, and I swear to the gods I'll find Pandora's box and suck you out by the balls.

You'd die. There was a tremor to the words.

You'd suffer. And we both know I'll spite myself to destroy my enemy.

Who would guard your precious Gwen?

Her sisters. Shall I go get them? Let you talk to them?

Silence. Sweet silence.

Sabin gently placed Gwen on the bed and tucked the covers around her. A loud knock echoed from his door, and he scowled. Gwen didn't move, didn't moan or act as if she was aware of the interruption in any way. That saved the intruder's life.

Three long strides and he was at the door, removing the barricade then ripping it open.

Kaia tried to push her way inside. "Where is she? You better not have hurt her, Mr. Pound On Gwen For Giggles."

"It wasn't for giggles. It was to strengthen her, and you know it. You should be thanking me, since you failed to do your job. Now go."

She glared up at him, hands on her hips. "I'm not leaving until I see her."

"We're busy."

Golden eyes, so eerily similar to Gwen's, darted down his naked body. "I see that. I still want to talk to her."

Don't let them see, Gwen had beseeched. "She's naked." Truth. "And I'd like to get back to her." Again, truth. "Your conversation can wait."

A wide grin spread over the Harpy's beautiful face, and his shoulders sagged in relief. Thank the gods sex wasn't against those damned Harpy rules.

He and Gwen were going to have a long talk when she awoke, and she was going to outline exactly what was permitted and what wasn't. And then the rules he didn't agree with would be demolished.

"Mom would be so proud! Little Gwennie, bagging an evil demon."

"Get lost." He slammed the door in her face. Then he grimaced and spun. Thankfully Gwen still hadn't moved.

Throughout the day, warriors, females and Harpies alike came knocking on his door. He couldn't relax because he couldn't get Gwen's words out of his head. Don't let *who* see what, damn it? The sisters had already seen her sleeping with him, the night of their arrival, so now he wasn't sure that was such a big deal. They hadn't tried to punish her or anything. Was Gwen ashamed of the wounds in her neck? Maybe he shouldn't have bitten her.

The first visitors were Maddox and a smiling Ashlyn, holding a plate of sandwiches. "After such an intense training session, I thought you and Gwen might be hungry."

Maddox hadn't been smiling, but he hadn't insisted Gwen be made to leave, either. "Thanks." Sabin took the plate and shut the door. He'd pulled on a robe, wanting to give the appearance of a sexual marathon—Kaia had seemed happy about that, so surely it wasn't shameful to the Harpies—while still maintaining his dignity.

Next came Anya and Lucien. "You and Gwen wanna watch a slasher movie with us while we pretend to read those dusty scrolls but really make everyone else do all the work?" Anya asked, waggling her eyebrows. "It's gonna be fun."

"No, thanks." Again, he shut the door.

A short while later, Bianka arrived. "I need to talk to my sister."

"She's still busy." *Sleeping.* He shut the door in her scowling face.

Finally the visits tapered off. Sabin texted Torin to let him know he was staying behind while the others went to Chicago.

Figured, was the reply. Which is why I already found you a replacement. Gideon's taking over the mission.

HIS RELIEF WAS almost palpable. Leaving Gwen like this wasn't even an option.

If any of the men are injured, you'll blame yourself, Doubt said.

Sabin didn't try to deny it. *With reason.*

What if you begin to resent Gwen?

Now he rolled his eyes. *I won't.*

How do you know? Sulky, whiny.

She's not to blame. I am. If I resent anyone, it will be myself.

Seriously, how could he resent this tenderhearted woman? If she'd known about the trip, he suspected she would have wanted to go herself.

Sabin watched the sun set, the moon rise and the sun reappear, unable to rest or relax. Why wasn't Gwen waking up? No one needed *this* much rest. Did she need blood again? He'd thought he'd given her plenty in the heat of their loving.

Sabin leaned back in the chair he'd dragged to the bedside. The wooden slats dug into his back, but he didn't mind. They kept him alert, his mind active.

Look at you. You're becoming everything you've ever despised, he thought. *Weak, because of a woman. Worried, over a woman. Vulnerable to attack, because of a woman.*

"Sabin," a breathless sigh rang out.

Sabin jerked upright in the chair, feet hitting the floor with a thump. His heart skipped a beat, his lungs nearly seized. Finally!

Gwen's eyes blinked open, but her eyelashes were matted together and she had to scrub them. Then their gazes collided, and he forgot to breathe. He'd wondered how she would react to awakening in his bed; he should have wondered how *he'd* react. He could have prepared himself. He was shaking, his blood heating at the sensual sight of her, rumpled and ready.

She frowned, attention sweeping the bedroom. "How'd I get here? Wait. Tell me when I return." She threw her legs over the side of the bed and lumbered to a stand.

Sabin was already on his feet, already swooping her up in his arms.

"I can walk," she protested.

"I know." He deposited her in the bathroom, stepped back into the room and shut the door behind him, allowing her a measure of privacy.

What if she falls and hurts herself?

Shut up. You're not going to affect me right now.

A horrified gasp pummeled through the wood, and he grinned. She must have only then realized she was naked. Holding her like that had affected him madly. He was hard as a steel pipe, her female scent in his nose.

When he heard the water switch on, he grabbed a change of clothes and stalked to the bedroom next to his. The door was open, so he walked inside without preamble. The three Harpies sat in a circle on the floor, stacks of groceries in the center. They were laughing about something—until they spotted him.

Kaia's eyes began to bleed black, and Sabin's demon quickly retreated. "Our food," she squawked and he grimaced. Funny. Didn't bother him when Gwen sounded like that. Rather, he just wanted to please her. "We stole it. It's ours."

"Calm down." Bianka slapped her arm, though her gaze never left Sabin. "About time you showed up. Where's Gwennie?"

"Showering. I need to use yours." He didn't wait for permission, but headed into the bathroom and gathered a towel.

"After hours and hours of nonstop sex, you guys can't share a stall?" one of them called. Sometimes, when he couldn't see the twins, it was hard to tell which was speaking.

"Maybe there'll be another marathon if they try and share," another teased.

They cackled.

"Did she put you in a coma? Has she been hiding you all this time to keep you from being shamed?" Taliyah had spoken this time; he recognized that cold timbre, which never failed to make him shudder.

She knew the truth, he realized. He wondered yet again if sleeping like that was against Harpy protocol. "What if she did?" he found himself saying.

Bianka and Kaia twittered. "Go little sis," one of them said.

Sabin kicked the door shut and jumped into the shower, moving quickly, afraid the females would burst in on Gwen and question her before he could. But they were exactly as he'd left them when he emerged, eating and laughing.

Taliyah, the only one not smiling, nodded at him. In gratitude?

He took a quick detour through the kitchen—someone had shopped, thank the gods—and rounded up a bag of chips, a brownie, a granola bar, an apple and a bottle of water. Loaded down, he entered his bedroom, shut the door with a backward kick, and found Gwen seated on the edge of the bed. She wore a pair of sweat shorts and a bright blue T-shirt, both of which she'd picked for herself in town the other day, her hair wet and dripping from a knot atop her head.

Doubt peeked from the shadowed corner in Sabin's mind, but decided not to risk incurring the Harpy's wrath and hid again.

Forcing his expression to remain neutral, he settled into the chair he'd occupied for far too long already. He balanced the tray on his stomach.

"We need to talk," she said, gazing at the food with longing. "About what happened in the forest…"

Before she could venture down that path, he told her how long she'd been out, how he'd guarded her, how no one had seen her neck, no one knew what she'd really been doing and how everyone assumed they'd been going at it like animals.

"There is a God," she said on a relieved breath.

Or gods. But whatever. Any other woman would have been horrified, he thought, fighting a grin. Still more proof that she was the only woman for him. "Now you're going to answer some questions for me."

She gulped, eyes luminous in the sunlight that streamed through a gap in the dark, heavy curtains. "All right."

"Why can you only eat stolen food?"

Her eyes narrowed. "I'm not supposed to discuss it."

"I think we're beyond that point."

"I guess we are," she said grudgingly. "Why do you want to know?"

"So I can understand." He popped open the brownie and bit into the end. "You've trusted me with your body. You've trusted me to guard you while you sleep. You've even trusted me with your weakness. Now trust me with your secrets."

Up and down her chest moved, her breath emerging shallow and raspy. Her stomach rumbled, and she rubbed it without looking away from him. Or rather, the food. "I—I—okay. Yes." She licked her lips. "Will you pay me?"

"Pay you? How much and for what?"

"Just say yes!" It was snarled.

"Yes?"

She licked her lips again, words tumbling from her. "The gods despise Harpies and consider us an abomination since we were the spawn of a prince of darkness. Long ago, they hoped to bring about our ruin in a manner that would not reflect poorly on them. A way that would seem as if we'd destroyed ourselves. So they cursed us in secret, stating that never again could we enjoy a meal freely given to us or one we had prepared ourselves. We sicken terribly if we disregard the curse; some even die. It only takes once to learn that lesson. As you saw for yourself at the camp in Egypt.

"Anyway, the first of my kind learned through trial and error that they could still eat, but only what they'd stolen or what was given to them in payment. The gods didn't succeed in destroying us, just making our lives difficult. So pay me. I gave you the answer you wanted, now you owe me."

Her demand for payment suddenly made sense. And hadn't Anya mentioned something about eating what they earned? Gods, he had to smarten up and listen better. "For the secret." He tossed the brownie at her and she caught it with a too-quick flick of her wrist. The dessert was consumed a second later. This was yet another similarity they shared, he reflected. Both their lives had been affected by a curse.

"You should have told me I could pay you with food," he chided. "I could have been feeding you all along."

"I didn't know you well enough to share the fundamentals of my race. And as my sisters say, knowledge is power. You didn't need more power over me."

He'd often said the same thing, though he thought he *did* need more power over her. "But now you do?" he asked softly, foolishly pleased with her. "Know me, that is?"

Her cheeks burned bright red. "Well, now I know you *better*."

Fair enough. Sabin dangled the bag of chips from pinched fingers. "Tell me who you didn't want to see you, what you didn't want them to see."

"My sisters. I didn't want them to see me sleeping."

So that *had* been the reason. "Wait. Tell me how you rested with your chicken, and then you'll get these."

"Sabin. Chips!"

"You haven't answered to my satisfaction."

"I never rested with a chick— Oh, you mean Tyson. For a long time, I didn't. Didn't rest, I mean. Does that count? Did I earn the chips?" She reached out, fingers waving eagerly.

He held firm. "How long were you with him?"

"Six months."

Six. Months. He gritted his teeth, not liking the thought of her with anyone that long. "You remained awake for all that time?"

"No. At first, I let him think I had insomnia. I'd stay up all night. But when the fatigue would get to be too much, I would call in sick at work and sleep in the trees. That's the only location we're supposed to sleep, since it's nearly impossible to be seen or reached. But as the months passed, I thought, why not rest with this man I trusted? So I started sleeping in bed with him. And before you ask, not sleeping around other people wasn't a command or curse of the gods, but a safety measure every Harpy is taught from birth."

He didn't recall her sisters leaving at night to head for the forest, but as silently as they moved, they certainly could have. "Why?"

She pushed out a frustrated breath. "Our wings can be bound while we sleep, as proven by my time in captivity. Now give. Me. The. Chips."

He tossed the bag.

Plastic ripped and orange-stained chips sprayed. Gwen popped one in her mouth, closed her eyes and moaned. Sabin had to swallow a moan of his own.

"Do you want to earn the apple?"

The tip of her tongue emerged, swiping over her lips. "Yes. Please."

"Tell me your thoughts about me. About what we did in the forest. And don't lie. I'm only paying for the truth."

She hesitated.

Why didn't she want him to know? *What* didn't she

want him to know? A minute ticked by in silence, and he feared she would simply content herself with the food she already had. Then she surprised him.

"I like you. More than I should. I'm attracted to you and want to be with you. When I'm not with you, I'm thinking about you. It's stupid. I'm stupid. But I love the way I feel when I'm with you. When your demon's quiet, I don't feel ashamed or forgettable or scared. I feel worthy, desired and protected."

Sabin tossed the apple at her and she caught it, her gaze avoiding him. "I feel the same about you," he admitted gruffly.

"You do?" Her eyes snapped to him, bright with hope.

"I do."

Slowly she grinned, but that grin soon fell away and her shoulders slumped. She bit into the apple, chewed, swallowed.

"Tell me what you're thinking," he said.

"I don't know if we can make anything work. You once said you could betray the woman you loved if it meant winning a battle. Not that I think you love me. I just, well, if you were to be with someone else, I would kill her. Then you." There at the end, there had been steel in her tone. Steel sharpened to a razor point.

"I won't. I wouldn't. I don't think I can." He scrubbed a hand down his face. "You're the only thing I can think about anymore. I doubt I could even fake it with someone else."

"But for how long will that last?" she asked softly, rolling the apple in her palms.

Forever, he suspected, guilt filling him. He'd already devoted more time to her than he should have.

He hadn't studied the names on Cronus's scrolls or done anything to find the two remaining artifacts. He hadn't been searching for Galen.

For so many years, he'd placed the war with the Hunters above everything else—and demanded the same from his men. Distractions hadn't been tolerated. They'd given him everything he'd asked for, and more. How could he, as their leader, now give himself fully to Gwen?

So, rather than answer her, he pushed to his feet, said, "I've neglected my duties to watch over you and now have a lot to do," and left her. If he hoped to keep her, he had a lot of shit to figure out first.

CHAPTER TWENTY

AND I WANTED TO BE A SOLDIER? Gwen wondered for
the thousandth time after another grueling session. She
was panting, sweaty and bruised as she flopped atop
Sabin's bed.

The last few days, Sabin had divided his time between his duties—whatever those were—and her training. She'd just spent the past few hours getting the crap
beaten out of her. Again. He gave no quarter, showed
no mercy. It sucked!

"You're stronger, aren't you?" he said, as if he could
read her thoughts.

"Yes." And she was.

"I won't apologize. You know you can take a punch
now."

"And dish out my own," she said smugly, recalling
how she'd sent the muscled warrior flying into the trees,
gasping for breath, only an hour ago. She also knew
when to duck and when to attack.

"You just have to learn how to summon your Harpy
faster. Good things happen when you do." He sat at the
edge of the bed, cupped a hand around the base of her
neck and drew her toward him. "Now drink."

As she sank her teeth into his artery, her cheeks
heated at the reminder of the way she'd taken him in

the forest. Then her eyelids drifted shut and she simply enjoyed the taste of this man.

He lifted her to his lap without breaking contact, and she immediately spread her legs, welcoming him against her body. He rubbed his erection between her thighs. She moaned at the bliss, the decadence. But when she tangled her fingers in his hair, withdrawing her teeth to lick and nip at him, he flung her back on the mattress, stood to shaky legs and strode toward the door.

"Time for round two," he said. "I'll meet you outside." He disappeared around the corner.

"You're really starting to piss me off," she called.

No reply.

She almost screeched in frustration. Twice before, he'd done this to her. Trained with her, brought her to his room to heal her injuries with that delicious blood, got her hot and ready, and then abandoned her for his "duties" or more training. Why? Since their little chat, he hadn't made love to her again. Again, why?

They'd declared their feelings for each other. Hadn't they? She knew she wanted him, however she could get him, for however long she could have him. No use denying that anymore. If they didn't last, at least she'd tried. And of course, it would be his fault so she'd have no regrets.

The thought of blaming him for any future discord caused her frustration to fade; she grinned. And the thought of a future with him had her sighing dreamily as she curled into a pillow. He was the kind of man every Harpy craved. Powerful, a little wild, a lot wicked. He could kill an enemy without guilt. He wasn't afraid of hard work. He could be ruthless, without mercy, yet he was tender with her.

The only question was, would he put Gwen before his war?

Wait. Two questions: Did she want him to?

With another sigh, she rose and headed back outside. The sun was high and warm as she searched for Sabin. The moment she saw him, she experienced a wave of pride. *Mine.* He was hunched over two daggers, sharpening them to razor points.

No reason to practice with fakes, he'd told her. Tomorrow, they planned to work with guns. Golden light caressed his bare chest, deepening his tan. Sweat beaded over his muscles, making them gleam—and her mouth water. The puncture wounds were already healing on his neck; she wished they'd remain forever, her brand on him.

I've had all that strength over me, inside me.

She wanted it again. Soon. The nights were the most difficult of all. He wouldn't enter the bedroom until close to morning—it didn't take his demon to make her wonder where he'd been, what he'd been doing—and then he would crawl in beside her, though he refused to touch her. She would feel his heat, hear his soft inhalations, and she would ache all over. Then she would fall asleep before she could do anything about it.

Tonight, if he continued to resist her, she would take matters into her own hands. Literally. He'd tangled with her Harpy once and survived; he could damn well do it again.

"Damn it," Ashlyn, wife to the keeper of Violence, said. It was surprising, hearing the gentle woman curse. "Not again!"

As usual, Ashlyn and Danika sat on the sidelines to cheer for her. They also liked to boo when Sabin knocked her down. Though she hadn't spent a lot of time with them, she already adored them. They were open and honest, kind and witty, and had somehow, despite everything, managed to make a relationship work with a Lord of the Underworld. Gwen planned to get the lowdown from them as to how they'd achieved such a feat, but hadn't yet had the time.

Currently, they were a bit distracted, playing some kind of game with Anya, Bianka and Kaia—who also liked to witness her sessions. Ashlyn and Danika had welcomed her sisters with open arms, claiming the fortress needed a little more estrogen to balance out the testosterone.

"It's my turn to roll," Bianka said in a mock growl. "So you can back off my dice or have your fingers removed. Your choice."

Maddox was inside, or he would have challenged her sister, Gwen knew. Game or not, he didn't like anyone threatening his woman.

The warrior called Kane stood off to the side, watching the women with a half smile on his face, his hazel eyes bright. He was out in the open, not leaning against a tree, not shaded by branches. And yet, even as Gwen watched, a twig snapped from the far black oak and hurtled straight into him, slapping him across the face.

He and a few of the others had apparently stayed behind to read scrolls Cronus, the god king, had given them—was that one of Sabin's duties?—while the rest of the men had traipsed off to Chicago on a mission to "kick Hunter ass." Odd that she missed them.

"—concentrating?" A hard weight slammed into her stomach, shoving her to her ass.

Sabin was on top of her a second later, glaring, the daggers just above her shoulders. "We've talked about allowing your mind to wander."

As her lungs were in the process of seizing, it took her a moment to form a reply. "We hadn't...started yet."

Do you really think you're...strong enough for this?

Doubt's voice drifted through her head, but the demon had sounded reluctant, afraid even to make itself known. It really was terrified of her, as Sabin had said. A sense of power accompanied the knowledge.

"I'm sorry for using the demon against you, but I want to train you against it, as well. And do you think a Hunter is going to ask your permission to begin and then wait until you nod?"

Good point. Perhaps it was time for her to make a point of her own. "First, your demon is like a tame little house cat now. Second..." Since her arms were free, she fisted her hands and slammed both into his temples. He grunted in surprise, cradling his head as he fell backward. She didn't waste any time. She kicked him in the chest so hard his ribs cracked.

The Harpy laughed. *More!*

For once, hearing that voice didn't terrify her, and she blinked in surprise. Was she...could she be...embracing her darker side?

"Go, Gwennie!" Kaia called.

"Kick him while he's down!" Bianka shouted.

He was still clutching the daggers as he blinked, trying to clear his vision. Gwen jumped to her feet, wings springing free in her back. Thankfully they were so small, they didn't rip her shirt away. Moving faster than anyone could possibly see, she raced behind him and wrapped her fingers around his wrists.

There wasn't time for him to resist.

Before he realized where she was and what she was doing, she had the sharp tips of the knives resting on his shoulders. A bead of blood formed around each one.

A moment passed in stunned silence.

"Okay. You've officially kicked my ass." Some men would have been humiliated by that, but there was pride in Sabin's tone.

Joy burst through her. Just like that, faster than a blink, she'd done it. She'd really done it. Winning a fight, no matter her opponent, was something she'd never thought to do, something she'd considered an impossibility. Yet she'd just defeated a freaking Lord of the Underworld, one of the most capable warriors in this world and any other. Gods trembled at the mere mention of their names.

Well, if they didn't, they should.

"Next time we fight, though, I want you to let your Harpy completely free," he said.

She nodded reluctantly. Letting the Harpy come out for lovemaking was one thing; battling was quite another.

"Just think about what you will soon be doing to the Hunters," Kaia said with awe. "Baby girl, I've never seen moves like yours."

"Mother would be proud." Taliyah strode beside her and slapped her on the back. "*If* we knew where she was, she might even welcome you back into her fold."

Gwen could have danced. She'd always been the anomaly, the weak link, the mistake. With one sweet victory, she finally felt like she was one of them. Like she was worthy.

Silent, Sabin reached up and plucked the daggers from her now shaky hands. What thoughts were tumbling through his mind?

"Good job." Ashlyn rubbed her rounded belly. "I'm truly impressed."

Grinning, Danika clapped. "Sabin, you should be embarrassed. You were brought down in less than a minute."

"And by a girl." But Kaia's amusement quickly faded. "Okay, now that the training is winding down, I have a question. When are we going to see some action?" She anchored her hands on her hips. "We're bored. We've been bored. And we've been on damn good behavior, waiting."

"Yeah. Hunters hurt baby sis, so now they need to pay," Bianka said.

"Soon," Sabin told them. "I swear it."

That scared Gwen a little. Not enough to change the course she'd set for herself, though.

"But at the moment, I'm going to spend some time with the woman of the hour. Alone." No one protested as Sabin ushered Gwen to a private alcove, where he'd already stashed a cooler. He motioned for her to sit inside a cool circle of shade. "Do you need more blood?"

"No." Seriously, what was he thinking? He was polite, but more distant than ever. Clearly "alone time" didn't require nudity and a bed. How disappointing. "I'm okay. Operating at full strength, even." To prove it, she too remained standing.

"Good. Much as I want to give it to you, I want to see how you recover from minor wounds without it."

"I'm not wounded, minor or otherwise."

"Really." His pointed gaze dropped to her arm.

She looked down and saw the bloody grooves in her forearm. "Oh." Wow. Getting shot must have inured her to the pain of other injuries.

"Let me know the moment it's gone."

Always the trainer. She liked that about him. Everything was a lesson meant to strengthen her, prepare her for what could happen. It really showed how much he cared, because he didn't do it for everyone. Only her, actually.

Now that she thought about it, he only reacted with violence when someone threatened *her*. Kaia and Bianka had verbally insulted and physically assaulted his friends on several occasions, and he'd grinned, even joined in the teasing. But the moment her sisters turned their teasing her way, Sabin's mood darkened. He never hesitated to shove them away, either. Really shove. To him, men and women were equal in every way and deserved the same treatment, something else she admired about him.

"Sit," he urged again. "I need to talk to you."

"Fine."

When she'd obeyed, he held up an ice-cold, dripping bottle of water. "If you want to earn it, you'll tell me what happens to a Harpy when she takes a consort. Tell me how long she has the consort, and what's expected of him."

Was he…could he be…thinking about signing on for the job? Her eyes were wide as he plopped a few feet in front of her and stretched out.

"Well?"

"Consorts are forever," she croaked, "and very rare.

A Harpy is a free spirit, but every so often one will en-
counter a male who…delights her. That's the best word
I can think of to describe the obsession. His smell and
touch become drugs to her. His voice soothes her fury
as nothing else is able, almost as if it strokes her feathers. As to what's expected of him, I don't know. I've
never met a Harpy with a consort."

He arched a brow. "You've never had one? A consort,
I mean. And if you dare say chicken man…"

"No, no consort." Tyson had *not* delighted her Harpy,
that was for sure. She waved her fingers at the water.
"I earned it." The bottle was soaring through the air a
second later. Cold liquid splashed her arms when she
caught it. In seconds, she had the contents drained.

"Do Harpies have to obey their consorts?"

A laugh bubbled from her. "No. Do you honestly
think a Harpy has to obey anyone?"

He shrugged, and she caught a glimpse of both resolve and disappointment in his dark gaze.

"Why do you want to know?" she asked.

"Your sisters seemed to think…" A muscle ticked in
his jaw. "Never mind."

"What?"

His gaze became piercing. "Sure you want to know?"

"Yes."

"They think *I* am your consort."

Her chin hit her sternum, her mouth forming a wide
O. "What?" she repeated, sounding foolish even to her
own ears. "Why would they think that?" And why
hadn't they talked to *her* about it, rather than Sabin?

"I calm you. You want me." He was almost defensive.

But if he…if she…holy hell. He *did* calm her. From
the first, he'd calmed her. And she craved him, his

blood, his presence, his body. She'd been such a failure at everything else in the Harpy world that she'd
always figured a true consort wasn't in the cards for
her. Was it?

When Sabin wasn't with her, she was looking for
him. When he *was* with her, she wanted to be snuggled
up to him, enjoying him. She had shared her secrets
with him and wasn't sorry.

Anya had told her Sabin belonged to her, but Gwen
hadn't believed the goddess back then. Now…holy hell,
she thought again, dazed.

Was that why Sabin had been so distant with her?
He didn't want to be her consort? Her stomach twisted
painfully. "I don't…I don't know if I love you, though,"
she said, trying to give him an out.

Something dark filled his eyes. Something hard and
hot. "You don't have to love me." The word "yet" hung
between them, unsaid but there all the same.

Did *he* love *her?* It was almost too much to hope for.
Because, if he loved her, he would have touched her
again. Right? "Let's talk about the war," she found herself saying, rather than asking what she really wanted
to know: *Why haven't you made love to me?* "Won't be
as uncomfortable."

He sighed. "Have it your way, then. I didn't go to
Chicago with the others, so I've been taking names from
scrolls that list other demon-possessed immortals out
there, looking for them in the books Lucien collected
over the years and trying to learn about them."

He'd stayed for her. She knew that, and couldn't stop
the delight that spread through her. Perhaps he didn't
hate the thought of being her consort, after all. "Found
anything?"

"I recognized a lot of the names from my days in the heavens. Most of the prisoners in Tartarus were placed there by me and the other Lords, so we won't be their favorite people. Might be best if we just hunt them down and kill them, so they don't help Galen. Then again, he helped lock them away, too, back when he was one of us, so maybe it's moot." He paused, sighed again. "Look, I brought up the consort thing because I wanted to talk to you about something."

Disappointment and eagerness dueled for supremacy. Eagerness won. She straightened, ears perking. This was clearly an important subject to him. "I'm listening."

Motions stiff, he dug into the cooler and withdrew another water.

"Payment?" she asked with a laugh. "I've already agreed to help you. No need to pay me."

Silent, he popped the lid and drained the contents.

Her grin faded, the silence edged with tension. "What's going on?"

He fell back against the tree, looking everywhere but at her. "When the time comes for battle, and it will, sooner rather than later, I want you to stay here, away from the action."

Yeah. Right. She laughed again, her humor restored. "Funny."

"I'm serious. I have your sisters. I don't need you."

But…he couldn't mean this. Could he? This driven warrior would use anyone against the Hunters, would not be happy with three Harpies when he could have four. Right?

"I would never joke about something like this," he added.

No, he wouldn't. Just then it felt as if a thousand of

Sabin's daggers were stabbing at her chest, each of them aimed for her heart. Several of them succeeded in puncturing the organ, for it throbbed and burned. "But you said you needed me. You did everything in your power to enlist my aid. I've been training. I've improved."

He scoured a hand down his face, looking exhausted all of a sudden. "I did say that. You have improved."

"But?"

"Damn it!" he suddenly growled, fist slamming into the ground. "*I'm* not ready for you to spring into active duty."

"I don't understand. What's going on? What changed your mind like this?" It would have taken something major, she knew.

"I just…damn it," he repeated. "Whatever goes down in Chicago will surely infuriate the Hunters. Look what happened after Egypt. They'll come here. They'll try to retaliate. I won't be able to concentrate with you by my side. All right? I'll worry. I'll be distracted. And my distraction will place my men at risk."

Gwen didn't know where she found the strength, but she pushed to her feet. Her eyes narrowed. He would worry. The female in her liked the thought of that. A lot. The blossoming warrior, the Harpy she now *wanted* to be, hated it, burning away the joy. She would never again be a coward.

"You can train yourself not to worry, then, because I'm joining you. It's my right."

He jumped to his feet, too, nostrils flared, hands fisted. "And it's my right as your lover—*consort,* to dispatch your enemy for you."

"I never said you were my consort. So you listen up. I've waited my entire life to be something. To prove myself. You will not take this away from me. I won't let you!"

"No, he won't," Taliyah suddenly interjected. She stood off to the side, Kaia and Bianka beside her. Each radiated fury. "No one stops a Harpy. No one."

"Big mistake, Doubt," Kaia told him. "Too bad—we were actually starting to like you."

"I knew eavesdropping was the smart thing to do," Bianka said through clenched teeth. "You might be wonderfully vicious, but you're still a man and we know better than to trust anything male. Look what happened the last time Gwen went down that road."

Taliyah ran her tongue over her straight, white teeth. "Gwen finally gave you what you wanted, and you decided you didn't want it anymore. Typical."

"Gwen," Kaia said. "Come. We're leaving the fortress. We'll take care of the Hunters on our own."

"No," Sabin said. "There'll be none of that."

For what seemed an eternity, Gwen simply stared over at him, silently begging him to tell her sisters they were wrong. Doubts consumed her, doubts that were all her own. Was he doing this to protect her, because he cared? Or did he simply have no faith in her abilities, even after all her hard work? Or was he planning to do something that would upset her—something with a female Hunter—and he didn't want her to witness it?

Or was his demon ruling his mind? If so, there had to be a way to combat it.

"Sabin," she said, hoping. "Let's talk this—"

"I want you to stay within these walls," he said flatly. "At all times."

"You'll leave me here, but you'll utilize my sisters, right?"

"Two of them. One will stay with you."

The women in question laughed. "As if," they said in unison.

Gwen raised her chin, glaring over at him. "They won't help you without me. Still think to leave me?"

"Yes." No hesitation.

How could he do this? How, when he'd worked so hard to win her and her sisters to his cause? Bile rose in her throat, burning like acid. "Do you want to win your war? Finally? Because you could. With us, with *all* of us, you very well could."

Silence. A silence that made her feel like she was being force-fed disappointment, regret and sadness, one rancid spoonful at a time.

"Gwen," Taliyah said, sharply this time. "Come."

Betrayed to her very soul, Gwen turned away from Sabin and followed her sisters.

CHAPTER TWENTY-ONE

CHICAGO WAS COOL and just a little windy. Still, the sun was like a glaring eye, following Gideon's every move. But he liked the towering buildings and the closeness of the water; one gave him the feel of being in a big city and the other a beach. The best of two worlds.

He and the other warriors had been here several days, yet had only now found the facility they'd come for. Somehow they'd passed it over and over again. Maybe because the numbers were off, or maybe because the twenty or so red brick buildings around it were exact copies of one another. Thin but tall, at least fourteen stories, two square windows on each floor.

Despite the fact that it was so well hidden, they should not have walked past it over and over again like they had. Made him wonder if something else was going on, something more than his "maybes." Something like magic.

A protective spell, perhaps? He'd met a few witches over the years and knew they were a powerful race. Though why any would choose to work with the Hunters was beyond him.

Finally, they'd come up with the brilliant idea of leaving Lucien out here alone, in spirit form, waiting for a Hunter to pass him. Hence another delay—Hunters weren't always easy to spot, their clothes normal, their weapons hidden—so Lucien had followed many a human. His efforts eventually paid off and Lucien spotted a likely candidate venturing inside a building none of them had noticed—or if they had, they didn't remember. Lucien had tagged the building with a small smear of his own blood, something Anya could track with her eyes closed.

Now everyone was settled across the street from it, hidden inside a construction site and peering through thick wooden beams as workers bustled behind them. A few people had possessed the courage to ask them to leave. A rose-scented, mismatched-eyes-swirling hypno-suggestion from Lucien, and everyone had forgotten they were even here. Gideon could scream, and they wouldn't even blink.

Gideon wanted a power like that. Or maybe a super rage like Maddox, who could rip the world to shreds just because he was pissed. Maybe the ability to read people's minds like Amun. Or to enjoy every cut, slash and injury inflicted upon him like Reyes. Or even to screw like a monkey like Paris. Or fly like Aeron. Or win everything like Strider. Or—he could name something he envied about every Lord of the Underworld. Even Cameo, the epitome of Misery. She could clear a room just by speaking. She could send grown men to their knees, sobbing like babies.

What could Gideon do? He could lie, that's what. And it sucked ass. (That was not a lie.) He couldn't tell a woman she was pretty unless she was ugly. He couldn't tell his friends he loved them. He had to tell them he hated them. He couldn't tell Hunters they were shitbags. He had to tell them they were sweetie pies.

Talk about a nightmare—which of course he'd have to call a dream come true.

And yet, through it all, he couldn't regret the fact that he was a demon-possessed warrior. He wore it like a badge of pride. He would have liked to act as if it disgusted him, which would have given him something in common with the others—all but Sabin and Strider, that is—but he never lied to himself.

Sometimes he thought he was the only warrior who *welcomed* his curse. There was nothing wrong with having a demon inside you. Nothing wrong with enjoying it, being glad you weren't alone—not that his demon ever spoke to him like the others' spoke to them. No, his was more a…presence in the back of his mind. Nothing wrong with being happy you were more powerful. But damn it, would it have killed the gods to stick him with Rage or Nightmare? Okay, now Nightmare would have been freaking awesome. Having the ability to turn Hunters' nightmares into reality would be the sweetest kind of heaven.

Suddenly a pang of longing swept through him and he blinked in surprise. Longing? For what? The ability? Or the demon itself?

Gideon waved the odd sensation aside. He didn't know if Nightmare had even been inside the box—there was another pang.

"We've been watching the place for over an hour, our guy has already left empty-handed and there's been no other movement. I think it's abandoned," Anya said, and there was a rare trace of confusion in her tone. "But I'm sensing chaos. A freaking lot of chaos." Chaos was the strongest source of her power, so if anyone would recognize it, it was this beautiful goddess.

"Couldn't possibly be witches and their spells," Gideon said.

Anya gasped. "Witches. Of course. Why didn't I think of that? I've had a run-in or two thousand with them over the years. Talk about abusers of power," she grumbled. "Wonder how they'll feel when I abuse mine and use their black hearts as our table's new centerpiece."

"Perhaps I should ghost inside," Lucien said. He would be invisible to those around him and could check things out without fear of being spotted.

"No. We talked about this," Anya said determinedly. She shook her head. Gideon stood on her right side, and felt the silky swish of her hair. "Something's wonky with that building, and I don't even want your spirit in it. And now that witches might be involved...hell, no."

Gideon adored women, and felt his skin heat at the brush of her hair. Last time he'd been with a woman had been mere hours after he'd returned from Egypt. The women of Buda knew, on some level, that he and the other Lords were different. They were considered "angels." He hadn't had to speak, just crook his finger, and this one had come running. But she wasn't enough to soothe the ache inside him. They were never enough.

"So let's keep standing here, doing nothing," he said. Which meant, let's raid the place, guns blazing, and well his friends knew it. They were well-versed in Gideon Speak. They had to be.

If he even attempted to utter a truth, any kind of truth, sharp pain burned through him. Pain far worse than one person should ever have to endure. Like knives dipped in acid, covered in salt and topped off with venom, then stabbed into his gut and raked all the way from his brain to his feet over and over again.

"We didn't survive a bomb a while back," he added, because yeah, they had. Only a few months had passed since the blast in question and he still remembered the shock and pain of it. But he would willingly endure it again. Too long had passed since he'd sunk his blade or fired off a round into his enemy. The dry spell made him twitchy. "So we damn sure can't survive anything else they throw at us. Even spells."

Gideon was proof the Lords could not only survive a bunch of shit but also come out grinning. Once, Hunters managed to capture and imprison him. The next three months of his life had been torture. Literally. He would rather have roasted in hell than endure the poking, prodding, testing and beatings that took him to the brink of death, only to be revived so that he could be beaten again.

Sabin had found and saved him, actually carting Gideon over his shoulder because Gideon had been unable to walk. They'd just cut off his feet to watch them regenerate. Perhaps that was why Gideon loved the warrior so much. Would do anything for him. *I'll kill a few Hunters just for him.* That Sabin wasn't here, when the boss man lived for this kind of shit…

It was the Harpy's fault, he was sure. Never had Sabin been so obsessed with a woman, locking himself away with her, ignoring his duties. Gideon was glad his friend had found someone, but unsure what it meant for their war.

"I have an idea," Strider said. Strider always had ideas. Since victory was necessary for his continued good health, he often planned and strategized for hours, days, weeks before marching into battle. "Ashlyn found the immortals for the Hunters. Hell, she probably found the witches for them. So we'll just have her find one for us. Our witch can undo whatever spell their witch cast, if it's actually a spell we're dealing with, and boom, victory."

"Time is not our friend right now. We need these kids out of our enemy's hands. We need to return to searching for the box," Lucien said.

"But, baby," Anya said, worry in her voice.

"I'll be fine, love. I won your heart, I can do anything." Lucien kissed her, lingering despite the urgency in his tone, before disappearing completely. The human workers continued to bustle around them, oblivious. If they could see and hear the warriors, they gave no indication.

Anya sighed, dreaming. "Gods, that man revs my engine."

Reyes chuckled.

Strider rolled his eyes.

Amun remained as stoic as ever.

No, not stoic, Gideon thought. But edged with something dark. Lines of tension branched from the man's dark eyes and set mouth. His shoulders were stiff, as though the muscles were knotted. The last trip inside the mind of that Hunter in the pyramid must have really messed him up.

If there were anything Gideon could do to help him, he would do it. Gideon loved the silent giant. No one was kinder, no one was more caring. As Gideon had recovered from his footbotomy, Amun had been the one to bring him food, make sure his bandages were clean and even carry him outside for fresh air.

Not knowing what else to do, he switched places with Strider so that he was standing next to Amun, and slapped the big guy on the back. Amun didn't face him, but his lips did twitch into a small smile.

"Quick, someone distract me," Anya said. "I'm bored."

Everyone groaned. A bored Anya was a troublesome Anya. But Gideon knew the truth. He still heard the worry in the goddess's voice. She didn't like to be parted from Lucien.

"We totally could *not* play How Am I Going To Kill The Hunters," he suggested.

"I'll stab them," Reyes said instantly, the gleam in his dark eyes ferocious.

"I'll shoot them," Strider replied. "In the groin."

"I'll snap their necks," Anya said, rubbing her palms together, "then make them watch me cut out their intestines." She'd do it, too. Anyone who threatened Lucien ended up on her Must Torture list. "No need to tell us you'd *kiss* them, Gideon. We already know."

A symphony of chuckles abounded.

So much for trying to be kind to Anya. He flipped each one of them off.

"I know what we can do," Reyes said. Normally he had a dagger in each hand and was cutting himself as he spoke. Not today. Not while parted from Danika. That was a pain all its own, he often said. "Let's take bets on how Sabin's doing with the Harpy."

"Man has balls, that's for sure," Strider said. "Gwen's pretty, but anyone who can rip out your throat…" He shuddered.

"Hey!" Anya leveled them with a scowl. "That wasn't Gwen's fault. Not that I think there's anything wrong with performing a throat extraction on a Hunter. Anyway, the way I hear it, she was scared. You don't scare a Harpy and live to brag. That's, like, one of the first things they teach you in deity school. The entire race is just violent by nature. I mean, you've met Gwen's sisters, right?"

This time, *everyone* shuddered.

"Sabin is a lucky bastard," Gideon said.

Anya's gaze locked on him, but her expression was suddenly dazed, as if she saw past him. A hum of power drifted from her, wrapping around him, squeezing. When she focused, a smile bloomed. "Better watch it," she said. "Or you're going to be fated to love a female far worse than a Harpy. The gods are fun that way."

The heat drained from his cheeks, and he clenched his hands into fists. "Do you know something?" She was a goddess and potentially privy to information they weren't.

"Maybe," she said with a dainty shrug.

"Don't you dare tell me!" He loved women, he did. But take one permanently, when a single one had never truly satisfied him? Hell, no. Violent as his life was, he needed something extreme to push him over the edge. When his partners asked how to please him, he had to tell them the opposite. How much worse would it be if he were strapped with a single female? He would never get sex the way he truly craved, not even accidentally.

"I'd absolutely tell you if I knew."

She was lying. He knew she was. Lying was a passion of hers. How did Lucien stand her? *Hey, wait a sec,* he thought, disgusted.

Suddenly Lucien materialized, his scarred face confused as everyone crowded around him. "The place is furnished but abandoned. No paperwork, but I did see clothing strewn about. Sizes only children can wear. Must have left in a hurry."

Frowning, Strider rubbed his temple. "That means we're too late, that we made the trip for nothing."

"There are strange markings on the wall, though," the scarred warrior added. "I could not decipher them. I want to flash you in one at a time so if the outside area is still being monitored, we won't be spotted. Surely someone among us will have seen the markings before and know what they mean."

Didn't take long. Within five minutes they were inside the building. Gideon was swaying from dizziness—flashing sucked—Strider was laughing, Reyes pale and clutching his stomach, Anya dancing around the empty room, and Amun staring into the distance.

"This way," Lucien said.

They stalked down narrow corridors, their booted footsteps echoing. Gideon traced a finger over the wall; it was painted a sickening gray. That had been the color of his cell while in captivity. The only furniture he'd been given was a bed with wrist and ankle straps.

Bad memories. He didn't like to venture down that brain path unless he was in the middle of a fight. Helped channel his rage. He looked around. There were multiple bedrooms. Well, they were more like barracks, with fifteen beds to a space. There were also what appeared to be classrooms.

Left, right, right, left and they entered a gymnasium, everyone remaining on guard. One wall was mirrored with a bar in front of it. For…ballet? he wondered. Of course, he thought next. Killers could be more effective when they were flexible.

Three of the walls were gray, just like the hall. But the last was painted in a multitude of colors. Gideon couldn't make out a single picture, only sharp, jagged lines and sweeping arches. They were a mess.

"It's lovely," he muttered.

"It's also a spell, as we suspected," Anya replied.

Bodies closed around him. Fingers were soon tracing, eyes following, searching for patterns.

"I've seen this before," Reyes said darkly. "In the books I used to learn more about Anya."

When Anya had first come to them, no one had known if she meant them harm. Not their fault, either. The woman was renowned throughout the ages for the trouble she caused.

"Oh, Panie. Your interest still flatters me, but really, get over your crush. I'm taken. Now about the spell. They definitely used the old language," she said. "Though they added their own flair, and I'm having trouble deciphering certain words. That one means dark, that one means power, and that one...helpless, I think."

"I don't want to leave now," Gideon said, spine suddenly tingling in warning. Danger was nearby.

Reyes sighed. "The lying is already getting on my nerves."

"I care. I do," Gideon told him dryly. "My heart is actually hurting for you. And just so you know, I can go without lying just like you can go without cutting yourself."

Another sigh. Then, "Sorry," Reyes said. "I shouldn't have gone there. Lie all you want."

"I won't."

Strider belted out a laugh and slapped him on the shoulder.

Gideon knew he was annoying. He did. But he couldn't stop.

Suddenly Anya, who had been muttering under her breath, reading, gasped. "Oh my gods." One step, two, she backed away from the wall. She was trembling, and in all the weeks Gideon had known her, all the battles they'd fought together, he'd never seen the courageous female tremble. "Flash us, Lucien. Now. All of us, if possible."

Lucien didn't hesitate, didn't waste time asking why. He stalked to her and wrapped his arms around her, clearly intending to flash her first—because whether she knew it or not, he couldn't transport more than he could touch. But it was too late. Dark, metal shades fell over the room's two windows, drowning out all hint of light.

Down the hall, he could hear the same shades closing over the other windows.

Gideon spun around, palming his daggers. He wanted to lash out, but it was now so dark he couldn't even see his hand in front of his face, much less his friends. He didn't want to cut the wrong person.

"Lucien," Anya cried.

"I'm here, baby, but I can't flash. I can't seem to force my body to dematerialize anymore." Lucien had never sounded so grim. "It's like there's some sort of a magnetic shield locking my spirit to my body."

"There is," Anya said. "Magic. I activated it the rest of the way when I read the spell aloud."

There was an ominous pause as everyone digested

that, realization bubbling in Gideon's throat, practically choking him.

"What do the designs mean?" Strider finally asked.

"Most of it is the spell, locking us in the dark, our powers gone, our bodies helpless. The last line, though, is a message to all of you. It says, Welcome to hell, Lords of the Underworld. You'll be here until you die."

CHAPTER TWENTY-TWO

THE FIRST WOMAN Aeron had found for Paris, the warrior had previously slept with. Not that Paris had known it by looking at her. His body's lack of response had given him away. So back to town she'd gone. Since receiving his demon, Paris had only once gotten hard for the same woman twice. And that was the female who had died and couldn't be reborn. *Because of me.*

The second woman Aeron had found for his friend had been a no go, as well. Same reason. The third had been a tourist, new to town, and had thankfully never crossed paths with the warrior. Aeron had abducted her right out of her hotel room while she slept so that his tattooed face and inhuman wings wouldn't frighten her. She'd woken up next to Paris and when she'd glimpsed his pretty face, she'd climbed on board for the ride of her life.

Today, Aeron was flying his friend into town. No more taking females back and forth. It was a waste of time. This way, Paris could choose whom he wanted and Aeron could quickly and efficiently procure her for him. The two could have their fun in Gilly's apartment, the safest place Aeron knew of, since Torin had the entire building wired like a maximum security prison to keep Danika's young friend safe. Aeron hadn't liked it when she had moved out of the fortress—she was too fragile, too skittish—but the warriors freaked her out and time hadn't calmed her. Aeron would take her to the coffee shop across the street, if she'd let him, and keep her company while they waited.

A perfect plan. Well, as perfect as he could work it.

If only Paris and the Harpies had gotten along. But Promiscuity had taken one look at the beautiful women and deemed them "too much effort." Aeron supposed he knew the feeling. He himself hadn't enjoyed a female in over a hundred years, and he wouldn't enjoy one for a hundred more. If ever. As he'd told his sweet Legion, they were simply too weak, too easily destroyed, while he would most likely live forever.

He wasn't sure he could survive having to watch another loved one die.

Speaking of loved ones, had Legion returned to hell? Was she in danger? She wasn't happy unless she was with Aeron and he wasn't complete unless she was perched on his shoulders.

The so-called angel hadn't visited him in days. Hopefully, she was gone for good and Legion would return.

He leaned to the left, turning smoothly. Pinks and purples streaked the sky, the sun setting perfectly. Wind whipped across his scalp, his hair too short to ruffle. Paris's, though, continually slapped his cheeks. The warrior was cradled against his chest, arms wrapped around his back, under his wings.

He remained low and in the shadows, out of view.

"I don't want to do this," Paris said flatly.

"Too bad. You need it."

"What are you? My pimp now?"

"If I have to be. Look, you found a woman you could

bed more than once. Surely you can find another. We just have to look for her."

"Damn you! That's like telling a man whose arm has been chopped off that you'll sew someone else's on him. It's not going to be the same. It won't be the right color, the right length. Nothing will be as perfect as the other."

"Then I'll petition Cronus for Sienna's return. You said her soul is in the heavens, yes?"

"Yes," was the grudging response. "He'll say no. He said I had a choice, and if I didn't pick her he would ensure she never returned to earth. He's probably already killed her. Again."

"I can sneak into the heavens. I can search for her."

There was a long pause, as though Paris was considering his words. "You could be caught, imprisoned. Then my sacrifice would be in vain. Just…forget about Sienna."

Problem was, Aeron couldn't forget about her until Paris did. He was going to have to ponder this, decide how to proceed. All he knew was that he wanted his friend back. The laughing, carefree warrior who had a smile for everyone.

"City's crowded tonight," he observed, hoping to bring them to a safer topic.

"Yes."

"Wonder what's going on." The moment he'd spoken, he experienced a twinge of dread. Last time it had been this crowded, the Hunters had invaded. He studied the people below more closely, looking for the telltale sign of the Hunters. A tattoo of infinity. But these people were wearing watches, long sleeves, and he couldn't see their wrists. Besides, while he knew Hunters were proud of their brands, he also knew they could have started hiding them, marking themselves in discreet locations. Would have been the smart thing to do. "I'm sorry, but we need to go back to the fortress."

"Good."

Aeron was already heavily armed, and he never minded fighting on his own, but he had Paris with him. Paris, who was still fuzzed from those massive amounts of ambrosia and would be more a hindrance than a help.

"Wait. Stop!" Paris had tensed against him, and his tone had been disbelieving, hopeful and dripping with wonder.

"What?"

"I think I saw…I think…Sienna." He said her name as if it was a prayer.

"How is that possible?" Aeron scanned the ground. There were so many faces and he was moving so quickly, he couldn't really distinguish one from another. But if Paris *had* seen Sienna, if she was somehow once again alive, then Hunters were definitely here. "Where?"

"Back. Go back. She was heading south." There was so much excitement in Paris's voice, Aeron couldn't resist.

Despite the danger, he turned. He wanted to toss out a warning, *don't get your hopes up,* but couldn't. Stranger things had happened.

Suddenly Paris jerked, grunted. "Find shelter! *Now!*"

Aeron felt something warm and wet slide over his arms where he gripped Paris's waist. Then a barrage of arrows pierced Aeron's wings, tearing the membrane. His arms and legs were next, the muscles ripped open, the bones nicked. As he jerked in pain, understanding dawned. Hunters were indeed here, and they'd spotted him. Had probably been watching and waiting for just such an opportunity.

My fault, he thought. *Again.* He began to fall...fall... twisting and turning. Crashing.

TORIN LEANED BACK in his chair, hands locked behind his head, feet propped on his desk. He'd been glued here for days, barely leaving to eat, shower or, hell, live. Cameo hadn't come to see him since the night of her return, and maybe that was for the best. He couldn't concentrate when she was near and he had more work on his plate than ever before.

He kept the warriors well-moneyed, playing with stocks and bonds. He monitored the surrounding area for intruders. He made all travel arrangements. He researched any leads on Pandora's box, the artifacts or the Hunters. He was even scouring news sites for any sign of a man-with-wings sighting. Aka Galen. To the best of Torin's knowledge, Galen and Aeron were the only warriors who possessed the means of flight.

Torin didn't mind his many jobs because he had the time to do it all; he never left the fortress. To do so could quite possibly kill everyone in the world. *So dramatic,* he thought dryly. But true. One touch of his skin against another's was all that was needed to jumpstart a plague. Last one he'd started, thanks to the Hunters, had been here in Buda. At least it had been contained by doctors before it could do too much damage.

But, oh, how he wanted to touch Cameo. Would have given anything for the chance. He pictured her in his mind. Small, slender, that long dark hair, those sad gray eyes.

Would he still want her if he could have his pick of

women? he found himself wondering for the thousandth time that day. Would he still want her if he could touch anyone he wished? Go into town anytime? As a man, yeah, he'd want her. She was pretty, smart, amusing if you got past her suicidal voice. But anything permanent? He just didn't know. Because…his gaze strayed to the monitor to his left.

Every so often he would catch a glimpse of a beautiful woman walking through town. Long black hair, exotic eyes that were bright one moment and glazed the next. She'd pause in her stride, smile, frown, then kick back into gear. When the wind caressed her, ruffling her hair, Torin would catch the barest hint of…pointed ears? Whether he was seeing things or not, the sight of those ears made him hard as a rock. He had the strangest urge to lick them.

She wore a T-shirt that said Nixie's IAD House O' Fun, and she had earbuds in her ears. What was a Nixie? A quick Google search and he figured it—she?—was some sort of Immortal After Dark. Interesting. Because he'd like nothing more than to explore her after dark.

What type of music was she listening to? Judging by the brisk nod of her head, it was something fast and hard. Where had she come from? What *was* she? *Delicious, I bet…*

Lusting after the strange woman had shaken him, sent those questions about Cameo spiraling through him. If he could desire another, he wasn't in love with Cameo. And if he wasn't in love with her, was it cruel of him to mess around with her? Would he eventually hurt her? Hurt himself?

He'd never be able to touch her, and as passionate as she was, she would eventually need a man who could.

He'd never had to worry about these things before because he'd never been with a woman. Not even before his possession. He'd been too busy then, too involved in his job. Maybe he needed to join Workaholics Anonymous, he thought dryly. He had to be the only millennia-old virgin in history.

One of his monitors flashed, and he gave it a detailed scan. Nothing out of the ordinary. No sign of his pointy-eared brunette, either. Another question popped into his head: if Cameo weren't worried about her demon inflicting untold misery upon a human, would she have chosen another man to dally with?

At the thought of her with another man, there was no intense surge of jealousy, as a taken male should feel. Okay, so there was more confirmation. Much as he adored her, much as he craved her sexually, much as he couldn't resist her when she stepped inside this room, he wouldn't have chosen her had circumstances been different.

Damn. What kind of moron was he?

To his right, there was a flash of azure light. Torin twisted to face it, dread already pooling in his stomach. Cronus.

Sure enough, when the light faded, the god king was standing in the middle of Torin's bedroom. "Hello again, Disease," said that imperial voice. A white robe draped one of Cronus's deceptively fragile-looking shoulders and flowed to his ankles. On his feet were leather sandals. What always struck Torin was the claw-like curve of the immortal's toenails. They just didn't fit with the man's old world nobility.

"Your Lordship." Torin didn't stand, as he knew Cronus expected. Already this god had too much power over him and his friends. He would keep what he could. Even this, so small a thing.

"Have you been searching for the possessed prisoners as I commanded?"

Torin studied him more intently. Something was different about the god. He looked…younger, maybe. His silver beard wasn't as thick as usual, and there were streaks of blond mixed with his white hair. If the heavenly sovereign had been going for Botox and highlights, he should have had time for a pedicure.

"Well?"

Wait. What did Cronus want to know? Oh, yeah. "Some of the warriors have been searching for them, yes."

A muscle ticked in the king's jaw. "Not good enough. I want the other possessed men and women found as soon as possible."

Well, Torin wanted to touch a female skin to skin without killing her, or in the case of an immortal, ruining the rest of her endless existence. Not everyone got what they wanted, did they? "Our hands are a little full at the moment."

Silver eyes narrowed on him. "Un-fill them."

As if it were that easy. "Wouldn't matter if I had all the time in the world. Some of the names have been removed from the list, so there's no way I'll be able to find them all."

There was a pause. Then, "I removed them. You did not need those names."

O-kay. "Why?"

"So many questions, demon. So little action. Find the possessed or suffer my wrath. That is all you need know. I am not asking for the impossible. I have given you the names you require. Now all you must do is find them. You can identify them by the butterflies tattooed on their bodies." There at the end, the god's tone had been dry. Almost...amused.

Again, as if it were that easy. "Why butterflies, anyway?" he grumbled, knowing it would do no good to argue. No one was more stubborn than Cronus. But he also knew that Cronus needed him to find and contain Galen. What he didn't know—what nobody knew—was why the god king couldn't do so on his own. Cronus wasn't exactly forthcoming.

"Many reasons."

"I'm un-filling my time, as commanded, so I've got enough to spare to listen to every one of those reasons."

Cronus's jaw clenched. "Someone considers himself more useful than he actually is, I see."

"My apologies," he said through gritted teeth. "I am lower than low, a nothing, unneeded, useless."

Cronus inclined his head in acknowledgment. "As my pet so quickly learned his place, I will give him a reward. You wish to know about the butterflies. Butterflies my children, the Greeks, bestowed upon you."

Torin nodded stiffly, not daring to speak lest he talk the god out of this boon.

"Before your possession, you were limited in what you could do, where you could go. Trapped in a cocoon, you could say. Now look at you." He waved his hand along Torin's body. "You emerged as something dark but beautiful. That's why I would have chosen the mark, at least. My children, well..." He opened his mouth to say more, paused, and then his head tilted to the side. "You have another visitor. Next time *I* visit you, Disease, I expect results. Or you will not find me so lenient." And then the god was gone and there was a knock at the door.

Torin flicked a glance to the monitor at his left. Cameo waved up at him, as if his earlier thoughts had summoned her. He shoved Cronus and the god's warnings to the back of his mind. He planned to help the king, but he would not jump when the bastard said jump. Pet, indeed.

Body still prepped and ready because of the glimpses he'd gotten of Lickable Ears, he pressed the button that unlocked his door. Cameo sailed inside, closing the wood behind her with a determined click. He swiveled in his chair, studying her with new understanding. Her color was high, pretty, and tension hummed from her. But that was all. Tension. The need for release.

No, she wouldn't have chosen him, either.

"Let me ask you a question," he said, twining his fingers over his middle.

Her hips swayed as she approached him, and her lips curled into a slow smile. "All right." She'd probably meant to sound husky, sexy, but that tragic voice only reached I-might-not-kill-myself-after-all.

"Why me? You could have any man here."

That had her grinding to a stop. Then her smile inched into a frown as she hopped onto the edge of his desk, out of reach, legs swinging. "You really want to talk about this?"

"Yes."

"It won't be pleasant."

"What is, these days?"

"Okay, then. You understand me, my demon. My curse."

"So do the others here."

Her fingers twisted in her lap. "Again, I have to ask if you really want to go there. Especially since we could be doing something else…"

Did he? It might alter the good thing they had going. Pleasure for both of them. Pleasure he wouldn't—and couldn't—get anywhere else. "Yeah. I want to go there." *Idiot.* But every day he saw Maddox and Ashlyn, Lucien and Anya, Reyes and Danika, and now Sabin and the Harpy, and he wanted something like that for himself.

Not that he could ever have it. He'd tried once, about four hundred years ago. All he'd had to do to ruin it was take off his gloves, caress his would-be-lover's face— and then watch her die the next day, her body ravaged by the disease he'd given her.

He couldn't go through that again.

Since then, he'd purposely stayed away from all things female. Until Cameo. She was the first woman he'd looked at, truly looked at, in too many years to count.

Her gaze darted away from him. "You're here. You never leave. You won't be killed in a battle. The man I loved was taken from me, tortured by my enemy and sent back in pieces. I don't have to worry about that with you. And I like you. I really do."

But she didn't love him, and the potential for love, the forever, die-without-you kind of love, anyway, wasn't there.

And wasn't that just about on par with the rest of his life?

"So…do you want to stop?" she asked softly.

He glanced at the monitor again. No sign of his pointy-eared babe. "Do I look stupid?"

A laugh escaped her, chasing away her sadness. "Good. We'll continue on as we have been. Right?"

"Right. But what happens when you meet a man you could love?"

She bit her bottom lip and shrugged. "We'll stop." She didn't ask him the same question. Except, of course, switching "man" for "woman." Both of them knew he'd never meet a woman who could live with him in any sense of the word.

One of his computers beeped, catching his attention. He straightened, scanning until he found the proper screen. A breath whistled from between his teeth. "Holy hell, I did it!"

"What?" Cameo asked.

"I found Galen. And, shit, you aren't going to believe where he is."

"You're not leaving me," Sabin told Gwen. Then, to her sisters, he said, "You're not taking her away from me." They'd spent the last hour packing their stuff—and some of his—and were now standing in the foyer of the fortress.

They were ready to leave, but Gwen kept stalling, "remembering" something she'd left in his room.

He knew the Harpies meant to take her away, for now and always. Right in front of him, they'd talked about how they didn't want him around Gwen anymore. They thought she was breaking too many rules, softening too much for a man who could never place her first on his list of priorities. More than that, they didn't like that he'd made love to her out in the open, where anyone, even an enemy, could have snuck up on him.

They liked him, appreciated what he'd done to

toughen Gwen up—that had been admitted grudg-ingly—but still considered him bad for her. And not the good kind of bad.

Hearing them talk, thinking about being without her, was screwing with his head. He *couldn't* be without her. *Wouldn't* be without her. He wouldn't lose her to her sisters and he damn sure wouldn't lose her to his war. He needed her.

"We'll do anything we damn well please," Bianka said, her tone daring him to contradict her again. "Soon as Gwen finds her…whatever she mentioned this time… we're gone."

"We'll see about that." His phone beeped, signaling a message. Frowning, he withdrew the device from his pocket. A text from Torin.

Galen in Buda. With an army. Prepare.

Then Cameo was racing down the stairs. "Did you hear?" she demanded.

"Yeah."

"What?" the Harpies asked. Even though they were planning to leave, they still felt entitled to know his business. Figured.

"He probably never left," Cameo continued as if they hadn't spoken. She stopped in front of him. "He's probably been here the whole time, waiting, watching, growing his numbers. And now that we're down half *our* number…"

"Shit." Sabin scoured his face with a hard hand. "What better time to punish us for what happened in Egypt. And let's not forget he wants those women back." Gwen included.

"Yeah. Torin's alerting the others," she said. "They're

not headed here, at least, but they are assembling in town."

"What the hell is going on?" Bianka demanded.

"Hunters are here and ready for battle," Sabin told her. "You said you'd fight for me, help me defeat them. Well, now's your chance." First, though, he had to figure out what to do about Gwen while he—they?—were gone. If they dared try to abscond with her while his back was turned...

A snarl rose in his throat, tickling his voice box.

And yeah, the thought of leaving a strong, capable warrior behind was foreign to him. Even straight-up ridiculous. Especially since he'd thought to send Gwen into battle from the very beginning. But he wasn't going to change his mind. Somehow, some way, Gwen had become the most important thing in his life.

He'd left her alone these past few days, trying to diminish her importance to him, as well as straighten out his priorities. Hadn't worked. She'd become more important—and his number one priority.

Just then Kane rushed past them. He was carrying the still-broken portrait of Galen that Danika had painted, one half in each hand.

"What are you doing with that?" Sabin called.

"Torin wants me to lock it up," was the reply. "Just in case."

Gaping, Kaia grabbed Kane by the arm, stopping him. "How did you get that? I hope you know you're going to pay for breaking it, you bast—" She released him with a yelp and rubbed her palm. "How the hell did you shock me like that?"

"I have no—"

"Oh, my God!" Gwen pounded down the steps, her

gaze riveted on the portrait. Her skin was pale, her mouth hanging open. "How did you get that?"

"What's wrong?" Sabin crossed the threshold to stand beside her. He wrapped an arm around her waist. She was trembling.

Taliyah's cool gaze shot from Gwen to the portrait, the portrait to Gwen. She, too, was paling, her already pallid skin revealing deep blue veins. "We need to go," she said, and for the first time since Sabin had met her, there was emotion in her tone. Dread. Worry.

Bianka pounded forward and grabbed for Gwen's wrist. "Don't say a word. Let's get out of here, go home."

"Gwen," Sabin said, holding tight. What the hell was going on?

A tug-of-war began, but Gwen barely seemed to notice.

"My father," she finally said, the words so quiet he had to strain to hear.

"What about your father?" he prompted. She'd never spoken of the man before, so he'd just assumed whoever it was was not a part of her life.

"They don't like me to talk about him. He's not like us. But how did you get this? It was hanging in my room in Alaska."

"Wait." He glanced at the portrait. "Are you saying…"

"That man is my father, yes."

No. *No.* "That's not possible. Look more closely and you'll see that you're mistaken." *Be mistaken. Please be mistaken.* He gripped her shoulders and forced her to face the painting.

"I'm not mistaken. That's him. I never knew him,

but I've studied this painting my entire life." Her tone was wistful. "It's the only link I have to my good side."

"Impossible."

"Gwen!" the Harpies shouted as one. "Enough."

She ignored them. "I'm telling you, that's my father. Why? What's wrong with you? And how did you get the painting? Why is it broken?"

Another wave of denial burst through him, followed quickly by shock and more slowly by acceptance. With the acceptance came fury. So much fury, blended with the very dread and worry Taliyah had expressed. Galen was Gwen's father. Galen, his greatest enemy, the immortal responsible for the worst days of his long, long life, was Gwen's fucking father.

"Shit," Kane said. "Shit, shit, shit. This is bad. Very bad."

Sabin popped his jaw and did his best to gather his composure. "The portrait is hanging in your room? This exact portrait?"

She nodded. "My mother gave it to me. She painted it years ago, when she realized she carried me. She wanted me to see the angel, to want to be different from him."

"Gwen," Kaia snapped, pulling on her sister all the harder. "We told you to stop."

She didn't. It was as though the words were leaving her of their own free will, bottled up too long and spilling over. And maybe, having learned to fight, she was no longer afraid to stand up for what she desired. "She had a broken wing and crawled into a cave to heal. He was chasing a demon disguised as a human, a demon who ran inside that cave and tried to use her as a shield. He saved her, got rid of the demon.

"He doctored her, and she slept with him, even

though she hated what he was. She said she couldn't help herself, that she felt hopeful of a future with him. A future she had somehow convinced herself she wanted. Afterward, the dark-haired woman you see there arrived with a message, something about catching sight of a spirit, and he had to leave. He told her to wait, that he'd come back for her. But when he was gone, my mother regained her senses, realized she wanted nothing to do with a real live angel, and left. She's an artist, and when I was born she painted his portrait with the woman. The last vision she had of him was to be my first, she said."

Dear. Gods. "Do you know who your father is, Gwen?" he demanded.

Finally her eyes tore from the portrait and landed on him, confusion swimming in their depths. "Yes. An angel, like I said. An angel my mother seduced. That's why I'm the way I am. Weaker, less aggressive."

She wasn't that way any longer, but now was hardly the time to point that out. "Galen is no angel," Sabin said, his disgust loud and clear. "The man you're look-ing at, naming your father, is a demon, the keeper of Hope. I guarantee he's the reason your mother experi-enced that false sense of hope for a future with him and why she wised up so soon after he left."

A heavy gasp escaped her, and she shook her head violently. "No. No, that can't be right. If I possessed demon blood, I would have been strong like my sisters."

"You always were, you just refused to see it," Bianka said. "Mom beat down your confidence, is my guess."

Sabin closed his eyes, opened them. Why did this have to happen *now?*

"That man is just like me, except for one important distinction. He's the leader of the Hunters. He's responsible for the rape of those women. He's commander of the men who captured you. He's here, in Buda, and he's itching for battle." As he spoke, he realized his mistake. Delight sparked in her eyes at the knowledge that her father was nearby.

Not so long ago, Sabin had entertained the thought that the Hunters had planted her in that cell, thinking to use her as Bait to learn his secrets and lure him to his death. He'd discarded that thought immediately. He still discarded it, even though Doubt was shouting in his head, tossing out other possibilities.

She was more dangerous than Bait. Galen could play the father card to get her to betray Sabin.

Damn this!

"That just can't be right," Gwen repeated, delight replaced by disbelief as she faced her sisters. "I've never been like you, despite what Bianka said. I've always been too soft. Like an angel. How could my father be a demon? I would have been worse than you! Right? I mean…I can't…did you know anything about this?"

Ignoring her, Kaia stepped forward, getting in Sabin's face, placing them nose to nose. "You're lying. Much as we have always wished otherwise, her father is not a demon. And he's certainly not leading those Hunters. If Gwen were half demon, we would have known it. She wouldn't have—there's just been some sort of mistake. Gwen's father is not the leader of your enemy, so don't even think about hurting her!"

Gwen's goddamn father. The words echoed through his mind, though he almost couldn't process them. Any future he'd imagined with Gwen was most likely ruined. Even if she was completely innocent and hadn't aided her bastard of a father, which he knew she was,

Sabin planned to lock him away for eternity. How could she live with the warrior who'd imprisoned her father?

Besides, most people wouldn't turn on family, no matter the circumstances. He wouldn't. His friends—his makeshift family—were everything to him. Always had been. And it had to stay that way.

No matter how much his mind might be screaming not to do what he was now planning.

Gwen might not have aided her father, but that could change at any moment, now that she knew who he was. Fucking Fate!

"Maybe Kaia's right and you're mistaken," she said hopefully, clutching his shirt. "Maybe—"

"I spent a thousand years with that man, guarding the king of gods in the heavens. I spent a few thousand more hating him with every fiber of my being. I damn well know who he is."

"Why would a demon lead the Hunters? Why does he want to find the box that will destroy all of you if it will destroy him, too? Huh? Tell me that!"

"I don't know how he'll save himself. But I do know he's the reason we opened that damn box in the first place! He would do anything, even send his own daughter into our midst, to ruin us. And since our possession, he's fooled those humans into thinking he's an angel. That's how he's able to lead them."

She scrubbed a hand down her face, a mimic of him. "Maybe you're right about him, maybe you're wrong. Either way, I didn't know." Her eyes were luminous, even half-circled as they were by fading bruises. "And I didn't conspire against you."

He drew in a shuddering breath, released it. "I know you didn't."

"What is it, then? Do you think I'll aid him one day, now that I know who he is? I won't. I would never do that to you. Yeah, I'm leaving as planned," her voice broke at that, "because you don't trust me to fight with you. But you can trust me to keep your secrets safe."

"Save it," he said. "You're not going anywhere." And then he went for her wings.

CHAPTER TWENTY-THREE

A DUNGEON. SABIN had locked her in a freaking dungeon. Worse, he'd locked her in a dungeon next to the Hunters, who were moaning and crying and begging to be set free. And he'd done this after he'd bound her wings. *After* she'd trusted him with her secrets.

"I'm sorry," he'd said, and there'd been true remorse in his tone. "But this is for the best."

Like that mattered now.

She'd known he would do anything to win his war. She'd known it, hated it, yet she'd foolishly begun to believe his feelings had changed since he'd met her. He'd stayed with her, rather than go with his friends to Chicago. He'd taught her how to kick major ass. He'd asked her about a Harpy's consort, for gods' sake. And then he'd decided to leave her behind, and she hadn't known if it was because he cared or because he had no faith in her ability.

Now she knew. He hadn't cared. He thought her father was his enemy, thought *she* was his enemy.

Was she?

If he was right and the man in the portrait was Galen, leader of the Hunters, then Galen was indeed her father. She'd spent days, months, years staring at that same likeness: same pale hair and sky-colored eyes, same strong shoulders and white wings. Same broad back and carved chin. She'd traced her fingertips over it, imagining she felt actual skin. How many times had she dreamed of him coming for her, gathering her in his arms, begging forgiveness for taking so long to find her, then flying her to the heavens? Countless. Now he was nearby…they could be reunited….

No. There would be no happy reunion. To learn that he was actually a demon…that he hurt people…that he wanted to kill Sabin…Sabin, whom she hungered for constantly, but who had locked her up in squalor as if she meant nothing to him.

Gwen spun in a circle, laughing bitterly. The floor was comprised of dirt. Three of the walls were made of stone. No crackable mortar, just smooth rock. One was made of thick metal bars. There wasn't even a cot to sleep on or a chair to sit on.

Last thing he'd said before leaving her in this shithole? "We'll discuss this when I return."

Like hell they would.

One, she wouldn't be here. Two, she was going to break his jaw with her fist so he wouldn't be able to talk ever again. And three, she was going to kill him. And her anger was nothing compared to the Harpy's. It squawked inside her head, demanding retribution. How could Sabin have done this? How could he have taken her newly awakened need for vengeance away from her? How could he have left her here, after the way they'd made love?

Sabin's betrayal was an even bigger blow than the newfound knowledge of her father's evil.

"Son of a bitch!" Bianka growled, stomping from one corner to another. Dark grains of sand flew around her booted feet. "He had all of our wings clipped before I even knew what was going on. He shouldn't have been able to do that. No one should have been able to do that."

"I'm going to hang him with his own intestines." Kaia slammed a fist into a bar. It held steady, her strength basically that of a human's now. "I'm going to remove his limbs, one by one. I'm going to feed him to my snake and let him rot in her belly."

"He's mine. I'll take care of him." The sad thing was, Gwen didn't want her sisters to punish him. She wanted to do it herself. Yes, that was part of it. Also, despite everything—even her own desire to maim and kill him—she didn't want to see him hurt. How stupid was that? As he'd locked her up, relief had blazed in his eyes, even alongside the regret, so he deserved whatever she did to him. Deserved all but softening from her.

It had taken her a while to piece the reasons for his relief together. But finally, she had. He'd gotten his wish: she couldn't leave the fortress, and she wouldn't be fighting Hunters. He'd considered that more important than allowing her her freedom even though his enemies had once done the same thing to her.

Gwen, too, slammed a fist into the bar. The metal whined as it bent backward. "Well, I'm going to— hey. Did you see that?" Shocked, she glanced down at her fist. There was a red line from the impact, but the bones were intact. Tentatively she punched the bar again. Again, it bent. "Oh, I am so getting out of here."

Kaia gaped at her. "How is that possible? I hit it, too, but it didn't budge."

"He damaged our wings, draining our strength," Taliyah said. Which had to have hurt like hell. "He only smashed Gwen's until he released her into this cage. She's as strong as she ever was. I wonder, though, how he knew to go for our wings and why he was so gentle with Gwen's."

The first part of her sister's speech drained a little of her elation. "I'm sorry. It's my fault. I didn't mean…I thought…I'm so, so sorry. I told him. I thought he could help me train against it."

"He's your first love," Bianka said, surprising her. "It's understandable."

Grateful as she was for her sister's forgiveness, Gwen bristled at her words. First implied there would be many more. She didn't like the thought of being with another man. Didn't like the thought of kissing and touching someone else. Especially since she hadn't had nearly enough of Sabin. Did she love him, though?

She couldn't. Not after this.

"You don't blame me?"

They gathered around her and hugged her, and her love for *them* swelled. Hands down, it was the best family moment ever. They supported her, no matter that she'd broken the rules and screwed up royally.

When they released each other, Taliyah gave her lower back a shove and motioned to the bars with a tilt of her chin. "Do it again. Harder."

"Time to blow this joint," Kaia said, clapping.

Gwen's heart pounded as she obeyed, throwing her fist into the metal again and again. The bar bent and whined and bent some more.

"Keep at it," Kaia and Bianka cheered in unison. "You're so close!"

Pouring every ounce of her fury and frustration into

the punches, she increased her velocity, watching as her
fist hammered away, moving so swiftly she saw only
a blur. Sabin must have assumed her utterly lacking in
strength and wits because he hadn't left a guard. Or
maybe all the warriors were now off fighting, only the
females and Torin remaining. Gwen hadn't seen much
of the reclusive Lord during her stay here, but Sabin
had mentioned he never left the fortress, his link to the
outside world the monitors in his chamber.

Was there a camera here? Probably.

Gwen didn't allow the thought to slow her. *Boom.
Boom. Boom!*

Finally, the bar snapped completely, leaving a gaping
space to shimmy through. Success—and it felt damn
good. They exited one at a time. When the Hunters
spotted them outside the cell, they gripped their own
bars in a frenzy.

"Let us out."

"Please. Show us more mercy than we showed you."

"We're not evil. They are. Help us!"

The voices were familiar. She'd heard them for a
year of her life—the worst year of her life. Hunters.
Close. Hurt. Gwen felt her Harpy overtaking her, all
but the colors of red and black fading from her vision.
Hurt. Destroy. Under her shirt, her wings were flutter-
ingly wildly.

These men had stolen twelve months from her. They
had raped other women in front of her. *They* were evil.
They were her enemy. Sabin's enemy. Led by her father.
A man who was not the benevolent angel she'd always
thought him. She should kill him, too. He'd destroyed
all her dreams. But the moment she imagined going

for his throat, even her Harpy shied away. Murder her own father? No...no.

No wonder Sabin had locked her up.

"Help!"

The cry drew her back to the present, back to her rage. Why hadn't Sabin killed these bastards yet? They needed to be killed. She had to kill them. Yes, kill... kill...

In the back of her mind, she was aware of her sisters grasping at her arms but they were too weak to stop her. Usually, *she* tried to stop herself. Not this time. No longer. She was learning to embrace her Harpy, right?

She pounded at the second set of bars, fists again hammering, mouth now watering. Teeth sharpening. Nails elongating. The sight of her must have frightened them, because the men backed away from the bars.

Enemy...enemy...

Finally, the bars crumbled under her ministrations and she burst inside the cell with a screech. One minute men were standing, backing away from her, the next they were on the ground, motionless. More...she wanted more...

Her Harpy cooed happily while Gwen panted, trying to catch her breath as a deep male voice entered her awareness.

"—Aeron and Paris are missing. Sabin, Cameo and Kane are in town, William and Maddox have the women in hiding, guarding them with their lives, so I'm the only one here and I can't touch her because I'm Disease. So do me a favor and calm her down or I'll have to do it and you won't like my methods."

The deep voice was unfamiliar to her. Good. Someone else for her to destroy. Where was...her gaze circled the room. Or rather, hallway. Oh, look there. Three bodies were vertical. They appeared feminine rather than masculine. All that meant was that they'd taste sweeter.

More. She stalked from the cage, determined to make them fall as the Hunters had.

"Gwen."

She recognized that voice. It wasn't from her nightmares, but it didn't slow her. She rammed the woman in the temple with her fist, heard a gasp, watched the form fly back and slam into a rocky wall. Dust must have plumed around the woman because it filled Gwen's nose.

"Gwen, honey, you have to stop," another voice said. "You did this once before. Remember?"

"Well, you did it twice, but the time we're referring to, you actually almost killed us, and we had to rip the wings from your back." A third familiar voice. "We hypnotized you to bury the memory, but it's there. Think back, Gwennie. Bianka, what's the damn code phrase to make her remember?"

"Butterscotch rum? Hopscotch butter buns? Something stupid like that."

The memory rose…higher…higher…pushing forward, and soon the shadows around it scattered and light pierced it, shining brightly. She'd been eight years old. Something had set her off…a cousin had eaten her birthday cake. Yes. That's right. She'd laughed while she'd done it, taunting Gwen, after she'd nearly gotten captured for stealing it.

The tether she'd kept the Harpy on had snapped inside her, and the next thing she'd known, the cousin and her sisters were hovering near death. The only reason they'd survived was that Taliyah had somehow ripped off her wings in the fray.

It had taken her weeks to regrow them. Weeks they'd taken from her memory, as well. *My memory,* the Harpy squawked. *Mine.*

Possessive bitch. *Memory loss was better than the alternative,* a rational part of her brain supplied. *The guilt would have destroyed me.*

They *are weak. They can't hurt you this time. You can—*

"Gods, who would have thought I'd want that stupid demon back in her life?"

"Torin, dude, can you get Sabin here? He's the only one who can calm her without hurting her."

Sabin. *Sabin.* Tendrils of her bloodlust faded, leaving room for Gwen's conscience to make itself known. *You don't want to kill your sisters. You love them.* In and out she breathed, slow and measured. Slowly colors sparked inside her mind, the black and red dispersing. Gray walls, brown floor. Taliyah's white hair, Kaia's red and Bianka's black. They were scratched up but alive, thank the heavens.

Then realization struck. *You did it. You calmed yourself down without killing everyone in the room.* Her eyes widened, and despite the chaos around her, joy burst through her. That had never happened before. Each time she'd lost control here at the fortress, Sabin had been here to talk her down. Maybe she didn't need to fear her Harpy anymore. Maybe, for once, they could live in harmony. Even without Sabin.

The thought nearly dropped her to her knees. She didn't want to live without him. She'd planned to leave,

yes, but if she were honest she'd admit that she'd expected him to come for her—or to return herself.

"You're okay?" Bianka asked, as surprised as she
was.

"Yes." She spun, purposely avoiding the Hunter's
cage, and found no trace of the man who had been
speaking. "Where's Torin?"

"He's not actually here," Kaia said. "He was talking
to us from a speaker."

"Then he knows we escaped," she said, clutching her
stomach and backing away. What if he came for them?
What if she killed him to keep him from locking her up
again? Sabin would never forgive her. Would believe
beyond any doubt—and that was saying something for
him—that she meant to aid the Hunters. *Wait, you don't
fear your Harpy anymore, remember?* Old habits died
hard, she supposed.

"He knows," Taliyah said as Torin echoed, "Yeah,
I know."

Kaia grabbed her shoulders and forced Gwen to still.
"He can't do anything because he can't touch us."

"Well, I can shoot you," that disembodied voice reminded them.

Gwen shuddered. Bullets were not fun.

"Let's gather Ashlyn and Danika," Kaia said, unconcerned with either their audience or Torin's threat.

"Torin said they're guarded by Maddox and William," Bianka reminded her. "Let's take them, too."

Nervous energy still pounded through Gwen, but
those words had her blood freezing. "Why do we want
them?" The girls were sweet and kind and didn't deserve to be hurt.

"Payback. Now come on." Bianka turned on her heel and pounded up the steps, headed into the main house.

"I don't understand," Gwen called, her voice shaking. "Payback how?"

Kaia released her and turned, as well. "Sabin damaged our wings, so now we're going to damage his precious army. When the rest of the warriors return and find the women missing, as well as their friends, they'll freak."

No, she thought. No. "I told you. Sabin's mine. I'll take care of him."

Both Kaia and Taliyah ignored her, following after Bianka.

"Don't worry. We may be weakened but that's what guns are for," Kaia said, grinning over her shoulder in the likely direction of Torin's camera. "Right, Tor-Tor?"

"I won't let you do this," he replied, his voice hard as steel.

"Watch us." Taliyah's voice was cold as ice. Quite a pair they made just then, both unwilling to bend.

Gwen watched her sisters disappear up the stairs. To capture the innocent females, to hurt her man. Well, not her man. Not anymore. But she realized she had a choice to make. Allow things to play out as they were, or stop her sisters, maybe hurting them in the process, and take matters into her own hands.

"Gwen," Torin said, jolting her. "You can't let them do this."

"But I love them." They'd always been there for her. They'd forgiven her so easily for spilling their secrets. They'd even tried to protect her from her own memories. To do this…

"The men will fight to the death to protect those females. And if your sisters do manage to defeat them—which is a big *if* since they aren't operating at full strength—it'll mean war between the Lords and the Harpies."

Yes, it would.

"It will divide the warriors here, because I suspect Sabin will choose you. And that will make us vulnerable to the Hunters. They'll have the advantage. If they don't already. I haven't been able to reach Lucien all day. Not Strider, Anya, or any of the others who went to Chicago, either. That's not like them, and I'm afraid something's happened to them. I need Sabin to go look for them, but he's stuck here, fighting."

Her first thought? She hoped the Lords in Chicago were okay. Her second? Sabin, choose her? Not likely. "He could have had my help, but he doesn't trust me."

"He trusts you. He just used that as an excuse to protect you. Even I know that, and I'm not that close to him." Heavy pause, breath crackling. "Well, you'd better make a decision fast because your sisters are indeed carrying guns and are closing in on their targets."

SABIN CROUCHED IN the shadows. Kane was at his left, Cameo at his right; they were loaded down with enough weapons to take out a small country. Sadly, that might not be enough for the coming battle.

Hunters were everywhere. Coming out of shops, striding down the sidewalks, eating at outdoor cafés. Like flies, they swarmed and buzzed and annoyed the hell out of him.

There were average-looking women, the bulge of knives and guns giving them away. Tall, muscled men who looked like they'd just come from war and were eager for another were positioned on the rooftops of buildings, gazing down at the town's happenings. Beside them, to Sabin's dismay, were children, ranging in age from roughly eight to eighteen. Sabin had already watched one of those teens walk through a wall. *Walk through it,* as if it weren't even there.

What could the others do?

He was outmanned, and he knew it. And even as depraved as he was, he also knew he wouldn't hurt the kids. Hunters had probably banked on that. *Could have used a Harpy right about now.*

His fingers curled tightly around his guns, his bones brittle. *Don't go there.* He'd been surveying the scene for a while, trying to decide, to work up a plan. Rather than feeling empowered, though, he felt more helpless than ever. He just didn't know what to do.

The worst part was that he'd left Gwen locked up— looked like he was going there, after all—and so another battle awaited him at home. Stupid. He'd allowed his concern for her to overrule his common sense. That was the danger of softening toward a woman. Emotions screwed with your thought processes, made you do stupid things. But he couldn't go back for her, apologize and ask for her aid. He'd hurt her sisters. Loyal and loving as they were with each other, she would never be able to forgive him.

Over and over he tried to tell himself that it was better this way. That he'd fought Hunters and won before her, and he could fight Hunters and win after her. And anyway, she was related to Galen. Sabin couldn't trust Gwen's motivation now. He couldn't trust her to help him and not also help her family.

Gwen could be your family. He scowled at the way-ward thought, scowled further when Doubt chimed in.

You don't deserve her. Not now. Maybe not even be-fore. She wouldn't want you anyway, so this is moot.

"Shut up," he muttered.

Kane flicked him a glance. "Your demon giving you trouble?"

"Always."

"So what are we going to do about the current situation? It's just the three of us."

"We've fought with worse odds," Cameo said, and Sabin cringed. Her voice always had that effect on him. Strangely, though, it didn't affect him as badly as usual this time. Maybe because he was already miserable. How could he have done that to Gwen?

I just wanted to protect her.

Well, you failed.

"No, we haven't," he said. "Because this time we have to make sure no kids get hurt in the fray."

Her finger flexed on her gun. "Well, we have to do something. We can't leave them out there unfettered."

Sabin studied the melee again. Just as crowded, just as dangerous. Those kids…shit. They complicated everything. Decision time. "Okay. Here's what we're gonna do. Split up, head in different directions, stay in the shadows, damn it, and take out the adults one by one. Kill on sight. Just…don't get *yourselves* killed. Do me a favor and—" His words stopped abruptly, his gaze slamming into the camo-clad Hunters stuffing two un-conscious men into their van at the end of the street. Several of the kids surrounded them, forming a wall.

Cameo followed the line of his gaze and gasped. "Is that…"

The chunk of earth underneath Kane split, and he fell into the widening hole. "Aeron and Paris? Shit. Yes. That's them."

Sabin cursed under his breath. "New plan. Kill as many of the men around them as possible, and I'll take care of the kids. If you can, drag Aeron and Paris back to the fortress and I'll meet you there."

CHAPTER TWENTY-FOUR

GWEN HAD LOCKED her sisters up. *I'm as bad as Sabin.*

She was inside Torin's room, standing behind him, arms crossed over her chest. He kept his back to her, as if he didn't have to worry about her approaching. He didn't. But at the very least, he should have feared a bullet in the brain. She was a Harpy, after all.

"I think I just made the biggest mistake of my life and it's too late to fix it." *If* her sisters forgave her, and *if* she forgave Sabin, they'd still want to punish her for her actions. Oh, who was she kidding? Everyone she loved—well, kind of liked, *sometimes,* in Sabin's case—was stubborn to their very cores. There'd be no forgiveness.

Her gaze landed on one of the monitors, the one that showed her sisters. They were pacing, cursing and beating at the bars, to no avail. They were fast healers, so she had perhaps a few days before they were able to bust out. And punish her for betraying them, of course. Gwen's chest constricted.

Taliyah had put up the greatest fight, and Gwen still bore the wounds. There were multiple gashes riding her ribs and neck. She couldn't believe she'd actually beaten them, even weakened as they'd been. All her life, they'd been the pinnacle she'd longed to reach. Stronger, prettier, smarter. Better. She'd constantly compared herself to them and always came up lacking.

Now, here she was, a warrior to the core. If she succeeded with the Hunters, would they be proud of her?

On one of the other monitors, Maddox and William paced, both weighed down with too many weapons to count. Ashlyn and Danika were behind them, wringing their hands.

"I'm worried," Danika could be heard saying. "The dream I had last night…I saw Reyes trapped in a dark box, his demon screaming and screaming and screaming for release."

Ashlyn rubbed her rounded belly, her features pale. "Maybe we should travel to Chicago. I can listen, learn whether Hunters have hidden them and where."

"No," Maddox said.

"Good idea," Danika said, speaking over him. "But what about what Torin told us? Hunters are out there in Buda even now."

"Better head into town," Torin suddenly said, drawing her attention from the monitors, his voice no longer dryly amused. "Just got a text from Sabin. Aeron and Paris are injured and being stuffed inside a van, Hunters are swarming and Sabin's about to initiate battle."

Gwen's stomach twisted painfully. "Where are they?"

"I've got a tracker in Sabin's cell and it's showing his location as two miles north of here. Head out the back door and down the hill. Don't take any turns and you'll run right into him."

"Thanks." She needed weapons. Lots and lots of weapons. An image of the chest in Sabin's closet filled her mind. Perfect! She spun on her heel, meaning to stalk out of Torin's bedroom.

"Oh, and Gwen."

She turned, faced him.

He opened a map of the surrounding forest on the far computer screen, a red line highlighting the way. "There are traps here, here and here, so be careful as you descend or you'll be blindsided."

"Thank you." With another sigh, she raced to Sabin's bedroom. The chest was no longer locked, thanks to her sisters, and nearly picked clean. There was only a gun and a knife. She took both. There'd been no time to train with a semiautomatic yet, but pointing and shooting didn't sound too difficult.

"Here goes," she muttered, wings fluttering frantically. Out of the fortress and down the hill she raced, not even glancing at the SUV parked in back. In Harpy form, she could get there faster.

The two-mile trek took her less than a minute to make. And it only took that long because she had to dodge the Lords' booby traps. The town was bursting with pedestrians. Thankfully, blur that she was, no one had spotted her yet. Some felt her, though, looking confused as she breezed by and wind caressed them.

Once she reached her destination she continued moving swiftly, eyes drinking in the scene. A group of military types surrounded an open van. As Torin had said, there were two unconscious men lying inside. Three guards crouched beside them, guns at the ready, smoke wafting from their barrels.

There was not a driver in front. Odd, she thought, until she realized Kane was behind a building and killing anyone who approached the wheel. The front glass was already shattered, blood dripping from the wheel. Four bodies were sprawled outside the open door.

When a Hunter approached him, Kane simply switched locations and hid, keeping his gun trained on the van.

Where was Sabin?

Why weren't humans screaming?

Even as she questioned herself, her gaze fell on a young girl who had her arms outstretched. A soft voice whispered through Gwen's mind: *Stay calm. Go home. Forget that you came into town. Forget what you saw.*

That beguiling voice made Gwen want to do as it suggested, the memories already fading, her body already spinning toward the fortress. Perhaps she would have obeyed completely if not for her Harpy. The dark side of her nature squawked and clawed inside her mind, drowning out the voice, reminding her of her purpose.

What should I do? And what was up with all the kids she was suddenly seeing? One of them, a little boy, was moving through the town almost as fast as Gwen was. Only reason she saw him was that he left a slight trail of light in his wake. He was obviously searching for the Lords, and when he spotted one—Cameo, this time— he stopped and began to yell.

Frowning, clearly reluctant to hurt him, Cameo grabbed the boy and pinched his carotid. He went down like a brick. Sweat ran down her face, along her chest, soaking her T-shirt to her body. Gwen had never seen the female warrior so upset and tired.

But at least one question had been answered. The kids were obviously helping the Hunters.

There was an infuriated growl behind her. "Come out, come out wherever you are. You can't beat us, and you can't call for reinforcements. We've got your friends. You've never been more ripe for the plucking."

Gwen spun, but another voice called out, "Why don't you give yourselves up, save yourselves the humiliation of failing?"

"You claim you're not evil—well, now's the time to prove it! Turn yourselves over to us and give us the girl. Let us find a way to remove the demons from your bodies. Help us return the world to what it once was—good and right and pure."

"Maybe beg us for forgiveness, too," a male sneered. "Had you been locked up as intended, sickness would never have been introduced into the world and my son would still be alive."

Wow, Gwen mused. Hunters really were fanatics. As if the Lords were responsible for all of the world's evil. Humans had free will. Hunters, too. They'd chosen to lock Gwen up. They'd chosen to rape females of the otherworld. That made the Hunters evil—and unworthy of mercy.

Someone screamed, drawing Gwen's attention. Her eyes widened when she saw Sabin dance through a mass of men, two daggers clutched in his hands. His arms moved gracefully, slicing through humans with lethal procession. One by one they fell around him.

Nearly every inch of his clothes was bright crimson, as though his entire body was cut up. Hopefully, that was not the case. Hopefully, he wore his enemy's blood.

Gwen felt the now familiar surge of her Harpy taking over, mind and body, nothing holding it back. At first, she experienced her instinctive fear. Then the fear faded. *I can do this. I* will *do this.* Her vision tunneled to red and black, and her mouth watered for a taste of that sweet red nectar. Her hands itched to hurt…maim.

Just before she gave over completely, she thought: *Please don't hurt Sabin or his friends. Please don't hurt the children. Please take as many as you can to the fortress and lock them up.* That's what Sabin would want.

Wings swishing more frantically than ever, Gwen scooped up the sleeping child Cameo had taken down— *don't hurt, don't hurt, don't hurt*—and carted his motionless body with her as she swooped through the masses and chop-blocked Hunters, fractured their kneecaps so they couldn't stand and slammed the hilt of her blade into their temples.

Should have brought the SUV, after all, she thought as she gathered one of the unconscious Hunters in her other arm and headed toward the fortress. She deposited her cargo in one of the dungeon cells and rejoined the fray. The total journey took five minutes. She repeated the action sixteen times before realizing she was shaking, slowing a little. The crowd, at least, was thinning.

Sabin was still on his feet and Cameo was at his back, each dispatching threats from a different direction. Kane still had his weapon trained on the van.

Aeron and Paris, she thought, working her way toward them. She had to remove them from the area. They were clearly injured and in dire need of help. But a Hunter stepped into her path and she slammed into him, losing her breath as she soared backward. When she landed, broken pieces of concrete jabbed into her back, cutting.

Sabin dispatched him and was at her side a moment later, as if he'd known exactly where she was the entire time despite her speed, and jerking her to her feet.

"Torin texted me, told me you were here. You okay?" he rasped.

The feel of his hand on her...divine. Momentarily made her forget where she was and what she was doing. The sweat and blood glistening off him reminded her. "Yes," she rasped. She was panting, tired, overheated, aching and trembling. "I'm fine."

He swayed, scrubbing a hand down his face as if to clear his line of vision. Never had she seen the fierce, vibrant warrior so near the end of his tolerance. "Can you get Aeron and Paris to safety?"

At least he wasn't trying to send her away. "Yes." She hoped. But just then she wanted to take Sabin to safety, rather than his friends.

Sabin grabbed the semiautomatic from the back of her waist and removed the safety. "You mind?"

"Not at all."

"I'll get you to the van," he said before she could grab him, and off he went. A rapid boom, boom, boom followed.

Even with the blocks her ears were sensitive and the sound of that gunfire had her cringing. In fact, she felt warm liquid trickle from her eardrums. Thankfully, the blood somehow muted the volume.

Once again bodies began falling around him. Gwen moved forward, noticing that only one child remained among the masses. The little girl keeping the townspeople at bay. Gwen had several kids locked up, but thought the Hunters must have taken some of the others and run. What kind of monsters brought children into war?

When she reached the van, Sabin continued to fire, even though there were no longer any Hunters around the vehicle, the last few having taken off to hide. Or maybe they'd been nailed by Kane. She hefted a warrior on each shoulder, nearly toppling under their weight. No way she'd be able to cart them both at the same time.

She placed Aeron on the seat as gently as she could and tightened her grip on Paris. He wore the most blood. "Have to come back," she said, hoping Sabin heard her, and sprinted for the trees. This journey took a little longer, her sprint slowing. Finally, though, she reached her destination.

Huffing, she deposited the hulking warrior in the foyer of the fortress. Torin must have seen her coming and alerted Maddox and William, because the men had let the women out of hiding. When Ashlyn and Danika spotted Paris, they rushed forward.

Fear gleamed in Danika's dark green eyes. "Is he…"

"No. He's breathing."

"What's going—" Ashlyn began.

"No time. Have to go back for the others." Gwen didn't wait for a reply but rushed back to the city.

Sabin was still at the van, a group of Hunters now holding shields and pushing their way toward him. Clearly they'd come prepared for anything. Still trembling, and fatigued beyond imagining, Gwen lifted Aeron and took off at a run.

Before she reached the forest's edge, a bullet pierced her left thigh.

She cried out, dropped to the ground. Aeron grunted, but didn't wake, and blood gushed from her. Damn it! An artery had been hit. The trembling became almost violent, but she pushed to her feet. Black winked in and out of her vision. *Keep going. You can do it.* She surged ahead. Took her ten minutes this time, but reaching the finish line had never been sweeter.

Again, both Danika and Ashlyn were waiting for her, doctoring Paris there in the foyer while Maddox and William rushed to get them whatever they needed.

Gwen dropped Aeron beside his friend, too weak to be gentle this time. When she stumbled to the door, Danika grabbed her arm.

"You can't go back. You can barely stand."

She jerked loose. "Have to."

"You won't make it. You'll faint on the hill."

"Then I'll drive." 'Cause there was no way she was staying here. Sabin was out there, needed her.

"No." There was steel in Danika's tone. "I'll drive you. Just let me get the keys."

"William," Maddox called.

The warrior sighed. "I know what that means. I'm supposed to do the driving."

Still Danika rushed off. Ashlyn stepped up and placed two fingertips at the base of Gwen's neck. "Your pulse is too fast," she said on a sigh. "Breathe slower. That's the way. In. Out. Good girl."

She must have closed her eyes because the next thing she knew, her leg was bandaged and William was at her side, grabbing her hand and ushering her toward the door.

"Danni gave me the keys. If we're gonna do this, let's do it."

"Be careful," Ashlyn called.

Once they were settled in the SUV, William peeled out, burning rubber through the forest. Gwen was thrown against the door, and her temple slapped into the window. *That's gonna leave a mark,* she thought dizzily.

"You holding on?"

"Yes," she said, the word weak, even to her own ears.

"Hey, listen. Thank you for bringing Aeron and Paris home. Anya loves them and would have been devastated if they'd been killed. Much as she irritates me, I want her happy."

"My pleasure." And pain.

When they reached their destination, the battle had already wound down. Sabin, Kane and Cameo were bleeding profusely, cut up and nearly broken, but they continued fighting the stragglers.

Seeing the SUV, they jumped back, out of the way. Gwen braced herself as William hit the gas and ran over the humans. "Gods, this is fun," he said on a laugh. The vehicle bounced once, twice. Before it stopped, Gwen threw open her door. Sabin sprinted to her side and dove in. The others claimed the backseat just as swiftly.

"Go, go, go," Sabin commanded, and William once again burned rubber. Sabin's arm wound around Gwen's waist, squeezing tight.

Now that he was with her, alive, what little energy she possessed drained away completely. Weakness consumed her, overshadowing all else. Even the Harpy was eerily silent.

"Gwen," Sabin said, concern drenching his tone. "Gwen, can you hear me?"

She tried to respond, but no words would form. No sound would push past the sudden lump in her throat. She didn't know what to say, anyway. She was still furious with him, still wanted to hurt him for what he'd done to her, still wanted to cry for the way he'd doubted her.

"Gwen! Stay with me, darling. Okay? Just stay with me."

William must have hit another body because Gwen bounced back and forth again. Or maybe Sabin was shaking her. There were two white-hot bands wrapped around her forearms.

"Stay with me! That's an order."

She'd just saved his life, and he thought to order her around? "Go to...hell..." she managed, then darkness claimed her and she knew nothing more.

CHAPTER TWENTY-FIVE

SABIN PRESSED HIS WRIST into Gwen's mouth, her teeth sinking deep into his vein. The feel of those soft lips… that hot suction… He was so hard his cock could be considered a dangerous weapon. This was Gwen's second feeding, and she was healing nicely. She had flat-out refused to take his neck, even though she would have received a better flow of blood and thereby healed much faster. Worse, she refused to talk to him.

So he talked for both of them. He told her the kids she'd captured were still contained, but comfortable and safe. He told her that her sisters had escaped the dungeon about an hour ago and had once again taken up residence in the chamber beside his. Despite the anger they had to feel, they'd been strangely quiet.

So had Doubt, for that matter.

He'd known the demon feared the Harpies. He'd known the little shit retreated deep inside his mind every time Gwen became riled. But now the fiend remained silent even if she wasn't. Striking distance was all that was required now. Almost seemed as if Doubt, well, doubted itself and its ability to take her in a battle of wills. Poetic justice, if you asked Sabin.

The demon turned on Sabin every time he ventured away from Gwen, of course, and still sought other victims constantly. But not Gwen, not any longer, and it never dared say anything *about* Gwen. After the way she'd ripped through those Hunters… The demon had also stopped trying to convince Sabin that he couldn't have her, too afraid to piss Gwen off.

A little anger from her wouldn't have been a bad thing, though. Anything was preferable to the silent treatment.

Sabin sighed. So badly he wanted to hop a plane and search for the missing warriors. But first, he had to recover from yesterday's battle. He and the others were no good to anyone right now. What's more, he knew he couldn't divide their forces more than they already were. Hunters were still in Buda, and those Hunters had to be dealt with before the fortress fell or the women were injured.

This morning Torin had pegged one of the new captured with a tracking dye and "accidentally" let him escape, following his every move from his computer and waiting for the bastard to lead the warriors to their hiding place.

Waiting was difficult, though. He'd tried to talk the Harpies into going to Chicago, had promised them a fortune, but they'd shut their door in his face. He knew they didn't want money. They wanted him to send Gwen packing. That, however, he couldn't do.

He loved her. More than before, even.

More than his war, more than his hatred for the Hunters, he loved her. She was Galen's daughter—so what. Sabin carried the demon of Doubt inside him, so like he really had room to judge. Gwen wouldn't aid her father. She wouldn't. Sabin knew that soul-deep. And yeah, he also knew that Gwen would be giving up a chance at a relationship with her dad to be with him, which was why he needed to prove to Gwen that *he* was now her family.

She was number one in his life. He shouldn't have locked her away. He should have trusted her, should have allowed her to fight. Hell, he would have lost without her—and he *would* rather lose than be without her ever again.

The pressure of her mouth eased, and then she was pulling away from him. He was seated on a recliner he'd dragged to his bedroom—more than taking from his neck, Gwen had refused to drink from him on the bed. She was seated across from him in the other recliner he'd confiscated because she'd also refused to sit on his lap.

Her lips were bright red and puffy, as though she'd been kissed. "Thanks," she muttered.

Thanks—her first word since waking from her injuries this morning. He closed his eyes, smiling as her beautiful voice drifted through his head. "My pleasure."

"I can tell," she said dryly.

Slowly his eyelids cracked open. She hadn't flounced to the bed as she had earlier but remained in the chair, her back ramrod straight, peering just over his shoulder, determination pulsing off her. Dread coursed through him. What, exactly, was she determined to do? Leave him still?

"How are Aeron and Paris?" she asked.

Needed to work up to it, did she? "Healing like the rest of us. Thanks to you."

"Thanks to William. I'd pushed myself too far and wouldn't have been able—"

"Because of *you*," he interjected. "You did more, fought harder, than anyone I've ever seen. And you had no reason to do it and every reason not to. Yet still you saved us all. I'll never be able to thank you enough for that."

"I don't want your thanks," she said, cheeks heating. Not in embarrassment, nor in desire. But…anger? Why would she be angry at his gratitude? She released a shuddering breath, which seemed to calm her. "I'm healed, my strength almost completely returned."

"Yes."

"Which means…I'm leaving." Her voice cracked there at the end.

And there it was. He'd suspected that was coming, but was still devastated by the words. *You can't leave,* he wanted to shout. *You're mine. Now and always.* But he, more than anyone, knew the consequences of trying to control such a fierce soldier. "Why?" was all he managed to get out.

Jerkily she hooked a lock of hair behind her ear. "You know why."

"Spell it out for me."

Finally her eyes slid to him. Fire sizzled in their depths. "You want to hear it? Fine. You used my weakness against me, my *secrets.* You hurt my sisters, forced me to hurt them and lock them away to save you. You didn't trust me and you almost died for it." She jumped to her feet, hands fisted. "You almost died!"

Okay, the thought of his death upset her most. She'd mentioned it twice. Hope flared inside him, and Sabin was out of his chair and tossing her on the bed before she had time to blink. As she bounced from the impact, he pinned her with his weight.

Rather than struggle against him, she glared up at him. "I could snap your neck."

"I know." Actually, this position left her vulnerable. Left her wings immobile, which drained her strength. Her weakness, the one he'd used against her before. There'd be no more of that. He flipped to his back, placing her atop him. "I thought I was doing it for your own good. I didn't want you fighting. Didn't want you hurt. Didn't want you pitted against your own father."

"That wasn't your choice."

"I know," he repeated. "To be honest, I did it for me. I needed to know you were safe. That was stupid of me. Stupid and wrong. I won't be leaving you behind again. You're a better soldier than I've ever been."

Her legs straddled his waist, placing the heat of her directly above his throbbing erection. He groaned, gripped her hips to keep her still.

"I can't trust you anymore," she said.

"You can. You can trust me. You, more than anyone."

"Liar!" She slapped him, hard enough to crack bone. His cheek exploded in pain, but he didn't make a sound, didn't retaliate or release her. Just slowly faced her, ready for anything else she wanted to dish. He deserved it. He'd let her flay the skin from his body if it meant working this out between them. "I question everything you say now, something I didn't do even when your demon was drifting through my head at every possible opportunity. More than that, I will never truly believe *you* trust me. After everything you've done—"

"I have weaknesses, too." The words left him in a desperate rush, quieting her. "You gave me your secrets. Now let me give you mine. To prove that I trust you, that I'll never leave you behind again." He didn't give her a chance to respond. "While guarding the king of gods, I lost an eye. Zeus had to give me another. I can't see great distances like the other warriors."

As he spoke, her shoulders relaxed a little. Her fingers curled in his shirt, bunching the material and lifting it from his stomach. His hope intensified. "You could be lying."

"I told you. I can't lie. I pass out if I try. That's part of my curse—and another weakness."

"You said you wouldn't use my secrets against me. That was a lie, but you didn't pass out."

"I meant it at the time."

She remained silent.

"I hold two daggers while fighting because I have a tendency to grab my opponent if a hand is free. I've lost fingers that way more times than I can count. If you can disarm me of a single blade, you can more easily defeat me." He'd never told anyone these things. Even his men, though they'd probably noticed over the years. Still, he was surprised by how easily—and willingly— he shared with her.

"I—I think I noticed that." Her tone was softer, gentler. "During practice."

Encouraged, he continued. "Everyone is sensitive in some place, some way. It's a weakness, an Achilles heel. Mine is my left knee. The slightest pressure can send me to the ground. That's why I fight with my body half-turned."

She blinked, as if she were reliving their practice sessions in her mind, trying to judge the truth of his claim for herself. A few minutes ticked by in silence. Sabin concentrated on breathing deep and even, drawing her scent into his nose.

"To be honest, though, there is one weakness that

slays me more than any other. Right now, always, that's you." His voice dropped, husky, intent. "If you still want to leave, leave. But know that I'll be leaving with you. Try to lose me, and I'll just hunt you down. Where you go, I go. If you decide to stay and wish me to stop fighting, I'll never again fight the Hunters. *You* are more important. I'd rather die than live without you, Gwendolyn."

She was shaking her head, disbelief warring with hope in her expression. "My father—"

"Doesn't matter."

"But...but..."

"I love you, Gwen." More than he'd ever loved another. More than he loved even himself. And he loved himself a great deal—most of the time. "I never thought I'd find myself grateful to Galen for anything, but I am. I could almost forgive him for every wrong he's committed because he brought you into the world."

She licked her lips, still hesitant to accept his claim. "But other women—"

"Don't even tempt me. I am your consort. Not for any reason, even to win a battle, would I turn to someone else. Ever. I'd rather lose the battle than lose you. You are it for me. The only one. Hurting you destroys me. I know that now."

"I want to believe you. I do." Her gaze fell to his chest, to where her fingers rested. Those fingers relaxed their grip, even traced squiggly lines. "I'm afraid."

"Give me time. Let me prove it. Please. I don't deserve a second chance, but I'm willing to beg for one. Anything you desire, anything you—"

"What I desire is you." Her eyes met his, pupils consuming the irises. "You're here, and you're alive, and that's all I can seem to make matter at the moment. Let me have you." She ripped his shirt in half and dove down, mouth suddenly sucking one of his nipples. "I don't know about the future, but I know that I need you. Show me what you want me to believe. Show me you love me."

Sabin's hands tangled in her hair, and he rolled them over. Joy burst through him. Joy and shock, love and white-hot desire. She hadn't offered the everlasting declaration he'd hoped for, but this would do. For now.

He tugged at her clothing, his own. Soon they were both naked, hot skin pressed against hot skin. He sucked in a breath at the bliss. She moaned, her nails spearing deep in his shoulders.

Sabin kissed his way to her chest, laved his tongue over each of her nipples, kneaded her breasts, and then continued his trail of kisses. His tongue swooped into her navel, and she quivered, writhing against him.

"Grab the headboard," he commanded.

"Wh-what?"

"Headboard. Hold it. Don't let go."

She was blinking up at him in confusion, the scent of desire wafting from her. She was lost in the pleasure, drowning in it, but finally she obeyed. Her back arched, her breasts now high in the air, nipples hard as little pearls.

"Drape your legs over my shoulders," he rasped out, reaching up to roll one of those beautiful nipples between his fingers.

This time she obeyed without hesitation, gasping, trying to grind up against him. When he felt her heels digging into his lower back, he parted the damp folds guarding the new center of his world and bent his head for a taste.

Her flavor was intoxicating. Addicting. Rich and sweet, the perfection he remembered. He circled her clitoris, teasing it, while he sank two fingers inside her. Her cry echoed throughout the bedroom.

"I can't believe I resisted you, even for a second."

"More."

"Have I told you yet how beautiful you are? How much I love you?"

"More!"

He chuckled. On and on he tongued her, his fingers never ceasing their ministrations. Her head thrashed back and forth, strawberry curls flying in every direction, body writhing.

"More," she chanted. "More, more, more."

When he brought a third finger into play, she immediately began spasming, holding him inside, muscles locking tight. He sucked her clit harder…longer…drawing out her climax.

Only when she screamed his name, only when she collapsed against the mattress limply, did he release her. He crawled up her body, cock begging to penetrate her tight little sheath. But he didn't. Not yet.

Her eyelids blinked open. Luminous amber irises peered up at him, white teeth nibbling at her bottom lip.

"I'm not going to hurt you, ever again," he vowed, and then flipped her to her stomach. "Let me prove it."

She gasped, instantly reared back to knock his weight off her, but he reached down and flattened his chest to her back, stopping the frantic flutter of her wings. She stilled. *Don't panic on me, darling.* Next he flattened his hands over hers, meshing his cock between her lower cheeks, his legs outside hers. He was panting, warm breath trekking wildly over her shoulders.

"I owe these precious wings a proper apology," he said, lifting his weight. "Will you allow me to touch them?"

Thankfully, she didn't try to buck him off again. She did stop breathing, though. He heard the hitch of it in her throat. Unable to speak, she nodded.

"Make them stop," he said. "Please."

Gradually, the wings calmed.

Inch by inch, he covered each delicate wing with a kiss. They were soft, like silk, and cool to the touch, the perfect contrast to his heat. There wasn't a single hint of feathers, which surprised him. They were nearly translucent, blue veins intertwining from top to bottom, flowing like crystal rivers.

Just then he hated himself for what he'd done to her. How could he have bound these beautiful wings, even for a moment?

"I'm sorry," he said. "So sorry. I shouldn't have done it. No excuse is good enough."

"I—I forgive you." The words were husky, wine-rich. "I do understand why you did it. I don't like that you did it, but I do understand."

"I'll make it up to you, I swear it. I—"

"Need you inside me. Now." Frantically she moved her backside against him, seeking the head of his shaft. "You've made me desperate. I need more."

"Yes. Yes." Wait. *Slow down.* "Fertile yet?"

"No."

Speed back up. Sabin gripped her hips and slammed all the way to the hilt. They cried out in unison. So good. Felt so good. Better than before, hotter, wetter.

More fulfilling. They were connected, one being, fused together. She belonged to him, and he to her.

Bending down, he pressed his stomach to her back, reached around and thrummed her clit with one hand and kneaded her breasts with the other, attacking every possible pleasure-point. She lifted her body, grabbing the headboard again and sinking deeper onto his cock.

Shit, he wasn't going to last much longer. He was at the edge, had been at the edge for days already. But over and over he hammered inside her, slipping, sliding, no longer Sabin, only Gwen's man.

A scream suddenly reverberated through the room, and she was once again locking down on him, milking him. Just like that, Sabin hurtled over, pleasure consuming him, washing him in great waves of sensation.

They stayed like that forever, still joined, before collapsing against the mattress. Sabin quickly rolled to her side, not wanting to smash her with his weight. Well, not wanting to smash her *again*.

Unable to release her, even for a second, he pulled her into his side and she eagerly snuggled against him. This, he decided, must be what heaven was like.

"Twice now you've asked me if I was fertile, which leads me to believe you can have children," she said between breaths, the husky announcement breaking the silence. "Even Ashlyn is pregnant, though I assumed she had gotten that way before she arrived here. Oh, wait. Galen helped make me, so you guys *can* reproduce."

"Yes, and yes, Ashlyn's child is Maddox's. The conditions for conceiving have to be just right, but we can indeed father kids. I'm sure you've read the stories of the gods impregnating humans."

"Yeah, but you guys weren't born in the traditional

way," she countered. "You were created by Zeus him-self. I would think you'd be…lacking in…you know…baby serum."

Baby serum? He had to cut back a laugh. "We have a lot more hormones, white blood cells and other neces-sary components than humans. It's one of the reasons we're able to heal so quickly. Most females' bodies can-not handle that potent a…serum, so they begin fight-ing and killing it."

"Think I could handle it?"

"I think you could handle anything."

Gradually she relaxed against him. Might even have smiled. "Do you ever want to have kids?"

He never had before. His life had been too turbulent. But he liked the thought of creating a baby with Gwen. A baby just like her, increasing this new blessing in his life. "Yeah. Someday, just not yet. Not until it's safe."

Her expression was pensive. "Safe." She sighed and changed the subject. "I don't want you to stop fighting Hunters, but I don't know if I'll stay with you."

"Fair enough." Though he'd use his dying breath to convince her to stay. And he hadn't lied. He'd follow her. Wherever she went, he'd follow. Getting rid of him was going to be a bitch of a problem. "But don't expect me to watch you walk away and do nothing."

"Well, you don't have to worry about that just yet. First, I'm going to help you find your friends. Can you trust me to do that?"

"Yes. I could discover you hugging Galen and I wouldn't doubt you." He said it with confidence. Meant it. Gwen was the one thing in his life that he would never have to doubt.

A laugh bubbled from her. "That I would have to see

to believe." She traced her fingertips along his chest. "I need to talk to my sisters."

"Good luck with that." He captured them and brought them to his lips.

Another sigh. "I half expected them to leave. But deep down I knew they'd stay just to punish me for what I did to them."

"They won't hurt you." He wouldn't allow it.

She twined their hands and gave a gentle squeeze. "How are Danika and Ashlyn?"

"Grateful to you, worried about the missing men."

Frowning, Gwen sat up, hair tumbling gloriously down her back. "I'm going to shower, clear my head. Will you call a meeting with everyone here in, say... an hour?"

He didn't ask why she wished to have the meeting, he simply trusted her, as he'd said he would. "Consider it done."

CHAPTER TWENTY-SIX

GIDEON WAS SLOWLY GOING INSANE. He'd lost track of time and didn't know how long he'd been trapped. A day? Two? A year? There wasn't a sliver of light to cling to, nothing to remind himself that there was a world out there—a world he would soon return to by fair means or foul.

First, he needed a little peace and quiet to think up an escape plan.

His demon, usually just a presence in the back of his mind, had yet to stop screaming inside his head. "In, in, in," it cried, meaning, "Out, out, out." "Need dark, need dark," it sobbed, meaning, "Need light, need light." Lies thought it was locked inside Pandora's box once more, unable to escape, forgotten, abandoned.

Apparently, the other demons thought the same. Lucien moaned frequently, though Anya was always there to soothe him. Reyes was surprisingly calm. He'd mutter Danika's name, then wouldn't speak again for hours. Amun growled and snarled low in his throat, as though he were fighting a horde of demons Gideon couldn't even imagine. The secrets that must be playing through his head…

Strider, who had been outsmarted and therefore had lost a mind game, constantly banged his head against the wall, his demon probably screeching, his body definitely agonized. Gideon had seen the warrior lose only once, hundreds of years ago, but the consequences of that loss were imprinted in his memory. Never had he seen a grown man writhe with such force, tears streaming down his ashen face, eyes flashing anguish rather than the usual pride, teeth grinding so vigorously blood poured from them.

Concentrate, dummy. Many times the entire group had tried prying the window shutters open or hacking through the brick walls. Anya, the only one who still had use of her abilities, muted though they were, had blasted tornados through the chamber, but she'd only hurt the men, not the building. Everything had been fortified and then refortified—with spells?—until their prison was seemingly unbreachable.

"I'm going to look for a way out again," Anya said. She was the calmest of the group—an ironic twist, since she thrived on chaos. There was a rustle of clothing, a moan from Lucien, a coo from Anya, and then the shuffle of footsteps.

Gideon had always been reluctant to commit to a woman, preferring variety. Right now that seemed stupid. He had no one to think about, wish for, or dream of. No one to keep him focused, as Reyes had. No one to comfort him, as Lucien had.

What female would have you long-term?

What, he was possessed by Doubt now?

Thump.

"Sorry," Anya muttered. "Who'd I hit?"

"I need—" Strider's breath sawed in and out, shallow and raspy, pained. "Help. Help me. *Please.*"

"Soon," Anya promised, then cooed at him for a few minutes. More footsteps.

Bang. Scrape.

"Well, well, well. What do we have here?" a voice boomed from what Gideon assumed were hidden speakers. And it didn't belong to anyone he knew. "Is it my birthday?"

The room grew eerily quiet, until Anya beat a hasty path back to Lucien, her heels clacking against the tiled floor.

Lights flickered on, chasing away the shadows. In that moment, sweet peace claimed Gideon. He blinked against the spots clouding his vision, seeing his friends for the first time in forever. Lucien was splayed across the floor, his head resting in Anya's lap as the goddess clutched him protectively. Reyes was slumped against the wall, grinning eerily. Strider was on his side, clutching his stomach, knees drawn to his chest, and Amun was beside him, petting his head, his own features glazed.

No sign of Hunters, though. The windows were still blocked, the door still closed.

"I wondered who had tripped my silent alarm. Had to take care of your friends in Buda before I could return here, though." Cruel laugh. "We've been hoping you'd come here, ever since that article was published. I see our denial of this facility's existence had the desired effect and convinced you there was no way this could be a trap."

With the sudden quiet in his mind, Gideon was able to sift that voice through his mental files, and *hello*. It belonged to someone he knew, after all. Dean Stefano. Second in command of the Hunters, answerable only to that sick fuck, Galen. Stefano hated Sabin for stealing Darla, his wife; said Darla would still be alive if the Lords and the evil they housed were in hell where they belonged.

Stefano's evil knew no bounds. He'd sent Danika, an innocent, to spy on them, planning to use her to capture—and torture—the Lords one by one. Not that his plan had worked. But he'd sent her in, and then tried to bomb the fortress with her in it.

Dread tightened Gideon's stomach, followed quickly by rage and sorrow as Stefano's words took root and spread. *Had to take care of your friends.* Understanding dawned. Hunters had been to Budapest. They'd fought—and they'd won, or they wouldn't be here now. Sabin would never have let them escape.

Where was Sabin now? Until the box was found, Hunters wouldn't kill the Lords, believing their demons would escape and cause more trouble. Had they imprisoned him? Tortured him? Pushing to his feet proved difficult, but Gideon did it. Swayed, but managed to stay upright. All but Strider did the same, extending their weapons, ready to do what was necessary despite their infirmities.

"Come in here." Reyes waved his fingers in challenge. "I dare you."

Stefano gave another laugh, this one genuinely amused. "Why should I? I can starve you, watch you waste away. I can poison your air, watch you suffer. And I can do all of those things without ever touching your filthy bodies." There at the end, his voice had hardened, eagerness dripping from the sharp edges.

"Let the woman go," Lucien called. "She's done nothing to you."

"Hell, no." Anya shook her head, pale hair flying in every direction. "I stay here."

"How sweet," Stefano said mockingly. "She wants to stay with her demon. Well, I think I'll remove her. Just for you, Death. I don't think you'll like what I do to her, though."

Snarling, Lucien crouched, preparing to engage. His semiautomatic was raised, aimed. Ready. He looked brutal and savage, every inch Death. "Try."

That's when a boy, around eleven years old, walked through the far wall as though he were a ghost. Gideon's eyes widened, his mind replaying the scene in hopes of processing the extraordinary event.

"Come with me," the boy said to Anya. "Please."

"Neat trick." She slowly spun, arms spread. "You sent a child into the lion's den. Cowardly, don't you think? And do you really think your little pet can force *me* to do something I don't want to do?"

"Yes, I can," the boy responded in all seriousness. "But there's no need to engage in violence."

Lucien shoved Anya behind him, his eyes glowing red, his teeth sharp and bared. Seeing the usually stoic warrior worked into such a frenzy was almost painful. The man loved his woman and would die for her. Would rather die, actually, than to see her hurt.

Stealthily Gideon moved beside Death, unsure of what to do but knowing he couldn't passively watch. But really, who reeked of evil here? The men in the cage or the men who had sent a child into the midst of war?

Reyes, Strider and Amun flanked Gideon's other side, forming a protective wall around Anya.

"Come," the boy said again, frowning now. "Please. I don't want to hurt you."

"Isn't he wonderful?" Stefano asked with a laugh. "I do hope you like him, my newest weapon against you.

I didn't plan to use him for a while yet. Then you had to venture into Egypt and steal my incubators. Incubators I *will* find and use again. Especially the one our friend Sabin so favors."

"So glad to hear from you, Stefano," Gideon said, ignoring the taunts. "This is wondrous—" sick "—even for you."

A pause. Then, "Ahh, Lies. A *delight,* as always. How tedious your demon must be. But I have good news for you. We've found a way to draw the demons from your bodies and place them inside someone else. Someone weaker, someone who will accept their imprisonment for the good of mankind. Which is what we've already done to Sabin. After we defeated him, of course. He put up quite a fight, Sabin did, but in the end he fell. Just. Like. You."

Hell, no. Sabin wasn't dead. Sabin couldn't be dead. He was too virile, too determined. More than that, sucking out their demons and placing them in another body wasn't possible. It couldn't be possible.

"You don't believe me." Stefano laughed again. "That's fine. You will when it happens to you. Besides, why do you think your friend isn't here, saving you?"

A fear Gideon had entertained himself. *Don't let Stefano get to you. He's lying. Later you can—*

Gideon slammed a fist into the wall at his right. Dust plumed around him. He hit it again and again, tears burning his eyes. He hit it so many times his bones cracked and his muscles tore. He'd spent thousands of years with Sabin, had thought to spend a thousand more.

"Poor Lies." Stefano *tsk*ed under his tongue. "Without a leader. Whatever will you do now?"

"Fuck you!" Gideon screamed. "I'll kill you. Fucking kill you." And he meant it with everything inside of him, it was the truth, something he planned to do, wanted to do, *would* do. "You will die by my hand, motherfucker!"

As the heated words echoed around him, his demon gave a shocked cry—then a pained one. The pain shoved its way into Gideon, tearing him apart cell by cell. Felt like every one of his organs were splintering, his bones popping from their joints. Lies was clawing at his skull, falling to his feet, grasping for an anchor, biting at his toes as the pain drove it to madness. Still that wasn't enough. The demon swept through the rest of him, screaming, tearing his veins, leaving only acid behind.

Gideon's knees gave out, and he collapsed to the floor. The dagger he'd held in his good hand skidded out of reach. He'd known better. Allowing his emotions to overtake him was always his downfall. That's why he'd learned to hide everything he felt behind sarcasm. Idiot! *Stefano's defeated you now. Your enemy has the advantage. He can walk in here, grab you up, beat you, cut off your limbs, and there's not a fucking thing you can do about it.*

"Hate…you…" he gritted out. Hell, he'd already told the truth once. Why not do it again? Say what he'd longed to say for so long. "Hate you to the depths of my soul."

Again, the demon screamed. Screamed and screamed and screamed. Again the pain ripped through him, tore him apart.

He opened his mouth to reveal another truth.

"Ly-ing," Amun said haltingly. "He's…lying… Sabin… alive."

They were the first words the keeper of Secrets had spoken in centuries. His voice was raw, as though his voice box had been wiped with sandpaper and run through a shredder, each word like rubbing salt in a wound.

"You don't know that," Stefano blustered. "You weren't there. He's dead, I promise you."

Gideon stilled. Despite the agony, the torment of his current condition, he stilled. Stefano had lied to him. Fucking lied to him, and he'd believed it. Gideon, who could sniff out a lie from a thousand feet away. He'd uttered so many over his lifetime, identifying them was as natural as breathing.

Amun roared and fell to his knees beside Gideon. The floodgates had been opened, it seemed, for one word, then one sentence, then one story after another rushed from the warrior, all told in the different voices of their creators. He spoke of murder, rape and abuse of every kind. He spoke of jealousy, greed and infidelity. Incest, suicide and depression.

None of the crimes were his own, but they might as well have been. They belonged to the people he'd encountered over the years, the Hunters he had drained of memory, and they were as clear to him as if he had lived them himself.

Eyes squeezed shut tightly, Amun rubbed his temples, writhing, grimacing, the spew of poison never slowing. "He didn't love me anymore, even though I did everything for him." His voice was high, like a woman's. Gideon thought he heard a gasp over the speakers, but couldn't be sure. "Cooked and cleaned and slept with him even when I was too tired. All he cared about was his precious war. Though he still found time to screw our whore of a neighbor, over and over again. He treated me like I was garbage!"

"How are you projecting that voice? That's Darla's voice. How, damn you?" Stefano barked. There was no answer, only more of Darla's secrets. Gideon had no idea how the warrior had learned them. "Shut him up. Shut him up right now!"

The little boy jumped, startled, before rushing forward. When Lucien and Reyes grabbed at him, their arms misted through him, and both warriors screamed in agony, the sounds of their pain blending with Gideon's, with Amun's. Then both men dropped like weights in an ocean, their bodies twitching as if they'd just received the shock of a lifetime. Anya crouched behind them, ready to spring forward if the boy tried to touch them again.

Can't let the kid hurt Amun like that, Gideon thought, forcing himself to stand. He was unsteady, dizzy, hurting so badly there were tears in his eyes. He had to hunch over and grip his stomach to keep from vomiting. With his free hand, he grabbed his dagger and held it out in warning. But really, how was he going to stop someone he couldn't grab?

Anya stretched one arm toward the boy, who now crouched beside Amun, about to reach inside his throat. And do what? She stopped herself just before contact.

"Don't touch him," she shouted. Tiny golden flames branched from her fingers, but they were muted, mere outlines. "I have power in this realm and the other. Touch him, and you'll burn. Trust me. I won't hesitate. I've done worse."

Puppy dog brown eyes implored her to understand, to allow him to act as he'd been commanded. Poor kid.

His arm was shaking and remorse pulsed from him in powerful waves.

"There are two liars in the room, I see," Stefano said. "I don't care what powers you have. That boy is the son of a necromancer, able to live and walk among the dead. He can enter each world at will and nothing and no one can touch him while he's in the other."

"I sleep with a necromancer, you idiot. Lucien can walk among the dead himself." Anya raised her chin, blue eyes tearing and flashing at the same time. "Plus, I'm Anarchy and I have no mercy. Your pet comes any closer and you'll get to see me in action."

Knowing her as he did, Gideon knew when she was faking. The woman was operating on pure bravado. She would never be able to harm a child. At home, she constantly rubbed Ashlyn's belly and cooed to the baby. *Auntie Anya is gonna teach you to steal everything your little heart desires,* she was fond of saying.

Gideon reached out, unsteady, vision glazed, and circled his fingers around her hand. "I would find no joy in taking care of this," he managed to squeeze past the lump in his throat.

"I—I—yes." Slowly the flames died, and Anya nodded. There was relief in her eyes. She bent and grabbed Lucien by the shoulders, dragging him away from the boy. Amun was still babbling, Stefano still demanding the kid somehow shut him up.

As he wobbled on his feet, Gideon met the boy's grim, determined stare. "I won't make the warrior be quiet."

Though he spoke a lie, the boy seemed to understand what he meant and nodded. Fighting the weakness and pain beating through him, Gideon leaned down, placing his lips at Amun's ear. And for the first time in centuries, he was able to offer reassurance without having to resort to the truth. "You're all right. This is going to be fine. We're all going to get out of this alive. Shh, shh now. Everything's going to be all right."

Gradually the boom of Amun's voice faded until he was merely muttering under his breath. He still clutched his head, his eyes closed, his body curled into a fetal ball. Back and forth he rocked.

An arm wrapped around Gideon's waist, and he turned. The swift action caused his stomach to roll and his vision to momentarily blacken before he saw who'd touched him. Anya. How much longer could he stay upright? How much longer could he act as though he was racer ready?

Her strawberry scent wafted to his nose as she tugged him upright, and he nearly toppled. "I've been thinking. I'll willingly go with the brat," she said quietly. To keep Lucien from overhearing?

"Yes," Gideon said, even as he shook his head *no*. He experienced another stomach cramp, spots once again winking in his line of sight.

She cupped his face, drew him to her as if she meant to kiss him, did kiss him lightly, then moved her lips to his ear, purring, "Out of this room, my strength might fully return. I could finally take Stefano out."

If Lucien awoke and discovered Anya missing... No, Gideon couldn't allow his friend to suffer that kind of agony.

When it came to Lucien, Gideon hadn't quite shaken his guilt. From the onset of their possession, Lucien had been like a brother to him, taking him under his wing, talking Gideon down when he became too wild.

Yet when the time had come to choose between Lucien and Sabin, Gideon had chosen Sabin because he'd believed, with all his heart, that the Hunters deserved to die for what they'd done to Baden, keeper of Distrust. Yet Lucien had desired peace. Gideon still believed that, but he also knew Lucien had deserved better from him.

"Time for you to leave your man," Stefano announced. "Don't worry, after I'm done with you I'll let you return and tell him all about it."

"Come," the boy said, standing. He motioned Anya over with a wave of his hand. "I will force you if I must."

Gideon had to stop her. But how? His strength was still draining, replaced by more and more pain. Soon he would be completely incapacitated, unable to rise on his own for hours, perhaps days.

Too, the others couldn't take much more. Would Stefano send in the troops, subduing the warriors by sheer force and separating them? Or did he have to leave the warriors in here to prevent their powers from returning, as Anya suspected? Didn't matter, he supposed. There was only one way to buy time and figure out how to escape.

"I don't want you to take me instead. Don't want you to question me," Gideon said. "Stefano, tell the boy to take Anya and leave me."

There was a pause as his lie was interpreted.

"No," Anya gasped. Then, as if the denial wasn't enough for her, she grabbed Gideon's arms and shoved him to the ground. One kick, two, right in his stomach. Unable to stop himself, he vomited, over and over again, until there was nothing left. "See? He's in no condition to talk. You'll take me," she said firmly, "or no one."

"Bring them both," Stefano said, glee in his tone, as if that's what he'd wanted all along.

After a slight hesitation, the boy stepped into Anya's body, disappearing from view. Maybe he had possessed her, because she walked from the room without complaint. Holy shit.

When the boy returned a short while later, Gideon held up his hand. "Don't want to do it on my own."

That earned him a relieved nod.

Gideon lumbered to his feet and, with a last backward glance, abandoned his friends.

CHAPTER TWENTY-SEVEN

GWEN WAS SURPRISED to see her sisters in the media room—grrr, the *entertainment* room, but same thing, really—when she stepped inside. She was equally surprised that they didn't spring from the couch and stab her.

Her gaze shifted to take in the rest of the attendees. Who would support her, and who wouldn't? Ashlyn, Danika and Cameo were seated at the far table, two heads bent over scrolls, the yellow paper crackling, while one typed on a laptop. Ashlyn's pretty face was scrunched in concentration. Danika was pale and sickly-looking. Cameo was scowling.

William, Kane and Maddox were missing, and she suspected they were in town, searching for any lingering Hunters. Across from the women, Aeron and Paris were playing pool while talking strategy, their bruises mostly faded. Well, Paris's were mostly faded. It was hard to tell with Aeron, since his entire body was covered in tattoos.

"I'm telling you, I saw her," Paris said.

"Wishful thinking or ambrosia-induced hallucinations," Aeron replied. "When we fell, you were conscious. Did you see her again?"

"No. She probably hid."

Aeron was merciless. "I've been gentle with you to

this point, Paris, and that seems to have done no good. You have to let go of your grief. This morning we interrogated a few of the newest Hunters. They knew nothing about her. Afterward you summoned Cronus, asked him if she'd been sent back. And what did he say?"

Paling, Paris slammed his cue into one of the balls. "Without a body, her soul withered. Died."

A tiny, scaled…thing was sliding around Aeron's shoulders, stopping to pet the top of his head and kiss his cheek. Aeron reached up and gently scratched the fiend's neck as though it was a treasured pet, as though touching it was natural, welcome. Not once did he falter in his conversation. "Would the god king lie to you?"

"Yes!"

"Why? He wants our help."

"I don't know," Paris snarled.

"What *is* that thing?" Gwen asked, gaze still riveted on the creature winding itself around Aeron.

Sabin, who stood beside her in the doorway, burning her exposed skin with his presence, tempting her to forgive and forget and focus on the future, a future with him, smiled. "That's Legion. She's a demon—and a friend. Aeron would rather die than see her hurt, so please don't try and take her out."

That…thing was a girl? *Doesn't matter. You've got things to do.* Gwen's eyes were wide as she finished her study of the chamber's occupants. Torin leaned a shoulder against the wall, as far away from everyone as he could get. He clutched a handheld monitor in his gloved hands, his attention riveted on the small screen.

He'd support her, she knew it. One thing she'd noticed about him, he placed his friends above his own welfare.

"Gonna pretend we're not here?" Kaia stretched her arms over her head, preening like a kitten without a care.

Yes. No. "Hey." Finally meeting her sisters' gazes, she offered them a half smile and a wave. She'd spent the last hour thinking about what to say to them—if they were interested in listening to her. Nothing had come to her. An apology wouldn't work because she wasn't exactly sorry for what she'd done.

Taliyah stood, expression as blank as usual. Bristling, Sabin stepped in front of Gwen.

"Fine," Taliyah said, ignoring him. "You're not going to say anything about what happened, I'll get us started." A pause, then, "I'm proud of you."

"Wh-what?" Gwen asked, her voice broken. That was *so* not what she'd expected to hear. She peeked around her warrior's big bulk, her oldest sister once more coming into view. Taliyah was proud of her? Nothing could have surprised her more.

"You did what you had to do." Taliyah closed the distance between them and tried to shove Sabin out of the way. "You were a Harpy in every sense of the word."

Sabin didn't budge.

The ice in Taliyah's eyes would have frozen anyone else. "Let me hug my sister."

"No."

Gwen could see the stiff set of his shoulders, feel the tension in his back. "Sabin."

"No," he said, knowing what she wanted. "This could be a trick." Then, to Taliyah, he added, "You're not going to hurt her."

Bianka and Kaia joined Taliyah, forming a half circle

around the warrior. They could have attacked him, but somewhat to Gwen's surprise, they didn't.

"Seriously, let us hug our sister," Kaia said stiffly. That she didn't threaten to cause him bodily harm… a miracle. "Please." The last was offered grudgingly.

"Please, Sabin," Gwen said, flattening her palms against his shoulder blades.

He drew in a deep, shuddering breath, as if trying to sift through their scents for the truth. "No tricks. Or else." He pivoted out of the way and they immediately swept past him.

Three sets of arms wound around Gwen.

"Like I said, I'm so unbelievably proud of you."

"I've never seen anyone so fierce."

"Color me shocked. You totally kicked my ass!"

Gwen was frozen, baffled to her core. "You're not angry?"

"Hell, no," Kaia said, then backtracked. "Well, maybe at first. But this morning, when we were plotting ways to kidnap you and have our revenge on Sabin, we saw you feeding from him. Made us realize he is your family now, and we stepped over the line. You don't threaten a Harpy's family, ever, and we knew better."

Okay. Wow. Gwen's gaze skidded to Sabin, who was watching her with fire in his dark eyes. He wanted to be with her, he'd said. He would give up the war for her. He wanted to put her first, make her the top priority in his life. He trusted her not to betray him. He loved her.

She wanted to believe him, so badly she wanted to believe him, but she couldn't quite bring herself to. Not just because he'd locked her up, but because, as she'd lain in bed, recovering, she'd realized that she was now a weapon, the weapon he'd always wanted her to be.

She'd proven herself in battle. He wouldn't have to leave her behind anymore, wouldn't have to worry about her. How better to get what he wanted from her than to seduce her, body and soul?

Did he truly love her? *That's* what she wanted to know.

He claimed he wouldn't care if he caught her embracing her father. Maybe that was the truth. But, if he loved her now, would he one day grow to resent her for who and what she was? Would his hatred of the Hunters and their leader extend to her? Would his friends turn on him for bringing an enemy into their house? Would her every word and action be suspect?

Those doubts weren't swimming inside her head because of his demon. They were hers. All hers. And she didn't know how to get rid of them, even though she desperately wanted to be with Sabin.

When she'd seen him in town, bloody and lethal, her heart had truly stopped—absolute proof it belonged to him. What a fierce picture he'd presented. Any woman would be proud to have such a strong, competent man at her side. She'd wanted to be that woman. Then and always. She lacked the confidence to grab on to the dream, though. Which was funny if you thought about it. Physically, she'd never been stronger.

"I'm gonna hate leaving you," Bianka said, releasing her, and stepped back.

"Well…" *Now for the hard part.* "Then why try? I need you to stay here, at the fortress, and help Torin guard it and the humans."

"And where will you be going?" Taliyah released her, too, pale eyes studying Gwen's face. At least they hadn't denied her request.

She squared her shoulders, determination rushing through her. "That's actually why I called this meeting. Could I have everyone's attention please?" She clapped her hands, waiting for the room's other occupants to turn their gazes her way. "Sabin and I will be going to Chicago to find his missing friends. They've gone silent, and we think something is wrong."

At that, Sabin blinked. That was his only reaction. She knew he was waiting for information from Torin, but she figured it was better to be en route while they waited than stuck here, ineffective.

"I'm so glad you're going," Ashlyn said. "I don't know if anyone told you, but Aeron, Cameo and, yeah, your sister Kaia, took me into town this morning. I heard some things."

Uh-oh. There was gonna be some trouble in the fortress. "You shouldn't have gone into town. Your man will be ticked if he finds out." She'd seen Maddox with the pregnant woman only a few times, but once had been enough to assure her of his fierce need to protect.

Ashlyn waved a hand through the air. "He knew about it. He can't take me himself because I can't hear conversations when he's with me, so the compromise was to let me go with guards. He knew I'd just sneak out later otherwise. Anyway, some of the Hunters were headed to Chicago, as well. They were afraid of you, unsure of what you could do to them."

Hunters, afraid of her. They'd feared her while she'd been trapped in that pyramid, but there had been nothing she could truly do to them. No longer was she helpless. The thought made her smile. Sabin, too, practically glowed with pride.

Her stomach quivered at the sight, and breath heated

in her lungs. When he looked at her like that, she could almost believe he truly loved her and would do anything for her. *Mind on the task at hand.* "What about the prisoners?"

"Still locked up." Facing her, Paris rested his cue on the floor and leaned against it. He was paler than usual, lines of stress around his eyes. "Aeron and I, multitaskers that we are, have taken over their…care."

"Me helping," Legion the female demon piped up.

Care. Aka torture. Had Sabin interrogated them? She knew he liked to do so, yet he'd barely left her side since that battle. "The children…"

"Like I mentioned earlier, they've already been separated and moved to nicer quarters. They're scared and haven't used whatever powers they have. Yet. So we're unsure what we're dealing with. But we'll get it out of the adults, don't worry," Sabin said.

Paris nodded with grim determination. "I'll do it when we get back. I'm going with you."

Sabin and Aeron shared a heavy look.

"You're staying here," Sabin corrected. "All of you are. We need as many warriors here as we can get. We don't know how many Hunters remained behind."

"More than that, Torin saw Galen in town," Cameo said. "We haven't yet caught sight of him, which could mean he's hiding, planning to strike again."

Sabin approached Gwen's side and banded a strong arm around her waist. She didn't protest. Though her mind was unsure about him, her body knew she belonged with him. His lemon scent wafted to her nose, a drug she'd become addicted to. "But you, Paris…your new favorite thing to do puts everyone at risk. You'll stay here and get yourself cleaned up."

Paris opened his mouth to protest.

"Torin can take care of our travel arrangements," Sabin continued, cutting him off. Up and down, he caressed her arm, perhaps not even aware of what he was doing.

"You'll have to fly commercial," Torin said, "since the boys have the jet we always charter in the States with them."

"What if we're spotted by Hunters? And how will we get our weapons past security?" If they were caught with even one blade, they'd be questioned—a waste of time—and arrested.

"I have ways." Sabin kissed her temple. "Trust me. I've been doing this for a long time. We won't be spotted."

"Bring Reyes and the others home safely." Danika's fingers twined, as if she were saying a prayer. "Please."

"Please," Ashlyn echoed.

"And don't forget Anya," Kaia said. "No telling what kind of trouble she's stirred up."

"I'll do my best," Gwen told them, and she meant it. But would her best be good enough?

"TELL ME, WHAT'S a goddess doing with a demon?"

Anya eyed her lover's sworn enemy: Galen, keeper of the demon of Hope. He occupied one side of her new prison, and she the other. His long white wings were tucked into his back, the top arches rising over his shoulders. His eyes were blue like the sky, and the more she looked into them, the more she would swear she saw fluffy white clouds. Those eyes were meant to lull, to relax.

They only managed to piss her off.

Ghost Boy had "escorted" her—damned kid had taken control of her body as if it were his own—into this small, sparse hellhole and left her. Where she'd waited. And waited. Alone, enraged. Now she knew the Hunters had left her for their leader—who had remained in Buda until he'd been told of the bounty here.

Meanwhile, though, Gideon's screams had echoed through the halls—and with his screams, gleeful laughter from his captors. Poor Lies. She felt a little guilty for kicking him earlier. Had he spilled any secrets?

"Have you no answer, beauty?"

"I'm having fun, that's what." They'd made the mistake of leaving her unfettered. Although Ghost Boy had accompanied Galen, of course. Apparently, he was their insurance policy. Well, they'd soon learn they should have picked a better policy. Without that strange metal walling her in, her strength was returning. Soon, she would be a living nightmare. And they would suffer.

Was Lucien recovering as she was? Anya hated being away from him.

Slowly Galen's lips curled with amusement. "You're feisty. I like that. Lucien is a lucky man. More than lucky. Such an ugly man capturing the heart of one such as you is nothing short of a miracle."

Even his voice was meant to calm. Actually, everything about him seemed purposely honed to offer hope, like a bright light in a room of darkness and fear. What he didn't know was that Anya preferred the darkness. Always had.

"He isn't ugly," she said, pacing from one side of the back wall to the other. The more she stayed in motion, the less her actions would be watched, she suspected. "He's honorable and loving and wonderfully fierce."

A scoff. "But he's a demon."

She stopped to arch a brow at him. "Well, yeah. And so the hell are you."

"No." Patient, Galen shook his head. "I'm an angel, sent from the heavens to cleanse this earth of evil."

"Ha!" She kicked back into motion. "That's a good one. Believing our own press, are we?"

"I won't argue my origins with a demon whore." No longer did he sound amused or tolerant. "Now, tell me what the Lords know of the two artifacts that remain missing."

"Who says they're missing?" she taunted.

There were several beats of silence. "True. For all you know, I have one."

Bastard. Did he?

"If they had all four, they would not be here, at my mercy. They would be searching for the box. Or would have found it."

She rolled her eyes, though she trembled inside. "Sure you have any mercy, *angel?*"

His shoulders lifted in a shrug. "You're alive, aren't you?"

Her heels clicked against the tile. "But then, I'm sure you think you can use me in some way."

He crossed his arms over his massive chest, stretching the fabric of his white shirt. His pants were white, too. Overkill if you asked Anya, but whatever. She doubted he'd want fashion advice from her. "I'm growing weary of you, goddess. Perhaps I should have Death brought in."

Meaning he'd rather amuse himself with Lucien's torture? "Look, I'll talk to you, tell you everything you want to know, but only if you get rid of the kid. He annoys me." She didn't want someone so young to be hurt by her hand.

"I apologize if I gave you the impression that I'm foolish." Galen's mouth curled into a half smile. "He stays."

It had been worth a shot. Time for Plan B. Distraction, then fury. If she couldn't fly at him, she would make him fly at her. The boy wouldn't interfere with his leader. "Why do you hate the Lords so much, anyway? What'd they ever do to you?"

"A better question is this: why *shouldn't* I hate them? They want to ruin me. Therefore, I will ruin them first." He splayed his arms, an it's-that-simple gesture. "All these years, we've only been able to injure them, too afraid of releasing their demons. If that happened, the gods would curse me anew. I've already been warned." He smiled faintly. "But we're close, so close to changing that. Any day now I'll know if the demon of Distrust was able to bond with my female. If so…I will lead the most powerful army this world has ever seen."

"Your spineless servant seemed to think you'd use weaklings and lock them away for the *good* of this world."

He shrugged. "However would he get that idea?"

Okay, thinking cap time. He'd said he would be cursed somehow if he killed the Lords and freed their demons. But not, obviously, if he had somewhere to store those demons. Taking them from the Lords, though, would destroy the immortals. Destroy—kill— Lucien.

The bottom dropped out of her stomach, and her blood ran cold. "How did you find Distrust? How did you capture it, a crazed demon?" Stefano had claimed they'd already successfully bonded the demon with another body. Clearly, he'd lied. Again. But the fact that they were trying to do so was just as frightening.

"Unlike Amun, I'm not one to spill all my secrets," Galen said.

"Well, until you do, I'm afraid I can't believe you."

He gave her another of those half smiles. "I'm devastated, of course."

Gods, I hate him! She tapped a nail against her chin, as if she were deep in thought. She'd managed to distract him, and now she would piss him off. "Let's see, let's see. If I were a cowardly, jealous demon pretending to be an angel and I wanted to find and control an evil spirit, I would…what? Have others do my dirty work, definitely. Maybe even use children," she said, gaze flicking past Ghost Boy. Her eyes widened as his narrowed. She'd meant to enrage him with the taunt, but she'd done more than that, she realized.

She'd found the answer. Somehow, some way, one—or more—of those Halfling children were capable of finding an otherworldly spirit. Maybe even Ghost Boy himself.

"We'll take them from you," she said, meeting Galen's eyes once more. "Prevent you from using them ever again. We've won every other battle with you. This will be no different. I mean, we even have a Harpy on our side now. Have you perchance heard of what a Harpy can do?"

"You will shut your mouth," the "angel" growled at her.

She'd gotten to him. Excellent. An emotional man was a man who made mistakes. "And you know what's worse than a Harpy? Cronus, the new god king. He wants you dead. Did you know that?"

Galen straightened. "You lie."

"Do I? The All-Seeing Eye—the Eye you lost to us—had a vision. In it, she saw you try and murder Cronus. Now he's after you. I don't know why he hasn't killed you himself. I'm sure he has his reasons. But believe me, I've been his target. He won't leave you alone until he has what he wants."

Galen's jaw hardened more with every word she spoke. "I would never hurt a Titan."

"Wouldn't you? You betrayed your closest friends."

"They weren't my friends," he shouted, slamming a fist into the wall and rattling the foundation.

That's the way, big boy. "Too bad they didn't realize that earlier. But no matter. They still managed to defeat you. Just as they'll defeat you every time you challenge them. It's science, after all. You're weaker."

Fury sizzled from him, snapping under his skin. "Your precious Lucien wasn't strong enough to lead us, Zeus's elite army. He shouldn't have been placed in charge."

"So rather than challenge him like an honorable soldier, you convinced him to open Pandora's box, then told the gods of *his* decision to betray them? You formed an army of your own and tried to stop him. Nope, that's not cowardly at all."

He stalked two steps forward before catching himself and halting. His hands fisted. "I did what I had to do. A good soldier wins by any means necessary. Just ask your friend Sabin."

Push harder. You almost had him. "Ah, but like I said, you didn't win, did you? Even though you knew what Lucien and the others were going to do, you weren't able to stop them and prove them weak. *You* lost. *You* were made to look weak. *You* got cursed to house a demon inside you just like the others. You, you, you." She laughed. "How humiliating."

"Enough!"

"Want to hit me?" Again, she laughed cruelly. "Does the sweet little angel want to cut out Anya's tongue? What would your followers think then, hmm? But I'm sure they've seen you do much worse. Or do you always have Stefano order that done, so you can appear merciful?"

For a long moment, he watched her, silent, not lunging toward her as she'd hoped. Then, to her surprise, he smiled. "Stefano's not here, and I'm not feeling merciful. But don't worry. This will only hurt for a second." With that, he whipped a small crossbow from between his wings. Before she had time to duck, he fired two arrows, propelling her into the back wall. One cut through her left shoulder, the other her right, pinning her to the brick.

Pain exploded through her, her vision blurring. Blood cascaded down her arms, so hot it burned her. Sweat beaded on her brow and upper lip, but it didn't cool her down.

The boy, she noticed distantly, had paled. His lower lip was trembling.

"I think it's time for Lucien to join our little party," Galen said. "He'll watch everything we do to you. Strip you, take you, hurt you. Let's see if he's strong enough to save you, shall we?"

"Touch him," she managed to work through clenched teeth, "and I'll eat your heart in front of you."

He laughed, and oh, how she despised the sound of his amusement. But his laughter was cut short as a boom erupted and the building actually shook.

"Looks like the cavalry's here," Anya said, grinning despite the throbbing in her shoulders. "I knew the others would come for us. I believe I mentioned the Harpy, yes?"

He looked at her, the first stirring of panic in his eyes, then turned his gaze to the door.

Another boom, another shake.

"This isn't over. If she fights her way down, fine," he told the boy as he stomped to the exit, "but do not let her out of this room."

CHAPTER TWENTY-EIGHT

THOUGH SABIN AND Gwen hadn't been spotted by any Hunters or frisked by security—Doubt had earned its keep, making everyone around them doubt everything they saw—the flight to the States had been hard, in every sense of the word. Gwen had snuggled up next to Sabin, hour after hour, and he hadn't been able to touch her the way he craved. And he wouldn't, not in front of witnesses and not until she trusted him. Winning her heart and her trust was the most important battle of his life, and for once he'd decided not to rush it.

I will have her.

When they'd deplaned, Sabin, who was used to being around humans, having them stare at his height and muscled strength, hadn't liked the way males had stared at his woman. Their desire had been obvious.

Drove him freaking insane. Which was why he'd allowed Doubt to swoop into those human minds and fill them with insecurities about their appearance, their prowess in bed—and why he'd been tempted to erupt into one of Maddox's famous violent fits. He'd managed to control himself, keeping his eye on the prize: the safe return of his friends. But only because Gwen hadn't seemed to notice the gaping, the drooling mouths, and the stopping dead in their tracks.

They'd immediately driven to the house the warriors had been staying at, a house miles from anything and everything. They'd watched it for a bit, ascertaining two things: one, the warriors weren't there and two, Hunters hadn't been there and planted little presents. Too bad about the lack of Hunters, if you asked Sabin. He was ready for action.

He and Gwen had loaded themselves with weapons, each grabbed a ball cap to hide their hair and shield their faces, and headed to the only other place he knew his friends would have gone. Now they walked the street in front of a row of buildings, and he knew he was close to the training facility, but…he couldn't find it. Each building blended into the next. And each time he counted off, he lost track of their numbers.

Gwen paused and rubbed the back of her neck, staring up into the sky. "This is hopeless. We're in the right place. Why can't we find it?"

He sighed. Maybe it was time to bring out the big guns. *If* the god king would respond to him for once. "Cronus," he muttered, "a little help would be nice. You want us to succeed, right?"

A moment passed, then another. Nothing happened.

He was just about to give up when suddenly Gwen gasped. "Look."

Sabin followed her gaze, experienced a jolt of shock. There, on the roof of the building to their right, a building Sabin had somehow overlooked time and time again, stood the god king. The building seemed to shake beneath him. His white robe whipped around his ankles. After being ignored for so long, Sabin was being aided? And so easily?

"Now you owe me, Doubt, and I always collect." Cronus disappeared a second later.

It would benefit Cronus for Sabin to win this day. The god should have been happy to aid the cause, not demanding favors in return.

"Who was that?" Gwen asked. "How did he do that? And do you think my...Galen is in there?"

Sabin explained about Cronus. "Galen...I don't know. What if he is? Do you still want to do this?"

"Yes." No hesitation this time, though there'd been an edge to her tone.

Was he asking too much of her? Sabin didn't have parents. The Greeks had created him already fully formed. As there was no love lost between him and the former gods, he couldn't even fathom a guess as to how Gwen was feeling.

"I'll be fine," she added, as if she read his thoughts. "After everything he's done, he needs to be taken down."

There at the end, her voice had trembled. Sabin decided then and there to intervene if Galen opted to join the fray—which wasn't likely to happen as the bastard always cut and run, leaving his lackeys to do his dirty work. Hope placed himself before others, and always had. But Sabin didn't want Gwen regretting anything; he didn't want her to later blame him for her actions—or his own, he thought with a sinking stomach. He'd wondered before but couldn't help doing so again: Would she hate him if he was the one to defeat and restrain her father?

Only two things mattered to Sabin right now: Gwen and his friends' safety. In that order. She came first, now and always. Nothing would change that.

"Let's do this," she said softly, and trekked forward.

"Before we go in there," he said, keeping pace beside

her, "I want to tell you again that I love you. I love you so much I ache with it. I just…I wanted you to know in case anything happens."

"Nothing's going to happen." She stumbled, caught herself. "But I love you, too. I do. There's no denying that anymore. I'm still not sure about you, though. I, just, I don't know. Doubt is like my pet now, and I like that. Really. I just—"

"It's okay." She loved him. Thank the gods, she loved him. He drew her to a halt and pulled her into his embrace, hating her words, but understanding nonetheless. He should have trusted her. From the beginning, he should have placed her first. "We'll figure all of that out later. I promise. I don't want any worries on your mind right now. Distractions can get you—"

"Killed," she finished for him, smiling. "I paid attention to your lessons." She tentatively wrapped her arms around his waist, resting her head in the hollow of his neck. Her hair was soft against his skin. "You be careful in there."

Gods, he adored this woman. Her strength, her courage, her wit. "You, too. Whatever you do, save yourself. Understand me?" he said fiercely. "I'd be lost without you."

"I will." She gave a half-amused, half-strained smile. "That's Harpy code, after all."

He kissed the top of her head. She looked up at him then, her lips puffy and red and he couldn't resist. He meshed their mouths together, his tongue sweeping inside hers with a possessive thrust. Her hands lifted, tangling in his hair, and she moaned.

He swallowed the sound, savoring it, letting it fill him up. Here was his life, in his arms, all he needed. But he forced himself to pull away. "Come on. I want to get this over with so that you and I can talk. Why don't you go through the front door, and I'll take the back. We'll scope out each entrance, meet in the middle."

With another swift kiss to her mouth, Sabin started forward again. The sun burned bright, glaring down at him. He kept his face down, hoping he wouldn't be recognized if cameras were scanning the area.

Can you do this?

Yes.

What if you fail?

I won't.

What if Gwen is hurt?

She won't be. He would make sure of it.

"Pick up the pace, slowpoke." A slight breeze caressed his face as Gwen jumped into hyperdrive and passed him, her wings giving her a speed he could never hope to match. That didn't stop him from trying, though. He didn't want her in that building alone. He quickened his steps and raced around back. There he found a fence with spikes that stretched toward the sky and electric wires that circled every slat.

Usually he took his time and disabled such wires. Today, he didn't have that luxury. He simply climbed. The shocks that worked through him would have killed a human. They were painful, stopped his heart twice, pushed the breath out of him continually, but he still didn't slow. Up, up, he shimmied, until he was falling to the ground. His boots thumped into concrete, rattling him, and he took off in a run, already going for his guns.

It didn't take him long to reach his first quarry. There were three Hunters seated at a round table, an umbrella shading them. Had they not felt the building shake? Their bad. Finally. The party could start.

"—pissed his pants," one laughed.

"Should have seen his face when I shoved those spikes under his nails. And when I cut off his hands…" More laughter. "I hope he continues the silence. I've never had so much fun in my life."

"Demons. They deserve this and more."

Sabin's heart sank even as his demon stirred. *I want to play,* Doubt said gleefully.

Have fun.

Needing no more encouragement, the demon swooped out of his mind and into theirs.

The other Lords are going to be angry. They'll come for you, make you pay. Everything you've done to their brethren will be done to you—magnified by a thousand, I'm sure.

One of the men shuddered. "We know the other demons will come for their friends when they've healed from that last battle. Maybe we should, I don't know, pack up soon."

"I'm not a coward. I'm staying here and doing whatever's necessary to pry information from our prisoners."

Then you'll be gutted like a fish, I bet.

Now the second speaker shuddered.

"Uh, guys. Save it. My beeper just vibrated. An alarm has been tripped. Either someone's escaped or we're under attack."

They jumped to their feet. None of them had spotted Sabin yet. Silencer on—check. Chamber loaded—check. At one time, he would have drawn their attention, taunted them about their coming death and taken joy as they paled. Now, he simply shot them one after the other in the back of the head. They slumped in their chairs, what was left of their foreheads hitting the glass tabletop with a thump.

He kept moving, rounding the corner. A group of children were splashing around in a pool. One of the boys had a hand extended, water rising and balancing above it.

"Throw it at me," a little girl implored. "See if it can get through my shielding spell."

With a laugh, the boy tossed the water at the girl. Not a single drop touched her.

Sabin had suspected they would be here, but was still shocked to see them. Despite their unusual abilities, they were just children. How could the Hunters use them like this? Place them in such danger?

Sabin replaced one of his semiautomatics with a tranq gun. He didn't want to do this, but it was the best—and safest—solution for everyone involved. What was Gwen doing? Was she inside? Hurt? Without pause, he began nailing the kids with darts. One by one, they sank into unconsciousness. He quickly dragged them out of the water and laid them in the shade, never once releasing his weapons.

Finally, he was ready to enter the house. To help Gwen.

"You filthy animal! What have you done?"

Sabin whipped around. A Hunter had just taken aim at him, fired. A bullet slammed into his right shoulder. Wincing, he hammered out another round from his Sig. One bullet hit the Hunter's neck, the other his chest. He slumped over, gasping. When his skull cracked against the ground, the gasping stopped.

Bleeding, unconcerned by the pain, Sabin rushed

inside the building, sheathing the tranq in favor of the second semiautomatic. Already Hunters littered the floor, motionless. Gwen. Sabin's heart swelled with pride. Maybe it was wrong of him, but he really loved her dark side. She was magic on a battlefield.

He followed the trail of adult bodies through the winding hallways. Some of the rooms were bedrooms with multiple bunk beds, some were classrooms. There were tiny desks and artwork on the walls; every single piece showed a demon being tortured. There were even signs. *A perfect world is a world without demons. When the demons are gone, there will be no sickness, no death. No evil. Lost someone you love? You know who to blame.*

Oh, yes. The children were being trained to hate the Lords from birth. Fabulous. Sabin had done some bad shit in his life, but never had he taught hatred to an innocent.

"Bastard!" he heard Gwen shout, followed by a howl of pain.

Increasing his speed, Sabin followed the sound, saw a man hunched over and grabbing his crotch. He didn't know what had happened and he didn't care to stop and ask. He simply aimed his Sig and fired three rounds. No one hurt Gwen.

Gwen whirled around, claws bared. Those tiny wings fluttered madly under her shirt. The death-glaze faded when she realized who stood before her. "Thanks."

"Anytime."

"I found your friends. They're hurt, but alive. I released them, but two are missing. Gideon and Anya."

First—she'd already found and released them? Holy hell. She was faster and better than even he had known.

Second—where the hell were the others? Locked up? "Anya?" he shouted. "Gideon?"

"Sabin? Sabin, is that you?" a woman called from down the hall. Anya. "It's about damn time. I'm back here. With a guard."

Sabin looked at Gwen just as three males flew into the room, their expressions wild. "Got 'em?" he asked.

"Go on." She faced the newest challenge. "Get Anya."

He took off in a run. He would have left any of his men, and Gwen was a better fighter than all of them put together, so he had no doubt of her success. *No doubt.* The thought made him smile.

As he moved, he exchanged a gun for a blade. He was almost out of bullets. Thankfully, a knife never needed refilling. *Where are you, Anya?* He burst through one door—empty. He shouldered his way through another, hinges splintering. Nothing. Three more rooms, and there she was, eyeing a little boy, both her shoulders stained crimson.

That boy turned to him, expression determined. There was something…off about him, as though he wasn't three-dimensional.

"Sabin!" When Anya darted to one side, the boy quickly followed, swiping out an arm.

"I have to keep her here," he said, but he didn't sound happy about it.

Slowly Sabin sheathed his blade and reached behind him, curling his fingers around the handle of the tranq gun.

"Don't touch him," Anya rushed out, "and don't let him touch you. You'll go down without warning."

"Anya!"

Sabin recognized the voice as Death's, so he didn't turn as footsteps approached. He kept his gaze on the boy, ready to jump at him despite Anya's warning if he went after the goddess again.

"Lucien! Stay back, baby, but tell me you're okay?" Anya's face lit with a mixture of pleasure and worry. "I have to know you're okay."

"I'm fine. You? Oh, gods." Lucien came up behind him and sucked in a breath. Sabin could feel waves of fury pulsing off him. "Your shoulders."

"Just a little scratch." There was fire in the words, a promise of retribution.

Keeping his hand behind his back, Sabin held the tranq out to Lucien. "Not sure it'll do any good, but I'm going to leave you to it. Gideon's still missing." The warrior took the weapon without a word, and Sabin spun on his heel.

He continued bursting into rooms. Several were padded. One was filled with computers and other technology. One was stuffed with enough canned food to last a lifetime. Down another hall he turned, shouting Gideon's name. These rooms had thicker locks and fingerprint IDs. Heart pounding, Sabin pressed his ear to each door until he finally, blessedly heard a whimper.

Gideon.

Urgency flooding him, he pried at the slit in the center. His muscles strained, his bones nearly popped out of joint, his wound reopened, but he worked the edge until the metal opened enough to squeeze through. First thing he noticed was the broken and bleeding form strapped to a gurney. A sickening sense of déjà vu hit him.

He crossed the distance, bile rising in his throat. Gideon's eyelids were so swollen it looked as if rocks were buried underneath them. Bruises colored every inch of his naked body. Many of his bones were broken and protruding through skin.

Both of his hands had been chopped off.

"They'll grow back, I swear to the gods they'll grow back," Sabin whispered as he pulled at the bonds. They were strong. Too strong, comprised of some sort of—godly?—metal. He couldn't even hack through them with a blade.

"Key. Not there." Gideon's voice was so weak, Sabin barely heard it. But the warrior motioned to a cabinet with a tilt of his chin. Sure enough, a key dangled there. "Didn't taunt me…with it."

"Save your strength, my friend." He spoke gently, but rage was pouring through him, consuming him, becoming the only thing he knew. Those bastards were going to pay for this. Every single one of them and a thousand times over. He needed to be punished as well, he thought. He'd sworn never to let this kind of thing happen to his comrade again, yet here they were, practically reliving the past.

When Gideon was free, Sabin gently gathered him in his arms and carried him into the hall. Strider had been in the process of turning the corner, pale and trembling and stumbling. When the warrior spotted Sabin's bundle, he released a savage cry.

"Is he…"

"He's alive." Barely.

"Thank the gods. Lucien's got Anya. He managed to tranq the kid guarding her. Reyes is somewhere in back. Stefano's called for retreat, but you'll never believe who's stuck around."

At the moment, Sabin didn't care. "Have you seen Gwen?"

"Yeah. Down the hall and to the right." Strider gulped. "I've been searching for you. I'll take Gideon. You go help your woman."

Dread instantly mixed with his rage as Sabin carefully handed Gideon over. "Did something happen to her?"

"Just go."

He ran, arms pumping, legs shaking, until he reached the chamber where he'd left her. She was still there, but she was no longer fighting human Hunters. She was fighting her father. And she was losing.

Guess who stuck around, Strider had said. Of all the times for the bastard to grow some balls. Gwen was winded, panting, bloody, stumbling every time she lashed out as though her legs could no longer hold her weight. Galen had a long snakelike whip. No, not snakelike. It *was* a snake. Hissing, teeth gleaming with venom. And every time Gwen managed to cut off the snake's head, another grew in its place.

"The big, strong Lords of the Underworld, relying on a woman. And they call me the coward," Galen sneered.

"I'm not just any woman," Gwen gritted out. "I'm a Harpy."

"As if that makes a difference."

"It should. I'm also a half demon. Don't you recognize me?" She closed in despite the snake chomping on her calf and slashed for the warrior's heart.

"Should I? All their women look the same to me. Filthy whores." He expertly dodged, jerking the whip out of her and making her cry out before cracking it again. This time it coiled around her wrist. He gave another tug. Once more she cried out. She fell to her knees, her entire body spasming.

Sabin couldn't watch this. Couldn't let the bastard destroy Gwen, no matter how much Gwen might resent him for interfering. "Leave her alone. I'm the one you want." Teeth gnashing, he withdrew several daggers and tossed all but one at the whip, severing its hold on Gwen. He threw the last at Galen, nailing him in the stomach. The warrior roared, fell, and Gwen lumbered to her feet.

Sabin jumped in front of her, blocking her from the crouching Galen. "Finally ready to do this? To admit defeat?"

Scowling, Galen pulled the knife from his gut. "You really think you're strong enough to best me?"

"I already have. We've plowed through most of your forces." He was grinning as he palmed and aimed his Sig. "All that remains is your imprisonment. And it looks like that won't be too difficult to obtain."

"Stop it. Just stop it." Gwen staggered to a halt in front of him, shoulders squared. She swayed, but didn't fall, her gaze locked on Galen. "I don't want you taken until you hear what I have to say. I've waited for this day my entire life, dreamed of telling you that I'm the daughter of Tabitha Skyhawk. That I'm twenty-seven years old, and thought to be sired by an angel."

Galen laughed as he stood, but that laugh couldn't hide his wince. He was bleeding profusely now. "Is that supposed to mean something to me?"

"You tell me. About twenty-eight years ago, you slept with a Harpy," Gwen said. "She had red hair and brown eyes. She was injured. You patched her up. Then you left but said you'd be back."

His lingering smirk faded as he studied her. "And?" He didn't sound as if he cared, but he didn't try to escape when he'd clearly lost the battle, either.

Gwen's entire body trembled, and Sabin's rage darkened. "And the past has a way of catching up with people, doesn't it? So, surprise. Here I am." She splayed her arms. "Your long-lost daughter."

"No." Galen shook his head. At least his amusement didn't return. "You're lying. I would have known."

"Because you would have gotten a birth announcement?" Now *Gwen* laughed, the sound tinged with darkness.

"No," he repeated. "It's impossible. I'm no one's father."

Behind them, the battle was winding down. The screams were stopping, the grunts fading. No more gunshots. No more pounding footsteps. Then the rest of the Lords were filling the doorway, each wearing expressions of hate and fury. Each dripping in blood. Strider still carried Gideon, as if afraid to set him down.

"Well, well, well. Look who we have here," Lucien growled.

"Not so tough without a child around to shield you, Hope?" Anya laughed.

"Tonight I'll dine on your black heart," Reyes snarled.

Sabin studied the grim set of his friends' faces. These warriors had been tortured, and they weren't done exacting their revenge. Much as he sympathized, though, he couldn't let them have it yet.

"Galen is ours," Sabin told them. "Stay back. Gwen?"

GWEN KNEW WHAT Sabin was asking. Allow him to imprison her father, or let her father go. That he was leaving the choice up to her proved his love as nothing else could have. If only she could give him what he wanted.

"I—I don't know," she said, voice cracking. Peering into those sky-eyes, eyes she'd once only dreamed about, she was struck anew with the knowledge that her father was here, in front of her, that he represented everything she'd ever wanted as a little girl and then as an adult, while she'd been trapped in that cell in Egypt. How often had she yearned to be held and protected by him?

He hadn't known about her. Now that he did, would he love her? Would he want her with him, as she'd craved all those years?

Galen eyed the warriors glaring at him menacingly. "Perhaps I spoke too soon. We will talk, you and I. Privately." He stepped forward and reached out to her.

Sabin snarled, and it was the type of sound a beast made just before it flew into attack. "You can leave, if she allows it, but you don't touch her. Ever."

For several seconds, it looked as if Galen would argue. The Lords certainly were. They wanted this man in chains and didn't like that Sabin had offered him freedom.

"No child of mine would choose to be with the Lords of the Underworld." Galen held out his hand and waved his fingers at her. "Come with me. We will leave, get to know each other."

Did he truly wish to learn about her or did he simply hope to use her as another weapon against his hated enemies? The suspicion hurt, and Gwen found herself grabbing Sabin's gun, barrel aimed at Galen's head. "No matter what happens, I'm not going anywhere with you."

Sabin hated him. This man had done cruel things. Would continue to do cruel things.

"You would kill your own father?" Galen asked, clutching his heart as if she'd truly injured his feelings.

In her mind, he was suddenly wrapping his arms around her, holding her close, telling her how much he loved her. Hope. It was there, in her chest, blooming through her entire body. Did it stem from him? Or from herself?

"You were so quick to dismiss me," she gritted out. "You said you had no children."

"I was merely in shock," he explained patiently. "Absorbing the news. After all, it's not every day a man is given the priceless gift of fatherhood."

Her hand trembled.

"Your mother...Tabitha. I remember. She was the most beautiful sight I'd ever beheld, or have since. I wanted her instantly and meant to keep her, but she left me. I was never able to find her. Had I known about you, I would have desired a place in your life."

Truth or lie? She lifted her chin even as her arm fell. Maybe there was good in him. Maybe he could be saved. Maybe not. But... "Go."

He reached for her.

"Go," she repeated, a hot tear streaming down her cheek.

"Daughter..."

"I said go!"

Suddenly his wings jerked into motion, spreading, fast, too fast, flapping, wind gusting around them. Before anyone could blink, he burst up, through the ceiling and out of the building.

Unable to hold back any longer, the other warriors

fired at him, even tossed their blades. Someone must have nailed him, because there was a howl. It wasn't too bad an injury, though, because Galen didn't fall back inside. Gwen hated herself for the relief she felt.

The sound of heavy breathing filled the room, blending with muttered curses, stomping footsteps.

"Not again," Strider groaned, finally placing Gideon on the floor. "Why would you do that, Sabin? Why would you let *her* do that?" A second later, the hulking warrior was beside his friend, writhing in agony.

Sabin's hesitation had given Galen the chance to escape, and Galen's escape had meant defeat for the Lords. Defeat for Strider. *My fault,* she thought. She'd just proven Sabin right. She couldn't be trusted with his greatest enemy. She'd hesitated to do what was needed.

"I'm sorry," Sabin said to his friend.

I'll make it up to him. Somehow, some way. She spun, meaning to grab on to him and make him listen to her apology. Instead, she gasped. "You're bleeding."

"I'm fine. I'll heal. How are you?" His gaze raked her, taking in every bruise and cut. A muscle ticked below his eye. "I should have taken him down when I had the chance. He hurt you."

"I'll heal," she said, parroting him as she threw herself into his arms. "I'm sorry. I'm so sorry. Can you forgive me?"

He grunted, even as he kissed the top of her head. "I love you. There's nothing to forgive, darling."

"I wimped out. I let your greatest enemy go. I—"

"No, no, no. I'm not letting you blame yourself for this. *I* let him go." He cupped her jaw. "Now tell me what I want to hear. What I need to hear."

"I love you, too."

He closed his eyes for a moment, his relief palpable. "We're staying together."

"Yes. If you'll have me."

"What do you mean, if I'll have you? I told you, you're first in my life."

"I know." Slowly her lashes lifted and then she was peering up at him, tears now streaming freely down her cheeks. "You gave up a victory for me. I can't believe you did that."

"I would give up anything, everything for you."

"You really do love me. You mean it. Won't grow to hate me, won't let war come between us."

"Is that what's been worrying you?" He snorted. "Darling, I could have told you those things."

"But I wouldn't have believed you. I thought winning was the most important thing in your life."

"No. That's you."

She smiled radiantly up at him. But that smile faded as the murmurs of the other Lords filled her ears, reminding her of what she'd done. Or hadn't done. "I should have told you to lock him away forever. I'm sorry. I'm so sorry. He needs to be stopped, I know that, but there at the end, I just couldn't bring myself… couldn't let you…I'm so sorry. Now he's going to cause even more trouble."

"It's all right. It's all right. We'll deal with it. We've severely handicapped their army."

"Not sure how much good that will do us. Galen found Distrust," Anya said. "He's trying to place the demon inside someone else's body, hoping to create an immortal soldier he can control. He was pretty confident about his success."

Distrust, once Sabin's best friend, Gwen remembered. If Distrust were on her father's side, would Sabin be able to hurt whichever body it resided in? No matter what kind of destruction that person inflicted. She didn't want her man faced with the same type of decision she'd just had to make.

Sabin smoothed a hand through her damp hair. "I don't know what I'd do," he said as if he'd read her thoughts. "But I do now understand how difficult your decision must have been. If you need that bastard free to make you happy, then free he'll stay."

"Hey," several of the warriors muttered behind him.

"We get a say in that," Reyes growled, rifling through the pockets of the fallen Hunters.

Gwen sighed. "I'll come to terms with his capture, I know I will. Seeing him for the first time was just too shocking to process. Don't worry, though. Next time I'll do better."

"Yeah, but worrying is what I do best."

"Not anymore. Loving me is what you do best."

"That's the truth."

"Let's go home," she said, squeezing him tight. "We've got some kids to soothe, artifacts to find, Hunters to kill and a box to destroy. After you love the breath out of me, of course."

EPILOGUE

ONCE THEY WERE HOME, their injuries healed, they were able to make love like wild animals. Afterward, Gwen had too much energy to sleep. She popped up and started jumping on the bed, daring Sabin to do something about it. He propped himself against the headboard, watching her through bright, amused eyes.

She *tsk*ed under her tongue. "Look at you. Just sitting there, unable to keep up with a little girl who—ahhhhhh."

He'd kicked her legs out from under her, sending her tumbling to her back. Grinning, he dove on top of her. "Who's the tired one now, huh?"

She was laughing as she rolled him over, her hair falling around them like a curtain. "Not me, that's for sure."

"Let me see what I can do about that."

And he did.

A long while later, she found herself snuggled back into his side, having trouble catching her breath. "So what's next, hmm?" she asked, happier than she'd ever been. Who would have thought Gwendolyn the Timid would hook up with the fiercest Lord of the Underworld, throw herself into the midst of a war, and like it? Not her, that was for sure.

For the moment, though, things were calm. All the

couples were safe, secure and reunited. The women (and Legion) were finding new homes for the children, both the ones Gwen had captured during their Budapest battle and the ones they'd rescued from Hunter High. Anya even had a favorite, the one she called "Ghost Boy," and Gwen suspected the goddess would place him with a loving family here in Buda, where she could keep an eye on him.

Torin was searching for the people on Cronus's list, and the other warriors were plotting ways to find Galen—and Distrust. Gideon was still healing; that would take a while. Legion disappeared periodically, and both Paris and Aeron were acting strangely.

"What's next with us?" Sabin asked. "Well, after my heart starts beating again, I'm going to crawl my way down your body and—"

"No," she said with a laugh, batting his hand away as he tickled her stomach. "With the Hunters."

He sank deeper into the mattress, his arms tightening around her. "Danika thinks Galen is going to try and pair Distrust with the woman in the painting with him. If he succeeds, it's gonna be a free-for-all when it comes time for the next battle. They won't merely try to injure us, they'll go for our heads. They'll *want* our demons free so they can pair them with new hosts of their choosing."

She'd suspected that, but still shuddered. "Brilliant of my...Galen, to place a piece of your beloved friend inside the body of your enemy."

"Yeah, but I wouldn't have expected anything less from the man who fathered you. Your sisters wouldn't happen to have come into their powers or whatever it is, would they? If so, maybe we can convince them to stay." Sabin traced hearts along her spine. "I've heard that every Harpy develops some sort of ability after living a few centuries. An ability like time travel. It'd come in handy, that's for sure."

"Only Taliyah. She can shift into other forms, as her own father could." Talking about her race was becoming easier. She *wanted* Sabin to know about her.

"Even better." He sighed. "We've gotta find those artifacts before Galen does. If he hasn't already found one. That snake-whip…the more I think of it, the more it reminds me of the creature that was guarding the Cage of Compulsion. The same kind of creature that supposedly guards each of the artifacts. As he's the keeper of Hope, I don't think he'd have any trouble convincing even a monster to help him."

"If he has one, we'll just steal it. I mean, you've got a Harpy and the goddess of Anarchy on your side. The odds are in your favor."

He chuckled. "Maybe you and I can visit the Temple of the Unspoken Ones. Something there told us about Danika, the All-Seeing Eye. Maybe whoever—whatever—it was will help us find something else."

Gwen traced her finger over his chest, loving the contrasting tones of their skin. "And if we find those people listed on the scrolls, we can convince them to help us. You don't have to worry about Doubt causing trouble. He knows I'll spank him."

"That he does." He kissed her temple. "But yes, I'll do anything—within reason—to win this war, including convincing criminals I helped incarcerate to help me. And actually, that should be easy. After all, I convinced the fiercest Harpy of them all to give me her heart."

"And would you do anything—within reason—to keep that Harpy happy?"

"Don't you know it."

"Do I?" She grinned up at him. "Prove it."

"My pleasure."

She was on her back in the next instant, giggling like a schoolgirl, her body and soul Sabin's, just the way she liked it.

* * * * *

Lords of the Underworld
Glossary of Characters and Terms

Aeron—Keeper of Wrath

All-Seeing Eye—Godly artifact with the power to see into heaven and hell

Amun—Keeper of Secrets

Anya—(Minor) Goddess of Anarchy

Ashlyn Darrow—Human female with supernatural ability

Baden—Keeper of Distrust (deceased)

Bait—Human females, Hunters' accomplices

Bianka Skyhawk—Harpy; sister of Gwen

Cage of Compulsion—Godly artifact with the power to enslave anyone trapped inside

Cameo—Keeper of Misery; only female warrior

Cloak of Invisibility—Godly artifact with the power to shield its wearer from prying eyes

Cronus—King of the Titans

Danika Ford—Human female

Darla Stefano—wife of Dean Stefano; Sabin's lover (deceased)

Dean Stefano—Hunter; right-hand man of Galen

dimOuniak—Pandora's box

Galen—Keeper of Hope

Gideon—Keeper of Lies

Gilly—Human female, friend of Danika

Greeks—Former rulers of Olympus, now imprisoned in Tartarus

Gwen Skyhawk—half-Harpy, half-angel

Hunters—Mortal enemies of the Lords of the Underworld

Hydra—Multiheaded serpent with poisonous fangs

Kaia Skyhawk—Harpy; sister of Gwen

Kane—Keeper of Disaster

Legion—Demon minion, friend of Aeron

Lords of the Underworld—Exiled warriors to the Greek gods who now house demons inside them

Lucien—Keeper of Death; leader of the Budapest warriors

Maddox—Keeper of Violence

Pandora—Immortal warrior, once guardian of *dim-Ouniak* (deceased)

Paring Rod—Godly artifact, power unknown

Paris—Keeper of Promiscuity

Reyes—Keeper of Pain

Sabin—Keeper of Doubt; leader of the Greece warriors

Sienna Blackstone—Female Hunter

Strider—Keeper of Defeat

Tabitha Skyhawk—Harpy; mother of Gwen

Taliyah Skyhawk—Harpy; sister of Gwen

Tartarus—Greek, god of Confinement; also the immortal prison on Mount Olympus

Titans—Current rulers of Olympus

Torin—Keeper of Disease

Tyson—Human; ex-boyfriend of Gwen

William—Immortal, friend of Anya

Zeus—King of the Greeks